THE JUNGLE BOOK

by
RUDYARD
KIPLING

illustrated by
WILLIAM
DEMPSTER

cover by
DON IRWIN

classic press, incorporated • santa rosa, california

The special contents of this edition are
© Copyright, 1968 by Classic Press, Incorporated

Printed in the United States of America

Text for this book was completely photoset by
Allservice Phototypesetting Company, Glenview, Illinois

PUBLISHER'S PREFACE

The book you are about to read is composed of stories written by Rudyard Kipling. Originally, these stories were in two volumes entitled "The Jungle Book," and "The Second Jungle Book." The present volume combines all of the Mowgli Stories under one cover. In addition, "Rikki Tikki Tavi," "The Elephant Boy," and "The Miracle of Purun Bhagat" have been included. Certain other stories that appeared in the original books have been omitted due to limitations of space. The stories that do appear in this book are unabridged, exactly as Kipling originally published them.

PART	PAGE

BACKWORD

Mowgli's Brothers

Now Rann, the Kite, brings home the night
   That Mang, the Bat, sets free —
The herds are shut in byre and hut,
   For loosed till dawn are we.
This is the hour of pride and power,
   Talon and tush and claw.
Oh, hear the call! — Good hunting all
   That keep the Jungle Law!

                    Night-Song in the Jungle.

IT was seven o'clock of a very warm evening in the Seeonee hills when Father Wolf woke up from his day's rest, scratched himself, yawned, and spread out his paws one after the other to get rid of the sleepy feeling in the tips. Mother Wolf lay with her big gray nose dropped across her four tumbling, squealing cubs, and the moon shone into the mouth of the cave where they all lived. "Augrh!" said Father

The Jungle Book

Wolf, "it is time to hunt again"; and he was going to spring downhill when a little shadow with a bushy tail crossed the threshold and whined: "Good luck go with you, O Chief of the Wolves; and good luck and strong white teeth go with the noble children, that they may never forget the hungry in this world."

It was the jackal—Tabaqui, the Dish-licker—and the wolves of India despise Tabaqui because he runs about making mischief, and telling tales, and eating rags and pieces of leather from the village rubbish-heaps. They are afraid of him too, because Tabaqui, more than any one else in the jungle, is apt to go mad, and then he forgets that he was ever afraid of any one, and runs through the forest biting everything in his way. Even the tiger hides when little Tabaqui goes mad, for madness is the most disgraceful thing that can overtake a wild creature. We call it hydrophobia, but they call it *dewanee*—the madness—and run.

"Enter, then, and look," said Father Wolf, stiffly; "but there is no food here."

"For a wolf, no," said Tabaqui; "but for so mean a person as myself a dry bone is a good feast. Who are we, the Gidur-log [the Jackal People], to pick and choose?" He scuttled to the back of the cave, where he found the bone of a buck with some meat on it, and sat cracking the end merrily.

"All thanks for this good meal," he said, licking his lips. "How beautiful are the noble children! How large are their eyes! And so young too! Indeed, indeed, I might have remembered that the children of kings are men from the beginning."

Now, Tabaqui knew as well as any one else that there is nothing so unlucky as to compliment children to their faces; and it pleased him to see Mother and Father Wolf look uncomfortable.

Tabaqui sat still, rejoicing in the mischief that he had made, and then he said spitefully:

"Shere Khan, the Big One, has shifted his hunting-grounds. He will hunt among these hills during the next moon, so he has told me."

Shere Khan was the tiger who lived near the Waingunga River, twenty miles away.

"He has no right!" Father Wolf began angrily. "By the Law of the Jungle he has no right to change his quarters without fair warning. He will frighten every head of game within ten miles; and I—I have to kill for two, these days."

"His mother did not call him Lungri [the Lame One] for nothing," said Mother Wolf, quietly. "He has been lame in one foot from his birth. That is why he has only killed cattle.

Now the villagers of the Waingunga are angry with him, and he has come here to make *our* villagers angry. They will scour the jungle for him when he is far away, and we and our children must run when the grass is set alight. Indeed, we are very grateful to Shere Khan!"

"Shall I tell him of your gratitude?" said Tabaqui.

"Out!" snapped Father Wolf. "Out, and hunt with thy master. Thou hast done harm enough for one night."

"I go," said Tabaqui, quietly. "Ye can hear Shere Khan below in the thickets. I might have saved myself the message."

Father Wolf listened, and in the dark valley that ran down to a little river, he heard the dry, angry, snarly, singsong whine of a tiger who has caught nothing and does not care if all the jungle knows it.

"The fool!" said Father Wolf. "To begin a night's work with that noise! Does he think that our buck are like his fat Waingunga bullocks?"

"H'sh! It is neither bullock nor buck that he hunts to-night," said Mother Wolf; "it is Man." The whine had changed to a sort of humming purr that seemed to roll from every quarter of the compass. It was the noise that bewilders wood-cutters, and gypsies sleeping in the open, and makes them run sometimes into the very mouth of the tiger.

"Man!" said Father Wolf, showing all his white teeth. "Faugh! Are there not enough beetles and frogs in the tanks that he must eat Man—and on our ground too!"

The Law of the Jungle, which never orders anything without a reason, forbids every beast to eat Man except when he is killing to show his children how to kill, and then he must hunt outside the hunting-grounds of his pack or tribe. The real reason for this is that man-killing means, sooner or later, the arrival of white men on elephants, with guns, and hundreds of brown men with gongs and rockets and torches. Then everybody in the jungle suffers. The reason the beasts give among themselves is that Man is the weakest and most defenseless of all living things, and it is unsportsmanlike to touch him. They say too—and it is true—that man-eaters become mangy, and lose their teeth.

The purr grew louder, and ended in the full-throated "Aaarh!" of the tiger's charge.

Then there was a howl—an untigerish howl—from Shere Khan. "He has missed," said Mother Wolf. "What is it?"

Father Wolf ran out a few paces and heard Shere Khan muttering and mumbling savagely, as he tumbled about in the scrub.

"The fool has had no more sense than to jump at a wood-

tiger: Suprisingly, the TIGER is a fine swimmer and likes to roam about river-banks. Not only because he likes water, but because other animals come to drink —and he likes other animals. Deer, pig, and buffalo are his favorite meals.

Royal Tiger

man-killing: Ferocious though he be, a tiger will attack humans only when he is hurt, extremely hungry, or very old.

cutters' camp-fire, so he has burned his feet," said Father Wolf, with a grunt. "Tabaqui is with him."

"Something is coming uphill," said Mother Wolf, twitching one ear. "Get ready."

The bushes rustled a little in the thicket, and Father Wolf dropped with his haunches under him, ready for his leap. Then, if you had been watching, you would have seen the most wonderful thing in the world—the wolf checked in mid-spring. He made his bound before he saw what it was he was jumping at, and then he tried to stop himself. The result was that he shot up straight into the air for four or five feet, landing almost where he left ground.

"Man!" he snapped. "A man's cub. Look!"

Directly in front of him, holding on by a low branch, stood a naked brown baby who could just walk—as soft and as dimpled a little thing as ever came to a wolf's cave at night. He looked up into Father Wolf's face and laughed.

"Is that a man's cub?" said Mother Wolf. "I have never seen one. Bring it here."

A wolf accustomed to moving his own cubs can, if necessary, mouth an egg without breaking it, and though Father Wolf's jaws closed right on the child's back not a tooth even scratched the skin, as he laid it down among the cubs.

"How little! How naked, and—how bold!" said Mother Wolf, softly. The baby was pushing his way between the cubs to get close to the warm hide. "Ahai! He is taking his meal with the others. And so this is a man's cub. Now was there ever a wolf that could boast of a man's cub among her children?"

"I have heard now and again of such a thing, but never in our pack or in my time," said Father Wolf. "He is altogether without hair, and I could kill him with a touch of my foot. But see, he looks up and is not afraid."

The moonlight was blocked out of the mouth of the cave, for Shere Khan's great square head and shoulders were thrust into the entrance, Tabaqui, behind him, was squeaking: "My Lord, my Lord, it went in here!"

"Shere Khan does us great honour," said Father Wolf, but his eyes were very angry. "What does Shere Khan need?"

"My quarry. A man's cub went this way," said Shere Khan. "Its parents have run off. Give it to me."

Shere Khan had jumped at a wood-cutter's camp-fire, as Father Wolf had said, and was furious from the pain of his burned feet. But Father Wolf knew that the mouth of the cave was too narrow for a tiger to come in by. Even where he was, Shere Khan's shoulders and fore paws were cramped

I have heard: Perhaps the ancient legend of Romulus and Remus was repeated in Father Wolf's pack down through the centuries. These twins were nursed by a she-wolf. When they grew to manhood, they founded the great city of Rome.

for want of room, as a man's would be if he tried to fight in a barrel.

"The Wolves are a free people," said Father Wolf. "They take orders from the Head of the Pack, and not from any striped cattle-killer. The man's cub is ours—to kill if we choose."

"Ye choose and ye do not choose! What talk is this of choosing? By the Bull that I killed, am I to stand nosing into your dog's den for my fair dues? It is I, Shere Khan, who speak!"

The tiger's roar filled the cave with thunder. Mother Wolf shook herself clear of the cubs and sprang forward, her eyes, like two green moons in the darkness, facing the blazing eyes of Shere Khan.

"And it is I, Raksha [the Demon], who answer. The man's cub is mine, Lungri—mine to me! He shall not be killed. He shall live to run with the Pack and to hunt with the Pack; and in the end, look you, hunter of little naked cubs—frog-eater —fish-killer, he shall hunt *thee!* Now get hence, or by the Sambhur that I killed (*I* eat no starved cattle), back thou goest to thy mother, burned beast of the jungle, lamer than ever thou camest into the world! Go!"

Father Wolf looked on amazed. He had almost forgotten the days when he won Mother Wolf in fair fight from five other wolves, when she ran in the Pack and was not called the Demon for compliment's sake. Shere Khan might have faced Father Wolf, but he could not stand up against Mother Wolf, for he knew that where he was she had all the advantage of the ground, and would fight to the death. So he backed out of the cave-mouth growling, and when he was clear he shouted:

"Each dog barks in his own yard! We will see what the Pack will say to this fostering of man-cubs. The cub is mine, and to my teeth he will come in the end, O bush-tailed thieves!"

Mother Wolf threw herself down panting among the cubs, and Father Wolf said to her gravely:

"Shere Khan speaks this much truth. The cub must be shown to the Pack. Wilt thou still keep him, Mother?"

"Keep him!" she gasped. "He came naked, by night, alone and very hungry; yet he was not afraid! Look, he has pushed one of my babes to one side already. And that lame butcher would have killed him, and would have run off to the Waingunga while the villagers here hunted through all our lairs in revenge! Keep him? Assuredly I will keep him. Lie still, little frog. O thou Mowgli,—for Mowgli, the Frog, I will call thee,—the time will come when thou wilt hunt Shere Khan as he has hunted thee!"

"But what will our Pack say?" said Father Wolf.

The Law of the Jungle lays down very clearly that any wolf may, when he marries, withdraw from the Pack he belongs to; but as soon as his cubs are old enough to stand on their feet he must bring them to the Pack Council, which is generally held once a month at full moon, in order that the other wolves may identify them. After that inspection the cubs are free to run where they please, and until they have killed their first buck no excuse is accepted if a grown wolf of the Pack kills one of them. The punishment is death where the murderer can be found; and if you think for a minute you will see that this must be so.

Father Wolf waited till his cubs could run a little, and then on the night of the Pack Meeting took them and Mowgli and Mother Wolf to the Council Rock—a hilltop covered with stones and boulders where a hundred wolves could hide. Akela, the great gray Lone Wolf, who led all the Pack by strength and cunning, lay out at full length on his rock, and below him sat forty or more wolves of every size and colour, from badger-coloured veterans who could handle a buck alone, to young black three-year-olds who thought they could. The Lone Wolf had led them for a year now. He had fallen twice into a wolf-trap in his youth, and once he had been beaten and left for dead; so he knew the manners and customs of men.

There was very little talking at the Rock. The cubs tumbled over one another in the center of the circle where their mothers and fathers sat, and now and again a senior wolf would go quietly up to a cub, look at him carefully, and return to his place on noiseless feet. Sometimes a mother would push her cub far out into the moonlight, to be sure that he had not been overlooked. Akela from his rock would cry: "Ye know the Law—ye know the Law; Look well, O Wolves!" And the anxious mothers would take up the call: "Look—look well, O Wolves!"

At last—and Mother Wolf's neck-bristles lifted as the time came—Father Wolf pushed "Mowgli, the Frog," as they called him, into the center, where he sat laughing and playing with some pebbles that glistened in the moonlight.

Akela never raised his head from his paws, but went on with the monotonous cry, "Look well!" A muffled roar came up from behind the rocks—the voice of Shere Khan crying, "The cub is mine; give him to me. What have the Free People to do with a man's cub?"

Akela never even twitched his ears. All he said was, "Look

well, O Wolves! What have the Free People to do with the orders of any save the Free People? Look well!"

There was a chorus of deep growls, and a young wolf in his fourth year flung back Shere Khan's question to Akela: "What have the Free People to do with a man's cub?"

Now the Law of the Jungle lays down that if there is any dispute as to the right of a cub to be accepted by the Pack, he must be spoken for by at least two members of the Pack who are not his father and mother.

"Who speaks for this cub?" said Akela. "Among the Free People, who speaks?" There was no answer, and Mother Wolf got ready for what she knew would be her last fight, if things came to fighting.

Then the only other creature who is allowed at the Pack Council—Baloo, the sleepy brown bear who teaches the wolf cubs the Law of the Jungle, old Baloo—who can come and go where he pleases because he eats only nuts and roots and honey—rose up on his hind quarters and grunted.

"The man's cub—the man's cub?" he said. "*I* speak for the man's cub. There is no harm in a man's cub. I have no gift of words, but I speak the truth. Let him run with the Pack, and be entered with the others. I myself will teach him."

"We need yet another," said Akela. "Baloo has spoken, and he is our teacher for the young cubs. Who speaks besides Baloo?"

A black shadow dropped down into the circle. It was Bagheera, the Black Panther, inky black all over, but with the panther markings showing up in certain lights like the pattern of watered silk. Everybody knew Bagheera, and nobody cared to cross his path; for he was as cunning as Tabaqui, as bold as the wild buffalo, and as reckless as the wounded elephant. But he had a voice as soft as wild honey dripping from a tree, and a skin softer than down.

"O Akela, and ye, the Free People," he purred, "I have no right in your assembly; but the Law of the Jungle says that if there is a doubt which is not a killing matter in regard to a new cub, the life of that cub may be bought at a price. And the Law does not say who may or may not pay that price. Am I right?"

"Good! good!" said the young wolves, who are always hungry. "Listen to Bagheera. The cub can be bought for a price. It is the Law."

"Knowing that I have no right to speak here, I ask your leave."

"Speak then," cried twenty voices.

"To kill a naked cub is shame. Besides, he may make

Aswail, or Sloth-bear.

old Baloo: He is one of the sloth-bears of India. Also called honey-bears, they love to eat honey-comb. They like to eat roots, grubs, and ants, too.

Bagheera: The black panther, though seldom weighing more than 150 pounds, is one of the most fearsome of the big cats. Like the bears, his color can vary from reddish yellow to black. The panther—also called the Tree Tiger—stalks and kills baboons, antelope, pigs and even unwary birds.

Black Panther

7

better sport for you when he is grown. Baloo has spoken in his behalf. Now to Baloo's word I will add one bull, and a fat one, newly killed, not half a mile from here, if ye will accept the man's cub according to the Law. Is it difficult?"

There was a clamour of scores of voices, saying:

"What matter? He will die in the winter rains. He will scorch in the sun. What harm can a naked frog do us? Let him run with the Pack. Where is the bull, Bagheera? Let him be accepted." And then came Akela's deep bay, crying: "Look well—look well, O Wolves!"

Mowgli was still playing with the pebbles, and he did not notice when the wolves came and looked at him one by one. At last they all went down the hill for the dead bull, and only Akela, Bagheera, Baloo, and Mowgli's own wolves were left. Shere Khan roared still in the night, for he was very angry that Mowgli had not been handed over to him.

"Ay, roar well," said Bagheera, under his whiskers; "for the time comes when this naked thing will make thee roar to another tune, or I know nothing of Man."

"It was well done," said Akela. "Men and their cubs are very wise. He may be a help in time."

"Truly, a help in time of need; for none can hope to lead the Pack forever," said Bagheera.

Akela said nothing. He was thinking of the time that comes to every leader of every pack when his strength goes from him and he gets feebler and feebler, till at last he is killed by the wolves and a new leader comes up—to be killed in his turn.

"Take him away," he said to Father Wolf, "and train him as befits one of the Free People."

And that is how Mowgli was entered into the Seeonee wolf-pack for the price of a bull and on Baloo's good word.

Now you must be content to skip ten or eleven whole years, and only guess at all the wonderful life that Mowgli led among the wolves, because if it were written out it would fill ever so many books. He grew up with the cubs, though they of course were grown wolves almost before he was a child, and Father Wolf taught him his business, and the meaning of things in the jungle, till every rustle in the grass, every breath of the warm night air, every note of the owls above his head, every scratch of a bat's claws as it roosted for a while in a tree, and every splash of every little fish jumping in a pool, meant just as much to him as the work of his office means to a business man. When he was not learning he sat out in the sun and slept, and ate, and went to sleep again; when he felt dirty or hot he swam in the forest pools; and when he wanted honey (Baloo told him that honey and

owls: No common owls did Mowgli hear. These were probably the great eagle owl of Asia. With its two foot wingspread, this is the biggest and most powerful of the whole family of hooters.

nuts were just as pleasant to eat as raw meat) he climbed up
for it, and that Bagheera showed him how to do.

Bagheera would lie out on a branch and call, "Come along,
Little Brother," and at first Mowgli would cling like the
sloth, but afterward he would fling himself through the
branches almost as boldly as the gray ape. He took his place
at the Council Rock, too, when the Pack met, and there he
discovered that if he stared hard at any wolf, the wolf would
be forced to drop his eyes, and so he used to stare for fun.

At other times he would pick the long thorns out of the
pads of his friends, for wolves suffer terribly from thorns and
burs in their coats. He would go down the hillside into the
cultivated lands by night, and look very curiously at the
villagers in their huts, but he had a mistrust of men because
Bagheera showed him a square box with a drop-gate so cunningly hidden in the jungle that he nearly walked into it, and
told him it was a trap.

traps: The villagers sometimes set cunning traps for the jungle animals. One of these was a pit. At the bottom, sharp stakes were fixed; over the top, branches were spread. Sometimes a young goat was tied, as bait. When the big cats sprang for the goat, they went through the branches, and were impaled on the sharp stakes below.

He loved better than anything else to go with Bagheera
into the dark warm heart of the forest, to sleep all through the
drowsy day, and at night see how Bagheera did his killing.
Bagheera killed right and left as he felt hungry, and so did
Mowgli—with one exception. As soon as he was old enough
to understand things, Bagheera told him that he must never
touch cattle because he had been bought into the Pack at the
price of a bull's life. "All the jungle is thine," said Bagheera,
"And thou canst kill everything that thou art strong enough
to kill; but for the sake of the bull that bought thee thou must
never kill or eat any cattle young or old. That is the Law of
the Jungle." Mowgli obeyed faithfully.

And he grew and grew strong as a boy must grow who
does not know that he is learning any lessons, and who has
nothing in the world to think of except things to eat.

Mother Wolf told him once or twice that Shere Khan was
not a creature to be trusted, and that some day he must kill
Shere Khan; but though a young wolf would have remembered that advice every hour, Mowgli forgot it because he
was only a boy—though he would have called himself a wolf
if he had been able to speak in any human tongue.

Shere Khan was always crossing his path in the jungle, for
as Akela grew older and feebler the lame tiger had come to
be great friends with the younger wolves of the Pack, who
followed him for scraps, a thing Akela would never have
allowed if he had dared to push his authority to the proper
bounds. Then Shere Khan would flatter them and wonder
that such fine young hunters were content to be led by a
dying wolf and a man's cub. "They tell me," Shere Khan
would say, "that at Council ye dare not look him between

porcupine: Though the PORCU-PINE is not a very cuddly sort, he is a rather comical fellow as he waddles his way through the tanglewood. The reason he waddles is that he uses his big tail like a whisk broom to erase his trail.

peacock: The only jungle enemy of the shy and beautiful peacock is the leopard. The PEACOCK is revered by the Hindus, who call him "Mor." Throughout India, his feathers are sought because they were—and still are—used for making magic.

the eyes"; and the young wolves would growl and bristle.

Bagheera, who had eyes and ears everywhere, knew something of this, and once or twice he told Mowgli in so many words that Shere Khan would kill him some day; and Mowgli would laugh and answer: "I have the Pack and I have thee; and Baloo, though he is so lazy, might strike a blow or two for my sake. Why should I be afraid?"

It was one very warm day that a new notion came to Bagheera—born of something that he had heard. Perhaps Ikki, the Porcupine, had told him; but he said to Mowgli when they were deep in the jungle, as the boy lay with his head on Bagheera's beautiful black skin: "Little Brother, how often have I told thee that Shere Khan is thy enemy?"

"As many times as there are nuts on that palm," said Mowgli, who, naturally, could not count. "What of it? I am sleepy, Bagheera, and Shere Khan is all long tail and loud talk, like Mao, the Peacock."

"But this is no time for sleeping. Baloo knows it, I know it, the Pack know it, and even the foolish, foolish deer know. Tabaqui has told thee too."

"Ho! ho!" said Mowgli. "Tabaqui came to me not long ago with some rude talk that I was a naked man's cub, and not fit to dig pig-nuts; but I caught Tabaqui by the tail and swung him twice against a palm-tree to teach him better manners."

"That was foolishness; for though Tabaqui is a mischief-maker, he would have told thee of something that concerned thee closely. Open those eyes, Little Brother! Shere Khan dares not kill thee in the jungle for fear of those that love thee; but remember, Akela is very old, and soon the day comes when he cannot kill his buck, and then he will be leader no more. Many of the wolves that looked thee over when thou wast brought to the Council first are old too, and the young wolves believe, as Shere Khan has taught them, that a man-cub has no place with the Pack. In a little time thou wilt be a man."

"And what is a man that he should not run with his brothers?" said Mowgli. "I was born in the jungle; I have obeyed the Law of the Jungle; and there is no wolf of ours from whose paws I have not pulled a thorn. Surely they are my brothers!"

Bagheera stretched himself at full length and half shut his eyes. "Little Brother," said he, "feel under my jaw."

Mowgli put up his strong brown hand, and just under Bagheera's silky chin, where the giant rolling muscles were all hid by the glossy hair, he came upon a little bald spot.

"There is no one in the jungle that knows that I, Bagheera, carry that mark—the mark of the collar; and yet, Little

Brother, I was born among men, and it was among men that my mother died—in the cages of the King's Palace at Oodeypore. It was because of this that I paid the price for thee at the Council when thou wast a little naked cub. Yes, I too was born among men. I had never seen the jungle. They fed me behind bars from an iron pan till one night I felt that I was Bagheera, the Panther, and no man's plaything, and I broke the silly lock with one blow of my paw, and came away; and because I had learned the ways of men, I became more terrible in the jungle than Shere Khan. Is it not so?"

"Yes," said Mowgli; "all the jungle fear Bagheera—all except Mowgli."

"Oh, *thou* art a man's cub," said the Black Panther, very tenderly; "and even as I returned to my jungle, so thou must go back to men at last,—to the men who are thy brothers,— if thou art not killed in the Council."

"But why—but why should any wish to kill me?" said Mowgli.

"Look at me," said Bagheera; and Mowgli looked at him steadily between the eyes. The big panther turned his head away in half a minute.

"*That* is why," he said, shifting his paw on the leaves. "Not even I can look thee between the eyes, and I was born among men, and I love thee, Little Brother. The others they hate thee because their eyes cannot meet thine, because thou art wise; because thou hast pulled out thorns from their feet—because thou art a man."

"I did not know these things," said Mowgli, sullenly; and he frowned under his heavy black eyebrows.

"What is the Law of the Jungle? Strike first and then give tongue. By thy very carelessness they know that thou art a man. But be wise. It is in my heart that when Akela misses his next kill,—and at each hunt it costs him more to pin the buck,—the Pack will turn against him and against thee. They will hold a jungle Council at the Rock, and then—and then. . . . I have it!" said Bagheera, leaping up. "Go thou down quickly to the men's huts in the valley, and take some of the Red Flower which they grow there, so that when the time comes thou mayest have even a stronger friend than I or Baloo or those of the Pack that love thee. Get the Red Flower."

By Red Flower Bagheera meant fire, only no creature in the jungle will call fire by its proper name. Every beast lives in deadly fear of it, and invents a hundred ways of describing it.

"The Red Flower?" said Mowgli. "That grows outside their huts in the twilight. I will get some."

"There speaks the man's cub," said Bagheera, proudly. "Remember that it grows in little pots. Get one swiftly, and keep it by thee for time of need."

"Good!" said Mowgli. "I go. But art thou sure, O my Bagheera"—he slipped his arm round the splendid neck, and looked deep into the big eyes—"art thou sure that all this is Shere Khan's doing?"

"By the Broken Lock that freed me, I am sure, Little Brother."

"Then, by the Bull that bought me, I will pay Shere Khan full tale for this, and it may be a little over," said Mowgli; and he bounded away.

"That is a man. That is all a man," said Bagheera to himself, lying down again. "Oh, Shere Khan, never was a blacker hunting than that frog-hunt of thine ten years ago!"

Mowgli was far and far through the forest, running hard, and his heart was hot in him. He came to the cave as the evening mist rose, and drew breath, and looked down the valley. The cubs were out, but Mother Wolf, at the back of the cave, knew by his breathing that something was troubling her frog.

"What is it, Son?" she said.

"Some bat's chatter of Shere Khan," he called back. "I hunt among the ploughed fields to-night"; and he plunged downward through the bushes, to the stream at the bottom of the valley. There he checked, for he heard the yell of the Pack hunting, heard the bellow of a hunted Sambhur, and the snort as the buck turned at bay. Then there were wicked, bitter howls from the young wolves: "Akela! Akela! Let the Lone Wolf show his strength. Room for the leader of our Pack! Spring, Akela!"

The Lone Wolf must have sprung and missed his hold, for Mowgli heard the snap of his teeth and then a yelp as the Sambhur knocked him over with his fore foot.

He did not wait for anything more, but dashed on; and the yells grew fainter behind him as he ran into the crop-lands where the villagers lived.

"Bagheera spoke truth," he panted, as he nestled down in some cattle-fodder by the window of a hut. "To-morrow is one day for Akela and for me."

Then he pressed his face close to the window and watched the fire on the hearth. He saw the husbandman's wife get up and feed it in the night with black lumps; and when the morning came and the mists were all white and cold, he saw the man's child pick up a wicker pot plastered inside with earth, fill it with lumps of red-hot charcoal, put it under his blanket, and go out to tend the cows in the byre.

charcoal: Natives in many places pile pieces of wood, cover the pile with earth or sand, and fire it through openings at the bottom. Because oxygen is limited, the wood doesn't burn up completely, but becomes charcoal. These hard, black pieces make an excellent fuel, producing considerable heat without flame. Because charcoal smoulders so quietly, it can be carried around conveniently in clay pots or metal braziers.

"Is that all?" said Mowgli. "If a cub can do it, there is nothing to fear"; so he strode around the corner and met the boy, took the pot from his hand and disappeared into the mist while the boy howled with fear.

"They are very like me," said Mowgli, blowing into the pot, as he had seen the woman do. "This thing will die if I do not give it things to eat"; and he dropped twigs and dried bark on the red stuff. Half-way up the hill he met Bagheera with the morning dew shining like moonstones on his coat.

"Akela has missed," said the panther. "They would have killed him last night, but they needed thee also. They were looking for thee on the hill."

"I was among the ploughed lands. I am ready. Look!" Mowgli held up the fire-pot.

"Good! Now, I have seen men thrust a dry branch into that stuff, and presently the Red Flower blossomed at the end of it. Art thou not afraid?"

"No. Why should I fear? I remember—now if it is not a dream—how, before I was a wolf, I lay beside the Red Flower, and it was warm and pleasant."

All that day Mowgli sat in the cave tending his fire-pot and dipping dry branches into it to see how they looked. He found a branch that satisfied him, and in the evening when Tabaqui came to the cave and told him, rudely enough, that he was wanted at the Council Rock, he laughed till Tabaqui ran away. Then Mowgli went to the Council, still laughing.

Akela the Lone Wolf lay by the side of his rock as a sign that the leadership of the Pack was open, and Shere Khan with his following of scrap-fed wolves walked to and fro openly, being flattered. Bagheera lay close to Mowgli, and the fire-pot was between Mowgli's knees. When they were all gathered together, Shere Khan began to speak—a thing he would never have dared to do when Akela was in his prime.

"He has no right," whispered Bagheera. "Say so. He is a dog's son. He will be frightened."

Mowgli sprang to his feet. "Free People," he cried, "does Shere Khan lead the Pack? What has a tiger to do with our leadership?"

"Seeing that the leadership is yet open, and being asked to speak"—Shere Khan began.

"By whom?" said Mowgli. "Are we *all* jackals, to fawn on this cattle-butcher? The leadership of the Pack is with the Pack alone."

There were yells of "Silence, thou man's cub!"

"Let him speak; he has kept our law!" And at last the seniors of the Pack thundered: "Let the Dead Wolf speak!"

moonstone: Some translucent kinds of the mineral feldspar show a pearl-like display of color. It is one of the semi-precious stones.

When a leader of the Pack has missed his kill, he is called the Dead Wolf as long as he lives, which is not long, as a rule.

Akela raised his old head wearily:

"Free people, and ye too, jackals of Shere Khan, for twelve seasons I have led ye to and from the kill, and in all that time not one has been trapped or maimed. Now I have missed my kill. Ye know how that plot was made. Ye know how ye brought me up to an untried buck to make my weakness known. It was cleverly done. Your right is to kill me here on the Council Rock now. Therefore I ask, 'Who comes to make an end of the Lone Wolf?' For it is my right, by the Law of the Jungle, that ye come one by one."

There was a long hush, for no single wolf cared to fight Akela to the death. Then Shere Khan roared: "Bah! What have we to do with this toothless fool? He is doomed to die! It is the man-cub who has lived too long. Free People, he was my meat from the first. Give him to me. I am weary of this man-wolf folly. He has troubled the jungle for ten seasons. Give me the man-cub, or I will hunt here always, and not give you one bone! He is a man—a man's child, and from the marrow of my bones I hate him!"

Then more than half the Pack yelled: "A man—a man! What has a man to do with us? Let him go to his own place."

"And turn all the people of the villages against us?" snarled Shere Khan. "No; give him to me. He is a man, and none of us can look him between the eyes."

Akela lifted his head again, and said: "He has eaten our food; he has slept with us; he has driven game for us; he has broken no word of the Law of the Jungle."

"Also, I paid for him with a bull when he was accepted. The worth of a bull is little, but Bagheera's honour is something that he will perhaps fight for," said Bagheera in his gentlest voice.

"A bull paid ten years ago!" the Pack snarled. "What do we care for bones ten years old?"

"Or for a pledge?" said Bagheera, his white teeth bared under his lip. "Well are ye called the Free People!"

"No man's cub can run with the people of the jungle!" roared Shere Khan. "Give him to me."

"He is our brother in all but blood," Akela went on; "and ye would kill him here. In truth, I have lived too long. Some of ye are eaters of cattle, and of others I have heard that, under Shere Khan's teaching, ye go by dark night and snatch children from the villager's doorstep. Therefore I know ye to be cowards, and it is to cowards I speak. It is certain that I must die, and my life is of no worth or I would offer that in the man-cub's place. But for the sake of the Honour of the Pack,—a little matter that, by being without a leader, ye have forgotten,—I promise that if ye let the man-cub go to his own place, I will not, when my time comes to die, bare one tooth against ye. I will die without fighting. That will at least save the Pack three lives. More I cannot do; but, if ye will, I can save ye the shame that comes of killing a brother against whom there is no fault—a brother spoken for and bought into the Pack according to the Law of the Jungle."

"He is a man—a man—a man!" snarled the Pack; and most of the wolves began to gather round Shere Khan, whose tail was beginning to switch.

"Now the business is in thy hands," said Bagheera to Mowgli. "*We* can do no more except fight."

Mowgli stood upright—the fire-pot in his hands. Then he stretched out his arms, and yawned in the face of the Council; but he was furious with rage and sorrow, for, wolf-like, the wolves had never told him how they hated him.

"Listen, you!" he cried. "There is no need for this dog's jabber. Ye have told me so often to-night that I am a man (though indeed I would have been a wolf with you to my life's end) that I feel your words are true. So I do not call ye my brothers any more, but *sag* [dogs], as a man should. What ye will do, and what ye will not do, is not yours to say. That matter is with *me*; and that we may see the matter more plainly, I, the man, have brought here a little of the Red Flower which ye, dogs, fear."

He flung the fire-pot on the ground, and some of the red coals lit a tuft of dried moss that flared up as all the Council drew back in terror before the leaping flames.

Mowgli thrust his dead branch into the fire till the twigs lit and crackled, and whirled it above his head among the cowering wolves.

"Thou art the master," said Bagheera, in an undertone. "Save Akela from the death. He was ever thy friend."

Akela, the grim old wolf who had never asked for mercy in his life, gave one piteous look at Mowgli as the boy stood all naked, his long black hair tossing over his shoulders in the light of the blazing branch that made the shadows jump and quiver.

"Good!" said Mowgli, staring around slowly, and thrusting out his lower lip. "I see that ye are dogs. I go from you to my own people—if they be my own people. The jungle is shut to me, and I must forget your talk and your companionship; but I will be more merciful than ye are. Because I was all but your brother in blood, I promise that when I am a man among men I will not betray ye to men as ye have betrayed

red flower: All, or certainly almost all wild animals fear fire. Domestic animals do not. Cats or dogs will curl up by the fireplace, as they probably curled up by campfires and cavefires tens of centuries ago.

gullet: Throat.

me." He kicked the fire with his foot, and the sparks flew up. "There shall be no war between any of us and the Pack. But here is a debt to pay before I go." He strode forward to where Shere Khan sat blinking stupidly at the flames, and caught him by the tuft on his chin. Bagheera followed close, in case of accidents. "Up, dog!" Mowgli cried. "Up, when a man speaks, or I will set that coat ablaze!"

Shere Khan's ears lay flat back on his head, and he shut his eyes, for the blazing branch was very near.

"This cattle-killer said he would kill me in the Council because he had not killed me when I was a cub. Thus and thus, then, do we beat dogs when we are men! Stir a whisker, Lungri, and I ram the Red Flower down thy gullet!" He beat Shere Khan over the head with the branch, and the tiger whimpered and whined in an agony of fear.

"Pah! Singed jungle-cat—go now! But remember when next I come to the Council Rock, as a man should come, it will be with Shere Khan's hide on my head. For the rest, Akela goes free to live as he pleases. Ye will *not* kill him, because that is not my will. Nor do I think that ye will sit here any longer, lolling out your tongues as though ye were somebodies, instead of dogs whom I drive out— thus! Go!"

The fire was burning furiously at the end of the branch, and Mowgli struck right and left round the circle, and the wolves ran howling with the sparks burning their fur. At last there were only Akela, Bagheera, and perhaps ten wolves that had taken Mowgli's part. Then something began to hurt Mowgli inside him, as he had never been hurt in his life before, and he caught his breath and sobbed, and the tears ran down his face.

"What is it? What is it?" he said. "I do not wish to leave the jungle, and I do not know what this is. Am I dying, Bagheera?"

"No, Little Brother. Those are only tears such as men use," said Bagheera. "Now I know thou art a man, and a man's cub no longer. The jungle is shut indeed to thee henceforward. Let them fall, Mowgli; they are only tears." So Mowgli sat and cried as though his heart would break; and he had never cried in all his life before.

"Now," he said, "I will go to men. But first I must say farewell to my mother"; and he went to the cave where she lived with Father Wolf, and he cried on her coat, while the four cubs howled miserably.

"Ye will not forget me?" said Mowgli.

"Never while we can follow a trail," said the cubs. "Come to the foot of the hill when thou art a man, and we will talk to thee; and we will come into the crop-lands to play with thee by night."

"Come soon!" said Father Wolf. "Oh, wise little Frog, come again soon; for we be old, thy mother and I."

"Come soon," said Mother Wolf, "little naked son of mine; for, listen, child of man, I loved thee more than ever I loved my cubs."

"I will surely come," said Mowgli; "and when I come it will be to lay out Shere Khan's hide upon the Council Rock. Do not forget me! Tell them in the jungle never to forget me!"

The dawn was beginning to break when Mowgli went down the hillside alone to the crops to meet those mysterious things that are called men.

HUNTING-SONG OF THE SEEONEE PACK

As the dawn was breaking the Sambhur belled
 Once, twice, and again!
And a doe leaped up—and a doe leaped up
From the pond in the wood where the wild deer sup.
This I, scouting alone, beheld,
 Once, twice, and again!

As the dawn was breaking the Sambhur belled
 Once, twice, and again!
And a wolf stole back—and a wolf stole back
To carry the word to the waiting Pack;
And we sought and we found and we bayed on his track
 Once, twice, and again!

As the dawn was breaking the Wolf-pack yelled
 Once, twice, and again!
Feet in the jungle that leave no mark!
Eyes that can see in the dark—the dark!
Tongue—give tongue to it! Hark! O Hark!
 Once, twice, and again!

2

Kaa's Hunting

His spots are the joy of the Leopard: his horns are the
    Buffalo's pride—
Be clean, for the strength of the hunter is known by the gloss
    of his hide.

If ye find that the Bullock can toss you, or the heavy-browed
    Sambhur can gore;
Ye need not stop work to inform us; we knew it ten seasons
    before.

Oppress not the cubs of the stranger, but hail them as Sister
    and Brother,
For though they are little and fubsy, it may be the Bear is
    their mother.

"There is none like to me!" says the Cub in the pride of his
    earliest kill;
But the Jungle is large and the Cub he is small. Let him think
    and be still.

                                 Maxims of Baloo.

ALL that is told here happened some time before Mowgli was turned out of the Seeonee wolf-pack. It was in the days when Baloo was teaching him the Law of the Jungle. The big, serious, old brown bear was delighted to have so quick a pupil, for the young wolves will only learn as much of the Law of the Jungle as applies to their own pack and tribe, and run away as soon as they can repeat the Hunting Verse: "Feet that make no noise; eyes that can see in the dark; ears that can hear the winds in their lairs, and sharp white teeth—all these things are the marks of our brothers except Tabaqui and the Hyena, whom we hate." But Mowgli, as a man-cub, had to learn a great deal more than this. Sometimes Bagheera, the Black Panther, would come lounging through the jungle to see how his pet was getting on, and would purr with his head against a tree while Mowgli recited the day's lesson to Baloo. The boy could climb almost as well as he could swim, and swim almost as well as he could run; so Baloo, the Teacher of the Law, taught him the Wood and Water laws: how to tell a rotten branch from a sound one; how to speak politely to the wild bees when he came upon a hive of them fifty feet above-ground; what to say to Mang, the Bat, when he disturbed him in the branches at midday; and how to warn the water-snakes in the pools before he splashed down among them. None of the Jungle People like being disturbed, and all are very ready to fly at an intruder. Then, too, Mowgli was taught the Strangers' Hunting Call, which must be repeated aloud till it is answered, whenever one of the Jungle People hunts outside his own grounds. It means, translated: "Give me leave to hunt here because I am hungry"; and the answer is: "Hunt, then, for food, but not for pleasure."

All this will show you how much Mowgli had to learn by heart, and he grew very tired of repeating the same thing a hundred times; but, as Baloo said to Bagheera one day when Mowgli had been cuffed and had run off in a temper: "A man's cub is a man's cub, and he must learn *all* the Law of the Jungle."

"But think how small he is," said the Black Panther, who would have spoiled Mowgli if he had had his own way. "How can his little head carry all thy long talk?"

"Is there anything in the jungle too little to be killed? No. That is why I teach him these things, and that is why I hit him, very softly, when he forgets."

"Softly! What dost thou know of softness, old Iron-feet?" Bagheera grunted. "His face is all bruised to-day by thy—softness. Ugh!"

"Better he should be bruised from head to foot by me who

The Jungle Book

love him than that he should come to harm through ignorance," Baloo answered, very earnestly. "I am now teaching him the Master Words of the Jungle that shall protect him with the Birds and the Snake People, and all that hunt on four feet, except his own pack. He can now claim protection, if he will only remember the Words, from all in the jungle. Is not that worth a little beating?"

"Well, look to it then that thou dost not kill the man-cub. He is no tree-trunk to sharpen thy blunt claws upon. But what are those Master Words? I am more likely to give help than to ask it"— Bagheera stretched out one paw and admired the steel-blue ripping-chisel talons at the end of it— "Still I should like to know."

"I will call Mowgli and he shall say them—if he will. Come, Little Brother!"

"My head is ringing like a bee-tree," said a sullen voice over their heads, and Mowgli slid down a tree-trunk, very angry and indignant, adding, as he reached the ground: "I come for Bagheera and not for *thee*, fat old Baloo!"

"That is all one to me," said Baloo, though he was hurt and grieved. "Tell Bagheera, then, the Master Words of the Jungle that I have taught thee this day."

"Master Words for which people?" said Mowgli, delighted to show off. "The jungle has many tongues. *I* know them all."

"A little thou knowest, but not much. See, O Bagheera, they never thank their teacher! Not one small wolfling has come back to thank old Baloo for his teachings. Say the Word for the Hunting People, then,—great scholar!"

"We be of one blood, ye and I," said Mowgli, giving the words the Bear accent which all the Hunting People of the Jungle use.

"Good! Now for the Birds."

Mowgli repeated, with the Kite's whistle at the end of the sentence.

"Now for the Snake People," said Bagheera.

The answer was a perfectly indescribable hiss, and Mowgli kicked up his feet behind, clapped his hands together to applaud himself, and jumped on Bagheera's back, where he sat sideways, drumming with his heels on the glossy skin and making the worst faces that he could think of at Baloo.

"There—there! That was worth a little bruise," said the Brown Bear, tenderly. "Some day thou wilt remember me." Then he turned aside to tell Bagheera how he had begged the Master Words from Hathi, the Wild Elephant, who knows all about these things, and how Hathi had taken Mowgli down to a pool to get the Snake Word from a water-snake,

Carrion Kite

20

because Baloo could not pronounce it, and how Mowgli was now reasonably safe against all accidents in the jungle, because neither snake, bird, nor beast would hurt him.

"No one then is to be feared," Baloo wound up, patting his big furry stomach with pride.

"Except his own tribe," said Bagheera, under his breath; and then aloud to Mowgli: "Have a care for my ribs, Little Brother! What is all this dancing up and down?"

Mowgli had been trying to make himself heard by pulling at Bagheera's shoulder-fur and kicking hard. When the two listened to him he was shouting at the top of his voice: "And *so* I shall have a tribe of my own, and lead them through the branches all day long."

"What is this new folly, little dreamer of dreams?" said Bagheera.

"Yes, and throw branches and dirt at old Baloo," Mowgli went on. "They have promised me this, ah!"

"Whoof!" Baloo's big paw scooped Mowgli off Bagheera's back, and as the boy lay between the big fore paws he could see the bear was angry.

"Mowgli," said Baloo, "thou hast been talking with the Bandar-log—the Monkey People."

Mowgli looked at Bagheera to see if the panther was angry too, and Bagheera's eyes were as hard as jade-stones.

"Thou hast been with the Monkey People—the gray apes—the people without a Law—the eaters of everything. That is great shame."

"When Baloo hurt my head," said Mowgli (he was still down on his back), "I went away, and the gray apes came down from the trees and had pity on me. No one else cared." He snuffled a little.

"The pity of the Monkey People!" Baloo snorted.

"The stillness of the mountain stream! The cool of the summer sun! And then, man-cub?"

"And then—and then they gave me nuts and pleasant things to eat, and they—they carried me in their arms up to the top of the trees and said I was their blood-brother, except that I had no tail, and should be their leader some day."

"They have *no* leader," said Bagheera. "They lie. They have always lied."

"They were very kind, and bade me come again. Why have I never been taken among the Monkey People? They stand on their feet as I do. They do not hit me with hard paws. They play all day. Let me get up! Bad Baloo, let me up! I will go play with them again."

"Listen, man-cub," said the bear, and his voice rumbled like thunder on a hot night. "I have taught thee all the Law

jade-stones: Hard vitreous stones, usually green in color, but ranging into the whites, highly prized in lands of the East.

monkeys: Though the band described here are not very lovable, monkeys individually are probably the smartest of all animals. They can learn and they can reason. Monkeys were among the very first astronauts, and were able to carry out special duties— pushing buttons—on signal while in space.

of the Jungle for all the Peoples of the Jungle—except the Monkey Folk who live in the trees. They have no Law. They are outcasts. They have no speech of their own but use the stolen words which they overhear when they listen and peep and wait up above in the branches. Their way is not our way. They are without leaders. They have no remembrance. They boast and chatter and pretend that they are a great people about to do great affairs in the jungle, but the falling of a nut turns their minds to laughter, and all is forgotten. We of the jungle have no dealings with them. We do not drink where the monkeys drink; we do not go where the monkeys go; we do not hunt where they hunt; we do not die where they die. Has thou ever heard me speak of the Bandar-log till to-day?"

"No," said Mowgli in a whisper, for the forest was very still now that Baloo had finished.

"The Jungle People put them out of their mouths and out of their minds. They are very many, evil, dirty, shameless, and they desire, if they have any fixed desire, to be noticed by the Jungle People. But we do *not* notice them even when they throw nuts and filth on our heads."

He had hardly spoken when a shower of nuts and twigs spattered down through the branches; and they could hear coughings and howlings and angry jumpings high up in the air among the thin branches.

"The Monkey People are forbidden," said Baloo, "forbidden to the Jungle People. Remember."

"Forbidden," said Bagheera; "but I still think Baloo should have warned thee against them."

"I—I? How was I to guess he would play with such dirt. The Monkey People! Faugh!"

A fresh shower came down on their heads, and the two trotted away, taking Mowgli with them. What Baloo had said about the monkeys was perfectly true. They belonged to the tree-tops, and as beasts very seldom look up, there was no occasion for the monkeys and the Jungle People to cross one another's path. But whenever they found a sick wolf, or a wounded tiger or bear, the monkeys would torment him, and would throw sticks and nuts at any beast for fun and in the hope of being noticed. Then they would howl and shriek senseless songs, and invite the Jungle People to climb up their trees and fight them, or would start furious battles over nothing among themselves, and leave the dead monkeys where the Jungle People could see them.

They were always just going to have a leader and laws and customs of their own, but they never did, because their memories would not hold over from day to day, and so they settled things by making up a saying: "What the Bandar-log think now the Jungle will think later"; and that comforted them a great deal. None of the beasts could reach them, but on the other hand none of the beasts would notice them, and that was why they were so pleased when Mowgli came to play with them, and when they heard how angry Baloo was.

They never meant to do any more,—the Bandar-log never mean anything at all,—but one of them invented what seemed to him a brilliant idea, and he told all the others that Mowgli would be a useful person to keep in the tribe, because he could weave sticks together for protection from the wind; so, if they caught him, they could make him teach them. Of course Mowgli, as a wood-cutter's child, inherited all sorts of instincts, and used to make little playhuts of fallen branches without thinking how he came to do it. The Monkey People, watching in the trees, considered these huts most wonderful. This time, they said, they were really going to have a leader and become the wisest people in the jungle—so wise that every one else would notice and envy them. Therefore they followed Baloo and Bagheera and Mowgli through the jungle very quietly till it was time for the midday nap, and Mowgli, who was very much ashamed of himself, slept between the panther and the bear, resolving to have no more to do with the Monkey People.

The next thing he remembered was feeling hands on his legs and arms,—hard, strong little hands,—and then a swash of branches in his face; and then he was staring down through the swaying boughs as Baloo woke the jungle with his deep cries and Bagheera bounded up the trunk with every tooth bared. The Bandar-log howled with triumph, and scuffled away to the upper branches where Bagheera dared not follow, shouting: "He has noticed us! Bagheera has noticed us! All the Jungle People admire us for our skill and our cunning!" Then they began their flight; and the flight of the Monkey People through tree-land is one of the things nobody can describe. They have their regular roads and cross-roads, uphills and downhills, all laid out from fifty to seventy or a hundred feet above ground, and by these they can travel even at night if necessary.

Two of the strongest monkeys caught Mowgli under the arms and swung off with him through the tree-tops, twenty feet at a bound. Had they been alone they could have gone twice as fast, but the boy's weight held them back. Sick and giddy as Mowgli was he could not help enjoying the wild rush, though the glimpses of earth far down below frightened him, and the terrible check and jerk at the end of the

Gibbon

Monkeys are very agile animals. The GIBBON, pictured here, is considered to be the finest acrobat of the entire monkey world.

swing over nothing but empty air brought his heart between his teeth.

His escort would rush him up a tree till he felt the weak topmost branches crackle and bend under them, and, then, with a cough and a whoop, would fling themselves into the air outward and downward, and bring up hanging by their hands or their feet to the lower limbs of the next tree. Sometimes he could see for miles and miles over the still green jungle, as a man on the top of a mast can see for miles across the sea, and then the branches and leaves would lash him across the face, and he and his two guards would be almost down to earth again.

So bounding and crashing and whooping and yelling, the whole tribe of Bandar-log swept along the tree-roads with Mowgli their prisoner.

For a time he was afraid of being dropped; then he grew angry, but he knew better than to struggle; and then he began to think. The first thing was to send back word to Baloo and Bagheera, for, at the pace the monkeys were going, he knew his friends would be left far behind. It was useless to look down, for he could see only the top sides of the branches, so he stared upward and saw, far away in the blue, Rann, the Kite, balancing and wheeling as he kept watch over the jungle waiting for things to die. Rann noticed that the monkeys were carrying something, and dropped a few hundred yards to find out whether their load was good to eat. He whistled with surprise when he saw Mowgli being dragged up to a tree-top, and heard him give the Kite call for "We be of one blood, thou and I." The waves of the branches closed over the boy, but Rann balanced away to the next tree in time to see the little brown face come up again. "Mark my trail!" Mowgli shouted. "Tell Baloo of the Seeonee Pack, and Bagheera of the Council Rock."

"In whose name, Brother?" Rann had never seen Mowgli before, though of course he had heard of him.

"Mowgli, the Frog. Man-cub they call me! Mark my tra—il!"

The last words were shrieked as he was being swung through the air, but Rann nodded, and rose up till he looked no bigger than a speck of dust, and there he hung, watching with his telescope eyes the swaying of the tree-tops as Mowgli's escort whirled along.

"They never go far," he said with a chuckle. "They never do what they set out to do. Always pecking at new things are the Bandar-log. This time, if I have any eyesight, they have pecked down trouble for themselves, for Baloo is no fledgling and Bagheera can, as I know, kill more than goats."

Then he rocked on his wings, his feet gathered up under him, and waited.

Meanwhile, Baloo and Bagheera were furious with rage and grief. Bagheera climbed as he had never climbed before, but the branches broke beneath his weight, and he slipped down, his claws full of bark.

"Why didst thou not warn the man-cub!" he roared to poor Baloo, who had set off at a clumsy trot in the hope of overtaking the monkeys. "What was the use of half slaying him with blows if thou didst not warn him?"

"Haste! O haste! We—we may catch them yet!" Baloo panted.

"At that speed! It would not tire a wounded cow. Teacher of the Law, cub-beater—a mile of that rolling to and fro would burst thee open. Sit still and think! Make a plan. This is no time for chasing. They may drop him if we follow too close."

"*Arrula! Whoo!* They may have dropped him already, being tired of carrying him. Who can trust the Bandar-log? Put dead bats on my head! Give me black bones to eat! Roll me into the hives of the wild bees that I may be stung to death, and bury me with the hyena; for I am the most miserable of bears! *Arulala! Wahooa!* O Mowgli, Mowgli! Why did I not warn thee against the Monkey Folk instead of breaking thy head? Now perhaps I may have knocked the day's lesson out of his mind, and he will be alone in the jungle without the Master Words!"

Baloo clasped his paws over his ears and rolled to and fro, moaning.

"At least he gave me all the Words correctly a little time ago," said Bagheera, impatiently. "Baloo, thou hast neither memory nor respect. What would the jungle think if I, the Black Panther, curled myself up like Ikki, the Porcupine, and howled?"

"What do I care what the jungle thinks? He may be dead by now."

"Unless and until they drop him from the branches in sport, or kill him out of idleness, I have no fear for the man-cub. He is wise and well-taught, and, above all, he has the eyes that make the Jungle People afraid. But (and it is a great evil) he is in the power of the Bandar-log, and they, because they live in trees, have no fear of any of our people." Bagheera licked his one fore paw thoughtfully.

"Fool that I am! Oh, fat, brown, root-digging fool that I am!" said Baloo, uncoiling himself with a jerk. "It is true what Hathi, the Wild Elephant, says: *To each his own fear*; and they, the Bandar-log, fear Kaa, the Rock Snake. He can

Though it seems fantastic to think that even a large snake can swallow a goat with one gulp, this is the truth. Some types can unhinge their jaws to take in an animal much larger than their heads. Their bodies stretch around the meal. The whole goat, or other animal, can be seen moving down the snake's rubbery body.

Python

climb as well as they can. He steals the young monkeys in the night. The mere whisper of his name makes their wicked tails cold. Let us go to Kaa."

"What will he do for us? He is not of our tribe, being footless and with most evil eyes," said Bagheera.

"He is very old and very cunning. Above all, he is always hungry," said Baloo, hopefully. "Promise him many goats."

"He sleeps for a full month after he has once eaten. He may be asleep now, and even were he awake, what if he would rather kill his own goats?" Bagheera, who did not know much about Kaa, was naturally suspicious.

"Then in that case, thou and I together, old hunter, may make him see reason." Here Baloo rubbed his faded brown shoulder against the panther, and they went off to look for Kaa, the Rock Python.

They found him stretched out on a warm ledge in the afternoon sun, admiring his beautiful new coat for he had been in retirement for the last ten days changing his skin, and now he was very splendid—darting his big blunt-nosed head along the ground, and twisting the thirty feet of his body into fantastic knots and curves, and licking his lips as he thought of his dinner to come.

"He has not eaten," said Baloo, with a grunt of relief, as soon as he saw the beautifully mottled brown and yellow jacket. "Be careful, Bagheera! He is always a little blind after he has changed his skin, and very quick to strike."

Kaa was not a poison snake—in fact he rather despised the Poison Snakes for cowards; but his strength lay in his hug, and when he had once lapped his huge coils round anybody there was no more to be said. "Good hunting!" cried Baloo, sitting up on his haunches. Like all snakes of his breed Kaa was rather deaf, and did not hear the call at first. Then he curled up ready for any accident, his head lowered.

"Good hunting for us all," he answered. "Oho, Baloo, what dost thou do here? Good hunting, Bagheera. One of us at least needs food. Is there any news of game afoot? A doe now, or even a young buck? I am as empty as a dried well."

"We are hunting," said Baloo, carelessly. He knew that you must not hurry Kaa. He is too big.

"Give me permission to come with you," said Kaa. "A blow more or less is nothing to thee, Bagheera or Baloo, but I—I have to wait and wait for days in a wood path and climb half a night on the mere chance of a young ape. *Pss naw!* The branches are not what they were when I was young. Rotten twigs and dry boughs are they all."

"Maybe thy great weight has something to do with the matter," said Baloo.

"I am a fair length—a fair length," said Kaa, with a little pride. "But for all that, it is the fault of this new-grown timber. I came very near to falling on my last hunt,—very near indeed,—and the noise of my slipping, for my tail was not tight wrapped round the tree, waked the Bandar-log, and they called me most evil names."

"'Footless, yellow earthworm,'" said Bagheera under his whiskers, as though he were trying to remember something.

"*Sssss!* Have they ever called me *that?*" said Kaa.

"Something of that kind it was that they shouted to us last moon, but we never noticed them. They will say anything—even that thou hast lost all thy teeth, and dare not face anything bigger than a kid, because (they are indeed shameless, these Bandar-log)—because thou art afraid of the he-goats' horns," Bagheera went on sweetly.

Now a snake, especially a wary old python like Kaa, very seldom shows that he is angry, but Baloo and Bagheera could see the big swallowing muscles on either side of Kaa's throat ripple and bulge.

"The Bandar-log have shifted their grounds," he said, quietly. "When I came up into the sun today I heard them whooping among the tree-tops."

"It—it is the Bandar-log that we follow now," said Baloo; but the words stuck in his throat, for this was the first time in his memory that one of the Jungle People had owned to being interested in the doings of the monkeys.

"Beyond doubt, then, it is no small thing that takes two such hunters—leaders in their own jungle, I am certain—on the trail of the Bandar-log," Kaa replied, courteously, as he swelled with curiosity.

"Indeed," Baloo began, "I am no more than the old, and sometimes very foolish, Teacher of the Law to the Seeonee wolf-cubs, and Bagheera here—"

"Is Bagheera," said the Black Panther, and his jaws shut with a snap, for he did not believe in being humble. "The trouble is this, Kaa. Those nut-stealers and pickers of palm-leaves have stolen away our man-cub, of whom thou hast perhaps heard."

"I heard some news from Ikki (his quills make him presumptuous) of a man-thing that was entered into a wolf-pack, but I did not believe. Ikki is full of stories half heard and very badly told."

"But it is true. He is such a man-cub as never was," said Baloo. "The best and wisest and boldest of man-cubs. My own pupil, who shall make the name of Baloo famous through all the jungles; and besides, I—we—love him, Kaa."

"*Ts! Ts!*" said Kaa, shaking his head to and fro. "I have also known what love is. There are tales I could tell that—"

"That need a clear night when we are all well fed to praise properly," said Bagheera, quickly. "Our man-cub is in the hands of the Bandar-log now, and we know that of all the Jungle People they fear Kaa alone."

"They fear me alone. They have good reason," said Kaa. "Chattering, foolish, vain—vain, foolish, and chattering—are the monkeys. But a man-thing in their hands is in no good luck. They grow tired of the nuts they pick, and throw them down. They carry a branch half a day, meaning to do great things with it, and then snap it in two. That manling is not to be envied. They called me also—'yellow fish,' was it not?"

"Worm—worm—earthworm," said Bagheera; "as well as other things which I cannot now say for shame."

"We must remind them to speak well of their master. *Aaa-sssh!* We must help their wandering memories. Now, whither went they with thy cub?"

"The jungle alone knows. Toward the sunset, I believe," said Baloo. "We had thought that thou wouldst know, Kaa."

"I? How? I take them when they come in my way, but I do not hunt the Bandar-log—or frogs—or green scum on a water-hole, for that matter."

"Up, up! Up, up! *Hillo! Illo! Illo!* Look up, Baloo of the Seeonee Wolf Pack!"

Baloo looked up to see where the voice came from, and there was Rann, the Kite, sweeping down with the sun shining on the upturned flanges of his wings. It was near Rann's bedtime, but he had ranged all over the jungle looking for the bear, and missed him in the thick foliage.

"What is it?" said Baloo.

"I have seen Mowgli among the Bandar-log. He bade me tell you. I watched. The Bandar-log have taken him beyond the river to the Monkey City—to the Cold Lairs. They may stay there for a night, or ten nights, or an hour. I have told the bats to watch through the dark time. That is my message. Good hunting, all you below!"

"Full gorge and a deep sleep to you, Rann!" cried Bagheera. "I will remember thee in my next kill, and put aside the head for thee alone, O best of kites!"

"It is nothing. It is nothing. The boy held the Master Word. I could have done no less," and Rann circled up again to his roost.

"He has not forgotten to use his tongue," said Baloo, with a chuckle of pride. "To think of one so young remembering the Master Word for the birds while he was being pulled across trees!"

"It was most firmly driven into him," said Bagheera. "But I am proud of him, and now we must go to the Cold Lairs."

They all knew where that place was, but few of the Jungle People ever went there, because what they called the Cold Lairs was an old deserted city, lost and buried in the jungle, and beasts seldom use a place that men have once used. The wild boar will, but the hunting-tribes do not. Besides, the monkeys lived there as much as they could be said to live anywhere, and no self-respecting animal would come within eye-shot of it except in times of drouth, when the half-ruined tanks and reservoirs held a little water.

"It is half a night's journey—at full speed," said Bagheera. Baloo looked very serious. "I will go as fast as I can," he said, anxiously.

"We dare not wait for thee. Follow, Baloo. We must go on the quick-foot—Kaa and I."

"Feet or no feet, I can keep abreast of all thy four," said Kaa, shortly.

Baloo made one effort to hurry, but had to sit down panting, and so they left him to come on later, while Bagheera hurried forward, at the rocking panther-canter. Kaa said nothing, but, strive as Bagheera might, the huge Rock Python held level with him. When they came to a hill-stream, Bagheera gained, because he bounded across while Kaa swam, his head and two feet of his neck clearing the water, but on level ground Kaa made up the distance.

"By the Broken Lock that freed me," said Bagheera, when twilight had fallen, "thou art no slowgoer."

"I am hungry," said Kaa. "Besides, they called me speckled frog."

"Worm—earthworm, and yellow to boot."

"All one. Let us go on," and Kaa seemed to pour himself along the ground, finding the shortest road with his steady eyes, and keeping to it.

In the Cold Lairs the Monkey People were not thinking of Mowgli's friends at all. They had brought the boy to the Lost City, and were very pleased with themselves for the time. Mowgli had never seen an Indian city before, and though this was almost a heap of ruins it seemed very wonderful and splendid. Some king had built it long ago on a little hill. You could still trace the stone causeways that led up to the ruined gates where the last splinters of wood hung to the worn, rusted hinges. Trees had grown into and out of the walls; the battlements were tumbled down and decayed, and wild creepers hung out of the windows of the towers on the walls in bushy hanging clumps.

A great roofless palace crowned the hill, and the marble of the courtyards and the fountains was split and stained

deserted city: Deserted or lost cities are found in deep jungles from time to time, and probably there are some still undiscovered. It happened, ages ago, that people built cities. Then they left them because of a war, a plague, a scarcity of food, or a change of trade routes. In short order the fertile jungle, unchecked, grew up around them.

The Jungle Book

the king's elephants: In earlier days, some of India's rulers were so wealthy they could afford to keep elephants as pets. "Elephant doors" are fairly common on Indian palaces; they are doors set in the walls tall and wide enough for an elephant and HOWDAH (special structure for the rider) to get through.

with red and green, and the very cobblestones in the court-yard where the king's elephants used to live had been thrust up and apart by grasses and young trees. From the palace you could see the rows and rows of roofless houses that made up the city, looking like empty honeycombs filled with blackness; the shapeless block of stone that had been an idol in the square where four roads met; the pits and dimples at street corners where the public wells once stood, and the shattered domes of temples with wild figs sprouting on their sides.

The monkeys called the place their city, and pretended to despise the Jungle People because they lived in the forest. And yet they never knew what the buildings were made for nor how to use them. They would sit in circles on the hall of the king's council-chamber, and scratch for fleas and pre-

tend to be men; or they would run in and out of the roofless houses and collect pieces of plaster and old bricks in a corner, and forget where they had hidden them, and fight and cry in scuffling crowds, and then break off to play up and down the terraces of the king's garden, where they would shake the rose-trees and the oranges in sport to see the fruit and flowers fall. They explored all the passages and dark tunnels in the palace and the hundreds of little dark rooms; but they never remembered what they had seen and what they had not, and so drifted about in ones and twos or crowds, telling one another that they were doing as men did. They drank at the tanks and made the water all muddy, and then they fought over it, and then they would all rush together in mobs and shout: "There are none in the jungle so wise and good and clever and strong and gentle as the Bandar-log." Then all would begin again till they grew tired of the city and went back to the tree-tops, hoping the Jungle People would notice them.

Mowgli, who had been trained under the Law of the Jungle, did not like or understand this kind of life. The monkeys dragged him into the Cold Lairs late in the afternoon, and instead of going to sleep, as Mowgli would have done after a long journey, they joined hands and danced about and sang their foolish songs.

One of the monkeys made a speech, and told his companions that Mowgli's capture marked a new thing in the history of the Bandar-log, for Mowgli was going to show them how to weave sticks and canes together as a protection against rain and cold. Mowgli picked up some creepers and began to work them in and out, and the monkeys tried to imitate; but in a very few minutes they lost interest and began to pull their friends' tails or jump up and down on all fours, coughing.

"I want to eat," said Mowgli. "I am a stranger in this part of the jungle. Bring me food, or give me leave to hunt here."

Twenty or thirty monkeys bounded away to bring him nuts and wild pawpaws; but they fell to fighting on the road, and it was too much trouble to go back with what was left of the fruit. Mowgli was sore and angry as well as hungry and he roamed through the empty city giving the Strangers' Hunting Call from time to time, but no one answered him, and Mowgli felt that he had reached a very bad place indeed.

"All that Baloo has said about the Bandar-log is true," he thought to himself. "They have no Law, no Hunting Call, and no leaders—nothing but foolish words and little picking, thievish hands. So if I am starved or killed here, it will be all my own fault. But I must try to return to my own jun-

paw-paws: Also called papaya or tree melon. Unripe paw-paws contain papain, which is sold in our grocery stores as a meat tenderizer.

31

Greek Frets.
a, from the Parthenon, above cella frieze; *b*, from vases.

fretwork: This is carving in ornamental patterns, often cut with a fretsaw. India is particularly rich in fine fretwork. The fretwork walls here, set with precious stones, must have been very beautiful.

Diamond Frets.
a, from Church of Retaud, France; *b*, from Lincoln Cathedral, England.

gle. Baloo will surely beat me, but that is better than chasing silly rose-leaves with the Bandar-log."

But no sooner had he walked to the city wall than the monkeys pulled him back, telling him that he did not know how happy he was, and pinching him to make him grateful. He set his teeth and said nothing, but went with the shouting monkeys to a terrace above the red sand-stone reservoirs that were half full of rain-water. There was a ruined summer-house of white marble in the center of the terrace, built for queens dead a hundred years ago. The domed roof had half fallen in and blocked up the underground passage from the palace by which the queens used to enter; but the walls were made of screens of marble tracery—beautiful, milk-white fretwork, set with agates and cornelians and jasper and lapis lazuli, and as the moon came up behind the hill it shone through the openwork, casting shadows on the ground like black-velvet embroidery.

Sore, sleepy, and hungry as he was, Mowgli could not help laughing when the Bandar-log began, twenty at a time, to tell him how great and wise and strong and gentle they were, and how foolish he was to wish to leave them. "We are great. We are free. We are wonderful. We are the most wonderful people in all the jungle! We all say so, and so it must be true," they shouted. "Now as you are a new listener and can carry our words back to the Jungle People so that they may notice us in future, we will tell you all about our most excellent selves."

Mowgli made no objection, and the monkeys gathered by hundreds and hundreds on the terrace to listen to their own speakers singing the praises of the Bandar-log, and whenever a speaker stopped for want of breath they would all shout together: "This is true; we all say so."

Mowgli nodded and blinked, and said "Yes" when they asked him a question, and his head spun with the noise. "Tabaqui, the Jackal, must have bitten all these people," he said to himself, "and now they have the madness. Certainly this is *dewanee*—the madness. Do they never go to sleep? Now there is a cloud coming to cover that moon. If it were only a big enough cloud I might try to run away in the darkness. But I am tired."

That same cloud was being watched by two good friends in the ruined ditch below the city wall, for Bagheera and Kaa, knowing well how dangerous the Monkey People were in large numbers, did not wish to run any risks. The monkeys never fight unless they are a hundred to one, and few in the jungle care for those odds.

"I will go to the west wall," Kaa whispered, "and come down swiftly with the slope of the ground in my favour. They will not throw themselves upon *my* back in their hundreds, but—"

"I know it," said Bagheera. "Would that Baloo were here; but we must do what we can. When that cloud covers the moon I shall go to the terrace. They hold some sort of council there over the boy."

"Good hunting," said Kaa, grimly, and glided away to the west wall. That happened to be the least ruined of any, and the big snake was delayed a while before he could find a way up the stones.

The cloud hid the moon, and as Mowgli wondered what would come next he heard Bagheera's light feet on the terrace. The Black Panther had raced up the slope almost without a sound, and was striking—he knew better than to waste time in biting—right and left among the monkeys, who were seated round Mowgli in circles fifty and sixty deep. There was a howl of fright and rage, and then as Bagheera tripped on the rolling, kicking bodies beneath him, a monkey shouted: "There is only one here! Kill him! Kill!" A scuffling mass of monkeys, biting, scratching, tearing, and pulling, closed over Bagheera, while five or six laid hold of Mowgli, dragged him up the wall of the summer-house, and pushed him through the hole of the broken dome. A man-trained boy would have been badly bruised, for the fall was a good ten feet, but Mowgli fell as Baloo had taught him to fall, and landed light.

"Stay there," shouted the monkeys, "till we have killed thy friend. Later we will play with thee, if the Poison People leave thee alive."

"We be of one blood, ye and I," said Mowgli, quickly giving the Snake's Call. He could hear rustling and hissing in the rubbish all round him, and gave the Call a second time to make sure.

"Down hoods all," said half a dozen low voices. Every old ruin in India becomes sooner or later a dwelling-place of snakes, and the old summer-house was alive with cobras. "Stand still, Little Brother, lest thy feet do us harm."

Mowgli stood as quietly as he could, peering through the openwork and listening to the furious din of the fight round the Black Panther—the yells and chatterings and scufflings, and Bagheera's deep, hoarse cough as he backed and bucked and twisted and plunged under the heaps of his enemies. For the first time since he was born, Bagheera was fighting for his life.

cobra: Best known of these deadly serpents is the COBRA DE CAPELLO (KO-bra dee ka-PELL-o). Close relatives are the hamadryads or king cobras, and the African asp, which Cleopatra used to kill herself. All cobras have the remarkable habit of swelling out the sides of their necks and heads when disturbed. They rise up, braced on their coiled bodies, prepared to strike. The poison, driven into the victim through hollow fangs, is deadly. Without medical help, people or animals usually die in a few minutes. There are estimates that cobras kill around 4,000 people a year in India.

"Baloo must be at hand; Bagheera would not have come alone," Mowgli thought; and then he called aloud: "To the tank, Bagheera! Roll to the water-tanks! Roll and plunge! Get to the water!"

Bagheera heard, and the cry that told him Mowgli was safe gave him new courage. He worked his way desperately, inch by inch, straight for the reservoirs, hitting in silence.

Then from the ruined wall nearest the jungle rose up the rumbling war-shout of Baloo. The old bear had done his best, but he could not come before. "Bagheera," he shouted, "I am here! I climb! I haste! *Ahuwora!* The stones slip under my feet! Wait my coming, O most infamous Bandar-log!"

He panted up the terrace only to disappear to the head in a wave of monkeys, but he threw himself squarely on his haunches, and spreading out his fore paws, hugged as many as he could hold, and then began to hit with a regular *bat-bat-bat*, like the flipping strokes of a paddle-wheel.

A crash and a splash told Mowgli that Bagheera had fought his way to the tank, where the monkeys could not follow. The panther lay gasping for breath, his head just out of water, while the monkeys stood three deep on the red stone steps, dancing up and down with rage, ready to spring upon him from all sides if he came out to help Baloo. It was then that Bagheera lifted up his dripping chin, and in despair gave the Snake's Call for protection,—"We be of one blood, ye and I,"—for he believed that Kaa had turned tail at the last minute. Even Baloo, half smothered under the monkeys on the edge of the terrace, could not help chuckling as he heard the big Black Panther asking for help.

coping stone: A coping is the highest row of bricks or stones in a wall; a coping stone is one of the pieces that make up the coping.

Kaa had only just worked his way over the west wall, landing with a wrench that dislodged a coping-stone into the ditch. He had no intention of losing any advantage of the ground, and coiled and uncoiled himself once or twice, to be sure that every foot of his long body was in working order.

All that while the fight with Baloo went on, and the monkeys yelled in the tank round Bagheera, and Mang, the Bat, flying to and fro, carried the news of the great battle over the jungle, till even Hathi, the Wild Elephant, trumpeted, and, far away, scattered bands of the Monkey Folk woke and came leaping along the tree-roads to help their comrades in the Cold Lairs, and the noise of the fight roused all the day-birds for miles round.

Then Kaa came straight, quickly, and anxious to kill. The fighting strength of a python is in the driving blow of his head, backed by all the strength and weight of his body. If you can imagine a lance, or a battering-ram, or a hammer, weighing nearly half a ton driven by a cool, quiet mind living in the handle of it, you can imagine roughly what Kaa was like when he fought. A python four or five feet long can knock a man down if he hits him fairly in the chest, and Kaa was thirty feet long, as you know. His first stroke was delivered into the heart of the crowd round Baloo—was sent home with shut mouth in silence, and there was no need of a second. The monkeys scattered with cries of "Kaa! It is Kaa! Run! Run!"

Generations of monkeys have been scared into good behaviour by the stories their elders told them of Kaa, the night-thief, who could slip along the branches as quietly as moss grows, and steal away the strongest monkey that ever lived; of old Kaa, who could make himself look so like a dead branch or a rotten stump that the wisest were deceived till the branch caught them, and then—

Kaa was everything that the monkeys feared in the jungle, for none of them knew the limits of his power, none of them could look him in the face, and none had ever come alive out of his hug. And so they ran, stammering with terror, to the walls and the roofs of the houses, and Baloo drew a deep breath of relief. His fur was much thicker than Bagheera's, but he had suffered sorely in the fight. Then Kaa opened his mouth for the first time and spoke one long hissing word, and the faraway monkeys, hurrying to the defense of the Cold Lairs, stayed where they were, cowering, till the loaded branches bent and crackled under them. The monkeys on the walls and the empty houses stopped their cries, and in the stillness that fell upon the city Mowgli heard Bagheera shaking his wet sides as he came up from the tank.

Then the clamour broke out again. The monkeys leaped higher up the walls; they clung round the necks of the big stone idols and shrieked as they skipped along the battlements; while Mowgli, dancing in the summer-house, put his eye to the screenwork and hooted owl-fashion between his front teeth, to show his derision and contempt.

"Get the man-cub out of that trap; I can do no more," Bagheera gasped. "Let us take the man-cub and go. They may attack again."

"They will not move till I order them. Stay you sssso!" Kaa hissed, and the city was silent once more. "I could not come before, Brother, but I *think* I heard thee call"—this was to Bagheera.

battlements: The top part of a wall, used for defense. There are often holes in the wall, through which defenders of the castle fire arrows.

35

"I—I may have cried out in the battle," Bagheera answered. "Baloo, art thou hurt?"

"I am not sure that they have not pulled me into a hundred little bearlings," said Baloo, gravely shaking one leg after the other. "Wow! I am sore. Kaa, we owe thee, I think, our lives—Bagheera and I."

"No matter. Where is the manling?"

"Here, in a trap. I cannot climb out," cried Mowgli. The curve of the broken dome was above his head.

"Take him away. He dances like Mao, the Peacock. He will crush our young," said the cobras inside.

"Hah!" said Kaa, with a chuckle, "he has friends everywhere, this manling. Stand back, Manling; and hide you, O Poison People. I break down the wall."

Kaa looked carefully till he found a discoloured crack in the marble tracery showing a weak spot, made two or three light taps with his head to get the distance, and then lifting up six feet of his body clear of the ground, sent home half a dozen full-power, smashing blows, nose-first. The screenwork broke and fell away in a cloud of dust and rubbish, and Mowgli leaped through the opening and flung himself between Baloo and Bagheera—an arm round each big neck.

"Art thou hurt?" said Baloo, hugging him softly.

"I am sore, hungry, and not a little bruised; but, oh, they have handled ye grievously, my Brothers! Ye bleed."

"Others also," said Bagheera, licking his lips and looking at the monkey-dead on the terrace and round the tank.

"It is nothing, it is nothing if thou art safe, O my pride of all little frogs!" whimpered Baloo.

"Of that we shall judge later," said Bagheera, in a dry voice that Mowgli did not at all like. "But here is Kaa, to whom we owe the battle and thou owest thy life. Thank him according to our customs, Mowgli."

Mowgli turned and saw the great python's head swaying a foot above his own.

"So this is the manling," said Kaa. "Very soft is his skin, and he is not so unlike the Bandar-log. Have a care, Manling, that I do not mistake thee for a monkey some twilight when I have newly changed my coat."

"We be of one blood, thou and I," Mowgli answered. "I take my life from thee, to-night. My kill shall be thy kill if ever thou art hungry, O Kaa."

"All thanks, Little Brother," said Kaa, though his eyes twinkled. "And what may so bold a hunter kill? I ask that I may follow when next he goes abroad."

"I kill nothing,—I am too little,—but I drive goats toward such as can use them. When thou art empty come to me and see if I speak the truth. I have some skill in these [he held out his hands], and if ever thou art in a trap, I may pay the debt which I owe to thee, to Bagheera, and to Baloo, here. Good hunting to ye all, my masters."

"Well said," growled Baloo, for Mowgli had returned thanks very prettily. The python dropped his head lightly for a minute on Mowgli's shoulder. "A brave heart and a courteous tongue," said he. "They shall carry thee far through the jungle, Manling. But now go hence quickly with thy friends. Go and sleep, for the moon sets, and what follows it is not well that thou shouldst see."

The moon was sinking behind the hills and the lines of trembling monkeys huddled together on the walls and battlements looked like ragged, shaky fringes of things. Baloo went down to the tank for a drink, and Bagheera began to put his fur in order, as Kaa glided out into the center of the terrace and brought his jaws together with a ringing snap that drew all the monkeys' eyes upon him.

"The moon sets," he said. "Is there yet light to see?"

From the walls came a moan like the wind in the tree-tops: "We see, O Kaa!"

"Good! Begins now the Dance—the Dance of the Hunger of Kaa. Sit still and watch."

He turned twice or thrice in a big circle, weaving his head from right to left. Then he began making loops and figures of eight with his body, and soft, oozy triangles that melted into squares and five-side figures, and coiled mounds, never resting, never hurrying, and never stopping his low, humming song. It grew darker and darker, till at last the dragging, shifting coils disappeared, but they could hear the rustle of the scales.

Baloo and Bagheera stood still as stone, growling in their throats, their neck-hair bristling, and Mowgli watched and wondered.

"Bandar-log," said the voice of Kaa at last, "can ye stir foot or hand without my order? Speak!"

"Without thy order we cannot stir foot or hand, O Kaa!"

"Good! Come all one pace nearer to me."

The lines of the monkeys swayed forward helplessly, and Baloo and Bagheera took one stiff step forward with them.

"Nearer!" hissed Kaa, and they all moved again.

Mowgli laid his hands on Baloo and Bagheera to get them away, and the two great beasts started as though they had been waked from a dream.

"Keep thy hand on my shoulder," Bagheera whispered. "Keep it there, or I must go back—must go back to Kaa. *Aah!*"

"It is only old Kaa making circles on the dust," said Mowgli; "let us go"; and the three slipped off through a gap in the walls to the jungle.

"*Whoof!*" said Baloo, when he stood under the still trees again. "Never more will I make an ally of Kaa," and he shook himself all over.

"He knows more than we," said Bagheera, trembling. "In a little time, had I stayed, I should have walked down his throat."

"Many will walk that road before the moon rises again," said Baloo. "He will have good hunting—after his own fashion."

"But what was the meaning of it all?" said Mowgli, who did not know anything of a python's powers of fascination. "I saw no more than a big snake making foolish circles till the dark came. And his nose was all sore. Ho! Ho!"

"Mowgli," said Bagheera, angrily, "his nose was sore on *thy* account; as my ears and sides and paws, and Baloo's neck and shoulders are bitten on *thy* account. Neither Baloo nor Bagheera will be able to hunt with pleasure for many days."

"It is nothing," said Baloo; "we have the man-cub again."

"True; but he has cost us most heavily in time which might have been spent in good hunting, in wounds, in hair, —I am half plucked along my back,—and last of all, in honour. For, remember, Mowgli, I, who am the Black Panther, was forced to call upon Kaa for protection, and Baloo and I were both made stupid as little birds by the Hunger-Dance. All this, Man-cub, came of thy playing with the Bandar-log."

"True; it is true," said Mowgli, sorrowfully. "I am an evil man-cub, and my stomach is sad in me."

"*Mf!* What says the Law of the Jungle, Baloo?"

Baloo did not wish to bring Mowgli into any more trouble, but he could not tamper with the Law, so he mumbled, "Sorrow never stays punishment. But remember, Bagheera, he is very little."

"I will remember; but he has done mischief; and blows must be dealt now. Mowgli, hast thou anything to say?"

"Nothing. I did wrong. Baloo and thou art wounded. It is just."

Bagheera gave him half a dozen love-taps; from a panther's point of view they would hardly have waked one of his own cubs, but for a seven-year-old boy they amounted to as severe a beating as you could wish to avoid. When it was all over Mowgli sneezed, and picked himself up without a word.

"Now," said Bagheera, "jump on my back, Little Brother, and we will go home."

One of the beauties of Jungle Law is that punishment settles all scores. There is no nagging afterward.

Mowgli laid his head down on Bagheera's back and slept so deeply that he never waked when he was put down by Mother Wolf's side in the home-cave.

ROAD-SONG OF THE BANDAR-LOG

Here we go in a flung festoon,
Half-way up to the jealous moon!
Don't you envy our pranceful bands?
Don't you wish you had extra hands?
Wouldn't you like if your tails were—so—
Curved in the shape of a Cupid's bow?
    Now you're angry, but—never mind,
    Brother, thy tail hangs down behind!

Here we sit in a branchy row,
Thinking of beautiful things we know;
Dreaming of deeds that we mean to do,
All complete, in a minute or two—
Something noble and grand and good,
Won by merely wishing we could.
    Now we're going to—never mind,
    Brother, thy tail hangs down behind!

Guenon, or Common Green
Monkey

All the talk we ever have heard
Uttered by bat or beast or bird—
Hide or fin or scale or feather—
Jabber it quickly and all together!
Excellent! Wonderful! Once again!
Now we are talking just like men.
    Let's pretend we are . . . never mind,
    Brother, thy tail hangs down behind!
    This is the way of the Monkey-kind.

Then join our leaping lines that scumfish through the pines,
That rocket by where, light and high, the wild-grape swings,
By the rubbish in our wake, and the noble noise we make,
Be sure, be sure, we're going to do some splendid things!

3

Tiger! Tiger!

jog trot: This is moving along faster than a walk, but not quite as fast as a run.

What of the hunting, hunter bold?
    Brother, the watch was long and cold.
What of the quarry ye went to kill?
    Brother, he crops in the jungle still.
Where is the power that made your pride?
    Brother, it ebbs from my flank and side.
Where is the haste that ye hurry by?
    Brother, I go to my lair—to die.

NOW we must go back to the last tale but one. When Mowgli left the wolf's cave after the fight with the Pack at the Council Rock, he went down to the plowed lands where the villagers lived, but he would not stop there because it was too near to the jungle, and he knew that he had made at least one bad enemy at the Council. So he hurried on, keeping to the rough road that ran down the valley, and followed it at a steady jog-trot for nearly twenty miles, till he came to a country that he did not know. The valley opened

40

out into a great plain dotted over with rocks and cut up by ravines. At one end stood a little village, and at the other the thick jungle came down in a sweep to the grazing-grounds, and stopped there as though it had been cut off with a hoe. All over the plain, cattle and buffaloes were grazing, and when the little boys in charge of the herds saw Mowgli they shouted and ran away, and the yellow pariah dogs that hang about every Indian village barked. Mowgli walked on, for he was feeling hungry, and when he came to the village gate he saw the big thorn-bush that was drawn up before the gate at twilight, pushed to one side.

"Umph!" he said, for he had come across more than one such barricade in his night rambles after things to eat. "So men are afraid of the People of the Jungle here also." He sat down by the gate, and when a man came out he stood up, opened his mouth, and pointed down it to show that he wanted food. The man stared and ran back up the one street of the village shouting for the priest, who was a big, fat man dressed in white, with a red and yellow mark on his forehead. The priest came to the gate, and with him at least a hundred people who stared and talked and shouted and pointed at Mowgli.

"They have no manners, these Men Folk," said Mowgli to himself. "Only the gray ape would behave as they do." So he threw back his long hair and frowned at the crowd.

"What is there to be afraid of?" said the priest. "Look at the marks on his arms and legs. They are the bites of wolves. He is but a wolf-child run away from the jungle."

Of course, in playing together, the cubs had often nipped Mowgli harder than they intended, and there were white scars all over his arms and legs. But he would have been the last person in the world to call these bites; for he knew what real biting meant.

"Arré! Arré!" said two or three women together. "To be bitten by wolves, poor child! He is a handsome boy. He has eyes like red fire. By my honour, Messua, he is not unlike thy boy that was taken by the tiger."

"Let me look," said a woman with heavy copper rings on her wrists and ankles, and she peered at Mowgli under the palm of her hand. "Indeed he is not. He is thinner, but he has the very look of my boy."

The priest was a clever man, and he knew that Messua was wife to the richest villager in the place. So he looked up at the sky for a minute, and said solemnly: "What the jungle has taken the jungle has restored. Take the boy into thy house, my sister, and forget not to honour the priest who sees so far into the lives of men."

ravines: Deep, narrow gorges in mountains, usually formed by rushing waters or cut by streams.

priest: The red and yellow mark on his forehead is a caste mark, showing that he is a Brahmin.

lacquered: The bedstead was covered with a hard, glossy finish. Oriental lacquers came from the sap of a variety of sumac tree. Today the word refers to a mixture of cellulose compounds, resins and plasticizers. Modern lacquers are water resistant, give a brilliant finish, can be sprayed on, and dry quickly.

"By the Bull that bought me," said Mowgli to himself, "but all this talking is like another looking-over by the Pack! Well, if I am a man, a man I must become."

The crowd parted as the woman beckoned Mowgli to her hut, where there was a red lacquered bedstead, a great earthen grain-chest with curious raised patterns on it, half a dozen copper cooking-pots, an image of a Hindu god in a little alcove, and on the wall a real looking-glass, such as they sell at the country fairs.

She gave him a long drink of milk and some bread, and then she laid her hand on his head and looked into his eyes; for she thought perhaps that he might be her real son come back from the jungle where the tiger had taken him. So she said: "Nathoo, O Nathoo!" Mowgli did not show that he knew the name. "Dost thou not remember the day when I gave thee thy new shoes?" She touched his foot, and it was almost as hard as horn. "No," she said sorrowfully; "those feet have never worn shoes, but thou art very like my Nathoo, and thou shalt be my son."

Mowgli was uneasy, because he had never been under a roof before; but as he looked at the thatch, he saw that he could tear it out any time if he wanted to get away, and that the window had no fastenings. "What is the good of a man," he said to himself at last, "if he does not understand man's talk? Now I am as silly and dumb as a man would be with us in the jungle. I must learn their talk."

It was not for fun that he had learned while he was with the wolves to imitate the challenge of bucks in the jungle and the grunt of the little wild pig. So as soon as Messua pronounced a word Mowgli would imitate it almost perfectly, and before dark he had learned the names of many things in the hut.

There was a difficulty at bedtime, because Mowgli would not sleep under anything that looked so like a panther-trap as that hut, and when they shut the door he went through the window. "Give him his will," said Messua's husband. "Remember he can never till now have slept on a bed. If he is indeed sent in the place of our son he will not run away."

So Mowgli stretched himself in some long, clean grass at the edge of the field, but before he had closed his eyes a soft gray nose poked him under the chin.

"Phew!" said Gray Brother (he was the eldest of Mother Wolf's cubs). "This is a poor reward for following thee twenty miles. Thou smellest of wood-smoke and cattle — altogether like a man already. Wake, Little Brother; I bring news."

"Are all well in the jungle?" said Mowgli, hugging him.

"All except the wolves that were burned with the Red Flower. Now, listen. Shere Khan has gone away to hunt far off till his coat grows again, for he is badly singed. When he returns he swears that he will lay thy bones in the Waingunga."

"There are two words to that. I also have made a little promise. But news is always good. I am tired to-night,—very tired with new things, Gray Brother,—but bring me the news always."

"Thou wilt not forget that thou art a wolf? Men will not make thee forget?" said Gray Brother, anxiously.

"Never. I will always remember that I love thee and all in our cave; but also I will always remember that I have been cast out of the Pack."

"And that thou mayest be cast out of another pack. Men are only men, Little Brother, and their talk is like the talk of frogs in a pond. When I come down here again, I will wait for thee in the bamboos at the edge of the grazing-ground."

For three months after that night Mowgli hardly ever left the village gate, he was so busy learning the ways and customs of men. First he had to wear a cloth round him, which annoyed him horribly; and then he had to learn about money, which he did not in the least understand, and about plowing, of which he did not see the use. Then the little children in the village made him very angry. Luckily, the Law of the Jungle had taught him to keep his temper, for in the jungle, life and food depend on keeping your temper; but when they made fun of him because he would not play games or fly kites, or because he mispronounced some word, only the knowledge that it was unsportsmanlike to kill little naked cubs kept him from picking them up and breaking them in two.

He did not know his own strength in the least. In the jungle he knew he was weak compared with the beasts, but in the village, people said he was as strong as a bull.

And Mowgli had not the faintest idea of the difference that caste makes between man and man. When the potter's donkey slipped in the clay-pit, Mowgli hauled it out by the tail, and helped to stack the pots for their journey to the market at Khanhiwara. That was very shocking, too, for the potter is a low-caste man, and his donkey is worse. When the priest scolded him, Mowgli threatened to put him on the donkey, too, and the priest told Messua's husband that Mowgli had better be set to work as soon as possible; and the village head-man told Mowgli that he would have to go out with the buffaloes next day, and herd them while they grazed. No one was more pleased than Mowgli; and that night, because he

caste: In India, people are born into certain classes, or CASTES. There are four main castes: the priests, the soldiery, the merchants, and the peasants. These are further divided up into many hundreds. One caste cannot marry into another or eat food cooked by another.

43

tower musket: **tower musket:** A muzzle-loading, single-shot, flint-lock gun used early in the 19th century by the British army. They bore the "Tower of London" stamp.

money lender: The very poor have often been victimized by money lenders. These people lend money at very great rates of interest and demand security worth many times the loan. In the United States and other modern nations, lending—or financing—is kept under reasonable control by laws.

had been appointed a servant of the village, as it were, he went off to a circle that met every evening on a masonry platform under a great fig-tree. It was the village club, and the head-man and the watchman and the barber (who knew all the gossip of the village), and old Buldeo, the village hunter, who had a Tower musket, met and smoked. The monkeys sat and talked in the upper branches, and there was a hole under the platform where a cobra lived, and he had his little platter of milk every night because he was sacred; and the old men sat around the tree and talked, and pulled at the big *huqas* (the water-pipes) till far into the night. They told wonderful tales of gods and men and ghosts; and Buldeo told even more wonderful ones of the ways of beasts in the jungle, till the eyes of the children sitting outside the circle bulged out of their heads. Most of the tales were about animals, for the jungle was always at their door. The deer and the wild pig grubbed up their crops, and now and again the tiger carried off a man at twilight, within sight of the village gates.

Mowgli, who naturally knew something about what they were talking of, had to cover his face not to show that he was laughing, while Buldeo, the Tower musket across his knees, climbed on from one wonderful story to another, and Mowgli's shoulders shook.

Buldeo was explaining how the tiger that had carried away Messua's son was a ghost-tiger, and his body was inhabited by the ghost of a wicked old money-lender, who had died some years ago. "And I know that this is true," he said, "because Purun Dass always limped from the blow that he got in a riot when his account-books were burned, and the tiger that I speak of *he* limps, too, for the tracks of his pads are unequal."

"True, true; that must be the truth," said the graybeards, nodding together.

"Are all these tales such cobwebs and moon-talk?" said Mowgli. "That tiger limps because he was born lame, as every one knows. To talk of the soul of a money-lender in a beast that never had the courage of a jackal is child's talk."

Buldeo was speechless with surprise for a moment, and the head-man stared.

"Oho! It is the jungle brat, is it?" said Buldeo. "If thou art so wise, better bring his hide to Khanhiwara, for the Government has set a hundred rupees [$30] on his life. Better still, do not talk when thy elders speak."

Mowgli rose to go. "All the evening I have lain here listening," he called back over his shoulder, "and, except once or twice, Buldeo has not said one word of truth concerning the jungle, which is at his very doors. How, then, shall I believe the tales of ghosts and gods and goblins which he says he has seen?"

"It is full time that boy went to herding," said the headman, while Buldeo puffed and snorted at Mowgli's impertinence.

The custom of most Indian villages is for a few boys to take the cattle and buffaloes out to graze in the early morning, and bring them back at night; and the very cattle that would trample a white man to death allow themselves to be banged and bullied and shouted at by children that hardly come up to their noses. So long as the boys keep with the herds they are safe, for not even the tiger will charge a mob of cattle. But if they straggle to pick flowers or hunt lizards, they are sometimes carried off. Mowgli went through the village street in the dawn, sitting on the back of Rama, the great herd bull; and the slaty-blue buffaloes, with their long, backward-sweeping horns and savage eyes, rose out of their byres, one by one, and followed him, and Mowgli made it very clear to the children with him that he was the master. He beat the buffaloes with a long polished bamboo, and told Kamya, one of the boys, to graze the cattle by themselves, while he went on with the buffaloes, and to be very careful not to stray away from the herd.

An Indian grazing-ground is all rocks and scrub and tussocks and little ravines, among which the herds scatter and disappear. The buffaloes generally keep to the pools and muddy places, where they lie wallowing or basking in the warm mud for hours. Mowgli drove them on to the edge of the plain where the Waingunga River came out of the jungle; then he dropped from Rama's neck, trotted off to a bamboo clump, and found Gray Brother. "Ah," said Gray Brother, "I have waited here very many days. What is the meaning of this cattle-herding work?"

"It is an order," said Mowgli. "I am a village herd for a while. What news of Shere Khan?"

"He has come back to this country, and has waited here a long time for thee. Now he has gone off again, for the game is scarce. But he means to kill thee."

"Very good," said Mowgli. "So long as he is away do thou or one of the brothers sit on that rock, so that I can see thee as I come out of the village. When he comes back wait for me in the ravine by the *dhâk-* tree in the center of the plain. We need not walk into Shere Khan's mouth."

Then Mowgli picked out a shady place and lay down and slept while the buffaloes grazed round him. Herding in India is one of the laziest things in the world. The cattle move and

45

crunch, and lie down, and move on again, and they do not even low. They only grunt, and the buffaloes very seldom say anything, but get down into the muddy pools one after another, and work their way into the mud till only their noses and staring china-blue eyes show above the surface, and there they lie like logs. The sun makes the rocks dance in the heat, and the herd-children hear one kite (never any more) whistling almost out of sight overhead, and they know that if they died, or a cow died, that kite would sweep down, and the next kite miles away would see him drop and follow, and the next, and the next, and almost before they were dead there would be a score of hungry kites come out of nowhere. Then they sleep and wake and sleep again, and weave little baskets of dried grass and put grasshoppers in them; or catch two praying-mantises and make them fight; or string a necklace of red and black jungle-nuts; or watch a lizard basking on a rock, or a snake hunting a frog near the wallows. Then they sing long, long songs with odd native quavers at the end of them, and the day seems longer than most people's whole lives, and perhaps they make a mud castle with mud figures of men and horses and buffaloes, and put reeds into the men's hands, and pretend that they are kings and the figures are their armies or that they are gods to be worshiped. Then evening comes, and the children call, and the buffaloes lumber up out of the sticky mud with noises like gun-shots going off one after the other, and they all string across the gray plain back to the twinkling village lights.

Day after day Mowgli would lead the buffaloes out to their wallows, and day after day he would see Gray Brother's back a mile and a half away across the plain (so he knew that Shere Khan had not come back), and day after day he would lie on the grass listening to the noise round him, and dreaming of old days in the jungle. If Shere Kahn had made a false step with his lame paw up in the jungles by the Waingunga, Mowgli would have heard him in those long still mornings.

At last a day came when he did not see Gray Brother at the signal place, and he laughed and headed the buffaloes for the ravine by the *dhâk*-tree, which was all covered with golden-red flowers. There sat Gray Brother, every bristle on his back lifted.

"He has hidden for a month to throw thee off thy guard. He crossed the ranges last night with Tabaqui, hot-foot on thy trail," said the wolf, panting.

Mowgli frowned. "I am not afraid of Shere Khan, but Tabaqui is very cunning."

"Have no fear," said Gray Brother, licking his lips a little.

praying mantis: Don't let the prayer-like attitude of this pious-looking insect fool you. Those front legs are really in that position to grab smaller insects that venture too close. Because it destroys many such insects, the PRAYING MANTIS is considered beneficial.

Praying-mantis, adult male, reduced one fourth.

The **Dhak Tree** is very common in India. It has bright orange-red flowers that are used to make dye. Oil is made from the seeds and the bark is used to make rope. The gum of this tree contains 70 per cent tannin, and is used in making leather.

I met Tabaqui in the dawn. Now he is telling all his wisdom to the kites, but he told *me* everything before I broke his back. Shere Khan's plan is to wait for thee at the village gate this evening—for thee and for no one else. He is lying up now in the big dry ravine of the Waingunga."

"Has he eaten to-day, or does he hunt empty?" said Mowgli, for the answer meant life or death to him.

"He killed at dawn,—a pig,—and he has drunk too. Remember, Shere Khan could never fast even for the sake of revenge."

"Oh! Fool, fool! What a cub's cub it is! Eaten and drunk too, and he thinks that I shall wait till he has slept! Now, where does he lie up? If there were but ten of us we might pull him down as he lies. These buffaloes will not charge unless they wind him, and I cannot speak their language. Can we get behind his track so that they may smell it?"

"He swam far down the Waingunga to cut that off," said Gray Brother.

"Tabaqui told him that, I know. He would never have thought of it alone." Mowgli stood with his finger in his mouth, thinking. "The big ravine of the Waingunga. That opens out on the plain not half a mile from here. I can take the herd round through the jungle to the head of the ravine and then sweep down—but he would slink out at the foot. We must block that end. Gray Brother, canst thou cut the herd in two for me?"

"Not I, perhaps—but I have brought a wise helper." Gray Brother trotted off and dropped into a hole. Then there lifted up a huge gray head that Mowgli knew well, and the hot air was filled with the most desolate cry of all the jungle—the hunting-howl of a wolf at midday.

"Akela! Akela!" said Mowgli, clapping his hands. "I might have known that thou wouldst not forget me. We have a big work in hand. Cut the herd in two, Akela. Keep the cows and calves together, and the bulls and the plow-buffaloes by themselves."

The two wolves ran, ladies'-chain fashion, in and out of the herd, which snorted and threw up its head and separated into two clumps. In one the cow-buffaloes stood, with their calves in the center, and glared and pawed, ready, if a wolf would only stay still, to charge down and trample the life out of him. In the other the bulls and the young bulls snorted and stamped; but, though they looked more imposing, they were much less dangerous, for they had no calves to protect. No six men could have divided the herd so neatly.

"What orders!" panted Akela. "They are trying to join again."

Mowgli slipped on to Rama's back. "Drive the bulls away to the left, Akela. Gray Brother, when we are gone hold the cows together, and drive them into the foot of the ravine."

"How far?" said Gray Brother, panting and snapping.

"Till the sides are higher than Shere Khan can jump," shouted Mowgli. "Keep them there till we come down." The bulls swept off as Akela bayed, and Gray Brother stopped in front of the cows. They charged down on him, and he ran just before them to the foot of the ravine, as Akela drove the bulls far to the left.

"Well done! Another charge and they are fairly started. Careful, now—careful, Akela. A snap too much, and the bulls will charge. *Hujah!* This is wilder work than driving black-buck. Didst thou think these creatures could move so swiftly?" Mowgli called.

"I have—have hunted these too in my time," gasped Akela in the dust. "Shall I turn them into the jungle?"

"Ay, turn! Swiftly turn them. Rama is mad with rage. Oh, if I could only tell him what I need of him to-day!"

The bulls were turned to the right this time, and crashed into the standing thicket. The other herd-children, watching with the cattle half a mile away, hurried to the village as fast as their legs could carry them, crying that the buffaloes had gone mad and run away.

But Mowgli's plan was simple enough. All he wanted to do was to make a big circle uphill and get at the head of the ravine, and then take the bulls down it and catch Shere Khan between the bulls and the cows, for he knew that after a meal and a full drink Shere Khan would not be in any condition to fight or to clamber up the sides of the ravine. He was soothing the buffaloes now by voice, and Akela had dropped far to the rear, only whimpering once or twice to hurry the rear-guard. It was a long, long circle, for they did not wish to get too near the ravine and give Shere Khan warning. At last Mowgli rounded up the bewildered herd at the head of the ravine on a grassy patch that sloped steeply down to the ravine itself. From that height you could see across the tops of the trees down to the plain below; but what Mowgli looked at was the sides of the ravine, and he saw with a great deal of satisfaction that they ran nearly straight up and down, and the vines and creepers that hung over them would give no foothold to a tiger who wanted to get out.

"Let them breathe, Akela," he said, holding up his hand. "They have not winded him yet. Let them breathe. I must tell Shere Khan who comes. We have him in the trap."

He put his hands to his mouth and shouted down the ravine,—it was almost like shouting down a tunnel,—and the echoes jumped from rock to rock.

After a long time there came back the drawling, sleepy snarl of a full-fed tiger just awakened.

"Who calls?" said Shere Khan, and a splendid peacock fluttered up out of the ravine, screeching.

"I, Mowgli. Cattle-thief, it is time to come to the Council Rock! Down—hurry them down, Akela. Down, Rama, down!"

The herd paused for an instant at the edge of the slope, but Akela gave tongue in the full hunting-yell, and they pitched over one after the other just as steamers shoot rapids, the sand and stones spurting up round them. Once started, there was no chance of stopping, and before they were fairly in the bed of the ravine Rama winded Shere Khan and bellowed.

winded: Many animals have an extremely acute sense of smell. They can detect the scent of another animal, or man, at great distances. A hunter will sometimes speak of an animal "getting wind of him." That is, detecting the hunter's presence—and fleeing the area.

"Ha! Ha!" said Mowgli, on his back. "Now thou knowest!" and the torrent of black horns, foaming muzzles, and staring eyes whirled down the ravine like boulders in flood-time; the weaker buffaloes being shouldered out to the sides of the ravine where they tore through the creepers. They knew what the business was before them—the terrible charge of the buffalo-herd, against which no tiger can hope to stand. Shere Khan heard the thunder of their hoofs, picked himself up, and lumbered down the ravine, looking from side to side for some way of escape, but the walls of the ravine were straight, and he had to keep on, heavy with his dinner and his drink, willing to do anything rather than fight. The herd splashed through the pool he had just left, bellowing till the narrow cut rang. Mowgli heard an answering bellow from the foot of the ravine, saw Shere Khan turn (the tiger knew if the worst came to the worst it was better to meet the bulls than the cows with their calves), and then Rama tripped, stumbled, and went on again over something soft, and, with the bulls at his heels, crashed full into the other herd, while the weaker buffaloes were lifted clean off their feet by the shock of the meeting. That charge carried both herds out into the plain, goring and stamping and snorting. Mowgli watched his time, and slipped off Rama's neck, laying about him right and left with his stick.

"Quick, Akela! Break them up. Scatter them, or they will be fighting one another. Drive them away, Akela. *Hai*, Rama! *Hai! hai! hai!* my children. Softly now, softly! It is all over."

Akela and Gray Brother ran to and fro nipping the buffaloes' legs, and though the herd wheeled once to charge up the ravine again, Mowgli managed to turn Rama, and the others followed him to the wallows.

Shere Khan needed no more trampling. He was dead, and the kites were coming for him already.

"Brothers, that was a dog's death," said Mowgli, feeling for the knife he always carried in a sheath round his neck now that he lived with men. "But he would never have shown fight. His hide will look well on the Council Rock. We must get to work swiftly."

A boy trained among men would never have dreamed of skinning a ten-foot tiger alone, but Mowgli knew better than any one else how an animal's skin is fitted on, and how it can be taken off. But it was hard work, and Mowgli slashed and tore and grunted for an hour, while the wolves lolled out their tongues, or came forward and tugged as he ordered them.

Presently a hand fell on his shoulder, and looking up he saw Buldeo with the Tower musket. The children had told the village about the buffalo stampede, and Buldeo went out angrily, only too anxious to correct Mowgli for not taking better care of the herd. The wolves dropped out of sight as soon as they saw the man coming.

"What is this folly?" said Buldeo, angrily. "To think that thou canst skin a tiger! Where did the buffaloes kill him? It is the Lame Tiger too, and there is a hundred rupees on his head. Well, well, we will overlook thy letting the herd run off, and perhaps I will give thee one of the rupees of the reward when I have taken the skin to Khanhiwara." He fumbled in his waist-cloth for flint and steel, and stooped down to singe Shere Khan's whiskers. Most native hunters singe a tiger's whiskers to prevent his ghost haunting them.

"Hum!" said Mowgli, half to himself as he ripped back the skin of a fore paw. "So thou wilt take the hide to Khanhiwara for the reward, and perhaps give me one rupee? Now it is in my mind that I need the skin for my own use. Heh! old man, take away that fire!"

"What talk is this to the chief hunter of the village? Thy luck and the stupidity of thy buffaloes have helped thee to this kill. The tiger has just fed, or he would have gone twenty miles by this time. Thou canst not even skin him properly, little beggar-brat, and forsooth I, Buldeo, must be told not to singe his whiskers. Mowgli, I will not give thee one anna of the reward, but only a very big beating. Leave the carcass!"

"By the Bull that bought me," said Mowgli, who was trying to get at the shoulder, "must I stay babbling to an old ape all noon? Here, Akela, this man plagues me."

Buldeo, who was still stooping over Shere Khan's head, found himself sprawling on the grass, with a gray wolf standing over him, while Mowgli went on skinning as though he were alone in all India.

"Ye-es," he said, between his teeth. "Thou art altogether right, Buldeo. Thou wilt never give me one anna of the reward. There is an old war between this lame tiger and myself—a very old war, and—I have won."

To do Buldeo justice, if he had been ten years younger he would have taken his chance with Akela had he met the wolf in the woods, but a wolf who obeyed the orders of this boy who had private wars with man-eating tigers was not a common animal. It was sorcery, magic of the worst kind, thought Buldeo, and he wondered whether the amulet round his neck would protect him. He lay as still as still, expecting every minute to see Mowgli turn into a tiger, too.

"Maharaj! Great King," he said at last, in a husky whisper.

"Yes," said Mowgli, without turning his head, chuckling.

Tiger!
Tiger!

flint and steel: Though matches were in use at this time, they were also too expensive for the very poor of the villages. Many still preferred to strike a piece of steel against a piece of glass-like flint rock. This made a spark which they could use to kindle dry moss or shavings, and so build a fire.

rupee . . . anna: A rupee is a silver coin, equal to sixteen annas.

Obverse.   Reverse.
Rupee, 1862—British Museum.
(Size of the original.)

amulet: A charm, worn around neck or wrist, with magic power to ward off evil.

51

conches: These are shells—conch shells—which can be blown as horns.

sorcerer: A magician. They were supposedly capable of "white magic" to do good, but often used their powerful "black magic" for evil purposes.

"I am an old man. I did not know that thou wast anything more than a herd-boy. May I rise up and go away, or will thy servant tear me to pieces?"

"Go, and peace go with thee. Only, another time do not meddle with my game. Let him go, Akela."

Buldeo hobbled away to the village as fast as he could, looking back over his shoulder in case Mowgli should change into something terrible. When he got to the village he told a tale of magic and enchantment and sorcery that made the priest look very grave.

Mowgli went on with his work, but it was nearly twilight before he and the wolves had drawn the great gay skin clear of the body.

"Now we must hide this and take the buffaloes home! Help me to herd them, Akela."

The herd rounded up in the misty twilight, and when they got near the village Mowgli saw lights, and heard the conches and bells in the temple blowing and banging. Half the village seemed to be waiting for him by the gate. "That is because I have killed Shere Khan," he said to himself; but a shower of stones whistled about his ears, and the villagers shouted: "Sorcerer! Wolf's brat! Jungle-demon! Go away! Get hence quickly, or the priest will turn thee into a wolf again. Shoot, Buldeo, shoot!"

The old Tower musket went off with a bang, and a young buffalo bellowed in pain.

"More sorcery!" shouted the villagers. "He can turn bullets. Buldeo, that was *thy* buffalo."

"Now what is this?" said Mowgli, bewildered, as the stones flew thicker.

"They are not unlike the Pack, these brothers of thine," said Akela, sitting down composedly. "It is in my head that, if bullets mean anything, they would cast thee out."

"Wolf! Wolf's cub! Go away!" shouted the priest, waving a sprig of the sacred *tulsi* plant.

"Again? Last time it was because I was a man. This time it is because I am a wolf. Let us go, Akela."

A woman—it was Messua—ran across to the herd, and cried: "Oh, my son, my son! They say thou art a sorcerer who can turn himself into a beast at will. I do not believe, but go away or they will kill thee. Buldeo says thou art a wizard, but I know thou hast avenged Nathoo's death."

"Come back, Messua!" shouted the crowd. "Come back, or we will stone thee."

Mowgli laughed a little short ugly laugh, for a stone had hit him in the mouth. "Run back, Messua. This is one of the foolish tales they tell under the big tree at dusk. I have at least paid for thy son's life. Farewell; and run quickly, for I shall send the herd in more swiftly than their brickbats. I am no wizard, Messua. Farewell!

"Now, once more, Akela," he cried. "Bring the herd in."

The buffaloes were anxious enough to get to the village. They hardly needed Akela's yell, but charged through the gate like a whirlwind, scattering the crowd right and left.

"Keep count!" shouted Mowgli, scornfully. "It may be that I have stolen one of them. Keep count, for I will do your herding no more. Fare you well, children of men, and thank Messua that I do not come in with my wolves and hunt you up and down your street."

He turned on his heel and walked away with the Lone Wolf; and as he looked up at the stars he felt happy. "No more sleeping in traps for me, Akela. Let us get Shere Khan's skin and go away. No; we will not hurt the village, for Messua was kind to me."

When the moon rose over the plain, making it look all milky, the horrified villagers saw Mowgli, with two wolves at his heels and a bundle on his head, trotting across at the steady wolf's trot that eats up the long miles like fire. Then they banged the temple bells and blew the conches louder than ever; and Messua cried, and Buldeo embroidered the story of his adventures in the jungle, till he ended by saying that Akela stood up on his hind legs and talked like a man.

The moon was just going down when Mowgli and the two wolves came to the hill of the Council Rock, and they stopped at Mother Wolf's cave.

"They have cast me out from the Man Pack, Mother," shouted Mowgli, "but I come with the hide of Shere Khan to keep my word." Mother Wolf walked stiffly from the cave with the cubs behind her, and her eyes glowed as she saw the skin.

"I told him on that day, when he crammed his head and shoulders into this cave, hunting for thy life, Little Frog—I told him that the hunter would be the hunted. It is well done."

"Little Brother, it is well done," said a deep voice in the thicket. "We were lonely in the jungle without thee," and Bagheera came running to Mowgli's bare feet. They clambered up the Council Rock together, and Mowgli spread the skin out on the flat stone where Akela used to sit, and pegged it down with four slivers of bamboo, and Akela lay down upon it, and called the old call to the Council, "Look—look well, O Wolves!" exactly as he had called when Mowgli was first brought there.

brickbats: Half-bricks, or pieces broken and left after a mason has worked on a wall or chimney.

Ever since Akela had been deposed, the Pack had been without a leader, hunting and fighting at their own pleasure. But they answered the call from habit, and some of them were lame from the traps they had fallen into, and some limped from shot-wounds, and some were mangy from eating bad food, and many were missing; but they came to the Council Rock, all that were left of them, and saw Shere Khan's striped hide on the rock, and the huge claws dangling at the end of the empty, dangling feet. It was then that Mowgli made up a song without any rhymes, a song that came up into his throat all by itself, and he shouted it aloud, leaping up and down on the rattling skin, and beating time with his heels till he had no more breath left, while Gray Brother and Akela howled between the verses.

"Look well, O Wolves. Have I kept my word?" said Mowgli when he had finished; and the wolves bayed "Yes," and one tattered wolf howled:

"Lead us again, O Akela. Lead us again, O Man-cub, for we be sick of this lawlessness, and we would be the Free People once more."

"Nay," purred Bagheera, "that may not be. When ye are full-fed, the madness may come upon ye again. Not for nothing are ye called the Free People. Ye fought for freedom, and it is yours. Eat it, O Wolves."

"Man Pack and Wolf Pack have cast me out," said Mowgli. "Now I will hunt alone in the jungle."

"And we will hunt with thee," said the four cubs.

So Mowgli went away and hunted with the four cubs in the jungle from that day on. But he was not always alone, because years afterward he became a man and married.

But that is a story for grown-ups.

MOWGLI'S SONG

THAT HE SANG AT THE COUNCIL ROCK WHEN HE DANCED ON SHERE KHAN'S HIDE

The Song of Mowgli—I, Mowgli, am singing. Let the jungle listen to the things I have done.

Shere Khan said he would kill—would kill! At the gates in the twilight he would kill Mowgli, the Frog!

He ate and he drank. Drink deep, Shere Khan, for when wilt thou drink again? Sleep and dream of the kill.

I am alone on the grazing-grounds. Gray Brother, come to me! Come to me, Lone Wolf, for there is big game afoot.

Bring up the great bull-buffaloes, the blue-skinned herd-bulls with the angry eyes. Drive them to and fro as I order.

Sleepest thou still, Shere Khan? Wake, O wake! Here come I, and the bulls are behind.

Rama, the King of the Buffaloes, stamped with his foot. Waters of the Waingunga, whither went Shere Khan?

He is not Ikki to dig holes, nor Mao, the Peacock, that he should fly. He is not Mang, the Bat, to hang in the branches. Little bamboos that creak together, tell me where he ran?

Ow! He is there. Ahoo! He is there. Under the feet of Rama lies the Lame One! Up, Shere Khan! Up and kill! Here is meat; break the necks of the bulls!

Hsh! He is asleep. We will not wake him, for his strength is very great. The kites have come down to see it. The black ants have come up to know it. There is a great assembly in his honour.

Alala! I have no cloth to wrap me. The kites will see that I am naked. I am ashamed to meet all these people.

Lend me thy coat, Shere Khan. Lend me thy gay striped coat that I may go to the Council Rock.

By the Bull that bought me I have made a promise—a little promise. Only thy coat is lacking before I keep my word.

With the knife—with the knife that men use—with the knife of the hunter, the man, I will stoop down for my gift.

Waters of the Waingunga, bear witness that Shere Khan gives me his coat for the love that he bears me. Pull, Gray Brother! Pull, Akela! Heavy is the hide of Shere Khan.

The Man Pack are angry. They throw stones and talk child's talk. My mouth is bleeding. Let us run away.

Through the night, through the hot night, run swiftly with me, my brothers. We will leave the lights of the village and go to the low moon.

Waters of the Waingunga, the Man Pack have cast me out. I did them no harm, but they were afraid of me. Why?

Wolf Pack, ye have cast me out too. The jungle is shut to me and the village gates are shut. Why?

As Mang flies between the beasts and the birds so fly I between the village and the jungle. Why?

I dance on the hide of Shere Khan, but my heart is very heavy. My mouth is cut and wounded with the stones from the village, but my heart is very light because I have come back to the jungle. Why?

These two things fight together in me as the snakes fight in the spring. The water comes out of my eyes; yet I laugh while it falls. Why?

I am two Mowglis, but the hide of Shere Khan is under my feet.

All the jungle knows that I have killed Shere Khan. Look—look well, O Wolves!

Ahae! My heart is heavy with the things that I do not understand.

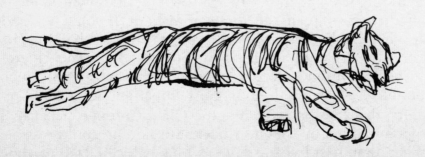

4

How
Fear
Came

"Now these are the Laws of the Jungle,
 and many and mighty are they;
But the head and the hoof of the Law
 and the haunch and the hump is—Obey!"

oldest law: It is true that laws exist among all living things. King Hammurabi of Babylonia set up the first known written people's laws in 2350 B.C., and an excellent set it was, for the times. There's little doubt he was actually putting on papyrus what had already been the law for centuries before. Another early set of laws is the Ten Commandments.

THE Law of the Jungle—which is by far the oldest law in the world—has arranged for almost every kind of accident that may befall the Jungle People, till now its code is as perfect as time and custom can make it. If you have read the other book about Mowgli, you will remember that he spent a great part of his life in the Seeonee Wolf-Pack, learning the Law from Baloo, the Brown Bear; and it was Baloo who told him, when the boy grew impatient at the constant orders, that the Law was like the Giant Creeper, because it dropped across every one's back and no one could escape. "When thou hast lived as long as I have, Little Brother, thou

58

wilt see how all the Jungle obeys at least one Law. And that will be no pleasant sight," said Baloo.

This talk went in at one ear and out at the other, for a boy who spends his life eating and sleeping does not worry about anything till it actually stares him in the face. But, one year, Baloo's words came true, and Mowgli saw all the Jungle working under the Law.

It began when the winter Rains failed almost entirely, and Ikki, the Porcupine, meeting Mowgli in a bamboo-thicket, told him that the wild yams were drying up. Now everybody knows that Ikki is ridiculously fastidious in his choice of food, and will eat nothing but the very best and ripest. So Mowgli laughed and said, "What is that to me?"

"Not much *now*," said Ikki, rattling his quills in a stiff, uncomfortable way, "but later we shall see. Is there any more diving into the deep rock-pool below the Bee-Rocks, Little Brother?"

"No. The foolish water is going all away, and I do not wish to break my head," said Mowgli, who, in those days, was quite sure that he knew as much as any five of the Jungle People put together.

"That is thy loss. A small crack might let in some wisdom." Ikki ducked quickly to prevent Mowgli from pulling his nose-bristles, and Mowgli told Baloo what Ikki had said. Baloo looked very grave, and mumbled half to himself: "If I were alone I would change my hunting-grounds now, before the others began to think. And yet—hunting among strangers ends in fighting; and they might hurt the Man-cub. We must wait and see how the *mohwa* blooms."

That spring the *mohwa* tree, that Baloo was so fond of, never flowered. The greeny, cream-colored, waxy blossoms were heat-killed before they were born, and only a few bad-smelling petals came down when he stood on his hind legs and shook the tree. Then, inch by inch, the untempered heat crept into the heart of the Jungle, turning it yellow, brown, and at last black. The green growths in the sides of the ravines burned up to broken wires and curled films of dead stuff; the hidden pools sank down and caked over, keeping the last least footmark on their edges as if it had been cast in iron; the juicy-stemmed creepers fell away from the trees they clung to and died at their feet; the bamboos withered, clanking when the hot winds blew, and the moss peeled off the rocks deep in the Jungle, till they were as bare and as hot as the quivering blue boulders in the bed of the stream.

The birds and the monkey-people went north early in the

wild yams: These are sweet potatoes. Some tropical species grow three feet long and weigh 30 pounds. There are reports that yams may grow as large as 90 pounds.

Branch of Yam

untempered heat: Untempered heat would be the kind that isn't cooled by clouds or moisture-carrying breezes.

year, for they knew what was coming; and the deer and the wild pig broke far away to the perished fields of the villages, dying sometimes before the eyes of men too weak to kill them. Chil, the Kite, stayed and grew fat, for there was a great deal of carrion, and evening after evening he brought the news to the beasts, too weak to force their way to fresh hunting-grounds, that the sun was killing the Jungle for three days' flight in every direction.

Mowgli, who had never known what real hunger meant, fell back on stale honey, three years old, scraped out of deserted rock-hives—honey black as a sloe, and dusty with dried sugar. He hunted, too, for deep-boring grubs under the bark of the trees, and robbed the wasps of their new broods. All the game in the Jungle was no more than skin and bone, and Bagheera could kill thrice in a night, and hardly get a full meal. But the want of water was the worst, for though the Jungle People drink seldom they must drink deep.

And the heat went on and on, and sucked up all the moisture, till at last the main channel of the Waingunga was the only stream that carried a trickle of water between its dead banks; and when Hathi, the wild elephant, who lives for a hundred years and more, saw a long, lean blue ridge of rock show dry in the very center of the stream, he knew that he was looking at the Peace Rock, and then and there he lifted up his trunk and proclaimed the Water Truce, as his father before him had proclaimed it fifty years ago. The deer, wild pig, and buffalo took up the cry hoarsely; and Chil, the Kite, flew in great circles far and wide, whistling and shrieking the warning.

By the Law of the Jungle it is death to kill at the drinking-places when once the Water Truce has been declared. The reason of this is that drinking comes before eating. Every one in the Jungle can scramble along somehow when only game is scarce; but water is water, and when there is but one source of supply, all hunting stops while the Jungle People go there for their needs. In good seasons, when water was plentiful, those who came down to drink at the Waingunga— or anywhere else, for that matter—did so at the risk of their lives, and that risk made no small part of the fascination of the night's doings. To move down so cunningly that never a leaf stirred; to wade knee-deep in the roaring shallows that drown all noise from behind; to drink, looking backward over one shoulder, every muscle ready for the first desperate bound of keen terror; to roll on the sandy margin, and return, wet-muzzled and well plumped out, to the admiring

grubs: Thick, wormlike larva—the insect which has hatched from the egg, but is not yet in its final form, such as a beetle, butterfly, and the like.

June-bug larva (natural size)

herd, was a thing that all tall-antlered young bucks took a delight in, precisely because they knew that at any moment Bagheera or Shere Khan might leap upon them and bear them down. But now all that life-and-death fun was ended, and the Jungle People came up, starved and weary, to the shrunken river,—tiger, bear, deer, buffalo, and pig, all together,—drank the fouled waters, and hung above them, too exhausted to move off.

The deer and the pig had tramped all day in search of something better than dried bark and withered leaves. The buffaloes had found no wallows to be cool in, and no green crops to steal. The snakes had left the Jungle and come down to the river in the hope of finding a stray frog. They curled round wet stones, and never offered to strike when the nose of a rooting pig dislodged them. The river-turtles had long ago been killed by Bagheera, cleverest of hunters, and the fish had buried themselves deep in the dry mud. Only the Peace Rock lay across the shallows like a long snake, and the little tired ripples hissed as they dried on its hot side.

It was here that Mowgli came nightly for the cool and the companionship. The most hungry of his enemies would hardly have cared for the boy then. His naked hide made him seem more lean and wretched than any of his fellows. His hair was bleached to tow color by the sun; his ribs stood out like the ribs of a basket, and the lumps on his knees and elbows, where he was used to track on all fours, gave his shrunken limbs the look of knotted grass-stems. But his eye, under his matted forelock, was cool and quiet, for Bagheera was his adviser in this time of trouble, and told him to go quietly, hunt slowly, and never, on any account, to lose his temper.

"It is an evil time," said the Black Panther, one furnace-hot evening, "but it will go if we can live till the end. Is thy stomach full, Man cub?"

"There is stuff in my stomach, but I get no good of it. Think you, Bagheera, the Rains have forgotten us and will never come again?"

"Not I! We shall see the *mohwa* in blossom yet, and the little fawns all fat with new grass. Come down to the Peace Rock and hear the news. On my back, Little Brother."

"This is no time to carry weight. I can still stand alone, but —indeed we be no fatted bullocks, we two."

Bagheera looked along his ragged, dusty flank and whispered: "Last night I killed a bullock under the yoke. So low was I brought that I think I should not have dared to spring if he had been loose. *Wou!*"

shoals: The highest points of land under water are those that show first when the water-level drops.

warden: One who watches over others; a keeper. In ancient times, one who ruled while the King was away might be called a WARDEN. Today we call the chief officer of a prison a warden.

vanguard: Those who go first in a group of people or animals or an army.

Mowgli laughed. "Yes, we be great hunters now," said he. "I am very bold—to eat grubs," and the two came down together through the crackling undergrowth to the river-bank and the lace-work of shoals that ran out from it in every direction.

"The water cannot live long," said Baloo, joining them. "Look across. Yonder are trails like the roads of Man."

On the level plain of the further bank the stiff jungle-grass had died standing, and, dying, had mummied. The beaten tracks of the deer and the pig, all heading toward the river, had striped that colorless plain with dusty gullies driven through the ten-foot grass, and, early as it was, each long avenue was full of first-comers hastening to the water. You could hear the does and fawns coughing in the snuff-like dust.

Up-stream, at the bend of the sluggish pool round the Peace Rock, and Warden of the Water Truce, stood Hathi, the wild elephant, with his sons, gaunt and gray in the moon-light, rocking to and fro—always rocking. Below him a little were the vanguard of the deer; below these, again, the pig and the wild buffalo; and on the opposite bank, where the tall trees came down to the water's edge, was the place set apart for the Eaters of Flesh—the tiger, the wolves, the panther, and the bear, and the others.

"We are under one Law, indeed," said Bagheera, wading into the water and looking across at the lines of clicking horns and starting eyes where the deer and the pig pushed each other to and fro. "Good hunting, all you of my blood," he added, lying down at full length, one flank thrust out of the shallows; and then, between his teeth, "But for that which is the Law it would be *very* good hunting."

The quick-spread ears of the deer caught the last sentence, and a frightened whisper ran along the ranks. "The Truce! Remember the Truce!"

"Peace there, peace!" gurgled Hathi, the wild elephant. "The Truce holds, Bagheera. This is no time to talk of hunting."

"Who should know better than I?" Bagheera answered, rolling his yellow eyes up-stream. "I am an eater of turtles—a fisher of frogs. *Ngaayah!* Would I could get good from chewing branches!"

"*We* wish so, very greatly," bleated a young fawn, who had only been born that spring, and did not at all like it. Wretched as the Jungle People were, even Hathi could not help chuckling; while Mowgli, lying on his elbows in the warm water, laughed aloud, and beat up the scum with his feet.

fawn: A deer that is less than a year old is spoken of as a fawn.

"Well spoken, little bud-horn," Bagheera purred. "When the Truce ends that shall be remembered in thy favor," and he looked keenly through the darkness to make sure of recognizing the fawn again.

Gradually the talking spread up and down the drinking-places. One could hear the scuffling, snorting pig asking for more room; the buffaloes grunting among themselves as they lurched out across the sand-bars, and the deer telling pitiful stories of their long foot-sore wanderings in quest of food. Now and again they asked some question of the Eaters of Flesh across the river, but all the news was bad, and the roaring hot wind of the Jungle came and went between the rocks and the rattling branches, and scattered twigs and dust on the water.

"The men-folk, too, they die beside their plows," said a young sambhur. "I passed three between sunset and night. They lay still, and their bullocks with them. We also shall lie still in a little."

sambhur: This is the large Indian elk.

"The river has fallen since last night," said Baloo. "O Hathi, hast thou ever seen the like of this drought?"

"It will pass, it will pass," said Hathi, squirting water along his back and sides.

"We have one here that cannot endure long," said Baloo; and he looked toward the boy he loved.

"I?" said Mowgli indignantly, sitting up in the water. "I have no long fur to cover my bones, but—but if *thy* hide were taken off, Baloo—"

Hathi shook all over at the idea, and Baloo said severely:

"Man-cub, that is not seemly to tell a Teacher of the Law. *Never* have I been seen without my hide."

"Nay, I meant no harm, Baloo; but only that thou art, as it were, like the cocoanut in the husk, and I am the same cocoanut all naked. Now that brown husk of thine—" Mowgli was sitting cross-legged, and explaining things with his fore-finger in his usual way, when Bagheera put out a paddy paw and pulled him over backward into the water.

"Worse and worse," said the Black Panther, as the boy rose spluttering. "First, Baloo is to be skinned, and now he is a cocoanut. Be careful that he does not do what the ripe cocoanuts do."

"And what is that?" said Mowgli, off his guard for the minute, though that is one of the oldest catches in the Jungle.

"Break thy head," said Bagheera quietly, pulling him under again.

"It is not good to make a jest of thy teacher," said the bear, when Mowgli had been ducked for the third time.

"Not good! What would ye have? That naked thing run-

63

ning to and fro makes a monkey-jest of those who have once been good hunters, and pulls the best of us by the whisker for sport." This was Shere Khan, the Lame Tiger, limping down to the water. He waited a little to enjoy the sensation he made among the deer on the opposite bank; then he dropped his square, frilled head and began to lap, growling: "The Jungle has become a whelping-ground for naked cubs now. Look at me, Man-cub!"

Mowgli looked—stared, rather—as insolently as he knew how, and in a minute Shere Khan turned away uneasily. "Man-cub this, and Man-cub that," he rumbled, going on with his drink, "the cub is neither man nor cub, or he would have been afraid. Next season I shall have to beg his leave for a drink. *Aurgh!*"

"That may come, too," said Bagheera, looking him steadily between the eyes. "That may come, too—Faugh, Shere Khan!—what new shame hast thou brought here?"

The Lame Tiger had dipped his chin and jowl in the water, and dark oily streaks were floating from it downstream.

"Man!" said Shere Khan coolly, "I killed an hour since." He went on purring and growling to himself.

The line of beasts shook and wavered to and fro, and a whisper went up that grew to a cry: "Man! Man! He has killed Man!" Then all looked toward Hathi, the wild elephant, but he seemed not to hear. Hathi never does anything till the time comes, and that is one of the reasons why he lives so long.

"At such a season as this to kill Man! Was no other game afoot?" said Bagheera scornfully, drawing himself out of the tainted water, and shaking each paw, cat-fashion, as he did so.

"I killed for choice—not for food." The horrified whisper began again, and Hathi's watchful little white eye cocked itself in Shere Khan's direction. "For choice," Shere Khan drawled. "Now come I to drink and make me clean again. Is there any to forbid?"

Bagheera's back began to curve like a bamboo in a high wind, but Hathi lifted up his trunk and spoke quietly.

"Thy kill was from choice?" he asked; and when Hathi asks a question it is best to answer.

"Even so. It was my right and my Night. Thou knowest, O Hathi." Shere Khan spoke almost courteously.

"Yes, I know," Hathi answered; and, after a little silence, "Hast thou drunk thy fill?"

"For to-night, yes."

"Go, then. The river is to drink, and not to defile. None but the Lame Tiger would so have boasted of his right at

tainted water: Dirtied, blemished, dishonored water.

64

this season when—when we suffer together—Man and Jungle People alike. Clean or unclean, get to thy lair, Shere Khan!"

The last words rang out like silver trumpets, and Hathi's three sons rolled forward half a pace, though there was no need. Shere Khan slunk away, not daring to growl, for he knew—what every one else knows—that when the last comes to the last, Hathi is the Master of the Jungle.

"What is this right Shere Khan speaks of?" Mowgli whispered in Bagheera's ear. "To kill Man is *always* shameful. The Law says so. And yet Hathi says—"

"Ask him. I do not know, Little Brother. Right or no right, if Hathi had not spoken I would have taught that lame butcher his lesson. To come to the Peace Rock fresh from a kill of Man—and to boast of it—is a jackal's trick. Besides, he tainted the good water."

Mowgli waited for a minute to pick up his courage, because no one cared to address Hathi directly, and then he cried: "What is Shere Khan's right, O Hathi?" Both banks echoed his words, for all the People of the Jungle are intensely curious, and they had just seen something that none, except Baloo, who looked very thoughtful, seemed to understand.

"It is an old tale," said Hathi; "a tale older than the Jungle. Keep silence along the banks, and I will tell that tale."

There was a minute or two of pushing and shouldering among the pigs and the buffalo, and then the leaders of the herds grunted, one after another, "We wait," and Hathi strode forward till he was nearly knee-deep in the pool by the Peace Rock. Lean and wrinkled and yellow-tusked though he was, he looked what the Jungle knew him to be—their master.

"Ye know, children," he began, "that of all things ye most fear Man"; and there was a mutter of agreement.

"This tale touches thee, Little Brother," said Bagheera to Mowgli.

"I? I am of the Pack—a hunter of the Free People," Mowgli answered. "What have I to do with Man?"

"And ye do not know why ye fear Man?" Hathi went on. "This is the reason. In the beginning of the Jungle, and none know when that was, we of the Jungle walked together, having no fear of one another. In those days there was no drought, and leaves and flowers and fruit grew on the same tree, and we ate nothing at all except leaves and flowers and grass and fruit and bark."

"I am glad I was not born in those days," said Bagheera.

How
Fear
Came

lair: A place where an animal lives; usually a cave or place in the rocks.

65

"Bark is only good to sharpen claws."

"And the Lord of the Jungle was Tha, the First of the Elephants. He drew the Jungle out of deep waters with his trunk; and where he made furrows in the ground with his tusks, there the rivers ran; and where he struck with his foot, there rose ponds of good water; and when he blew through his trunk,—thus,—the trees fell. That was the manner in which the Jungle was made by Tha; and so the tale was told to me."

"It has not lost fat in the telling," Bagheera whispered, and Mowgli laughed behind his hand.

"In those days there was no corn or melons or pepper or sugar-cane, nor were there any little huts such as ye have all seen; and the Jungle People knew nothing of Man, but lived in the Jungle together, making one people. But presently they began to dispute over their food, though there was grazing enough for all. They were lazy. Each wished to eat where he lay down, as sometimes we can do now when the spring rains are good. Tha, the First of the Elephants, was busy making new jungles and leading the rivers in their beds. He could not walk in all places; therefore he made the First of the Tigers the master and the judge of the Jungle, to whom the Jungle People should bring their disputes. In those days the First of the Tigers ate fruit and grass with the others. He was as large as I am, and he was very beautiful, in color all over like the blossom of the yellow creeper. There was never stripe nor bar upon his hide in those good days when this the Jungle was new. All the Jungle People came before him without fear, and his word was the Law of all the Jungle. We were then, remember ye, one people.

"Yet upon a night there was a dispute between two bucks —a grazing-quarrel such as ye now settle with the horns and the fore feet—and it is said that as the two spoke together before the First of the Tigers lying among the flowers, a buck pushed him with his horns, and the First of the Tigers forgot that he was the master and judge of the Jungle, and, leaping upon that buck, broke his neck.

"Till that night never one of us had died, and the First of the Tigers, seeing what he had done, and being made foolish by the scent of the blood, ran away into the marshes of the North, and we of the Jungle, left without a judge, fell to fighting among ourselves; and Tha heard the noise of it and came back. Then some of us said this and some of us said that, but he saw the dead buck among the flowers, and asked who had killed, and we of the Jungle would not tell because the smell of the blood made us foolish. We ran to and fro in

judge: One who knows the law, and applies it to settle a dispute between two or more sides.

marshes: Like swamps, marshes are flat, wet areas, sometimes partly under water. There are both fresh and salt water marshes. They are often the home of marsh birds, frogs, turtles, water rats, and many kinds of aquatic insects.

circles, capering and crying out and shaking our heads. Then Tha gave an order to the trees that hang low, and to the trailing creepers of the Jungle, that they should mark the killer of the buck so that he should know him again, and he said, 'Who will now be master of the Jungle People?' Then up leaped the Gray Ape who lives in the branches, and said, 'I will now be master of the Jungle.' At this Tha laughed, and said, 'So be it,' and went away very angry.

"Children, ye know the Gray Ape. He was then as he is now. At the first he made a wise face for himself, but in a little while he began to scratch and to leap up and down, and when Tha came back he found the Gray Ape hanging, head down, from a bough, mocking those who stood below; and they mocked him again. And so there was no Law in the Jungle—only foolish talk and senseless words.

"Then Tha called us all together and said: 'The first of your masters has brought Death into the Jungle, and the second Shame. Now it is time there was a Law, and a Law that ye must not break. Now ye shall know Fear, and when ye have found him ye shall know that he is your master, and the rest shall follow.' Then we of the Jungle said, 'What is Fear?' And Tha said, 'Seek till ye find.' So we went up and down the Jungle seeking for Fear, and presently the buffaloes—"

"Ugh!" said Mysa, the leader of the buffaloes, from their sand-bank.

"Yes, Mysa, it was the buffaloes. They came back with the news that in a cave in the Jungle sat Fear, and that he had no hair, and went upon his hind legs. Then we of the Jungle followed the herd till we came to that cave, and Fear stood at the mouth of it, and he was, as the buffaloes had said, hairless, and he walked upon his hinder legs. When he saw us he cried out, and his voice filled us with the fear that we have now of that voice when we hear it, and we ran away, tramping upon and tearing each other because we were afraid. That night, so it was told to me, we of the Jungle did not lie down together as used to be our custom, but each tribe drew off by itself—the pig with the pig, the deer with the deer; horn to horn, hoof to hoof,—like keeping to like, and so lay shaking in the Jungle.

"Only the First of the Tigers was not with us, for he was still hidden in the marshes of the North, and when the word was brought to him of the Thing we had seen in the cave, he said: 'I will go to this Thing and break his neck.' So he ran all the night till he came to the cave; but the trees and the creepers on his path, remembering the order that Tha had given, let down their branches and marked him as he ran, drawing their fingers across his back, his flank, his forehead, and his jowl. Wherever they touched him there was a mark and a stripe upon his yellow hide. *And those stripes do his children wear to this day!* When he came to the cave, Fear, the Hairless One, put out his hand and called him 'The Striped One that comes by night,' and the First of the Tigers was afraid of the Hairless One, and ran back to the swamps howling."

Mowgli chuckled quietly here, his chin in the water.

"So loud did he howl that Tha heard him and said, 'What is the sorrow?' And the First of the Tigers, lifting up his muzzle to the new-made sky, which is now so old, said: 'Give me back my power, O Tha. I am made ashamed before all the Jungle, and I have run away from a Hairless One, and he has called me a shameful name.' 'And why?' said Tha. 'Because I am smeared with the mud of the marshes,' said the First of the Tigers. 'Swim, then, and roll on the wet grass, and if it be mud it will wash away,' said Tha; and the First of the Tigers swam, and rolled and rolled upon the grass, till the Jungle ran round and round before his eyes, but not one little bar upon all his hide was changed, and Tha, watching him, laughed. Then the First of the Tigers said, 'What have I done that this comes to me?' Tha said, 'Thou hast killed the buck, and thou hast let Death loose in the Jungle, and with Death has come Fear, so that the people of the Jungle are afraid one of the other, as thou art afraid of the Hairless One.' The First of the Tigers said, 'They will never fear me, for I knew them since the beginning.' Tha said, 'Go and see.' And the First of the Tigers ran to and fro, calling aloud to the deer and the pig and the sambhur and the porcupine and all the Jungle Peoples, and they all ran away from him who had been their judge, because they were afraid.

"Then the First of the Tigers came back, and his pride was broken in him, and, beating his head upon the ground, he tore up the earth with all his feet and said: 'Remember that I was once the Master of the Jungle. Do not forget me, O Tha! Let my children remember that I was once without shame or fear!' And Tha said: 'This much I will do, because thou and I together saw the Jungle made. For one night in each year it shall be as it was before the buck was killed—for thee and for thy children. In that one night, if ye meet the Hairless One—and his name is Man—ye shall not be afraid of him, but he shall be afraid of you, as though ye were judges of the Jungle and masters of all things. Show him mercy in that night of his fear, for thou hast known what Fear is.'

"Then the First of the Tigers answered, 'I am content';

but when next he drank he saw the black stripes upon his flank and his side, and he remembered the name that the Hairless One had given him, and he was angry. For a year he lived in the marshes, waiting till Tha should keep his promise. And upon a night when the Jackal of the Moon [the Evening Star] stood clear of the Jungle, he felt that his Night was upon him, and he went to that cave to meet the Hairless One. Then it happened as Tha promised, for the Hairless One fell down before him and lay along the ground, and the First of the Tigers struck him and broke his back, for he thought that there was but one such Thing in the Jungle, and that he had killed Fear. Then, nosing above the kill, he heard Tha coming down from the woods of the North, and presently the voice of the First of the Elephants, which is the voice that we hear now—"

The thunder was rolling up and down the dry, scarred hills, but it brought no rain—only heat lightning that flickered along the ridges—and Hathi went on: "*That* was the voice he heard, and it said: 'Is this thy mercy?' The First of the Tigers licked his lips and said: 'What matter? I have killed Fear.' And Tha said: 'O blind and foolish! Thou hast untied the feet of Death, and he will follow thy trail till thou diest. Thou hast taught Man to kill!'

"The First of the Tigers, standing stiffly to his kill, said: 'He is as the buck was. There is no Fear. Now I will judge the Jungle Peoples once more.'

"And Tha said: 'Never again shall the Jungle Peoples come to thee. They shall never cross thy trail, nor sleep near thee, nor follow after thee, nor browse by thy lair. Only Fear shall follow thee, and with a blow that thou canst not see he shall bid thee wait his pleasure. He shall make the ground to open under thy feet, and the creeper to twist about thy neck, and the tree-trunks to grow together about thee higher than thou canst leap, and at the last he shall take thy hide to wrap his cubs when they are cold. Thou hast shown him no mercy, and none will he show thee.'

"The First of the Tigers was very bold, for his Night was still on him, and he said: 'The Promise of Tha is the Promise of Tha. He will not take away my Night?' And Tha said: 'The one Night is thine, as I have said, but there is a price to pay. Thou hast taught Man to kill, and he is no slow learner.'

"The First of the Tigers said: 'He is here under my foot, and his back is broken. Let the Jungle know I have killed Fear.'

"Then Tha laughed, and said: 'Thou hast killed one of many, but thou thyself shalt tell the Jungle—for thy Night is ended.'

"So the day came; and from the mouth of the cave went out another Hairless One, and he saw the kill in the path, and the First of the Tigers above it, and he took a pointed stick—"

"They throw a thing that cuts now," said Ikki, rustling down the bank; for Ikki was considered uncommonly good eating by the Gonds—they called him Ho-Igoo—and he knew something of the wicked little Gondee axe that whirls across a clearing like a dragon-fly.

"It was a pointed stick, such as they put in the foot of a pit-trap," said Hathi, and throwing it, he struck the First of the Tigers deep in the flank. Thus it happened as Tha said, for the First of the Tigers ran howling up and down the Jungle till he tore out the stick, and all the Jungle knew that the Hairless One could strike from far off, and they feared more than before. So it came about that the First of the Tigers taught the Hairless One to kill—and ye know what harm that

pit traps: These are among the many kinds of traps set in jungles by the natives. In ancient—and also recent times—the maharajas and other royalty and their guests hunted tigers often from the backs of elephants. It was partly for sport, partly because a tiger in the area could terrorize a whole village.

70

has since done to all our peoples—through the noose, and the pitfall, and the hidden trap, and the flying stick, and the stinging fly that comes out of white smoke [Hathi meant the rifle], and the Red Flower that drives us into the open. Yet for one night in the year the Hairless One fears the Tiger, as Tha promised, and never has the Tiger given him cause to be less afraid. Where he finds him, there he kills him, remembering how the First of the Tigers was made ashamed. For the rest, Fear walks up and down the Jungle by day and by night."

"*Ahi! Aoo!*" said the deer, thinking of what it all meant to them.

"And only when there is one great Fear over all, as there is now, can we of the Jungle lay aside our little fears, and meet together in one place as we do now."

"For one night only does Man fear the Tiger?" said Mowgli.

"For one night only," said Hathi.

"But I—but we—but all the Jungle knows that Shere Khan kills Man twice and thrice in a moon."

"Even so. *Then* he springs from behind and turns his head aside as he strikes, for he is full of fear. If Man looked at him he would run. But on his one Night he goes openly down to the village. He walks between the houses and thrusts his head into the doorway, and the men fall on their faces and there he does his kill. One kill in that Night."

"Oh!" said Mowgli to himself, rolling over in the water. "*Now* I see why it was Shere Khan bade me look at him! He got no good of it, for he could not hold his eyes steady, and—and I certainly did not fall down at his feet. But then I am not a man, being of the Free People."

"Umm!" said Bagheera deep in his furry throat. "Does the Tiger know his Night?"

"Never till the Jackal of the Moon stands clear of the evening mist. Sometimes it falls in the dry summer and sometimes in the wet rains—this one Night of the Tiger. But for the First of the Tigers, this would never have been, nor would any of us have known fear."

The deer grunted sorrowfully, and Bagheera's lips curled in a wicked smile. "Do men know this—tale?" said he.

"None know it except the tigers, and we, the elephants—the children of Tha. Now ye by the pools have heard it, and I have spoken."

Hathi dipped his trunk into the water as a sign that he did not wish to talk.

"But—but—but," said Mowgli, turning to Baloo, "why

71

did not the First of the Tigers continue to eat grass and leaves and trees? He did but break the buck's neck. He did not *eat*. What led him to the hot meat?"

"The trees and the creepers marked him, Little Brother, and made him the striped thing that we see. Never again would he eat their fruit; but from that day he revenged himself upon the deer, and the others, the Eaters of Grass," said Baloo.

"Then *thou* knowest the tale. Heh? Why have I never heard?"

"Because the Jungle is full of such tales. If I made a beginning there would never be an end to them. Let go my ear, Little Brother."

The Law Of The Jungle

JUST to give you an idea of the immense variety of the Jungle Law, I have translated into verse (Baloo always recited them in a sort of sing-song) a few of the laws that apply to the wolves. There are, of course, hundreds and hundreds more, but these will do for specimens of the simpler rulings.

Now this is the Law of the Jungle—as old and as true as the sky;
And the Wolf that shall keep it may prosper, but the Wolf that shall break it must die.
As the creeper that girdles the tree-trunk the Law runneth forward and back—
For the strength of the Pack is the Wolf, and the strength of the Wolf is the Pack.

Wash daily from nose-tip to tail-tip; drink deeply, but never too deep;
And remember the night is for hunting, and forget not the day is for sleep.

The Jackal may follow the Tiger, but, Cub, when thy whiskers are grown,
Remember the Wolf is a hunter—go forth and get food of thine own.

Keep peace with the Lords of the Jungle—the Tiger, the Panther, the Bear;
And trouble not Hathi the Silent, and mock not the Boar in his lair.

When Pack meets with Pack in the Jungle, and neither will go from the trail,
Lie down till the leaders have spoken—it may be fair words shall prevail.

When ye fight with a Wolf of the Pack, ye must fight him alone and afar,
Lest others take part in the quarrel, and the Pack be diminished by war.

The Lair of the Wolf is his refuge, and where he has made him his
 home,
Not even the Head Wolf may enter, not even the Council may come.

The Lair of the Wolf is his refuge, but where he has digged it too plain,
The Council shall send him a message, and so he shall change it again.

If ye kill before midnight, be silent, and wake not the woods with your
 bay,
Lest ye frighten the deer from the crops, and the brothers go empty
 away.

Ye may kill for yourselves, and your mates, and your cubs as they need,
 and ye can:
But kill not for pleasure of killing, and seven times never kill Man.

If ye plunder his kill from a weaker, devour not all in thy pride;
Pack-Right is the right of the meanest; so leave him the head and the
 hide.

The Kill of the Pack is the meat of the Pack. Ye must eat where it lies;
And no one may carry away of that meat to his lair, or he dies.

The Kill of the Wolf is the meat of the Wolf. He may do what he will,
But, till he has given permission, the Pack may not eat of that Kill.

Cub-Right is the right of the Yearling. From all of his Pack he may claim
Full-gorge when the killer has eaten; and none may refuse him the same.

Lair-Right is the right of the Mother. From all of her year she may claim
One haunch of each kill for her litter, and none may deny her the same.

Cave-Right is the right of the Father—to hunt by himself for his own:
He is freed of all calls to the Pack; he is judged by the Council alone.

Because of his age and his cunning, because of his gripe and his paw,
In all that the Law leaveth open, the word of the Head Wolf is Law.

Now these are the Laws of the Jungle, and many and mighty are they;
But the head and the hoof of the Law and the haunch and the hump is—
 Obey!

5

Letting
In The
Jungle

Veil them, cover them, wall them round—
  Blossom, and creeper, and weed—
Let us forget the sight and the sound,
  The smell and the touch of the breed!

Fat black ash by the altar-stone,
  Here is the white-foot rain,
And the does bring forth in the fields unsown,
  And none shall affright them again;
And the blind walls crumble, unknown, o'erthrown,
  And none shall inhabit again!

YOU will remember, if you have read the tales in the
first Jungle Book, that, after Mowgli had pinned Shere
Khan's hide to the Council Rock, he told as many as were
left of the Seeonee Pack that henceforward he would hunt

in the Jungle alone; and the four children of Mother and Father Wolf said that they would hunt with him. But it is not easy to change one's life all in a minute—particularly in the Jungle. The first thing Mowgli did, when the disorderly Pack had slunk off, was to go to the home-cave, and sleep for a day and a night. Then he told Mother Wolf and Father Wolf as much as they could understand of his adventures among men; and when he made the morning sun flicker up and down the blade of his skinning-knife,—the same he had skinned Shere Khan with,—they said he had learned something. Then Akela and Gray Brother had to explain their share of the great buffalo-drive in the ravine, and Baloo toiled up the hill to hear all about it, and Bagheera scratched himself all over with pure delight at the way in which Mowgli had managed his war.

It was long after sunrise, but no one dreamed of going to sleep, and from time to time, during the talk, Mother Wolf would throw up her head, and sniff a deep snuff of satisfaction as the wind brought her the smell of the tiger-skin on the Council Rock.

"But for Akela and Gray Brother here," Mowgli said, at the end, "I could have done nothing. Oh, mother, mother! if thou hadst seen the black herd-bulls pour down the ravine, or hurry through the gates when the Man-Pack flung stones at me!"

"I am glad I did not see that last," said Mother Wolf, stiffly. "It is not *my* custom to suffer my cubs to be driven to and fro like jackals. *I* would have taken a price from the Man-Pack; but I would have spared the woman who gave thee the milk. Yes, I would have spared her alone."

"Peace, peace, Raksha!" said Father Wolf, lazily. "Our Frog has come back again—so wise that his own father must lick his feet; and what is a cut, more or less, on the head? Leave Men alone." Baloo and Bagheera both echoed: "Leave Men alone."

Mowgli, his head on Mother Wolf's side, smiled contentedly, and said that, for his own part, he never wished to see, or hear, or smell Man again.

"But what," said Akela, cocking one ear—"but what if men do not leave thee alone, Little Brother?"

"We be *five*," said Gray Brother, looking round at the company, and snapping his jaws on the last word.

"We also might attend to that hunting," said Bagheera, with a little *switch-switch* of his tail, looking at Baloo. "But why think of men now, Akela?"

"For this reason," the Lone Wolf answered: "when that yellow thief's hide was hung up on the rock, I went back along our trail to the village, stepping in my tracks, turning aside, and lying down, to make a mixed trail in case one should follow us. But when I had fouled the trail so that I myself hardly knew it again, Mang, the Bat, came hawking between the trees, and hung up above me. Said Mang 'The village of the Man-Pack, where they cast out the Man-cub, hums like a hornet's nest.'"

"It was a big stone that I threw," chuckled Mowgli, who had often amused himself by throwing ripe paw-paws into a hornet's nest, and racing off to the nearest pool before the hornets caught him.

"I asked of Mang what he had seen. He said the Red Flower blossomed at the gate of the village, and men sat about it carrying guns. Now I know, for I have good cause," —Akela looked down at the old dry scars on his flank and side,—"that men do not carry guns for pleasure. Presently, Little Brother, a man with a gun follows our trail—if, indeed, he be not already on it."

"But why should he? Men have cast me out. What more do they need?" said Mowgli, angrily.

"Thou art a man, Little Brother," Akela returned. "It is not for *us*, the Free Hunters, to tell thee what thy brethren do, or why."

He had just time to snatch up his paw as the skinning-knife cut deep into the ground below. Mowgli struck quicker than an average human eye could follow, but Akela was a wolf; and even a dog, who is very far removed from the wild wolf, his ancestor, can be waked out of deep sleep by a cart-wheel touching his flank, and can spring away unharmed before that wheel comes on.

"Another time," Mowgli said quietly, returning the knife to its sheath, "speak of the Man-Pack and of Mowgli in *two* breaths—not one."

"Phff! That is a sharp tooth," said Akela, snuffing at the blade's cut in the earth, "but living with the Man-Pack has spoiled thine eye, Little Brother. I could have killed a buck while thou wast striking."

Bagheera sprang to his feet, thrust up his head as far as he could, sniffed, and stiffened through every curve of his body. Gray Brother followed his example quickly, keeping a little to his left to get the wind that was blowing from the right, while Akela bounded fifty yards up wind, and, half crouching, stiffened too. Mowgli looked on enviously. He could smell things as very few human beings could, but he had never reached the hair-trigger-like sensitiveness of a Jungle nose; and his three months in the smoky village had set him back sadly. However, he dampened his finger, rubbed it on his nose, and stood erect to catch the upper scent, which, though it is the faintest, is the truest.

"Man!" Akela growled, dropping on his haunches.

"Buldeo!" said Mowgli, sitting down. "He follows our trail, and yonder is the sunlight on his gun. Look!"

It was no more than a splash of sunlight, for a fraction of a second, on the brass clamps of the old Tower musket, but nothing in the Jungle winks with just that flash, except when the clouds race over the sky. Then a piece of mica, or a little pool, or even a highly polished leaf will flash like a heliograph. But that day was cloudless and still.

"I knew men would follow," said Akela, triumphantly. "Not for nothing have I led the Pack."

The four cubs said nothing, but ran down hill on their bellies, melting into the thorn and underbrush as a mole melts into a lawn.

"Where go ye, and without word?" Mowgli called.

"H'sh! We roll his skull here before midday!" Gray Brother answered.

"Back! Back and wait! Man does not eat Man!" Mowgli shrieked.

"Who was a wolf but now? Who drove the knife at me for thinking he might be Man?" said Akela, as the four wolves turned back sullenly and dropped to heel.

"Am I to give a reason for all I choose to do?" said Mowgli, furiously.

"That is Man! There speaks Man!" Bagheera muttered under his whiskers. "Even so did men talk round the King's cages at Oodeypore. We of the Jungle know that Man is wisest of all. If we trusted our ears we should know that of all things he is most foolish." Raising his voice, he added, "The Man-cub is right in this. Men hunt in packs. To kill one, unless we know what the others will do, is bad hunting. Come, let us see what this Man means toward us."

"We will not come," Gray Brother growled. "Hunt alone, Little Brother. *We* know our own minds. That skull would have been ready to bring by now."

Mowgli had been looking from one to the other of his friends, his chest heaving and his eyes full of tears. He strode forward to the wolves, and, dropping on one knee, said: "Do I not know my mind? Look at me!"

They looked uneasily, and when their eyes wandered, he called them back again and again, till their hair stood up all over their bodies, and they trembled in every limb, while Mowgli stared and stared.

"Now," said he, "of us five, which is leader?"

"Thou art leader, Little Brother," said Gray Brother, and

heliograph: A signalling instrument that uses a mirror to flash sunlight to a distant point. Messages can be sent in Morse code. The word comes from Greek: helio (sun) and graph (writing).

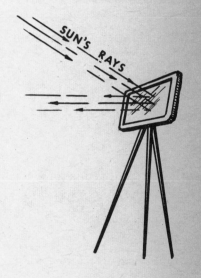

he licked Mowgli's foot.

"Follow, then," said Mowgli, and the four followed at his heels with their tails between their legs.

"This comes of living with the Man-Pack," said Bagheera, slipping down after them. "There is more in the Jungle now than Jungle Law, Baloo."

The old bear said nothing, but he thought many things.

Mowgli cut across noiselessly through the Jungle, at right angles to Buldeo's path, till, parting the undergrowth, he saw the old man, his musket on his shoulder, running up the trail of overnight at a dog-trot.

You will remember that Mowgli had left the village with the heavy weight of Shere Khan's raw hide on his shoulders, while Akela and Gray Brother trotted behind, so that the triple trail was very clearly marked. Presently Buldeo came to where Akela, as you know, had gone back and mixed it all up. Then he sat down, and coughed and grunted, and made little casts round and about into the Jungle to pick it up again, and all the time he could have thrown a stone over those who were watching him. No one can be so silent as a wolf when he does not care to be heard; and Mowgli, though the wolves thought he moved very clumsily, could come and go like a shadow. They ringed the old man as a school of porpoises ring a steamer at full speed, and as they ringed him they talked unconcernedly, for their speech began below the lowest end of the scale that untrained human beings can hear. [The other end is bounded by the high squeak of Mang, the Bat, which very many people cannot catch at all. From that note all the birds and bats and insect talk takes on.]

"This is better than any kill," said Gray Brother, as Buldeo stooped and peered and puffed. "He looks like a lost pig in the Jungles by the river. What does he say?" Buldeo was muttering savagely.

Mowgli translated. "He says that packs of wolves must have danced round me. He says that he never saw such a trail in his life. He says he is tired."

"He will be rested before he picks it up again," said Bagheera coolly, as he slipped round a tree-trunk, in the game of blindman's-buff that they were playing. "Now, what does the lean thing do?"

"Eat or blow smoke out of his mouth. Men always play with their mouths," said Mowgli, and the silent trailers saw the old man fill and light and puff at a water-pipe, and they took good note of the smell of the tobacco, so as to be sure of Buldeo in the darkest night, if necessary.

Then a little knot of charcoal-burners came down the path,

Bats are the only mammals that can fly. Most people don't know that bats can see well in the day time. At night, they make high pitched sounds, and guide themselves by the echoes. Human ears cannot hear their high-pitched cry.

water pipe: In a water pipe the tobacco smoke travels through water. This would give Buldeo a cooler smoke.

and naturally halted to speak to Buldeo, whose fame as a hunter reached for at least twenty miles round. They all sat down and smoked, and Bagheera and the others came up and watched while Buldeo began to tell the story of Mowgli, the Devil-child, from one end to another, with additions and inventions. How he himself had really killed Shere Khan; and how Mowgli had turned himself into a wolf, and fought with him all the afternoon, and changed into a boy again and bewitched Buldeo's rifle, so that the bullet turned the corner, when he pointed it at Mowgli, and killed one of Buldeo's own buffaloes; and how the village, knowing him to be the bravest hunter in Seeonee, had sent him out to kill this Devil-child. But meantime the village had got hold of Messua and her husband, who were undoubtedly the father and mother of this Devil-child, and had barricaded them in their own hut, and presently would torture them to make them confess they were witch and wizard, and then they would be burned to death.

"When?" said the charcoal burners, because they would very much like to be present at the ceremony.

Buldeo said that nothing would be done till he returned, because the village wished him to kill the Jungle Boy first. After that they would dispose of Messua and her husband, and divide their lands and buffaloes among the village. Messua's husband had some remarkably fine buffaloes, too. It was an excellent thing to destroy wizards, Buldeo thought; and people who entertained Wolf-children out of the Jungle were clearly the worst kind of witches.

But, said the charcoal-burners, what would happen if the English heard of it? The English, they had heard, were a perfectly mad people, who would not let honest farmers kill witches in peace.

Why, said Buldeo, the head-man of the village would report that Messua and her husband had died of snake-bite. *That* was all arranged, and the only thing now was to kill the Wolf-child. They did not happen to have seen anything of such a creature?

The charcoal-burners looked round cautiously, and thanked their stars they had not; but they had no doubt that so brave a man as Buldeo would find him if any one could. The sun was getting rather low, and they had an idea that they would push on to Buldeo's village and see that wicked witch. Buldeo said that, though it was his duty to kill the Devil-child, he could not think of letting a party of unarmed men go through the Jungle, which might produce the Wolf-demon at any minute, without his escort. He, therefore, would accompany them, and if the sorcerer's child appeared

haft: the handle of a knife.

—well, he would show them how the best hunter in Seeonee dealt with such things. The Brahmin, he said, had given him a charm against the creature that made everything perfectly safe.

"What says he? What says he? What says he?" the wolves repeated every few minutes; and Mowgli translated until he came to the witch part of the story, which was a little beyond him, and then he said that the man and woman who had been so kind to him were trapped.

"Does Man trap Man?" said Bagheera.

"So he says. I cannot understand the talk. They are all mad together. What have Messua and her man to do with me that they should be put in a trap; and what is all this talk about the Red Flower? I must look to this. Whatever they would do to Messua they will not do till Buldeo returns. And so—" Mowgli thought hard, with his fingers playing round the haft of the skinning-knife, while Buldeo and the charcoal-burners went off very valiantly in single file.

"I am going hot-foot back to the Man-Pack," Mowgli said at last.

"And those?" said Gray Brother, looking hungrily after the brown backs of the charcoal-burners.

"Sing them home," said Mowgli with a grin; "I do not wish them to be at the village gates till it is dark. Can ye hold them?"

Gray Brother bared his white teeth in contempt. "We can head them round and round in circles like tethered goats—if I know Man."

"That I do not need. Sing to them a little, lest they be lonely on the road, and, Gray Brother, the song need not be of the sweetest. Go with them, Bagheera, and help make that song. When the night is shut down, meet me by the village—Gray Brother knows the place."

"It is no light hunting to work for a Man-cub. When shall I sleep?" said Bagheera, yawning, though his eyes showed that he was delighted with the amusement. "Me to sing to naked men! But let us try."

He lowered his head so that the sound would travel, and cried a long, long, "Good hunting"—a midnight call in the afternoon, which was quite awful enough to begin with. Mowgli heard it rumble, and rise, and fall, and die off in a creepy sort of whine behind him, and laughed to himself as he ran through the Jungle. He could see the charcoal-burners huddled in a knot; old Buldeo's gun-barrel waving, like a banana-leaf, to every point of the compass at once. Then Gray Brother gave the *Ya-la-hi! Yalaha!* call for the buck-driving, when the Pack drives the nilghai, the big blue cow, before them, and it seemed to come from the very ends of the earth, nearer, and nearer, and nearer, till it ended in a shriek snapped off short. The other three answered, till even Mowgli could have vowed that the full Pack was in full cry, and then they all broke into the magnificent Morning-song in the Jungle, with every turn, and flourish, and grace-note, that a deep-mouthed wolf of the Pack knows. This is a rough rendering of the song, but you must imagine what it sounds like when it breaks the afternoon hush of the Jungle:

> One moment past our bodies cast
>   No shadow on the plain;
> Now clear and black they stride our track,
>   And we run home again.
> In morning hush, each rock and bush
>   Stands hard, and high, and raw:
> Then give the Call: "Good rest to all
>   That keep the Jungle Law!"
>
> Now horn and pelt our peoples melt
>   In covert to abide;
> Now, crouched and still, to cave and hill
>   Our Jungle Barons glide.
> Now, stark and plain, Man's oxen strain,
>   That draw the new-yoked plow;
> Now, stripped and dread, the dawn is red
>   Above the lit talao.
>
> Ho! Get to Lair! The sun's aflare
>   Behind the breathing grass:
> And creaking through the young bamboo
>   The warning whispers pass
> By day made strange, the woods we range
>   With blinking eyes we scan;
> While down the skies the wild duck cries:
>   "The Day—the Day to Man!"
>
> The dew is dried that drenched our hide,
>   Or washed about our way;
> And where we drank, the puddled bank
>   Is crisping into clay.
> The traitor Dark gives up each mark
>   Of stretched or hooded claw;
> Then hear the Call: "Good rest to all
>   That keep the Jungle Law!"

But no translation can give the effect of it, or the yelping scorn the Four threw into every word of it, as they heard the trees crash when the men hastily climbed up into the branches, and Buldeo began repeating incantations and charms. Then they lay down and slept, for, like all who live by their own exertions, they were of a methodical cast of mind; and no one can work well without sleep.

Meantime, Mowgli was putting the miles behind him, nine to the hour, swinging on, delighted to find himself so fit after all his cramped months among men. The one idea in his head was to get Messua and her husband out of the trap, whatever it was; for he had a natural mistrust of traps. Later on, he promised himself, he would pay his debts to the village at large.

It was twilight when he saw the well-remembered grazing grounds, and the *dhak*-tree where Gray Brother had waited for him on the morning that he killed Shere Khan. Angry as he was at the whole breed and community of Man, something jumped up in his throat and made him catch his breath when he looked at the village roofs. He noticed that every one had come in from the fields unusually early, and that, instead of getting to their evening cooking, they gathered in a crowd under the village tree, and chattered, and shouted.

"Men must always be making traps for men, or they are not content," said Mowgli. "Last night it was Mowgli—but that night seems many rains ago. To-night it is Messua and her man. To-morrow, and for very many nights after, it will be Mowgli's turn again."

He crept along outside the wall till he came to Messua's hut, and looked through the window into the room. There lay Messua, gagged, and bound hand and foot, breathing hard, and groaning: her husband was tied to the gaily painted bedstead. The door of the hut that opened into the street was shut fast, and three or four people were sitting with their backs to it.

Mowgli knew the manners and customs of the villagers very fairly. He argued that so long as they could eat, and talk, and smoke, they would not do anything else; but as soon as they had fed they would begin to be dangerous. Buldeo would be coming in before long, and if his escort had done its duty, Buldeo would have a very interesting tale to tell. So he went in through the window, and, stooping over the man and the woman, cut their thongs, pulling out the gags, and looked round the hut for some milk.

Messua was half wild with pain and fear (she had been beaten and stoned all the morning), and Mowgli put his hand over her mouth just in time to stop a scream. Her husband was only bewildered and angry, and sat picking dust and things out of his torn beard.

"I knew—I knew he would come," Messua sobbed at last. "Now do I *know* that he is my son!" and she hugged Mowgli to her heart. Up to that time Mowgli had been perfectly steady, but now he began to tremble all over, and that surprised him immensely.

"Why are these thongs? Why have they tied thee?" he asked, after a pause.

"To be put to the death for making a son of thee — what else?" said the man, sullenly. "Look! I bleed."

Messua said nothing, but it was at *her* wounds that Mowgli looked, and they heard him grit his teeth when he saw the blood.

"Whose work is this?" said he. "There is a price to pay."

"The work of all the village. I was too rich. I had too many cattle. *Therefore* she and I are witches, because we gave thee shelter."

"I do not understand. Let Messua tell the tale."

"I gave thee milk, Nathoo; dost thou remember?" Messua said timidly. "Because thou wast my son, whom the tiger took, and because I loved thee very dearly. They said that I was thy mother, the mother of a devil, and therefore worthy of death."

"And what is a devil?" said Mowgli. "Death I have seen."

The man looked up gloomily, but Messua laughed. "See!" she said to her husband, "I knew — I said that he was no sorcerer. He is my son — my son!"

"Son or sorcerer, what good will that do us?" the man answered. "We be as dead already."

"Yonder is the road to the Jungle" — Mowgli pointed through the window. "Your hands and feet are free. Go now."

"We do not know the Jungle, my son, as — as thou knowest," Messua began. "I do not think that I could walk far."

"And the men and women would be upon our backs and drag us here again," said the husband.

"H'm!" said Mowgli, and he tickled the palm of his hand with the tip of his skinning-knife; "I have no wish to do harm to any one of this village — *yet*. But I do not think they will stay thee. In a little while they will have much else to think upon. Ah!" he lifted his head and listened to shouting and trampling outside. "So they have let Buldeo come home at last?"

"He was sent out this morning to kill thee," Messua cried. "Didst thou meet him?"

"Yes — we — I met him. He has a tale to tell; and while he is telling it there is time to do much. But first I will learn what they mean. Think where ye would go, and tell me when I come back."

He bounded through the window and ran along again outside the wall of the village till he came within ear-shot of the crowd round the peepul-tree. Buldeo was lying on the ground, coughing and groaning, and every one was asking him questions. His hair had fallen about his shoulders; his hands and legs were skinned from climbing up trees, and he could hardly speak, but he felt the importance of his position keenly. From time to time he said something about devils and singing devils, and magic enchantment, just to give the crowd a taste of what was coming. Then he called for water.

"Bah!" said Mowgli. "Chatter—chatter! Talk, talk! Men are blood-brothers of the *Ban-dar-log*. Now he must wash his mouth with water; now he must blow smoke; and when all that is done he has still his story to tell. They are very wise people—men. They will leave no one to guard Messua till their ears are stuffed with Buldeo's tales. And—I grow as lazy as they!"

He shook himself and glided back to the hut. Just as he was at the window he felt a touch on his foot.

"Mother," said he, for he knew that tongue well, "what dost *thou* here?"

"I heard my children singing through the woods, and I followed the one I loved best. Little Frog, I have a desire to see that woman who gave thee milk," said Mother Wolf, all wet with the dew.

"They have bound and mean to kill her. I have cut those ties, and she goes with her man through the Jungle."

"I also will follow. I am old, but not yet toothless." Mother Wolf reared herself up on end, and looked through the window into the dark of the hut.

In a minute she dropped noiselessly, and all she said was: "I gave thee thy first milk; but Bagheera speaks truth: Man goes to Man at the last."

"Maybe," said Mowgli, with a very unpleasant look on his face; "but to-night I am very far from that trail. Wait here, but do not let her see."

"*Thou* wast never afraid of *me*, Little Frog," said Mother Wolf, backing into the high grass, and blotting herself out, as she knew how.

"And now," said Mowgli, cheerfully, as he swung into the hut again, "they are all sitting round Buldeo, who is saying that which did not happen. When his talk is finished, they say they will assuredly come here with the Red—with fire and burn you both. And then?"

"I have spoken to my man," said Messua. "Kanhiwara is thirty miles from here, but at Kanhiwara we may find the English—"

"And what Pack are they?" said Mowgli.

"I do not know. They be white, and it is said that they govern all the land, and do not suffer people to burn or beat each other without witnesses. If we can get thither to-night, we live. Otherwise we die."

"Live, then. No man passes the gates to-night. But what does *he* do?" Messua's husband was on his hands and knees digging up the earth in one corner of the hut.

"It is his little money," said Messua. "We can take nothing else."

"Ah, yes. The stuff that passes from hand to hand and never grows warmer. Do they need it outside this place also?" said Mowgli.

The man stared angrily. "He is a fool, and no devil," he muttered. "With the money I can buy a horse. We are too bruised to walk far, and the village will follow us in an hour."

"I say they will *not* follow till I choose; but the horse is well thought of, for Messua is tired." Her husband stood up and knotted the last of the rupees into his waist-cloth. Mowgli helped Messua through the window, and the cool night air revived her, but the Jungle in the starlight looked very dark and terrible.

"Ye know the trail to Kanhiwara?" Mowgli whispered.

They nodded.

"Good. Remember, now, not to be afraid. And there is no need to go quickly. Only—only there may be some small singing in the Jungle behind you and before."

"Think you we would have risked a night in the Jungle through anything less than the fear of burning? It is better to be killed by beasts than by men," said Messua's husband; but Messua looked at Mowgli and smiled.

"I say," Mowgli went on, just as though he were Baloo repeating an old Jungle Law for the hundredth time to a foolish cub—"I say that not a tooth in the Jungle is bared against you; not a foot in the Jungle is lifted against you. Neither man nor beast shall stay you till ye come within eyeshot of Kanhiwara. There will be a watch about you." He turned quickly to Messua, saying, "*He* does not believe, but thou wilt believe?"

"Ay, surely, my son. Man, ghost, or wolf of the Jungle, I believe."

"*He* will be afraid when he hears my people singing. Thou wilt know and understand. Go now, and slowly, for there is no need of any haste. The gates are shut."

Messua flung herself sobbing at Mowgli's feet, but he lifted her very quickly with a shiver. Then she hung about his neck and called him every name of blessing she could think of, but her husband looked enviously across his fields, and said: "*If* we reach Kanhiwara, and I get the ear of the English, I will bring such a lawsuit against the Brahmin and old Buldeo and the others as shall eat the village to the bone. They shall pay me twice over for my crops untilled and my buffaloes unfed. I will have a great justice."

Mowgli laughed. "I do not know what justice is, but— come next Rains and see what is left."

They went off toward the Jungle, and Mother Wolf leaped from her place of hiding.

"Follow!" said Mowgli; "and look to it that all the Jungle knows these two are safe. Give tongue a little. I would call Bagheera."

The long, low howl rose and fell, and Mowgli saw Messua's husband flinch and turn, half minded to run back to the hut.

"Go on," Mowgli called cheerfully. "I said there might be singing. The call will follow up to Kanhiwara. It is Favor of the Jungle."

Messua urged her husband forward, and the darkness of the Jungle shut down on them and Mother Wolf as Bagheera rose up almost under Mowgli's feet, trembling with delight of the night that drives the Jungle People wild.

"I am ashamed of thy brethen," he said, purring.

"What? Did they not sing sweetly to Buldeo?" said Mowgli.

"Too well! Too well! They made even *me* forget my pride, and, by the Broken Lock that freed me, I went singing through the Jungle as though I were out wooing in the spring! Didst thou not hear us?"

"I had other game afoot. Ask Buldeo if he liked the song. But where are the Four? I do not wish one of the Man-Pack to leave the gates to-night."

"What need of the Four, then?" said Bagheera, shifting from foot to foot, his eyes ablaze, and purring louder than ever. "I can hold them, Little Brother. Is it killing at last? The singing and the sight of the men climbing up the trees have made me very ready. What is Man that we should care for him—the naked brown digger, the hairless and toothless, the eater of earth? I have followed him all day—at noon—in the white sunlight. I herded him as the wolves herd buck. I am Bagheera! Bagheera! Bagheera! As I dance with my shadow, so danced I with those men. Look!" The great panther leaped as a kitten leaps at a dead leaf whirling overhead, struck left and right into the empty air, that sung under the strokes, landed noiselessly, and leaped again and again, while the half purr, half growl gathered head as steam rumbles in a boiler. "I am Bagheera—in the Jungle—in the night, and all my strength is in me. Who shall stay my stroke? Man-cub, with one blow of my paw I could beat thy head flat as a dead frog in the summer!"

"Strike, then!" said Mowgli, in the dialect of the village, *not* the talk of the Jungle, and the human words brought Bagheera to a full stop, flung back on haunches that quivered under him, his head just at the level of Mowgli's. Once more Mowgli stared, as he had stared at the rebellious cubs, full into the beryl-green eyes till the red glare behind their green went out like the light of a lighthouse shut off twenty miles across the sea; till the eyes dropped, and the big head with them—dropped lower and lower, and the red rasp of a tongue grated on Mowgli's instep.

"Brother—Brother—Brother!" the boy whispered, stroking steadily and lightly from the neck along the heaving back: "Be still, be still! It is the fault of the night, and no fault of thine."

"It was the smells of the night," said Bagheera penitently. "This air cries aloud to me. But how dost *thou* know?"

Of course the air round an Indian village is full of all kinds of smells, and to any creature who does nearly all his thinking through his nose, smells are as maddening as music and drugs are to human beings. Mowgli gentled the panther for a few minutes longer, and he lay down like a cat before a fire, his paws tucked under his breast, and his eyes half shut.

"Thou art of the Jungle and *not* of the Jungle," he said at last. "And I am only a black panther. But I love thee, Little Brother."

"They are very long at their talk under the tree," Mowgli said, without noticing the last sentence. "Buldeo must have told many tales. They should come soon to drag the woman and her man out of the trap and put them into the Red Flower. They will find that trap sprung. Ho! ho!"

"Nay, listen," said Bagheera. "The fever is out of my blood now. Let them find *me* there! Few would leave their houses after meeting me. It is not the first time I have been in a cage; and I do not think they will tie *me* with cords."

"Be wise, then," said Mowgli, laughing; for he was beginning to feel as reckless as the panther, who had glided into the hut.

"Pah!" Bagheera grunted. "This place is rank with Man, but here is just such a bed as they gave me to lie upon in the King's cages at Oodeypore. Now I lie down." Mowgli heard the strings of the cot crack under the great brute's weight. "By the Broken Lock that freed me, they will think they

have caught big game! Come and sit beside me, Little Brother; we will give them 'good hunting' together!"

"No; I have another thought in my stomach. The Man-Pack shall not know what share I have in the sport. Make thine own hunt. I do not wish to see them."

"Be it so," said Bagheera. "Ah, now they come!"

The conference under the peepul-tree had been growing noisier and noisier, at the far end of the village. It broke in wild yells, and a rush up the street of men and women, waving clubs and bamboos and sickles and knives. Buldeo and the Brahmin were at the head of it, but the mob was close at their heels, and they cried, "The witch and the wizard! Let us see if hot coins will make them confess! Burn the hut over their heads! We will teach them to shelter wolf-devils! Nay, beat them first! Torches! More torches! Buldeo, heat the gun-barrels!"

Here was some little difficulty with the catch of the door. It had been very firmly fastened, but the crowd tore it away bodily, and the light of the torches streamed into the room where, stretched at full length on the bed, his paws crossed and lightly hung down over one end, black as the Pit, and terrible as a demon, was Bagheera. There was one half-minute of desperate silence, as the front ranks of the crowd clawed and tore their way back from the threshold, and in that minute Bagheera raised his head and yawned—elaborately, carefully, and ostentatiously—as he would yawn when he wished to insult an equal. The fringed lips drew back and up; the red tongue curled; the lower jaw dropped and dropped till you could see half-way down the hot gullet; and the gigantic dog-teeth stood clear to the pit of the gums till they rang together, upper and under, with the snick of steel-faced wards shooting home round the edges of a safe. Next instant the street was empty; Bagheera had leaped back through the window, and stood at Mowgli's side, while a yelling, screaming torrent scrambled and tumbled one over another in their panic haste to get to their own huts.

"They will not stir till day comes," said Bagheera quietly. "And now?"

The silence of the afternoon sleep seemed to have overtaken the village, but, as they listened, they could hear the sound of heavy grain-boxes being dragged over earthen floors and set down against doors. Bagheera was quite right; the village would not stir till daylight. Mowgli sat still, and thought, and his face grew darker and darker.

"What have I done?" said Bagheera, at last, coming to his feet, fawning.

"Nothing but great good. Watch them now till the day. I

sleep." Mowgli ran off into the Jungle, and dropped like a dead man across a rock, and slept and slept the day round, and the night back again.

When he waked, Bagheera was at his side, and there was a newly-killed buck at his feet. Bagheera watched curiously while Mowgli went to work with his skinning-knife, ate and drank, and turned over with his chin in his hands.

"The man and the woman are come safe within eye-shot of Kanhiwara," Bagheera said. "Thy lair mother sent the word back by Chil, the Kite. They found a horse before midnight of the night they were freed, and went very quickly. Is not that well?"

"That is well," said Mowgli.

"And thy Man-Pack in the village did not stir till the sun was high this morning. Then they ate their food and ran back quickly to their houses."

"Did they, by chance, see thee?"

"It may have been. I was rolling in the dust before the gate at dawn, and I may have made also some small song to myself. Now, Little Brother, there is nothing more to do. Come hunting with me and Baloo. He has new hives that he wishes to show, and we all desire thee back again as of old. Take off that look which makes even me afraid! The man and woman will not be put into the Red Flower, and all goes well in the Jungle. Is it not true? Let us forget the Man-Pack."

"They shall be forgotten in a little while. Where does Hathi feed to-night?"

"Where he chooses. Who can answer for the Silent One? But why? What is there Hathi can do which we cannot?"

"Bid him and his three sons come here to me."

"But, indeed, and truly, Little Brother, it is not—it is not seemly to say 'Come,' and 'Go,' to Hathi. Remember, he is the Master of the Jungle, and before the Man-Pack changed the look on thy face, he taught thee the Master-words of the Jungle."

"That is all one. I have a Master-word for him now. Bid him come to Mowgli, the Frog, and if he does not hear at first, bid him come because of the Sack of the Fields of Bhurtpore."

"The Sack of the Fields of Bhurtpore," Bagheera repeated two or three times to make sure. "I go. Hathi can but be angry at the worst, and I would give a moon's hunting to hear a Master-word that compels the Silent One."

He went away, leaving Mowgli stabbing furiously with his skinning-knife into the earth. Mowgli had never seen human blood in his life before till he had seen, and—what meant much more to him—smelled Messua's blood on the thongs

sack: When soldiers capture a city they sometimes take what they want and destroy the rest: this is sacking.

plantain tree: A tropical plant much like the banana. Plantains are eaten cooked or dried and ground into meal. Millions of people in the tropics eat plantains and bananas as their main food.

reaping: The cutting of ripe grain.

that bound her. And Messua had been kind to him, and, so far as he knew anything about love, he loved Messua as completely as he hated the rest of mankind. But deeply as he loathed them, their talk, their cruelty, and their cowardice, not for anything the Jungle had to offer could he bring himself to take a human life, and have that terrible scent of blood back again in his nostrils. His plan was simpler but much more thorough; and he laughed to himself when he thought that it was one of old Buldeo's tales told under the peepul-tree in the evening that had put the idea into his head.

"It *was* a Master-word," Bagheera whispered in his ear. "They were feeding by the river, and they obeyed as though they were bullocks. Look, where they come now!"

Hathi and his three sons had arrived in their usual way, without a sound. The mud of the river was still fresh on their flanks, and Hathi was thoughtfully chewing the green stem of a young plantain-tree that he had gouged up with his tusks. But every line in his vast body showed to Bagheera, who could see things when he came across them, that it was not the Master of the Jungle speaking to a Man-cub, but one who was afraid coming before one who was not. His three sons rolled side by side, behind their father.

Mowgli hardly lifted his head as Hathi gave him "Good hunting." He kept him swinging and rocking, and shifting from one foot to another, for a long time before he spoke, and when he opened his mouth it was to Bagheera, not to the elephants.

"I will tell a tale that was told to me by the hunter ye hunted to-day," said Mowgli. "It concerns an elephant, old and wise, who fell into a trap, and the sharpened stake in the pit scarred him from a little above his heel to the crest of his shoulder, leaving a white mark." Mowgli threw out his hand, and as Hathi wheeled the moonlight showed a long white scar on his slaty side, as though he had been struck with a red-hot whip. "Men came to take him from the trap," Mowgli continued, "but he broke his ropes, for he was strong, and went away till his wound was healed. Then came he, angry, by night to the fields of those hunters. And I remember now that he had three sons. These things happened many, many Rains ago, and very far away—among the fields of Bhurtpore. What came to those fields at the next reaping, Hathi?"

"They were reaped by me and by my three sons," said Hathi.

"And to the plowing that follows the reaping?" said Mowgli.

"There was no plowing," said Hathi.

"And to the men that live by the green crops on the

ground?" said Mowgli.

"They went away."

"And to the huts in which the men slept?" said Mowgli.

"We tore the roofs to pieces, and the Jungle swallowed up the walls," said Hathi.

"And what more?" said Mowgli.

"As much good ground as I can walk over in two nights from the east to the west, and from the north to the south as much as I can walk over in three nights, the Jungle took. We let in the Jungle upon five villages; and in those villages, and in their lands, the grazing-ground and the soft crop-grounds, there is not one man to-day who takes his food from the ground. That was the Sack of the Fields of Bhurtpore, which I and my three sons did; and now I ask, Man-cub, how the news of it came to thee?" said Hathi.

"A man told me, and now I see even Buldeo can speak truth. It was well done, Hathi with the white mark; but the second time it shall be done better, for the reason that there is a man to direct. Thou knowest the village of the Man-Pack that cast me out? They are idle, senseless, and cruel; they play with their mouths, and they do not kill the weaker for food, but for sport. When they are full-fed they would throw their own breed into the Red Flower. This I have seen. It is not well that they should live here any more. I hate them!"

"Kill, then," said the youngest of Hathi's three sons, picking up a tuft of grass, dusting it against his fore legs, and throwing it away, while his little red eyes glanced furtively from side to side.

"What good are white bones to me?" Mowgli answered angrily. "Am I the cub of a wolf to play in the sun with a raw head? I have killed Shere Khan, and his hide rots on the Council Rock; but—but I do not know whither Shere Khan is gone, and my stomach is still empty. Now I will take that which I can see and touch. Let in the Jungle upon that village, Hathi!"

Bagheera shivered, and cowered down. He could understand, if the worst came to the worst, a quick rush down the village street, and a right and left blow into a crowd, or a crafty killing of men as they plowed in the twilight, but this scheme for deliberately blotting out an entire village from the eyes of man and beast frightened him. Now he saw why Mowgli had sent for Hathi. No one but the long-lived elephant could plan and carry through such a war.

"Let them run as the men ran from the fields of Bhurtpore, till we have the rain-water for the only plow, and the noise of the rain on the thick leaves for the pattering of their spindles—till Bagheera and I lair in the house of the Brah-

spindle: A thin rod used in spinning thread from a mass of fiber.

min, and the buck drink at the tank behind the temple! Let in the Jungle, Hathi!"

"But I—but we have no quarrel with them, and it needs the red rage of great pain ere we tear down the places where men sleep," said Hathi, doubtfully.

"Are ye the only eaters of grass in the Jungle? Drive in your peoples. Let the deer and the pig and the nilghai look to it. Ye need never show a hand's-breadth of hide till the fields are naked. Let in the Jungle, Hathi!"

"There will be no killing? My tusks were red at the Sack of the Fields of Bhurtpore, and I would not wake that smell again."

"Nor I. I do not wish even their bones to lie on the clean earth. Let them go and find a fresh lair. They cannot stay here. I have seen and smelled the blood of the woman that gave me food—the woman whom they would have killed but for me. Only the smell of the new grass on their door-steps can take away that smell. It burns in my mouth. Let in the Jungle, Hathi!"

"Ah!" said Hathi. "So did the scar of the stake burn on my hide till we watched the villages die under in the spring growth. Now I see. Thy war shall be our war. We will let in the Jungle!"

Mowgli had hardly time to catch his breath—he was shaking all over with rage and hate—before the place where the elephants had stood was empty, and Bagheera was looking at him with terror.

"By the Broken Lock that freed me!" said the Black Panther at last. "Art *thou* the naked thing I spoke for in the Pack when all was young? Master of the Jungle, when my strength goes, speak for me—speak for Baloo—speak for us all! We are cubs before thee! Snapped twigs under foot! Fawns that have lost their doe!"

The idea of Bagheera being a stray fawn upset Mowgli altogether, and he laughed and caught his breath, and sobbed and laughed again, till he had to jump into a pool to make himself stop. Then he swam round and round, ducking in and out of the bars of the moonlight like the frog, his namesake.

By this time Hathi and his three sons had turned, each to one point of the compass, and were striding silently down the valleys a mile away. They went on and on for two days' march—that is to say, a long sixty miles—through the Jungle; and every step they took, and every wave of their trunks, was known and noted and talked over by Mang and Chil and the Monkey People and all the birds. Then they began to feed, and fed quietly for a week or so. Hathi and his sons are like

Kaa, the Rock Python. They never hurry till they have to.

At the end of that time—and none knew who had started it—a rumor went through the Jungle that there was better food and water to be found in such and such a valley. The pig—who, of course, will go to the ends of the earth for a full meal—moved first by companies, scuffling over the rocks, and the deer followed, with the small wild foxes that live on the dead and dying of the herds; and the heavy-shouldered nilghai moved parallel with the deer, and the wild buffaloes of the swamps came after the nilghai. The least little thing would have turned the scattered, straggling droves that grazed and sauntered and drank and grazed again; but whenever there was an alarm some one would rise up and soothe them. At one time it would be Sahi the Porcupine, full of news of good feed just a little further on; at another Mang would cry cheerily and flap down a glade to show it was all empty; or Baloo, his mouth full of roots, would shamble alongside a wavering line and half frighten, half romp it clumsily back to the proper road. Very many creatures broke back or ran away or lost interest, but very many were left to go forward. At the end of another ten days or so the situation was this. The deer and the pig and the nilghai were milling round and round in a circle of eight or ten miles radius, while the Eaters of Flesh skirmished round its edge. And the center of that circle was the village, and round the village the crops were ripening, and in the crops sat men on what they call *machans*—platforms like pigeon-perches, made of sticks at the top of four poles—to scare away birds and other stealers. Then the deer were coaxed no more. The Eaters of Flesh were close behind them, and forced them forward and inward.

It was a dark night when Hathi and his three sons slipped down from the Jungle, and broke off the poles of the *machans* with their trunks; they fell as a snapped stalk of hemlock in bloom falls, and the men that tumbled from them heard the deep gurgling of the elephants in their ears. Then the vanguard of the bewildered armies of the deer broke down and flooded into the village grazing-grounds and the plowed fields; and the sharp-hoofed, rooting wild pig came with them, and what the deer left the pig spoiled, and from time to time an alarm of wolves would shake the herds, and they would rush to and fro desperately, treading down the young barley, and cutting flat the banks of the irrigating channels. Before the dawn broke the pressure on the outside of the circle gave way at one point. The Eaters of Flesh had fallen back and left an open path to the south, and drove upon drove of buck fled along it. Others, who were bolder,

barley: A grain. We use it sometimes in soups, but it can also be cooked as a cereal or used to make a heavy bread. Barley is a hardy plant that needs only a short growing season. It is grown in temperate zones, at the Arctic circle, at the equator, and even in Tibet, 10,000 feet above sea level.

lay up in the thickets to finish their meal next night.

But the work was practically done. When the villagers looked in the morning they saw their crops were lost. And that meant death if they did not get away, for they lived year in and year out as near to starvation as the Jungle was near to them. When the buffaloes were sent to graze the hungry brutes found that the deer had cleared the grazing-grounds, and so wandered into the Jungle and drifted off with their wild mates; and when twilight fell the three or four ponies that belonged to the village lay in their stables with their heads beaten in. Only Bagheera could have given those strokes, and only Bagheera would have thought of insolently dragging the last carcass to the open street.

The villagers had no heart to make fires in the fields that night, so Hathi and his three sons went gleaning among what was left; and where Hathi gleans there is no need to follow.

The men decided to live on their stored seed-corn until the rains had fallen, and then to take work as servants till they could catch up with the lost year; but as the grain-dealer was thinking of his well-filled crates of corn, and the prices he would levy at the sale of it, Hathi's sharp tusks were picking out the corner of his mud house, and smashing open the big wicker-chest, heaped with cow-dung, where the precious stuff lay.

When that last loss was discovered, it was the Brahmin's turn to speak. He had prayed to his own Gods without answer. It might be, he said, that, unconsciously, the village had offended some one of the Gods of the Jungle, for, beyond doubt, the Jungle was against them. So they sent for the head man of the nearest tribe of wandering Gonds — little, wise, and very black hunters, living in the deep Jungle, whose fathers came of the oldest race in India — the aboriginal owners of the land. They made the Gond welcome with what they had, and he stood on one leg, his bow in his hand, and two or three poisoned arrows stuck through his top-knot, looking half afraid and half contemptuously at the anxious villagers and their ruined fields. They wished to know whether his Gods — the old Gods — were angry with them, and what sacrifices should be offered. The Gond said nothing, but picked up a trail of the *Karela,* the vine that bears the bitter wild gourd, and laced it to and fro across the temple door in the face of the staring red Hindu image. Then he pushed with his hand in the open air along the road to Kanhiwara, and went back to his Jungle, and watched the Jungle people drifting through it. He knew that when the Jungle moves only white men can hope to turn it aside.

There was no need to ask his meaning. The wild gourd would grow where they had worshiped their God, and the sooner they saved themselves the better.

But it is hard to tear a village from its moorings. They stayed on as long as any summer food was left to them, and they tried to gather nuts in the Jungle, but shadows with glaring eyes watched them, and rolled before them even at midday; and when they ran back afraid to their walls, on the tree trunks they had passed not five minutes before the bark would be stripped and chiseled with the stroke of some great taloned paw. The more they kept to their village, the bolder grew the wild things that gamboled and bellowed on the grazing-grounds by the Waingunga. They had no time to patch and plaster the rear walls of the empty byres that backed on to the Jungle; the wild pig trampled them down, and the knotty-rooted vines hurried after and threw their elbows over the new-won ground, and the coarse grass bristled behind the vines like the lances of a goblin army following a retreat. The unmarried men ran away first, and carried the news far and near that the village was doomed. Who could fight, they said, against the Jungle, or the Gods of the Jungle, when the very village cobra had left his hole in the platform under the peepul-tree? So their little commerce with the outside world shrunk as the trodden paths across the open grew fewer and fainter. At last the nightly trumpetings of Hathi and his three sons ceased to trouble them; for they had no more to be robbed of. The crop on the ground and the seed in the ground had been taken. The outlying fields were already losing their shape, and it was time to throw themselves on the charity of the English at Kanhiwara.

Native fashion, they delayed their departure from one day to another till the first Rains caught them and the unmended roofs let in a flood, and the grazing-ground stood ankle deep, and all life came on with a rush after the heat of the summer. Then they waded out, men, women, and children, through the blinding hot rain of the morning, but turned naturally for one farewell look at their homes.

They heard, as the last burdened family filed through the gate, a crash of falling beams and thatch behind the walls. They saw a shiny, snaky black trunk lifted for an instant, scattering sodden thatch. It disappeared, and there was another crash, followed by a squeal. Hathi had been plucking off the roofs of the huts as you pluck water-lilies, and a rebounding beam had pricked him. He needed only this to unchain his full strength, for of all things in the Jungle the wild elephant enraged is the most wantonly destructive. He kicked backward at a mud wall that crumbled at the stroke, and, crumbling, melted to yellow mud under the torrent of rain. Then he wheeled and squealed, and tore through the narrow streets, leaning against the huts right and left, shivering the crazy doors, and crumpling up the eaves; while his three sons raged behind as they had raged at the Sack of the Fields of Bhurtpore.

"The Jungle will swallow these shells," said a quiet voice in the wreckage. "It is the outer wall that must lie down," and Mowgli, with the rain sluicing over his bare shoulders and arms, leaped back from a wall that was settling like a tired buffalo.

"All in good time," panted Hathi. "Oh, but my tusks were red at Bhurtpore! To the outer wall, children! With the head! Together! Now!"

The four pushed side by side; the outer wall bulged, split,

and fell, and the villagers, dumb with horror, saw the savage, clay-streaked heads of the wreckers in the ragged gap. Then they fled, houseless and foodless, down the valley, as their village, shredded and tossed and trampled, melted behind them.

A month later the place was a dimpled mound, covered with soft, green young stuff; and by the end of the Rains there was the roaring Jungle in full blast on the spot that had been under plow not six months before.

MOWGLI'S SONG AGAINST PEOPLE

I will let loose against you the fleet-footed
         vines —
I will call in the Jungle to stamp out your
         lines!
    The roofs shall fade before it,
      The house-beams shall fall,
    And the Karela, the bitter Karela,
      Shall cover it all!

In the gates of these your councils my
         people shall sing,
In the doors of these your garners the Bat-
         folk shall cling;
And the snake shall be your watchman,
  By a hearthstone unswept;
For the Karela, the bitter Karela,
  Shall fruit where ye slept!

Ye shall not see my strikers; ye shall hear them and
         guess;
By night, before the moon-rise, I will send for my cess,
    And the wolf shall be your herdsman
      By a landmark removed,
    For the Karela, the bitter Karela,
      Shall seed where ye loved!

I will reap your fields before you at the hands of a host;
Ye shall glean behind my reapers for the bread that is
         lost;
    And the deer shall be your oxen
      By a headland untilled,
    For the Karela, the bitter Karela,
      Shall leaf where ye build!

I have untied against you the club-footed vines,
I have sent in the Jungle to swamp out your lines!
    The trees — the trees are on you!
      The house-beams shall fall,
And the Karela, the bitter Karela,
    Shall cover you all!

6

The
King's
Ankus

These are the Four that are never content, that have never been
  filled since the Dews began—
Jacala's mouth, and the glut of the Kite, and the hands of the
  Ape, and the Eyes of Man.

                    —*Jungle Saying.*

KAA, the big Rock Python, had changed his skin for perhaps the two hundredth time since his birth; and Mowgli, who never forgot that he owed his life to Kaa for a night's work at Cold Lairs, which you may perhaps remember, went to congratulate him. Skin-changing always makes a snake moody and depressed till the new skin begins to shine and look beautiful. Kaa never made fun of Mowgli any more, but accepted him, as the other Jungle People did, for the Master of the Jungle, and brought him all the news that a python of his size would naturally hear. What Kaa did not tree bole: Tree trunk.

know about the Middle Jungle, as they call it,—the life that runs close to the earth or under it, the boulder, burrow, and the tree-bole life,—might have been written upon the smallest of his scales.

That afternoon Mowgli was sitting in the circle of Kaa's great coils, fingering the flaked and broken old skin that lay all looped and twisted among the rocks just as Kaa had left it. Kaa had very courteously packed himself under Mowgli's broad, bare shoulders, so that the boy was really resting in a living arm-chair.

"Even to the scales of the eyes it is perfect," said Mowgli, under his breath, playing with the old skin. "Strange to see the covering of one's own head at one's own feet!"

"Aye, but I lack feet," said Kaa; "and since this is the custom of all my people, I do not find it strange. Does thy skin never feel old and harsh?"

"Then go I and wash, Flathead; but, it is true, in the great heats I have wished I could slough my skin without pain, and run skinless."

"I wash, and *also* I take off my skin. How looks the new coat?"

Mowgli ran his hand down the diagonal checkerings of the immense back. "The Turtle is harder-backed, but not so gay." he said judgmatically "The Frog, my name-bearer, is more gay, but not so hard. It is very beautiful to see—like the mottling in the mouth of a lily."

"It needs water. A new skin never comes to full color before the first bath. Let us go bathe."

"I will carry thee," said Mowgli; and he stooped down, laughing, to lift the middle section of Kaa's great body, just where the barrel was thickest. A man might just as well have tried to heave up a two-foot water-main; and Kaa lay still, puffing with quiet amusement. Then the regular evening game began—the boy in the flush of his great strength, and the Python in his sumptuous new skin, standing up one against the other for a wrestling-match—a trial of eye and strength. Of course, Kaa could have crushed a dozen Mowglis if he had let himself go; but he played carefully, and never loosed one tenth of his power. Ever since Mowgli was strong enough to endure a little rough handling, Kaa had taught him this game, and it suppled his limbs as nothing else could. Sometimes Mowgli would stand lapped almost to his throat in Kaa's shifting coils, striving to get one arm free and catch him by the throat. Then Kaa would give way limply, and Mowgli, with both quick-moving feet, would try to cramp the purchase of that huge tail as it flung backward feeling for a rock or a stump. They would rock to and fro, head to head, each waiting for his chance, till the beautiful, statue-like group melted in a whirl of black-and-yellow coils and struggling legs and arms, to rise up again and again. "Now! now! now!" said Kaa, making feints with his head that even Mowgli's quick hand could not turn aside. "Look! I touch thee here, Little Brother! Here, and here! Are thy hands numb? Here again!"

The game always ended in one way—with a straight, driving blow of the head that knocked the boy over and over. Mowgli could never learn the guard for that lightning lunge, and, as Kaa said, there was not the least use in trying.

"Good hunting!" Kaa grunted at last; and Mowgli, as usual, was shot away half a dozen yards, gasping and laughing. He rose with his fingers full of grass, and followed Kaa to the wise snake's pet bathing-place—a deep, pitchy-black pool surrounded with rocks, and made interesting by sunken tree-stumps. The boy slipped in, Jungle-fashion, without a sound, and dived across; rose, too, without a sound, and turned on his back, his arms behind his head, watching the moon rising above the rocks, and breaking up her reflection in the water with his toes. Kaa's diamond-shaped head cut the pool like a razor, and came out to rest on Mowgli's shoulder. They lay still, soaking luxuriously in the cool water.

"It is *very* good," said Mowgli at last, sleepily. "Now, in the Man-Pack, at this hour, as I remember, they laid them down upon hard pieces of wood in the inside of a mud-trap, and, having carefully shut out all the clean winds, drew foul cloth over their heavy heads, and made evil songs through their noses. It is better in the Jungle."

A hurrying cobra slipped down over a rock and drank, gave them "Good hunting!" and went away.

"Sssh!" said Kaa, as though he had suddenly remembered something. "So the Jungle gives thee all that thou hast ever desired, Little Brother?"

"Not all," said Mowgli, laughing; "else there would be a new and strong Shere Khan to kill once a moon. Now, I could kill with my own hands, asking no help of buffaloes. And also I have wished the sun to shine in the middle of the Rains, and the Rains to cover the sun in the deep of summer; and also I have never gone empty but I wished that I had killed a goat; and also I have never killed a goat but I wished it had been buck; nor buck but I wished it had been nilghai. But thus do we feel, all of us."

"Thou hast no other desire?" the big snake demanded.

"What more can I wish? I have the Jungle and the favor of

buck: Male deer.

nilghai: A large Indian antelope with a bluish-gray hide. NILGHAI is Hindu for "blue cow."

the Jungle! Is there more anywhere between sunrise and sunset?"

"Now, the Cobra said—" Kaa began.

"What cobra? He that went away just now said nothing. He was hunting."

"It was another."

"Hast thou many dealings with the Poison People? I give them their own path. They carry death in the fore-tooth, and that is not good—for they are so small. But what hood is this thou hast spoken with?"

Kaa rolled slowly in the water like a steamer in a beam sea. "Three or four moons since," said he, "I hunted in Cold Lairs, which place thou hast not forgotten. And the thing I hunted fled shrieking past the tanks and to that house whose side I once broke for thy sake, and ran into the ground."

"But the people of Cold Lairs do not live in burrows." Mowgli knew that Kaa was talking of the Monkey People.

"This thing was not living, but seeking to live," Kaa replied, with a quiver of his tongue. "He ran into a burrow that led very far. I followed, and having killed, I slept. When I waked I went forward."

"Under the earth?"

"Even so, coming at last upon a White Hood [a white cobra], who spoke of things beyond my knowledge, and showed me many things I had never before seen."

"New game? Was it good hunting?" Mowgli turned quickly on his side.

"It was no game, and would have broken all my teeth; but the White Hood said that a man—he spoke as one that knew the breed—that a man would give the breath under his ribs for only the sight of those things."

"We will look," said Mowgli. "I now remember that I was once a man."

"Slowly—slowly. It was haste killed the Yellow Snake that ate the sun. We two spoke together under the earth, and I spoke of thee, naming thee as a man. Said the White Hood (and he is indeed as old as the Jungle): 'It is long since I have seen a man. Let him come, and he shall see all these things, for the least of which very many men would die.'"

"That *must* be new game. And yet the Poison People do not tell us when game is afoot. They are an unfriendly folk."

"It is *not* game. It is—it is—I cannot say what it is."

"We will go there. I have never seen a White Hood, and I wish to see the other things. Did he kill them?"

"They are all dead things. He says he is the keeper of them all."

"Ah! As a wolf stands above meat he has taken to his own

lair. Let us go."

Mowgli swam to bank, rolled on the grass to dry himself, and the two set off for Cold Lairs, the deserted city of which you may have heard. Mowgli was not the least afraid of the Monkey People in those days, but the Monkey People had the liveliest horror of Mowgli. Their tribes, however, were raiding in the Jungle, and so Cold Lairs stood empty and silent in the moonlight. Kaa led up to the ruins of the queen's pavilion that stood on the terrace, slipped over the rubbish, and dived down the half-choked staircase that went underground from the center of the pavilion. Mowgli gave the snake-call—"We be of one blood, ye and I,"—and followed on his hands and knees. They crawled a long distance down a sloping passage that turned and twisted several times, and at last came to where the root of some great tree, growing thirty feet overhead, had forced out a solid stone in the wall. They crept through the gap, and found themselves in a large vault, whose domed roof had been also broken away by tree-roots so that a few streaks of light dropped down into the darkness.

"A safe lair," said Mowgli, rising to his firm feet, "but over far to visit daily. And now what do we see?"

"Am I nothing?" said a voice in the middle of the vault; and Mowgli saw something white move till, little by little, there stood up the hugest cobra he had ever set eyes on—a creature nearly eight feet long, and bleached by being in darkness to an old ivory-white. Even the spectacle-marks of his spread hood had faded to faint yellow. His eyes were as red as rubies, and altogether he was most wonderful.

"Good hunting!" said Mowgli, who carried his manners with his knife, and that never left him.

"What of my city?" said the White Cobra, without answering the greeting. "What of the great, the walled city—the city of a hundred elephants and twenty thousand horses, and cattle past counting—the city of the King of Twenty Kings? I grow deaf here, and it is long since I heard their war-gongs."

"The Jungle is above our heads," said Mowgli. "I know only Hathi and his sons among elephants. Bagheera has slain all the horses in one village, and—what is a King?"

"I told thee," said Kaa softly to the Cobra—"I told thee, four moons ago, that thy city was not."

"The city—the great city of the forest whose gates are guarded by the King's towers—can never pass. They builded it before my father's father came from the egg, and it shall endure when my son's sons are as white as I! Salomdhi, son of Chandrabija, son of Viyeja, son of Yegasuri, made it in the

Cobras are usually 3 or 4 feet long. There is an old Hindu legend about cobras. Brahma, the God of Creation, once fell asleep in the hot sun. The cobra spread its hood and shaded him. In return, the priest of a Hindu temple or shrine often puts out milk for a pet cobra to drink.

102

days of Bappa Rawal. Whose cattle are *ye?*"

"It is a lost trail," said Mowgli, turning to Kaa. "I know not his talk."

"Nor I. He is very old. Father of Cobras, there is only the Jungle here, as it has been since the beginning."

"Then who is *he,*" said the White Cobra, "sitting down before me, unafraid, knowing not the name of the King, talking our talk through a man's lips? Who is he with the knife and the snake's tongue?"

"Mowgli they call me," was the answer. "I am of the Jungle. The Wolves are my people, and Kaa here is my brother. Father of Cobras, who art thou?"

"I am the Warden of the King's Treasure. Kurrun Raja builded the stone above me, in the days when my skin was dark, that I might teach death to those who came to steal. Then they let down the treasure through the stone, and I heard the song of the Brahmins my masters."

"Umm!" said Mowgli to himself. "I have dealt with one Brahmin already, in the Man-Pack, and—I know what I know. Evil comes here in a little."

"Five times since I came here has the stone been lifted, but always to let down more, and never to take away. There are no riches like these riches—the treasures of a hundred kings. But it is long and long since the stone was last moved, and I think that my city has forgotten."

"There is no city. Look up. Yonder are roots of the great trees tearing the stones apart. Trees and men do not grow together," Kaa insisted.

"Twice and thrice have men found their way here," the White Cobra answered savagely; "but they never spoke till I came upon them groping in the dark, and then they cried only a little time. But *ye* come with lies, Man and Snake both, and would have me believe the city is not, and that my wardship ends. Little do men change in the years. But *I* change never! Till the stone is lifted, and the Brahmins come down singing the songs that I know, and feed me with warm milk, and take me to the light again, I—I—*I*, and no other, am the Warden of the King's Treasure! The city is dead, ye say, and here are the roots of the trees? Stoop down, then, and take what ye will. Earth has no treasure like to these. Man with the snake's tongue, if thou canst go alive by the way that thou hast entered at, the lesser Kings will be thy servants!"

"Again the trail is lost," said Mowgli, coolly. "Can any jackal have burrowed so deep and bitten this great White Hood? He is surely mad. Father of Cobras, I see nothing

103

here to take away."

"By the Gods of the Sun and Moon, it is the madness of death upon the boy!" hissed the Cobra. "Before thine eyes close I will allow thee this favor. Look thou, and see what man has never seen before!"

"They do not well in the Jungle who speak to Mowgli of favors," said the boy, between his teeth; "but the dark changes all, as I know. I will look, if that please thee."

He stared with puckered-up eyes round the vault, and then lifted up from the floor a handful of something that glittered.

"Oho!" said he, "this is like the stuff they play with in the Man-Pack: only this is yellow and the other was brown."

He let the gold pieces fall, and moved forward. The floor of the vault was buried some five or six feet deep in coined gold and silver that had burst from the sacks it had been originally stored in, and, in the long years, the metal had packed and settled as sand packs at low tide. On it and in it, and rising through it, as wrecks lift through the sand, were jeweled elephant-howdahs of embossed silver, studded with plates of hammered gold, and adorned with carbuncles and turquoises. There were palanquins and litters for carrying queens, framed and braced with silver and enamel, with jade-handled poles and amber curtain-rings; there were golden candlesticks hung with pierced emeralds that quivered on the branches; there were studded images, five feet high, of forgotten gods, silver with jeweled eyes; there were coats of mail, gold inlaid on steel, and fringed with rotted and blackened seed-pearls; there were helmets, crested and beaded with pigeon's-blood rubies; there were shields of lacquer, of tortoise-shell and rhinoceros-hide, strapped and bossed with red gold and set with emeralds at the edge; there were sheaves of diamond-hilted swords, daggers, and hunting-knives; there were golden sacrificial bowls and ladles, and portable altars of a shape that never see the light of day; there were jade cups and bracelets; there were incense-burners, combs, and pots for perfume, henna, and eye-powder, all in embossed gold; there were nose-rings, armlets, head-bands, finger-rings, and girdles past any counting; there were belts, seven fingers broad, of square-cut diamonds and rubies, and wooden boxes, trebly clamped with iron, from which the wood had fallen away in powder, showing the pile of uncut star-sapphires, opals, cat's-eyes, sapphires, rubies, diamonds, emeralds, and garnets within.

The White Cobra was right. No mere money would begin to pay the value of this treasure, the sifted pickings of cen-

carbuncles: Violet-red garnets. The name means "little spark" in Latin.

turquoises: Blue green stones. The oldest piece of jewelry ever found is an Egyptian gold and turquoise bracelet, 8,000 years old.

pigeon's blood rubies: Rubies of a special, highly valued color. They are red with a slight mixture of purple, and a yellowish undertone.

henna: A reddish orange cosmetic. Indian women use it to beautify their nails, eyelids, and fingertips.

star-sapphires: A sapphire is a transparent deep blue stone. Some sapphires have tiny regular flaws inside. When one of these is properly cut and polished, a six-pointed star of light seems to be caught inside the stone.

turies of war, plunder, trade, and taxation. The coins alone were priceless, leaving out of count all the precious stones; and the dead weight of the gold and silver alone might be two or three hundred tons. Every native ruler in India to-day, however poor, has a hoard to which he is always adding; and though, once in a long while, some enlightened prince may send off forty or fifty bullock-cart loads of silver to be exchanged for Government securities, the bulk of them keep their treasure and the knowledge of it very closely to themselves.

But Mowgli naturally did not understand what these things meant. The knives interested him a little, but they did not balance so well as his own, and so he dropped them. At last he found something really fascinating laid on the front of a howdah half buried in the coins. It was a three-foot ankus, or elephant-goad—something like a small boat-hook. The top was one round shining ruby, and twelve inches of the handle below it were studded with rough turquoises close together, giving a most satisfactory grip. Below them was a rim of jade with a flower-pattern running round it— only the leaves were emeralds, and the blossoms were rubies sunk in the cool, green stone. The rest of the handle was a shaft of pure ivory, while the point—the spike and hook—was gold-inlaid steel with pictures of elephant-catching; and the pictures attracted Mowgli, who saw that they had something to do with his friend Hathi the Silent.

The White Cobra had been following him closely.

"Is this not worth dying to behold?" he said. "Have I not done thee a great favor?"

"I do not understand," said Mowgli. "The things are hard and cold, and by no means good to eat. But this"—he lifted the ankus—"I desire to take away, that I may see it in the sun. Thou sayest they are all thine? Wilt thou give it to me, and I will bring thee frogs to eat?"

The White Cobra fairly shook with evil delight. "Assuredly I will give it," he said. "All that is here I will give thee—till thou goest away."

"But I go now. This place is dark and cold, and I wish to take the thorn-pointed thing to the Jungle."

"Look by thy foot! What is that there?"

Mowgli picked up something white and smooth. "It is the bone of a man's head," he said quietly. "And here are two more."

"They came to take the treasure away many years ago. I spoke to them in the dark, and they lay still."

"But what do I need of this that is called treasure? If thou

The
King's
Ankus

government securities: The government would pay him with bonds. You may own United States Savings Bonds, which are government securities. A savings bond that you buy from the bank now for $18.75 will be worth $25.00 in about seven years.

ruby: A deep red, transparent stone, called "the gem of kings." A large flawless ruby is worth even more than a diamond. Burmese kings were so fond of rubies that when a new one was discovered they gave the whole court a holiday.

An Indian emperor, Jehangir, once had his name carved on a fine ruby. He wanted to be remembered after his death. And he is: every book on famous jewels mentions the Mongul ruby.

wilt give me the ankus to take away, it is good hunting. If not, it is good hunting none the less. I do not fight with the Poison People, and I was also taught the Master-word of thy tribe."

"There is but one Master-word here. It is mine!"

Kaa flung himself forward with blazing eyes. "Who bade me bring the Man?" he hissed.

"I surely," the old Cobra lisped. "It is long since I have seen Man, and this Man speaks our tongue."

"But there was no talk of killing. How can I go to the Jungle and say that I have led him to his death?" said Kaa.

"I talk not of killing till the time. And as to thy going or not going, there is the hole in the wall. Peace, now, thou fat monkey-killer! I have but to touch thy neck, and the Jungle will know thee no longer. Never Man came here that went away with the breath under his ribs. I am the Warden of the Treasure of the King's City!"

"But, thou white worm of the dark, I tell thee there is neither king nor city! The Jungle is all about us!" cried Kaa.

"There is still the Treasure. But this can be done. Wait a while, Kaa of the Rocks, and see the boy run. There is room for great sport here. Life is good. Run to and fro a while, and make sport, boy!"

Mowgli put his hand on Kaa's head quietly.

"The white thing has dealt with men of the Man-Pack until now. He does not know me," he whispered. "He has asked for this hunting. Let him have it." Mowgli had been standing with the ankus held point down. He flung it from him quickly, and it dropped crossways just behind the great snake's hood, pinning him to the floor. In a flash, Kaa's weight was upon the writhing body, paralyzing it from hood to tail. The red eyes burned, and the six spare inches of the head struck furiously right and left.

"Kill!" said Kaa, as Mowgli's hand went to his knife.

"No," he said, as he drew the blade; "I will never kill again save for food. But look you, Kaa!" He caught the snake behind the hood, forced the mouth open with the blade of the knife, and showed the terrible poison-fangs of the upper jaw lying black and withered in the gum. The White Cobra had outlived his poison, as a snake will.

"*Thuu*" ("It is dried up"), said Mowgli; and motioning Kaa away, he picked up the ankus, setting the White Cobra free.

"The King's Treasure needs a new Warden," he said gravely. "Thuu, thou hast not done well. Run to and fro and make sport, Thuu!"

"I am ashamed. Kill me!" hissed the White Cobra.

"There has been too much talk of killing. We will go now. I take the thorn-pointed thing, Thuu, because I have fought and worsted thee."

"See, then, that the thing does not kill thee at last. It is Death! Remember, it is Death! There is enough in that thing to kill the men of all my city. Not long wilt thou hold it, Jungle Man, nor he who takes it from thee. They will kill, and kill, and kill for its sake! My strength is dried up, but the ankus will do my work. It is Death! It is Death! It is Death!"

Mowgli crawled out through the hole into the passage again, and the last that he saw was the White Cobra striking furiously with his harmless fangs at the stolid golden faces of the gods that lay on the floor, and hissing, "It is Death!"

They were glad to get to the light of day once more; and when they were back in their own Jungle and Mowgli made the ankus glitter in the morning light, he was almost as pleased as though he had found a bunch of new flowers to stick in his hair.

"This is brighter than Bagheera's eyes," he said delightedly, as he twirled the ruby. "I will show it to him; but what did the Thuu mean when he talked of death?"

"I cannot say. I am sorrowful to my tail's tail that he felt not thy knife. There is always evil at Cold Lairs—above ground or below. But now I am hungry. Dost thou hunt with me this dawn?" said Kaa.

"No; Bagheera must see this thing. Good hunting!" Mowgli danced off, flourishing the great ankus, and stopping from time to time to admire it, till he came to that part of the Jungle Bagheera chiefly used, and found him drinking after a heavy kill. Mowgli told him all his adventures from beginning to end, and Bagheera sniffed at the ankus between whiles. When Mowgli came to the White Cobra's last words, the Panther purred approvingly.

"Then the White Hood spoke the thing which is?" Mowgli asked quickly.

"I was born in the King's cages at Oodeypore, and it is in my stomach that I know some little of Man. Very many men would kill thrice in a night for the sake of that one big red stone alone."

"But the stone makes it heavy to the hand. My little bright knife is better; and—see! the red stone is not good to eat. Then *why* would they kill?"

"Mowgli, go thou and sleep. Thou hast lived among men, and—"

"I remember. Men kill because they are not hunting; — for idleness and pleasure. Wake again, Bagheera. For what use was this thorn-pointed thing made?"

Bagheera half opened his eyes — he was very sleepy — with a malicious twinkle.

"It was made by men to thrust into the head of the sons of Hathi, so that the blood should pour out. I have seen the like in the street of Oodeypore, before our cages. That thing has tasted the blood of many such as Hathi."

"But why do they thrust into the heads of elephants?"

"To teach them Man's Law. Having neither claws nor teeth, men make these things — and worse."

"Always more blood when I come near, even to the things the Man-Pack have made," said Mowgli, disgustedly. He was getting a little tired of the weight of the ankus. "If I had known this, I would not have taken it. First it was Messua's blood on the thongs, and now it is Hathi's. I will use it no more. Look!"

The ankus flew sparkling, and buried itself point down thirty yards away, between the trees. "So my hands are clean of Death," said Mowgli, rubbing his palms on the fresh, moist earth. "The Thuu said Death would follow me. He is old and white and mad."

"White or black, or death or life, I am going to sleep, Little Brother. I cannot hunt all night and howl all day, as do some folk."

Bagheera went off to a hunting-lair that he knew, about two miles off. Mowgli made an easy way for himself up a convenient tree, knotted three or four creepers together, and in less time than it takes to tell was swinging in a hammock fifty feet above ground. Though he had no positive objection to strong daylight, Mowgli followed the custom of his friends, and used it as little as he could. When he waked among the very loud-voiced peoples that live in the trees, it was twilight once more, and he had been dreaming of the beautiful pebbles he had thrown away.

"At least I will look at the thing again," he said, and slid down a creeper to the earth; but Bagheera was before him. Mowgli could hear him snuffing in the half light.

"Where is the thorn-pointed thing?" cried Mowgli.

"A man has taken it. Here is the trail."

"Now we shall see whether the Thuu spoke truth. If the pointed thing is Death, that man will die. Let us follow."

"Kill first," said Bagheera. "An empty stomach makes a careless eye. Men go very slowly, and the Jungle is wet enough to hold the lightest mark."

They killed as soon as they could, but it was nearly three hours before they finished their meat and drink and buckled down to the trail. The Jungle People know that nothing makes up for being hurried over your meals.

"Think you the pointed thing will turn in the man's hand and kill him?" Mowgli asked. "The Thuu said it was Death."

"We shall see when we find," said Bagheera, trotting with his head low. "It is single-foot" (he meant that there was only one man), "and the weight of the thing has pressed his heel far into the ground."

"Hai! This is as clear as summer lightning," Mowgli answered; and they fell into the quick, choppy trail-trot in and out through the checkers of the moonlight, following the marks of those two bare feet.

"Now he runs swiftly," said Mowgli. "The toes are spread apart." They went on over some wet ground. "Now why does he turn aside here?"

"Wait!" said Bagheera, and flung himself forward with one superb bound as far as ever he could. The first thing to do when a trail ceases to explain itself is to cast forward without leaving your own confusing foot-marks on the ground. Bagheera turned as he landed, and faced Mowgli, crying, "Here comes another trail to meet him. It is a smaller foot, this second trail, and the toes turn inward."

Then Mowgli ran up and looked. "It is the foot of a Gond hunter," he said. "Look! Here he dragged his bow on the grass. That is why the first trail turned aside so quickly. Big Foot hid from Little Foot."

"That is true," said Bagheera. "Now, lest by crossing each other's tracks we foul the signs, let each take one trail. I am Big Foot, Little Brother, and thou art Little Foot, the Gond."

Bagheera leaped back to the original trail, leaving Mowgli stooping above the curious narrow track of the wild little man of the woods.

"Now," said Bagheera, moving step by step along the chain of footprints, "I, Big Foot, turn aside here. Now I hide me behind a rock and stand still, not daring to shift my feet. Cry thy trail, Little Brother."

"Now, I, Little Foot, come to the rock," said Mowgli, running up his trail. "Now, I sit down under the rock, leaning upon my right hand, and resting my bow between my toes. I wait long, for the mark of my feet is deep here."

"I also," said Bagheera, hidden behind the rock. "I wait, resting the end of the thorn-pointed thing upon a stone. It slips, for here is a scratch upon the stone. Cry thy trail, Little Brother."

"One, two twigs and a big branch are broken here," said Mowgli, in an undertone. "Now, how shall I cry *that*? Ah! It is plain now. I, Little Foot, go away making noises and tramplings so that Big Foot may hear me." He moved away from the rock pace by pace among the trees, his voice rising in the distance as he approached a little cascade. "I — go — far — away — to — where — the — noise — of — falling — water — covers — my — noise; and — here — I — wait. Cry thy trail, Bagheera, Big Foot!"

The panther had been casting in every direction to see how Big Foot's trail led away from behind the rock. Then he gave tongue:

"I come from behind the rock upon my knees, dragging the thorn-pointed thing. Seeing no one, I run. I, Big Foot, run swiftly. The trail is clear. Let each follow his own. I run!"

Bagheera swept on along the clearly marked trail, and Mowgli followed the steps of the Gond. For some time there was silence in the Jungle.

"Where art thou, Little Foot?" cried Bagheera. Mowgli's voice answered him not fifty yards to the right.

"Um!" said the panther, with a deep cough. "The two run side by side, drawing nearer!"

They raced on another half mile, always keeping about the same distance, till Mowgli, whose head was not so close to the ground as Bagheera's, cried: "They have met. Good hunting—look! Here stood Little Foot, with his knee on a rock—and yonder is Big Foot indeed!"

Not ten yards in front of them, stretched across a pile of broken rocks, lay the body of a villager of the district, a long, small-feathered Gond arrow through his back and breast.

"Was the Thuu so old and so mad, Little Brother?" said Bagheera gently. "Here is one death, at least."

"Follow on. But where is the drinker of elephant's blood—the red-eyed thorn?"

"Little Foot has it—perhaps. It is single-foot again now."

The single trail of a light man who had been running quickly and bearing a burden on his left shoulder, held on round a long, low spur of dried grass, where each footfall seemed, to the sharp eyes of the trackers, marked in hot iron.

Neither spoke till the trail ran up to the ashes of a camp-fire hidden in a ravine.

"Again!" said Bagheera, checking as though he had been turned into stone.

The body of a little wizened Gond lay with its feet in the ashes, and Bagheera looked inquiringly at Mowgli.

"That was done with a bamboo," said the boy, after one glance. "I have used such a thing among the buffaloes when I served in the Man-Pack. The Father of Cobras—I am sorrowful that I made a jest of him—knew the breed well, as I might have known. Said I not that men kill for idleness?"

"Indeed, they killed for the sake of the red and blue stones," Bagheera answered. "Remember, I was in the King's cages at Oodeypore."

"One, two, three, four tracks," said Mowgli, stooping over the ashes. "Four tracks of men with shod feet. They do not go so quickly as Gonds. Now, what evil had the little wood-man done to them? See, they talked together, all five, standing up, before they killed him. Bagheera, let us go back. My stomach is heavy in me, and yet it heaves up and down like an oriole's nest at the end of a branch."

"It is not good hunting to leave game afoot. Follow!" said

oriole's nest: Orioles weave hanging nests out of grasses and fibers.

111

the panther. "Those eight shod feet have not gone far."

No more was said for fully an hour, as they worked up the broad trail of the four men with shod feet.

It was clear, hot daylight now, and Bagheera said, "I smell smoke."

"Men are always more ready to eat than to run," Mowgli answered, trotting in and out between the low scrub bushes of the new Jungle they were exploring. Bagheera, a little to his left, made an indescribable noise in his throat.

"Here is one that has done with feeding," said he. A tumbled bundle of gay-colored clothes lay under a bush, and round it was some spilt flour.

"That was done by the bamboo again," said Mowgli. "See! that white dust is what men eat. They have taken the kill from this one,—he carried their food,—and given him for a kill to Chil, the Kite."

"It is the third," said Bagheera.

"I will go with new, big frogs to the Father of Cobras, and feed him fat," said Mowgli to himself. "The drinker of elephant's blood is Death himself—but still I do not understand!"

"Follow!" said Bagheera.

They had not gone half a mile further when they heard Ko, the Crow, singing the death-song in the top of a tamarisk under whose shade three men were lying. A half-dead fire smoked in the center of the circle, under an iron plate which held a blackened and burned cake of unleavened bread. Close to the fire, and blazing in the sunshine, lay the ruby-and-turquoise ankus.

"The thing works quickly; all ends here," said Bagheera. "How did *these* die, Mowgli? There is no mark on any."

A Jungle-dweller gets to learn by experience as much as many doctors know of poisonous plants and berries. Mowgli sniffed the smoke that came up from the fire, broke off a morsel of the blackened bread, tasted it, and spat it out again.

"Apple of Death," he coughed. "The first must have made it ready in the food for *these*, who killed him, having first killed the Gond."

"Good hunting, indeed! The kills follow close," said Bagheera.

"Apple of Death" is what the Jungle call thorn-apple or dhatura, the readiest poison in all India.

"What now?" said the panther. "Must thou and I kill each other for yonder red-eyed slayer?"

"Can it speak?" said Mowgli, in a whisper. "Did I do it a wrong when I threw it away? Between us two it can do no

Flowering Branch of Tamarisk.

tamarisk: A tree or shrub, also known as flowering cypress. The branches have a feathery appearance. Tannin from the bark is used in tanning leather. Some varieties give off a liquid with enough salt to be used in cooking.

wrong, for we do not desire what men desire. If it be left here, it will assuredly continue to kill men one after another as fast as nuts fall in a high wind. I have no love to men, but even I would not have them die six in a night."

"What matter? They are only men. They killed one another and were well pleased," said Bagheera. "That first little woodman hunted well."

"They are cubs none the less; and a cub will drown himself to bite the moon's light on the water. The fault was mine," said Mowgli, who spoke as though he knew all about everything. "I will never again bring into the Jungle strange things — not though they be as beautiful as flowers. This" — he handled the ankus gingerly — "goes back to the Father of Cobras. But first we must sleep, and we cannot sleep near these sleepers. Also we must bury *him*, lest he run away and kill another six. Dig me a hole under that tree."

"But, Little Brother," said Bagheera, moving off to the spot, "I tell thee it is no fault of the blood-drinker. The trouble is with men."

"All one," said Mowgli. "Dig the hole deep. When we wake I will take him up and carry him back."

.   .   .   .   .   .

Two nights later, as the White Cobra sat mourning in the darkness of the vault, ashamed, and robbed, and alone, the turquoise ankus whirled through the hole in the wall, and clashed on the floor of golden coins.

"Father of Cobras," said Mowgli (he was careful to keep the other side of the wall), "get thee a young and ripe one of thine own people to help thee guard the King's Treasure so that no man may come away alive any more."

"Ah-ha! It returns, then. I said the thing was Death. How comes it that thou art still alive?" the old Cobra mumbled, twining lovingly round the ankus-haft.

"By the Bull that bought me, I do not know! That thing has killed six times in a night. Let him go out no more."

THE SONG OF THE LITTLE HUNTER

Ere Mor the Peacock flutters, ere the Monkey People cry,
  Ere Chil the Kite swoops down a furlong sheer,
Through the Jungle very softly flits a shadow and a sigh—
  He is Fear, O Little Hunter, he is Fear!
Very softly down the glade runs a waiting, watching shade,
  And the whisper spreads and widens far and near;
And the sweat is on thy brow, for he passes even now—
  He is Fear, O Little Hunter, he is Fear!

Ere the moon has climbed the mountain, ere the rocks are ribbed with
    light,
  When the downward-dipping trails are dank and drear,
Comes a breathing hard behind thee—snuffle-snuffle through the night—
  It is Fear, O Little Hunter, it is Fear!
On thy knees and draw the bow; bid the shrilling arrow go;
  In the empty, mocking thicket plunge the spear;
But thy hands are loosed and weak, and the blood has left thy cheek—
  It is Fear, O Little Hunter, it is Fear!

When the heat-cloud sucks the tempest, when the slivered pine-trees fall,
  When the blinding, blaring rain-squalls lash and veer;
Through the war-gongs of the thunder rings a voice more loud than all—
  It is Fear, O Little Hunter, it is Fear!
Now the spates are banked and deep; now the footless boulders leap—
  Now the lightning shows each littlest leaf-rib clear—
But thy throat is shut and dried, and thy heart against thy side
  Hammers: Fear, O Little Hunter—this is Fear!

*For our white and our excellent nights—for the nights of swift
      running,*
Fair ranging, far-seeing, good hunting, sure cunning!
For the smells of the dawning, untainted, ere dew has departed!
For the rush through the mist, and the quarry blind-started!
*For the cry of our mates when the sambhur has wheeled and is
      standing at bay,*
*   For the risk and the riot of night!*
*   For the sleep at the lair-mouth by day,*
*   It is met, and we go to the fight.*
*   Bay! O bay!*

IT was after the letting in of the Jungle that the pleasantest
part of Mowgli's life began. He had the good conscience
that comes from paying debts; all the Jungle was his friend,
and just a little afraid of him. The things that he did and
saw and heard when he was wandering from one people to

crocodile: This largest of all reptiles can grow to 30 feet. His main diet is fish, but he'll eat anything that gets near him.

another, with or without his four companions, would make many stories, each as long as this one. So you will never be told how he met the Mad Elephant of Mandla, who killed two-and-twenty bullocks drawing eleven carts of coined silver to the Government Treasury, and scattered the shiny rupees in the dust; how he fought Jacala, the Crocodile, all one long night in the Marshes of the North, and broke his skinning-knife on the brute's back-plates; how he found a new and longer knife round the neck of a man who had been killed by a wild boar, and how he tracked that boar and killed him as a fair price for the knife; how he was caught up once in the Great Famine, by the moving of the deer, and nearly crushed to death in the swaying hot herds; how he saved Hathi the Silent from being once more trapped in a pit with a stake at the bottom, and how, next day, he himself fell into a very cunning leopard-trap, and how Hathi broke the thick wooden bars to pieces above him; how he milked the wild buffaloes in the swamp, and how—

But we must tell one tale at a time. Father and Mother Wolf died, and Mowgli rolled a big boulder against the mouth of their cave, and cried the Death Song over them; Baloo grew very old and stiff, and even Bagheera, whose nerves were steel, and whose muscles were iron, was a shade slower on the kill than he had been. Akela turned from gray to milky white with pure age; his ribs stuck out, and he walked as though he had been made of wood, and Mowgli killed for him. But the young wolves, the children of the disbanded Seeonee Pack, throve and increased, and when there were about forty of them, masterless, full-voiced, clean-footed five-year-olds, Akela told them that they ought to gather themselves together and follow the Law, and run under one head, as befitted the Free People.

This was not a question in which Mowgli concerned himself, for, as he said, he had eaten sour fruit, and he knew the tree it hung from; but when Phao, son of Phaona (his father was the Gray Tracker in the days of Akela's headship), fought his way to the leadership of the Pack, according to Jungle Law, and the old calls and songs began to ring under the stars once more, Mowgli came to the Council Rock for memory's sake. When he chose to speak the Pack waited till he had finished, and he sat at Akela's side on the rock above Phao. Those were days of good hunting and good sleeping. No stranger cared to break into the jungles that belonged to Mowgli's people, as they called the Pack, and the young wolves grew fat and strong, and there were many cubs to bring to the Looking-over. Mowgli always attended a

Looking-over, remembering the night when a black panther bought a naked brown baby into the Pack, and the long call, "Look, look well, O Wolves," made his heart flutter. Otherwise, he would be far away in the Jungle with his four brothers, tasting, touching, seeing, and feeling new things.

One twilight when he was trotting leisurely across the ranges to give Akela the half of a buck that he had killed, while the Four jogged behind him, sparring a little, and tumbling one another over for joy of being alive, he heard a cry that had never been heard since the bad days of Shere Khan. It was what they call in the Jungle the *pheeal*, a hideous kind of shriek that the jackal gives when he is hunting behind a tiger, or when there is a big killing afoot. If you can imagine a mixture of hate, triumph, fear, and despair, with a kind of leer running through it, you will get some notion of the *pheeal* that rose and sank and wavered and quavered far away across the Waingunga. The Four stopped at once, bristling and growling. Mowgli's hand went to his knife, and he checked, the blood in his face, his eyebrows knotted.

"There is no Striped One dare kill here," he said.

"That is not the cry of the Forerunner," answered Gray Brother. "It is some great killing. Listen!"

It broke out again, half sobbing and half chuckling, just as though the jackal had soft human lips. Then Mowgli drew deep breath, and ran to the Council Rock, overtaking on his way hurrying wolves of the Pack. Phao and Akela were on the Rock together, and below them, every nerve strained, sat the others. The mothers and the cubs were cantering off to their lairs; for when the *pheeal* cries it is no time for weak things to be abroad.

They could hear nothing except the Waingunga rushing and gurgling in the dark, and the light evening winds among the tree-tops, till suddenly across the river a wolf called. It was no wolf of the Pack, for they were all at the Rock. The note changed to a long, despairing bay; and "Dhole!" it said, "Dhole! dhole! dhole!" They heard tired feet on the rocks, and a gaunt wolf, streaked with red on his flanks, his right fore-paw useless, and his jaws white with foam, flung himself into the circle and lay gasping at Mowgli's feet.

"Good hunting! Under whose Headship?" said Phao gravely.

"Good hunting! Won-tolla am I," was the answer. He meant that he was a solitary wolf, fending for himself, his mate, and his cubs in some lonely lair, as do many wolves in the south. Won-tolla means an Outlier—one who lies out

dhole: This is the name of the wild dog of the Dekkan. Authorities say these vicious animals are not ancestors of our domestic dogs. They have only two molars to the jaw, while the true dogs, *Canis*, have three.

117

dekkan: A high flat plateau that stretches for many miles in southern India.

from any Pack. Then he panted, and they could see his heartbeats shake him backward and forward.

"What moves?" said Phao, for that is the question all the Jungle asks after the *pheeal* cries.

"The dhole, the dhole of the Dekkan—Red Dog, the Killer! They came north from the south saying the Dekkan was empty and killing out by the way. When this moon was new there were four to me—my mate and three cubs. She would teach them to kill on the grass plains, hiding to drive the buck, as we do who are of the open. At midnight I heard them together, full tongue on the trail. At the dawn-wind I found them stiff in the grass—four, Free People, four when this moon was new. Then sought I my Blood-Right and found the dhole."

"How many?" said Mowgli quickly; the Pack growled deep in their throats.

"I do not know. Three of them will kill no more, but at the last they drove me like the buck; on my three legs they drove me. Look, Free People!"

He thrust out his mangled fore-foot, all dark with dried blood. There were cruel bites low down on his side, and his throat was torn and worried.

"Eat," said Akela, rising up from the meat Mowgli had brought him, and the Outlier flung himself on it.

"This shall be no loss," he said humbly, when he had taken off the first edge of his hunger. "Give me a little strength, Free People, and I also will kill. My lair is empty that was full when this moon was new, and the Blood Debt is not all paid."

Phao heard his teeth crack on a haunch-bone and grunted approvingly.

"We shall need those jaws," said he. "Were their cubs with the dhole?"

"Nay, nay. Red Hunters all: grown dogs of their Pack, heavy and strong, for all that they eat lizards in the Dekkan."

What Won-tolla had said meant that the dhole, the red hunting-dog of the Dekkan, was moving to kill, and the Pack knew well that even the tiger will surrender a new kill to the dhole. They drive straight through the Jungle, and what they meet they pull down and tear to pieces. Though they are not as big nor half as cunning as the wolf, they are very strong and very numerous. The dhole, for instance, do not begin to call themselves a pack till they are a hundred strong; whereas forty wolves make a very fair pack indeed. Mowgli's wanderings had taken him to the edge of the high grassy downs of the Dekkan, and he had seen the fearless dholes sleeping and playing and scratching themselves in the little hollows and tussocks that they use for lairs. He despised and hated them because they did not smell like the Free People, because they did not live in caves, and, above all, because they had hair between their toes while he and his friends were clean-footed. But he knew, for Hathi had told him, what a terrible thing a dhole hunting-pack was. Even Hathi moves aside from their line, and until they are killed, or till game is scarce, they will go forward.

Akela knew something of the dholes, too, for he said to Mowgli quietly. "It is better to die in a Full Pack than leaderless and alone. This is good hunting, and—my last. But, as men live, thou hast very many more nights and days, Little Brother. Go north and lie down, and if any live after the dhole has gone by he shall bring thee word of the fight."

"Ah," said Mowgli, quite gravely, "must I go to the marshes and catch little fish and sleep in a tree, or must I ask help of the Bandar-log and crack nuts, while the Pack fight below?"

"It is to the death," said Akela. "Thou hast never met the dhole—the Red Killer. Even the Striped One—"

"*Aowa! Aowa!*" said Mowgli pettingly. "I have killed one striped ape, and sure am I in my stomach that Shere Khan would have left his own mate for meat to the dhole if he had winded a pack across three ranges. Listen now: There was a wolf, my father, and there was a wolf, my mother, and there was an old gray wolf (not too wise: he is white now) was my father and my mother. Therefore I—" he raised his voice, "I say that when the dhole come, and if the dhole come, Mowgli and the Free People are of one skin for that hunting; and I say, by the Bull that bought me—by the Bull Bagheera paid for me in the old days which ye of the Pack do not remember—*I* say, that the Trees and the River may hear and hold fast if I forget; *I* say that this my knife shall be as a tooth to the Pack—and I do not think it is so blunt. This is my Word which has gone from me."

"Thou dost not know the dhole, man with a wolf's tongue," said Won-tolla. "I look only to clear the Blood Debt against them ere they have me in many pieces. They move slowly, killing out as they go, but in two days a little strength will come back to me and I turn again for the Blood Debt. But for *ye*, Free People, my word is that ye go north and eat but little for a while till the dhole are gone. There is no meat in this hunting."

"Hear the Outlier!" said Mowgli with a laugh. "Free People, we must go north and dig lizards and rats from the

---

Red Dog

tussock: A clump of growing grass or swamp weeds.

blunt: Not sharp; dull or unable to cut well.

bank, lest by any chance we meet the dhole. He must kill out our hunting-grounds, while we lie hid in the north till it please him to give us our own again. He is a dog—and the pup of a dog—red, yellow-bellied, lairless, and haired between every toe! He counts his cubs six and eight at the litter, as though he were Chikai, the little leaping rat. Surely we must run away, Free People, and beg leave of the peoples of the north for the offal of dead cattle! Ye know the saying: 'North are the vermin; south are the lice. *We* are the Jungle.' Choose ye, O choose. It is good hunting! For the Pack—for the Full Pack—for the lair and the litter; for the in-kill and the out-kill; for the mate that drives the doe and the little, little cub within the cave; it is met!—it is met!—it is met!"

The Pack answered with one deep, crashing bark that sounded in the night like a big tree falling. "It is met!" they cried.

"Stay with these," said Mowgli to the Four. "We shall need every tooth. Phao and Akela must make ready the battle. I go to count the dogs."

"It is death!" Won-tolla cried, half rising. "What can such a hairless one do against the Red Dog? Even the Striped One, remember—"

"Thou art indeed an Outlier," Mowgli called back; "but we will speak when the dholes are dead. Good hunting all!"

He hurried off into the darkness, wild with excitement, hardly looking where he set foot, and the natural consequence was that he tripped full length over Kaa's great coils where the python lay watching a deer-path near the river.

"*Kssha!*" said Kaa angrily. "Is this jungle-work, to stamp and tramp and undo a night's hunting—when the game are moving so well, too?"

"The fault was mine," said Mowgli, picking himself up. "Indeed I was seeking thee, Flathead, but each time we meet thou art longer and broader by the length of my arm. There is none like thee in the Jungle, wise, old, strong, and most beautiful Kaa."

"Now, whither does *this* trail lead?" Kaa's voice was gentler. "Not a moon since there was a Manling with a knife threw stones at my head, and called me bad little tree-cat names, because I lay asleep in the open."

"Ay, and turned every driven deer to all the winds, and Mowgli was hunting, and this same Flathead was too deaf to hear his whistle, and leave the deer-roads free," Mowgli answered composedly, sitting down among the painted coils.

"Now this same Manling comes with soft, tickling words

rat: This common rodent is a dangerous and generally detested animal. He is a great food destroyer, and a vicious fighter for his size—which can be up to two feet. He sometimes carries disease, and multiplies with great rapidity.

composedly: This is the quality of being quietly confident. When you are COMPOSED, you are unworried; you know exactly what you are going to do, and how you are going to do it.

to this same Flathead, telling him that he is wise and strong and beautiful, and this same old Flathead believes and makes a place, thus, for this same stone-throwing Manling, and—. Art thou at ease now? Could Bagheera give thee so good a resting-place?"

Kaa had, as usual, made a sort of soft, half-hammock of himself under Mowgli's weight. The boy reached out in the darkness, and gathered in the supple cable-like neck till Kaa's head rested on his shoulder, and then he told him all that had happened in the Jungle that night.

"Wise I may be," said Kaa at the end; "but deaf I surely am. Else I should have heard the *pheeal*. Small wonder the Eaters of Grass are uneasy. How many be the dhole?"

"I have not yet seen. I came hot-foot to thee. Thou art older than Hathi. But oh, Kaa,"—here Mowgli wriggled with sheer joy,—"it will be good hunting. Few of us will see another moon."

"Dost *thou* strike in this? Remember thou art a Man; and remember what Pack cast thee out. Let the Wolf look to the Dog. Thou art a man."

"Last year's nuts are this year's black earth," said Mowgli. "It is true that I am a Man, but it is in my stomach that this night I have said that I am a Wolf. I called the River and the Trees to remember. I am of the Free People, Kaa, till the dhole has gone by."

"Free People," Kaa grunted. "Free thieves! And thou hast tied thyself into the death-knot for the sake of the memory of the dead wolves? This is no good hunting."

"It is my Word which I have spoken. The Trees know, the River knows. Till the dhole have gone by my Word comes not back to me."

"*Ngssh!* This changes all trails. I had thought to take thee away with me to the northern marshes, but the Word—even the Word of a little, naked, hairless manling—is the Word. Now I, Kaa, say—"

"Think well, Flathead, lest thou tie thyself into the death-knot also. I need no Word from thee, for well I know—"

"Be it so, then," said Kaa. "I will give no Word; but what is in thy stomach to do when the dhole come?"

"They must swim the Waingunga. I thought to meet them with my knife in the shallows, the Pack behind me; and so stabbing and thrusting we a little might turn them down-stream, or cool their throats."

"The dhole do not turn and their throats are hot," said Kaa. "There will be neither Manling nor Wolf-cub when that hunting is done, but only dry bones."

"*Alala!* If we die, we die. It will be most good hunting. But my stomach is young, and I have not seen many Rains. I am not wise nor strong. Hast thou a better plan, Kaa?"

"I have seen a hundred and a hundred Rains. Ere Hathi cast his milk-tushes my trail was big in the dust. By the First Egg I am older than many trees, and I have seen all that the Jungle has done."

"But *this* is new hunting," said Mowgli. "Never before have the dhole crossed our trail."

"What is has been. What will be is no more than a forgotten year striking backward. Be still while I count those my years."

For a long hour Mowgli lay back among the coils, while Kaa, his head motionless on the ground, thought of all that he had seen and known since the day he came from the egg. The light seemed to go out of his eyes and leave them like stale opals, and now and again he made little stiff passes with his head, right and left, as though he were hunting in his sleep. Mowgli dozed quietly, for he knew that there is nothing like sleep before hunting, and he was trained to take it at any hour of the day or night.

Then he felt Kaa's back grow bigger and broader below him as the huge python puffed himself out, hissing with the noise of a sword drawn from a steel scabbard.

"I have seen all the dead seasons," Kaa said at last, "and the great trees and the old elephants, and the rocks that were bare and sharp-pointed ere the moss grew. Art *thou* still alive, Manling?"

"It is only a little after moonset," said Mowgli. "I do not understand—"

"*Hssh!* I am again Kaa. I knew it was but a little time. Now we will go to the river, and I will show thee what is to be done against the dhole."

He turned, straight as an arrow, for the main stream of the Waingunga, plunging in a little above the pool that hid the Peace Rock, Mowgli at his side.

"Nay, do not swim. I go swiftly. My back, Little Brother!"

Mowgli tucked his left arm round Kaa's neck, dropped his right close to his body, and straightened his feet. Then Kaa breasted the current as he alone could, and the ripple of the checked water stood up in a frill round Mowgli's neck, and his feet were waved to and fro in the eddy under the python's lashing sides. A mile or two above the Peace Rock the Waingunga narrows between a gorge of marble rocks from eighty to a hundred feet high, and the current runs like a mill-race between and over all manner of ugly stones.

opals: There are several kinds of this valuable gem stone; fire opals, noble opals, black opals, common opals. Unlike most other gems, they show many bright colors in their depths, usually fire-red, green, yellow, blue. There are many superstitions about opals. One is that if you carry one wrapped in a bay leaf, it will make you invisible.

mill race: Old fashioned mills for the grinding of flour from wheat were often located on streams. The millers built dams, or other structures, and funneled the water flow into a narrow chute or tunnel in order to build up the force of the water. This narrow channel is the mill race. Water in the mill race ran very fast, to turn the big mill wheels.

But Mowgli did not trouble his head about the water; little water in the world could have given him a moment's fear. He was looking at the gorge on either side and sniffing uneasily, for there was a sweetish-sourish smell in the air, very like the smell of a big ant-hill on a hot day. Instinctively he lowered himself in the water, only raising his head to breathe from time to time, and Kaa came to anchor with a double twist of his tail round a sunken rock, holding Mowgli in the hollow of a coil, while the water raced on.

"This is the Place of Death," said the boy. "Why do we come here?"

"They sleep," said Kaa. "Hathi will not turn aside for the Striped One. Yet Hathi and the Striped One together turn aside for the dhole, and the dhole they say turn aside for nothing. And yet for whom do the Little People of the Rocks turn aside? Tell me, Master of the Jungle, who is the Master of the Jungle?"

"These," Mowgli whispered. "It is the Place of Death. Let us go."

"Nay, look well, for they are asleep. It is as it was when I was not the length of thy arm."

The split and weatherworn rocks of the gorge of the Waingunga had been used since the beginning of the Jungle by the Little People of the Rocks—the busy, furious, black wild bees of India; and, as Mowgli knew well, all trails turned off half a mile before they reached the gorge. For centuries the Little People had hived and swarmed from cleft to cleft, and swarmed again, staining the white marble with the stale honey, and made their combs tall and deep in the dark of the inner caves, where neither man nor beast nor fire nor water had ever touched them. The length of the gorge on both sides was hung as it were with black shimmery velvet curtains, and Mowgli sank as he looked, for those were the clotted millions of the sleeping bees. There were other lumps and festoons and things like decayed tree-trunks studded on the face of the rock, the old combs of past years, or new cities built in the shadow of the windless gorge, and huge masses of spongy, rotten trash had rolled down and stuck among the trees and creepers that clung to the rock-face. As he listened he heard more than once the rustle and slide of a honey-loaded comb turning over or falling away somewhere in the dark galleries; then a booming of angry wings and the sullen drip, drip, drip, of the wasted honey, guttering along till it lipped over some ledge in the open air and sluggishly trickled down on the twigs. There was a tiny little beach, not five feet broad, on one side

Red
Dog

gorge: A deep ravine, cut by a stream or river, with steep sides.

Neuter, or Worker.

wild bees: BEES are a numerous group, and come in several sizes, from one as big as your thumb to another not much bigger than a gnat. Some wild (and domestic) bees live in colonies. Many others are "solitary bees" and do not make their homes in hives.

Drone.

of the river, and that was piled high with the rubbish of uncounted years. There were dead bees, drones, sweepings, and stale combs, and wings of marauding moths that had strayed in after honey, all tumbled in smooth piles of the finest black dust. The mere sharp smell of it was enough to frighten anything that had no wings, and knew what the Little People were.

Kaa moved up-stream again till he came to a sandy bar at the head of the gorge.

"Here is this season's kill," said he. "Look!"

On the bank lay the skeletons of a couple of young deer and a buffalo. Mowgli could see that neither wolf nor jackal had touched the bones, which were laid out naturally.

"They came beyond the line: they did not know the Law," murmured Mowgli, "and the Little People killed them. Let us go ere they wake."

"They do not wake till the dawn," said Kaa. "Now I will tell thee. A hunted buck from the south, many, many Rains ago, came hither from the south, not knowing the Jungle, a Pack on his trail. Being made blind by fear, he leaped from above, the Pack running by sight, for they were hot and blind on the trail. The sun was high, and the Little People were many and very angry. Many too were those of the Pack who leaped into the Waingunga, but they were dead ere they took water. Those who did not leap died also in the rocks above. But the buck lived."

"How?"

"Because he came first, running for his life, leaping ere the Little People were aware, and was in the river when they gathered to kill. The Pack, following, was altogether lost under the weight of the Little People."

"The buck lived?" Mowgli repeated slowly.

"At least he did not die *then*, though none waited his coming down with a strong body to hold him safe against the water, as a certain old fat, deaf, yellow Flathead would wait for a Manling—yea, though there were all the dholes of the Dekkan on his trail. What is in thy stomach?" Kaa's head was close to Mowgli's ear; and it was a little time before the boy answered.

"It is to pull the very whiskers of Death, but—Kaa, thou art, indeed, the wisest of all the Jungle."

"So many have said. Look now, if the dhole follow thee—"

"As surely they will follow. Ho! ho! I have many little thorns under my tongue to prick into their hides."

"If they follow thee hot and blind, looking only at thy shoulders, those who do not die up above will take water either here or lower down, for the Little People will rise up and cover them. Now the Waingunga is hungry water, and they will have no Kaa to hold them, but will go down, such as live, to the shallows by the Seeonee lairs, and there thy Pack may meet them by the throat."

"*Ahai! Eowawa!* Better could not be till the Rains fall in the dry season. There is now only the little matter of the run and the leap. I will make me known to the dholes, so that they shall follow me very closely."

"Hast thou seen the rocks above thee? From the landward side?"

"Indeed, no. That I had forgotten."

"Go look. It is all rotten ground, cut and full of holes. One of thy clumsy feet set down without seeing would end the hunt. See, I leave thee here, and for thy sake only I will carry word to the Pack that they may know where to look for the dhole. For myself, I am not of one skin with *any* wolf."

When Kaa disliked an acquaintance he could be more unpleasant than any of the Jungle People, except perhaps Bagheera. He swam down-stream and opposite the Rock he came on Phao and Akela listening to the night noises.

"*Hssh!* Dogs," he said cheerfully. "The dholes will come down-stream. If ye be not afraid ye can kill them in the shallows."

"When come they?" said Phao. "And where is my Man-cub?" said Akela.

"They come when they come," said Kaa. "Wait and see. As for *thy* Man-cub, from whom thou has taken a Word and so laid him open to Death, *thy* Man-cub is with *me*, and if he be not already dead the fault is none of thine, bleached dog! Wait here for the dhole, and be glad that the Man-cub and I strike on thy side."

He flashed up-stream again, and moored himself in the middle of the gorge, looking upward at the line of the cliff. Presently he saw Mowgli's head move against the stars, and then there was a whizz in the air, the keen, clean *schloop* of a body falling feet first, and next minute the boy was at rest again in the loop of Kaa's body.

"It is no leap by night," said Mowgli quietly. "I have jumped twice as far for sport; but that is an evil place above —low bushes and gullies that go down very deep, all full of the Little People. I have put big stones one above the other by the side of three gullies. These I shall throw down with my feet in running, and the Little People will rise up behind me, very angry."

"That is Man's talk and Man's cunning," said Kaa. "Thou

bleached: To bleach is to drain or remove the color from something. Sometimes the sun will bleach; sometimes chemicals. Sometimes, as here, the bleaching is a natural aging process—a turning grey.

125

art wise, but the Little People are always angry."

"Nay, at twilight all wings near and far rest for a while. I will play with the dhole at twilight for the dhole hunts best by day. He follows now Won-tolla's blood-trail."

"Chil does not leave a dead ox, nor the dhole the blood-trail," said Kaa.

"Then I will make him a new blood-trail, of his own blood, if I can, and give him dirt to eat. Thou wilt stay here, Kaa, till I come again with my dholes?"

"Ay, but what if they kill thee in the Jungle or the Little People kill thee before thou canst leap down the river?"

"When to-morrow comes we will kill for to-morrow," said Mowgli, quoting a Jungle saying; and again, "When I am dead it is time to sing the Death Song. Good hunting Kaa!"

He loosed his arm from the python's neck and went down the gorge like a log in a freshet, paddling toward the far bank, where he found slack-water, and laughing aloud from sheer happiness. There was nothing Mowgli liked better than, as he himself said, "to pull the whiskers of Death," and make the Jungle know that he was their over-lord. He had often, with Baloo's help, robbed bees' nests in single trees, and he knew that the Little People hated the smell of wild garlic. So he gathered a small bundle of it, tied it up with a bark string, and then followed Won-tolla's blood-trail as it ran southerly from the lairs, for some five miles, looking at the trees with his head on one side, and chuckling as he looked.

"Mowgli the Frog have I been," said he to himself; "Mowgli the Wolf have I said that I am. Now Mowgli the Ape must I be before I am Mowgli the Buck. At the end I shall be Mowgli the Man. Ho!" and he slid his thumb along the eighteen-inch blade of his knife.

Won-tolla's trail, all rank with dark blood-spots, ran under a forest of thick trees that grew close together and stretched away northeastward, gradually growing thinner and thinner to within two miles of the Bee Rocks. From the last tree to the low scrub of the Bee Rocks was open country, where there was hardly cover enough to hide a wolf. Mowgli trotted along under the trees, judging distances between branch and branch, occasionally climbing up a trunk and taking a trial leap from one tree to another, till he came to the open ground, which he studied very carefully for an hour. Then he turned, picked up Won-tolla's trail where he had left it, settled himself in a tree with an outrunning branch some eight feet from the ground, and sat still, sharpening his knife on the sole of his foot and singing to himself.

A little before midday, when the sun was very warm, he

freshet: A flood of water, caused by melting snows or heavy rains. A log in a freshet would move very fast.

heard the patter of feet and smelt the abominable smell of the dhole pack as they trotted pitilessly along Won-tolla's trail. Seen from above, the red dhole does not look half the size of a wolf, but Mowgli knew how strong his feet and jaws were. He watched the sharp bay head of the leader snuffing along the trail and gave him "Good hunting!"

The brute looked up, and his companions halted behind him, scores and scores of red dogs with low-hung tails, heavy shoulders, weak quarters, and bloody mouths. The dholes are a silent people as a rule, and they have no manners even in their own Jungle. Fully two hundred must have gathered below him, but he could see that the leaders sniffed hungrily on Won-tolla's trail, and tried to drag the Pack forward. That would never do, or they would be at the Lairs in broad daylight, and Mowgli intended to hold them under his tree till dusk.

"By whose leave do ye come here?" said Mowgli.

"All Jungles are our Jungle," was the reply, and the dhole that gave it bared his white teeth. Mowgli looked down with a smile, and imitated perfectly the sharp chitter-chatter of Chikai, the leaping rat of the Dekkan, meaning the dholes to understand that he considered them no better than Chikai. The Pack closed up round the tree-trunk and the leader bayed savagely, calling Mowgli a tree-ape. For all answer Mowgli stretched down one naked leg and wriggled his bare toes just above the leader's head. That was enough, and more than enough, to wake the Pack to stupid rage. Those who have hair between their toes do not care to be reminded of it. Mowgli caught his foot away as the leader leaped up, and said sweetly: "Dog, red dog! Go back to the Dekkan and eat lizards. Go to Chikai thy brother—dog, dog—red, red, dog! There is hair between every toe!" He twiddled his toes a second time.

"Come down ere we starve thee out, hairless ape!" yelled the Pack, and this was exactly what Mowgli wanted. He laid himself down along the branch, his cheek to the bark, his right arm free, and there he told the Pack what he thought and knew about them, their manners, their customs, their mates, and their puppies. There is no speech in the world so rancorous and so stinging as the language the Jungle People use to show scorn and contempt. When you come to think of it you will see how this must be so. As Mowgli told Kaa, he had many little thorns under his tongue, and slowly and deliberately he drove the dholes from silence to growls, from growls to yells, and from yells to hoarse slavery ravings. They tried to answer his taunts, but a cub might as well have

abominable: Something very disgusting and offensive is ABOMINABLE.

tried to answer Kaa in a rage; and all the while Mowgli's right hand lay crooked at his side, ready for action, his feet locked round the branch. The big bay leader had leaped many times in the air, but Mowgli dared not risk a false blow. At last, made furious beyond his natural strength, he bounded up seven or eight feet clear of the ground. Then Mowgli's hand shot out like the head of a tree-snake, and gripped him by the scruff of his neck, and the branch shook with the jar as his weight fell back, almost wrenching Mowgli to the ground. But he never loosed his grasp, and inch by inch he hauled the beast, hanging like a drowned jackal, up on the branch. With his left hand he reached for his knife and cut off the red, bushy tail, flinging the dhole back to earth again. That was all he needed. The Pack would not go forward on Won-tolla's trail now till they had killed Mowgli or Mowgli had killed them. He saw them settle down in circles with a quiver of the haunches that meant they were going to stay, and so he climbed to a higher crotch, settled his back comfortably, and went to sleep.

After four or five hours he waked and counted the Pack. They were all there, silent, husky, and dry, with eyes of steel. The sun was beginning to sink. In half an hour the Little People of the Rocks would be ending their labors, and, as he knew, the dhole does not fight best in the twilight.

"I did not need such faithful watchers," he said politely, standing up on a branch, "but I will remember this. Ye be true dholes, but to my thinking over much of one kind. For that reason I do not give the big lizard-eater his tail again. Art thou not pleased, Red Dog?"

"I myself will tear out thy stomach!" yelled the leader, scratching at the foot of the tree.

"Nay, but consider, wise rat of the Dekkan. There will now be many litters of little tailless red dogs, yea, with raw red stumps that sting when the sand is hot. Go home, Red Dog, and cry that an ape has done this. Ye will not go? Come, then, with me, and I will make you very wise!"

He moved, Bandar-log fashion, into the next tree, and so on into the next and the next, the Pack following with lifted hungry heads. Now and then he would pretend to fall, and the Pack would tumble one over the other in their haste to be at the death. It was a curious sight—the boy with the knife that shone in the low sunlight as it shifted through the upper branches, and the silent Pack with their red coats all aflame, huddling and following below. When he came to the last tree he took the garlic and rubbed himself all over carefully, and the dholes yelled with scorn. "Ape with a wolf's tongue, dost thou think to cover thy scent?" they said. "We follow to the death."

"Take thy tail," said Mowgli, flinging it back along the course he had taken. The Pack instinctively rushed after it. "And follow now—to the death."

He had slipped down the tree-trunk, and headed like the wind in bare feet for the Bee Rocks, before the dholes saw what he would do.

They gave one deep howl, and settled down to the long, lobbing canter that can at the last run down anything that runs. Mowgli knew their pack-pace to be much slower than that of the wolves, or he would never have risked a two-mile run in full sight. They were sure that the boy was theirs at last, and he was sure that he held them to play with as he pleased. All his trouble was to keep them sufficiently hot

instinctively: When you do something instinctively, you do it without thinking. If someone makes a sudden, loud noise behind you, you jump.

behind him to prevent their turning off too soon. He ran cleanly, evenly, and springily; the tailless leader not five yards behind him; and the Pack tailing out over perhaps a quarter of a mile of ground, crazy and blind with the rage of slaughter. So he kept his distance by ear, reserving his last effort for the rush across the Bee Rocks.

The Little People had gone to sleep in the early twilight, for it was not the season of late-blossoming flowers; but as Mowgli's first footfalls rang hollow on the hollow ground he heard a sound as though all the earth were humming. Then he ran as he had never run in his life before, spurned aside one—two—three of the piles of stones into the dark, sweet-smelling gullies; heard a roar like the roar of the sea in a cave; saw with the tail of his eye the air grow dark behind him; saw the current of the Waingunga far below and a flat, diamond-shaped head in the water; leaped outward with all his strength, the tailless dhole snapping at his shoulder in mid-air, and dropped feet first to the safety of the river, breathless and triumphant. There was not a sting upon him, for the smell of the garlic had checked the Little People for just a few seconds that he was among them. When he rose Kaa's coils were steadying him and things were bounding over the edge of the cliff—great lumps, it seemed, of clustered bees falling like plummets; but before any lump touched water the bees flew upward and the body of a dhole whirled down-stream. Overhead they could hear furious short yells that were drowned in a roar like breakers—the roar of the wings of the Little People of the Rocks. Some of the dholes, too, had fallen into the gullies that communicated with the underground caves, and there choked and fought and snapped among the tumbled honeycombs, and at last, borne up even when they were dead on the heaving waves of bees beneath them, shot out of some hole in the river-face, to roll over on the black rubbish-heaps. There were dholes who had leaped short into the trees on the cliffs, and the bees blotted out their shapes; but the greater number of them, maddened by the stings, had flung themselves into the river; and, as Kaa said, the Waingunga was hungry water.

Kaa held Mowgli fast till the boy had recovered his breath.

"We may not stay here," he said. "The Little People are roused indeed. Come!"

Swimming low and diving as often as he could, Mowgli went down the river, knife in hand.

"Slowly, slowly," said Kaa. "One tooth does not kill a hundred unless it be a cobra's, and many of the dholes took water swiftly when they saw the Little People rise."

bees: The sting of a bee not only punctures, but carries an irritating poison as well, which can be very painful. Many stings, by many bees, can be deadly.

"The more work for my knife, then. *Phai!* How the Little People follow!" Mowgli sank again. The face of the water was blanketed with wild bees, buzzing sullenly and stinging all they found.

"Nothing was ever yet lost by silence," said Kaa—no sting could penetrate his scales—"and thou hast all the long night for the hunting. Hear them howl!"

Nearly half the pack had seen the trap their fellows rushed into, and turning sharp aside had flung themselves into the water where the gorge broke down in steep banks. Their cries of rage and their threats against the "tree-ape" who had brought them to their shame mixed with the yells and growls of those who had been punished by the Little People. To remain ashore was death, and every dhole knew it. Their pack was swept along the current, down to the deep eddies of the Peace Pool, but even there the angry Little People followed and forced them to the water again. Mowgli could hear the voice of the tailless leader bidding his people hold on and kill out every wolf in Seeonee. But he did not waste his time in listening.

"One kills in the dark behind us!" snapped a dhole. "Here is tainted water."

Mowgli had dived forward like an otter, twitched a struggling dhole under water before he could open his mouth, and dark rings rose as the body plopped up, turning on its side. The dholes tried to turn, but the current prevented them, and the Little People darted at their heads and ears, and they could hear the challenge of the Seeonee Pack growing louder and deeper in the gathering darkness. Again Mowgli dived, and again a dhole went under, and rose dead, and again the clamor broke out at the rear of the pack; some howling that it was best to go ashore, others calling on their leader to lead them back to the Dekkan, and others bidding Mowgli show himself and be killed.

"They come to the fight with two stomachs and several voices," said Kaa. "The rest is with thy brethren below yonder. The Little People go back to sleep. They have chased us far. Now, I, too, turn back, for I am not of one skin with any wolf. Good hunting, Little Brother, and remember the dhole bites low."

A wolf came running along the bank on three legs, leaping up and down, laying his head sideways close to the ground, hunching his back and breaking high into the air, as though he were playing with his cubs. It was Won-tolla, the Outlier, and he said never a word, but continued his horrible sport beside the dholes. They had been long in the water now, and were swimming wearily, their coats drenched and heavy, their bushy tails dragging like sponges, so tired and shaken that they, too, were silent, watching the pair of blazing eyes that moved abreast.

"This is no good hunting," said one, panting.

"Good hunting!" said Mowgli, as he rose boldly at the brute's side, and sent the long knife home behind the shoulder, pushing hard to avoid his dying snap.

"Art thou there, Man-cub?" said Won-tolla across the water.

"Ask of the dead, Outlier," Mowgli replied. "Have none come down-stream? I have filled these dogs' mouths with dirt; I have tricked them in the broad daylight, and their leader lacks his tail, but here be some few for thee still. Whither shall I drive them?"

"I will wait," said Won-tolla. "The night is before me."

Nearer and nearer came the bay of the Seeonee wolves. "For the Pack, for the Full Pack it is met!" and a bend in the river drove the dholes forward among the sands and shoals opposite the Lairs.

Then they saw their mistake. They should have landed half a mile higher up, and rushed the wolves on dry ground. Now it was too late. The bank was lined with burning eyes, and except for the horrible *pheeal* that had never stopped since sundown, there was no sound in the Jungle. It seemed as though Won-tolla were fawning on them to come ashore; and "Turn and take hold!" said the leader of the dholes. The entire Pack flung themselves at the shore, threshing and squattering through the shoal water, till the face of the Waingunga was all white and torn, and the great ripples went from side to side, like bow-waves from a boat. Mowgli followed the rush, stabbing and slicing as the dholes, huddled together, rushed up the river-beach in one wave.

Then the long fight began, heaving and straining and splitting and scattering and narrowing and broadening along the red, wet sands, and over and between the tangled tree-roots, and through and among the brushes, and in and out of the grass clumps; for even now the dholes were two to one. But they met wolves fighting for all that made the Pack, and not only the short, high, deep-chested, white-tusked hunters of the Pack, but the anxious-eyed lahinis—the she-wolves of the lair, as the saying is—fighting for their litters, with here and there a yearling wolf, his first coat still half woolly, tugging and grappling by their sides. A wolf, you must know, flies at the throat or snaps at the flank, while a dhole, by preference, bites at the belly; so when the dholes were

Red
Dog

struggling out of the water and had to raise their heads, the odds were with the wolves. On dry land the wolves suffered; but in the water or ashore, Mowgli's knife came and went without ceasing. The Four had worried their way to his side. Gray Brother, crouched between the boy's knees, was protecting his stomach, while the others guarded his back and either side, or stood over him when the shock of a leaping, yelling dhole who had thrown himself full on the steady blade, bore him down. For the rest, it was one tangled confusion—a locked and swaying mob that moved from right to left and from left to right along the bank; and also ground round and round slowly on its own center. Here would be a heaving mound, like a water-blister in a whirlpool, which would break like a water-blister, and throw up four or five mangled dogs, each striving to get back to the center; here would be a single wolf borne down by two or three dholes, laboriously dragging them forward, and sinking the while; here a yearling cub would be held up by the pressure round him, though he had been killed early, while his mother, crazed with dumb rage, rolled over and over, snapping, and passing on; and in the middle of the thickest press, perhaps, one wolf and one dhole, forgetting everything else, would be manœuvering for first hold till they were whirled away by a rush of furious fighters. Once Mowgli passed Akela, a dhole on either flank, and his all but toothless jaws closed over the loins of a third; and once he saw Phao, his teeth set in the throat of a dhole, tugging the unwilling beast forward till the yearlings could finish him. But the bulk of the fight was blind flurry and smother in the dark; hit, trip, and tumble, yelp, groan, and worry-worry-worry, round him and behind him and above him. As the night wore on, the quick, giddy-go-round motion increased. The dholes were cowed and afraid to attack the stronger wolves, but did not yet dare to run away. Mowgli felt that the end was coming soon, and contented himself with striking merely to cripple. The yearlings were growing bolder; there was time now and again to breathe, and pass a word to a friend, and the mere flicker of the knife would sometimes turn a dog aside.

"The meat is very near the bone," Gray Brother yelled. He was bleeding from a score of flesh-wounds.

"But the bone is yet to be cracked," said Mowgli. "*Eowawa! Thus* do we do in the Jungle!" The red blade ran like a flame along the side of a dhole whose hind-quarters were hidden by the weight of a clinging wolf.

"My kill!" snorted the wolf through his wrinkled nostrils.

manoeuvering: This is a shifting about, often for the purpose of making the most favorable attack. Enemy ships will MANOEUVER for the best position. The feints and sudden moves of wrestlers before they grapple would be manoeuvers, too.

133

"Leave him to me."

"Is thy stomach still empty, Outlier?" said Mowgli. Won-tolla was fearfully punished, but his grip had paralyzed the dhole, who could not turn round and reach him.

"By the Bull that bought me," said Mowgli, with a bitter laugh, "it is the tailless one!" And indeed it was the big bay-colored leader.

"It is not wise to kill cubs and lahinis," Mowgli went on, philosophically, wiping the blood out of his eyes, "unless one has also killed the Outlier; and it is in my stomach that this Won-tolla kills thee."

A dhole leaped to his leader's aid; but before his teeth had found Won-tolla's flank, Mowgli's knife was in his throat, and Gray Brother took what was left.

"And thus do we do in the Jungle," said Mowgli.

Won-tolla said not a word, only his jaws were closing and closing on the backbone as his life ebbed. The dhole shuddered, his head dropped, and he lay still, and Won-tolla dropped above him.

"*Huh!* The Blood Debt is paid," said Mowgli. "Sing the song, Won-tolla."

"He hunts no more," said Gray Brother; "and Akela, too, is silent this long time."

"The bone is cracked!" thundered Phao, son of Phaona. "They go! Kill, kill out, O hunters of the Free People!"

Dhole after dhole was slinking away from those dark and bloody sands to the river, to the thick Jungle, up-stream or down-stream as he saw the road clear.

"The debt! The debt!" shouted Mowgli. "Pay the debt! They have slain the Lone Wolf! Let not a dog go!"

He was flying to the river, knife in hand, to check any dhole who dared to take water, when, from under a mound of nine dead, rose Akela's red head and fore-quarters, and Mowgli dropped on his knees beside the Lone Wolf.

"Said I not it would be my last fight?" Akela panted. "It is good hunting. And thou, Little Brother?"

"I live, having killed many."

"Even so. I die, and I would—I would die by thee, Little Brother."

Mowgli took the terrible scarred head on his knees, and put his arms round the torn neck.

"It is long since the old days of Shere Khan, and a Man-cub that rolled naked in the dust."

"Nay, nay, I am a wolf. I am of one skin with the Free People," Mowgli cried. "It is no will of mine that I am a man."

"Thou art a man, Little Brother, wolfling of my watching. Thou art a man, or else the Pack had fled before the dhole. My life I owe to thee, and to-day thou hast saved the Pack even as once I saved thee. Hast thou forgotten? All debts are paid now. Go to thine own people. I tell thee again, eye of my eye, this hunting is ended. Go to thine own people."

"I will never go. I will hunt alone in the Jungle. I have said it."

"After the summer come the Rains, and after the Rains comes the spring. Go back before thou art driven."

"Who will drive me?"

"Mowgli will drive Mowgli. Go back to thy people. Go to Man."

"When Mowgli drives Mowgli I will go," Mowgli answered.

"There is no more to say," said Akela. "Little Brother, canst thou raise me to my feet? I also was a leader of the Free People."

Very carefully and gently Mowgli lifted the bodies aside, and raised Akela to his feet, both arms round him, and the Lone Wolf drew a long breath, and began the Death Song that a leader of the Pack should sing when he dies. It gathered strength as he went on, lifting and lifting, and ringing far across the river, till it came to the last "Good hunting!" and Akela shook himself clear of Mowgli for an instant, and, leaping into the air, fell backward dead upon his last and most terrible kill.

Mowgli sat with the head on his knees, careless of anything else, while the remnants of the flying dholes were being overtaken and run down by the merciless lahinis. Little by little the cries died away, and the wolves returned limping, as their wounds stiffened, to take stock of the losses. Fifteen of the Pack, as well as half a dozen lahinis, lay dead by the river, and of the others not one was unmarked. And Mowgli sat through it all till the cold daybreak, when Phao's wet, red muzzle was dropped in his hand, and Mowgli drew back to show the gaunt body of Akela.

"Good hunting!" said Phao, as though Akela were still alive, and then over his bitten shoulder to the others: "Howl, dogs! A Wolf has died to-night!"

But of all the Pack of two hundred fighting dholes, whose boast was that all Jungles were their Jungle, and that no living thing could stand before them, not one returned to the Dekkan to carry that word.

[This is the song that Chil sang as the kites dropped down one after another to the river-bed, when the great fight was finished. Chil is good friends with everybody, but he is a cold-blooded kind of creature at heart, because he knows that almost everybody in the Jungle comes to him in the long run.]

These were my companions going forth by night—
(For Chil! Look you, for Chil!)
Now come I to whistle them the ending of the fight.
(Chil! Vanguards of Chil!)
Word they gave me overhead of quarry newly slain,
Word I gave them underfoot of buck upon the plain.
Here's an end of every trail—they shall not speak again!

They that called the hunting-cry—they that followed fast—
(For Chil! Look you, for Chil!)
They that bade the sambhur wheel, and pinned him as he passed—
(Chil! Vanguards of Chil!)
They that lagged behind the scent—they that ran before,
They that shunned the level horn—they that overbore.
Here's an end of every trail—they shall not follow more.

These were my companions. Pity 't was they died!
(For Chil! Look you, for Chil!)
Now come I to comfort them that knew them in their pride.
(Chil! Vanguards of Chil!)
Tattered flank and sunken eye, open mouth and red,
Locked and lank and lone they lie, the dead upon their dead.
Here's an end of every trail—and here my hosts are fed!

Man goes to Man! Cry the challenge through the Jungle!
  He that was our Brother goes away.
Hear, now, and judge, O ye People of the Jungle,—
  Answer, who shall turn him—who shall stay?

Man goes to Man! He is weeping in the Jungle:
  He that was our Brother sorrows sore!
Man goes to Man! (Oh, we loved him in the Jungle!)
  To the Man-Trail where we may not follow more.

THE second year after the great fight with Red Dog and
   the death of Akela, Mowgli must have been nearly
seventeen years old. He looked older, for hard exercise, the
best of good eating, and baths whenever he felt in the least
hot or dusty, had given him strength and growth far beyond

his age. He could swing by one hand from a top branch for half an hour at a time, when he had occasion to look along the tree-roads. He could stop a young buck in mid-gallop and throw him sideways by the head. He could even jerk over the big, blue wild boars that lived in the Marshes of the North. The Jungle People who used to fear him for his wits feared him now for his strength, and when he moved quietly on his own affairs the mere whisper of his coming cleared the wood-paths. And yet the look in his eyes was always gentle. Even when he fought, his eyes never blazed as Bagheera's did. They only grew more and more interested and excited; and that was one of the things that Bagheera himself did not understand.

He asked Mowgli about it, and the boy laughed and said: "When I miss the kill I am angry. When I must go empty for two days I am very angry. Do not my eyes talk then?"

"The mouth is angry," said Bagheera, "But the eyes say nothing. Hunting, eating, or swimming, it is all one—like a stone in wet or dry weather." Mowgli looked at him lazily from under his long eyelashes, and, as usual, the panther's head dropped. Bagheera knew his master.

They were lying out far up the side of a hill overlooking the Waingunga, and the morning mist hung below them in bands of white and green. As the sun rose it changed into bubbling seas of red gold, churned off, and let the low rays stripe the dried grass on which Mowgli and Bagheera were resting. It was the end of the cold weather, the leaves and the trees looked worn and faded, and there was a dry, ticking rustle everywhere when the wind blew. A little leaf tap-tap-tapped furiously against a twig, as a single leaf caught in a current will. It roused Bagheera, for he snuffed the morning air with a deep, hollow cough, threw himself on his back, and struck with his fore-paws at the nodding leaf above.

"The year turns," he said. "The Jungle goes forward. The Time of New Talk is near. That leaf knows. It is very good."

"The grass is dry," Mowgli answered, pulling up a tuft. "Even Eye-of-the-Spring [that is a little trumpet-shaped, waxy red flower that runs in and out among the grasses]—even Eye-of-the-Spring is shut, and . . . Bagheera, *is* it well for the Black Panther so to lie on his back and beat with his paws in the air, as though he were the tree-cat?"

"Aowh?" said Bagheera. He seemed to be thinking of other things.

"I say, *is* it well for the Black Panther so to mouth and cough, and howl and roll? Remember, we be the Masters of the Jungle, thou and I."

"Indeed, yes: I hear, Man-cub." Bagheera rolled over hurriedly and sat up, the dust on his ragged, black flanks.

(He was just casting his winter coat.) "We be surely the Masters of the Jungle! Who is so strong as Mowgli? Who so wise?" There was a curious drawl in the voice that made Mowgli turn to see whether by any chance the Black Panther were making fun of him, for the Jungle is full of words that sound like one thing, but mean another. "I said we be beyond question the Masters of the Jungle," Bagheera repeated. "Have I done wrong? I did not know that the Man-cub no longer lay upon the ground. Does he fly, then?"

Mowgli sat with his elbows on his knees, looking out across the valley at the daylight. Somewhere down in the woods below a bird was trying over in a husky, reedy voice the first few notes of his spring song. It was no more than a shadow of the liquid, tumbling call he would be pouring later, but Bagheera heard it.

"I said the Time of New Talk is near," growled the panther, switching his tail.

"I hear," Mowgli answered. "Bagheera, why dost thou shake all over? The sun is warm."

"That is Ferao, the scarlet woodpecker," said Bagheera. "*He* has not forgotten. Now I, too, must remember my song," and he began purring and crooning to himself, harking back dissatisfied again and again.

"There is no game afoot," said Mowgli.

"Little Brother, are *both* thine ears stopped? That is no killing-word, but my song that I make ready against the need."

"I had forgotten. I shall know when the Time of New Talk is here, because then thou and the others all run away and leave me alone." Mowgli spoke rather savagely.

"But, indeed, Little Brother," Bagheera began, "we do not always—"

"I say ye do," said Mowgli, shooting out his forefinger angrily. "Ye *do* run away, and I, who am the Master of the Jungle, must needs walk alone. How was it last season, when I would gather sugar-cane from the fields of a Man-Pack? I sent a runner—I sent thee!—to Hathi, bidding him to come upon such a night and pluck the sweet grass for me with his trunk."

"He came only two nights later," said Bagheera, cowering a little; "and of that long, sweet grass that pleased thee so he gathered more than any Man-cub could eat in all the nights of the Rains. That was no fault of mine."

"He did not come upon the night when I sent him the word. No, he was trumpeting and running and roaring through the valleys in the moonlight. His trail was like the trail of three elephants, for he would not hide among the trees. He danced in the moonlight before the houses of the

casting his winter coat: Like most cats and some other mammals, Bagheera "shed" some of his heavy winter hair with the coming of warmer weather. Birds also shed, or moult, and so do many reptiles and shellfish. Crayfish, for example, cast *their* horny coats eight times a year. This is one way shellfish grow, since the shell is not elastic, like skin.

Man-Pack. I saw him, and yet he would not come to me; and *I* am the Master of the Jungle!"

"It was the Time of New Talk," said the panther, always very humble. "Perhaps, Little Brother, thou didst not that time call him by a Master-word? Listen to Ferao, and be glad!"

Mowgli's bad temper seemed to have boiled itself away. He lay back with his head on his arms, his eyes shut. "I do not know—nor do I care," he said sleepily. "Let us sleep, Bagheera. My stomach is heavy in me. Make me a rest for my head."

The panther lay down again with a sigh, because he could hear Ferao practising and repractising his song against the Springtime of New Talk, as they say.

In an Indian Jungle the seasons slide one into the other almost without division. There seem to be only two—the wet and the dry; but if you look closely below the torrents of rain and the clouds of char and dust you will find all four going round in their regular ring. Spring is the most wonderful, because she has not to cover a clean, bare field with new leaves and flowers, but to drive before her and to put away the hanging-on, over-surviving raffle of half-green things which the gentle winter has suffered to live, and to make the partly dressed stale earth feel new and young once more. And this she does so well that there is no spring in the world like the Jungle spring.

There is one day when all things are tired, and the very smells, as they drift on the heavy air, are old and used. One cannot explain this, but it feels so. Then there is another day —to the eye nothing whatever has changed—when all the smells are new and delightful, and the whiskers of the Jungle People quiver to their roots, and the winter hair comes away from their sides in long, draggled locks. Then, perhaps, a little rain falls, and all the trees and the bushes and the bamboos and the mosses and the juicy-leaved plants wake with a noise of growing that you can almost hear, and under this noise runs, day and night, a deep hum. *That* is the noise of the spring—a vibrating boom which is neither bees, nor falling water, nor the wind in tree-tops, but the purring of the warm, happy world.

Up to this year Mowgli had always delighted in the turn of the seasons. It was he who generally saw the first Eye-of-the-Spring deep down among the grasses, and the first bank of spring clouds which are like nothing else in the Jungle. His voice could be heard in all sorts of wet, starlighted, blossoming places, helping the big frogs through their choruses, or mocking the little up-side-down owls that hoot through the white nights. Like all his people, spring was the season

raffle: This means rubbish or refuse. We don't find this word used very often with this meaning. More often we're talking about a drawing, or game of chance.

he chose for his flittings—moving, for the mere joy of rushing through the warm air, thirty, forty, or fifty miles between twilight and the morning star, and coming back panting and laughing and wreathed with strange flowers. The Four did not follow him on these wild ringings of the Jungle, but went off to sing songs with other wolves. The Jungle People are very busy in the spring, and Mowgli could hear them grunting and screaming and whistling according to their kind. Their voices then are different from their voices at other times of the year, and that is one of the reasons why spring in the Jungle is called the Time of New Talk.

But that spring, as he told Bagheera, his stomach was changed in him. Ever since the bamboo shoots turned spotty-brown he had been looking forward to the morning when the smells should change. But when the morning came, and Mor the Peacock, blazing in bronze and blue and gold, cried it aloud all along the misty woods, and Mowgli opened his mouth to send on the cry, the words choked between his teeth, and a feeling came over him that began at his toes and ended in his hair—a feeling of pure unhappiness, so that he looked himself over to be sure that he had not trod on a thorn. Mor cried the new smells, the other birds took it over, and from the rocks by the Waingunga he heard Bagheera's hoarse scream—something between the scream of an eagle and the neighing of a horse. There was a yelling and scattering of *bandar-log* in the new-budding branches above, and there stood Mowgli, his chest, filled to answer Mor, sinking in little gasps as the breath was driven out of it by this unhappiness.

He stared all round him, but he could see no more than the mocking *bandar-log* scudding through the trees, and Mor, his tail spread in full splendor, dancing on the slopes below.

"The smells have changed," screamed Mor. "Good hunting, Little Brother! Where is thy answer?"

"Little Brother, good hunting!" whistled Chil the Kite and his mate, swooping down together. The two baffed under Mowgli's nose so close that a pinch of downy white feathers brushed away.

A light spring rain—elephant-rain they call it—drove across the Jungle in a belt half a mile wide, left the new leaves wet and nodding behind, and died out in a double rainbow and a light roll of thunder. The spring hum broke out for a minute, and was silent, but all the Jungle Folk seemed to be giving tongue at once. All except Mowgli.

"I have eaten good food," he said to himself. "I have drunk good water. Nor does my throat burn and grow small, as it did when I bit the blue-spotted root that Oo the Turtle said was clean food. But my stomach is heavy, and I have

blue-spotted root: Foods that agree with the reptilian, cold-blooded turtle may not always agree with warm-blooded mammals. Whatever plant this was may well have been slightly poisonous to Mowgli, causing his throat to feel burning and tight.

141

tree cat: The *Chaus* is the common wildcat of India. It's about 26 inches long, and yellowish gray in color, with reddish black, slightly tufted ears. Another type of jungle cat is the handsome *Felis ornata*, a well-spotted resident of India's deserts.

haughty: Mowgli walked with an air of great dignity; his manner would be like that of a king walking among the lowliest commoners.

given very bad talk to Bagheera and others, people of the Jungle and my people. Now, too, I am hot and now I am cold, and now I am neither hot nor cold, but angry with that which I cannot see. Huhu! It is time to make a running! Tonight I will cross the ranges; yes, I will make a spring running to the marshes of the North, and back again. I have hunted too easily too long. The Four shall come with me, for they grow as fat as white grubs."

He called, but never one of the Four answered. They were far beyond earshot, singing over the spring songs—the Moon and Sambhur Songs—with the wolves of the Pack; for in the springtime the Jungle People make very little difference between the day and the night. He gave the sharp, barking note, but his only answer was the mocking *maiou* of the little spotted tree-cat winding in and out among the branches for early birds' nests. At this he shook all over with rage, and half drew his knife. Then he became very haughty, though there was no one to see him, and stalked severely down the hillside, chin up and eyebrows down. But never a single one of his people asked him a question, for they were all too busy with their own affairs.

"Yes," said Mowgli to himself, though in his heart he knew that he had no reason. "Let the Red Dhole come from the Dekkan, or the Red Flower dance among the bamboos, and all the Jungle runs whining to Mowgli, calling him great elephant-names. But now, because Eye-of-the-Spring is red, and Mor, forsooth, must show his naked legs in some spring dance, the Jungle goes mad as Tabaqui. . . . By the Bull that bought me! am I the Master of the Jungle, or am I not? Be silent! What do ye here?"

A couple of young wolves of the Pack were cantering down a path, looking for open ground in which to fight. (You will remember that the Law of the Jungle forbids fighting where the Pack can see.) Their neck-bristles were as stiff as wire, and they bayed furiously, crouching for the first grapple. Mowgli leaped forward, caught one outstretched throat in either hand, expecting to fling the creatures backward as he had often done in games or Pack hunts. But he had never before interfered with a spring fight. The two leaped forward and dashed him aside, and without word to waste rolled over and over close locked.

Mowgli was on his feet almost before he fell, his knife and his white teeth were bared, and at that minute he would have killed both for no reason but that they were fighting when he wished them to be quiet, although every wolf has full right under the Law to fight. He danced round them with lowered shoulders and quivering hand, ready to send in a double blow when the first flurry of the scuffle should be over; but while he waited the strength seemed to ebb from his body, the knife-point lowered, and he sheathed the knife and watched.

"I have surely eaten poison," he sighed at last. "Since I broke up the Council with the Red Flower—since I killed Shere Khan—none of the Pack could fling me aside. And these be only tail-wolves in the Pack, little hunters! My strength is gone from me, and presently I shall die. Oh, Mowgli, why dost thou not kill them both?"

The fight went on till one wolf ran away, and Mowgli was left alone on the torn and bloody ground, looking now at his knife, and now at his legs and arms, while the feeling of unhappiness he had never known before covered him as water covers a log.

He killed early that evening and ate but little, so as to be in good fettle for his spring running, and he ate alone because all the Jungle People were away singing or fighting. It was a perfect white night, as they call it. All green things seemed to have made a month's growth since the morning. The branch that was yellow-leaved the day before dripped sap when Mowgli broke it. The mosses curled deep and warm over his feet, the young grass had no cutting edges, and all the voices of the Jungle boomed like one deep harpstring touched by the moon—the Moon of New Talk, who splashed her light full on rock and pool, slipped it between trunk and creeper, and sifted it through a million leaves. Forgetting his unhappiness, Mowgli sang aloud with pure delight as he settled into his stride. It was more like flying than anything else, for he had chosen the long downward slope that leads to the Northern Marshes through the heart of the main Jungle, where the springy ground deadened the fall of his feet. A man-taught man would have picked his way with many stumbles through the cheating moonlight, but Mowgli's muscles, trained by years of experience, bore him up as though he were a feather. When a rotten log or a hidden stone turned under his foot he saved himself, never checking his pace, without effort and without thought. When he tired of ground-going he threw up his hands monkey-fashion to the nearest creeper, and seemed to float rather than to climb up into the thin branches, whence he would follow a treeroad till his mood changed, and he shot downward in a long, leafy curve to the levels again. There were still, hot hollows surrounded by wet rocks where he could hardly breathe for the heavy scents of the night flowers and the bloom along the creeper-buds; dark avenues where the moonlight lay in belts as regular as checkered marbles in a

fettle: Condition.

rotten log: These are among the most interesting objects in any jungle or forest. Inside might be a family of squirrels, wood-rabbits, foxes, raccoons, or other small animals. Many kinds of insects and their larvae find shelter there, along with millions of micro-organisms, too small to be seen by the human eye. Use your magnifying glass, microscope, and collecting bottle for your next ROTTEN LOG —and don't poke your arm into a hollow too fast; those cubs and their parents have sharp bites!

church aisle; thickets where the wet young growth stood breast-high about him and threw its arms round his waist; and hilltops crowned with broken rock, where he leaped from stone to stone above the lairs of the frightened little foxes. He would hear, very faint and far off, the *chugdrug* of a boar sharpening his tusks on a bole; and would come across the great gray brute all alone, scribing and rending the bark of a tall tree, his mouth dripping with foam, and his eyes blazing like fire. Or he would turn aside to the sound of clashing horns and hissing grunts, and dash past a couple of furious sambhur, staggering to and fro with lowered heads, striped with blood that showed black in the moonlight. Or at some rushing ford he would hear Jacala the Crocodile bellowing like a bull, or disturb a twined knot of the Poison People, but before they could strike he would be away and across the glistening shingle, deep in the Jungle again.

So he ran, sometimes shouting, sometimes singing to himself, the happiest thing in all the Jungle that night, till the smell of the flowers warned him that he was near the marshes, and those lay far beyond his furthest hunting-grounds.

Here, again, a man-trained man would have sunk over-head in three strides, but Mowgli's feet had eyes in them, and they passed him from tussock to tussock and clump to quaking clump without asking help from the eyes in his head. He ran out to the middle of the swamp, disturbing the duck as he ran, and sat down on a moss-coated tree-trunk lapped in the black water. The marsh was awake all round him, for in the spring the Bird-People sleep very lightly, and companies of them were coming or going the night through. But no one took any notice of Mowgli sitting among the tall reeds humming songs without words, and looking at the soles of his hard brown feet in case of neglected thorns. All his unhappiness seemed to have been left behind in his own jungle, and he was just beginning a full-throat song when it came back again—ten times worse than before.

This time Mowgli was frightened. "It is here also!" he said half aloud. "It has followed me," and he looked over his shoulder to see whether the It were not standing behind him. "There is no one here." The night noises of the marsh went on, but never a bird or beast spoke to him, and the new feeling of misery grew.

"I have surely eaten poison," he said in an awe-stricken voice. "It must be that carelessly I have eaten poison, and my strength is going from me. I was afraid—and yet it was not *I* that was afraid—Mowgli was afraid when the two wolves fought. Akela, or even Phao, would have silenced

marsh: Swampy ground, like every other kind, seems to attract its own special residents—including, in India, the up-to-18-foot crocodile (sporting 76 teeth), swamp rabbits and hares, and birds with "stilt-type" legs for wading. Frogs, mice, insects and crustaceans live there. Plant life, too, is very varied, depending considerably on the kind of water, its motion, temperature availability, and salinity (salt-iness).

them; yet Mowgli was afraid. That is true sign I have eaten poison. . . . But what do they care in the Jungle? They sing and howl and fight, and run in companies under the moon, and I—*Hai-mai!*—I am dying in the marshes, of that poison which I have eaten." He was so sorry for himself that he nearly wept. "And after," he went on, "they will find me lying in the black water. Nay, I will go back to my own Jungle, and I will die upon the Council Rock, and Bagheera, whom I love, if he is not screaming in the valley—Bagheera, perhaps, may watch by what is left for a little, lest Chil use me as he used Akela."

A large, warm tear splashed down on his knee, and, miserable as he was, Mowgli felt happy that he was so miserable, if you can understand that upside-down sort of happiness. "As Chil the Kite used Akela," he repeated, "on the night I saved the Pack from Red Dog." He was quiet for a little, thinking of the last words of the Lone Wolf, which you, of course, remember. "Now Akela said to me many foolish things before he died, for when we die our stomachs change. He said . . . None the less, I *am* of the Jungle!"

In his excitement, as he remembered the fight on Waingunga bank, he shouted the last words aloud, and a wild buffalo-cow among the reeds sprang to her knees, snorting, "Man!"

"Uhh!" said Mysa the Wild Buffalo (Mowgli could hear him turn in his wallow), "*that* is no man. It is only the hairless wolf of the Seeonee Pack. On such nights runs he to and fro."

"Uhh!" said the cow, dropping her head again to graze, "I thought it was Man."

"I say no. Oh, Mowgli, is it danger?" lowed Mysa.

"Oh, Mowgli, is it danger?" the boy called back mockingly. "That is all Mysa thinks for: Is it danger? But for Mowgli, who goes to and fro in the Jungle by night, watching, what do ye care?"

"How loud he cries!" said the cow.

"Thus do they cry," Mysa answered contemptuously, "who, having torn up the grass, know not how to eat it."

"For less than this," Mowgli groaned to himself—"for less than this even last Rains I had pricked Mysa out of his wallow, and ridden him through the swamp on a rush halter." He stretched a hand to break one of the feathery reeds, but drew it back with a sigh. Mysa went on steadily chewing the cud, and the long grass ripped where the cow grazed. "I will not die *here*," he said angrily. "Mysa, who is of one blood with Jacala and the pig, would see me. Let us go beyond the swamp, and see what comes. Never have I run such a spring

wild buffalo: The Indian species is the true buffalo; the American animal that shares that name is really a bison. The Indian buffalo is truly a mean-tempered, amazingly powerful, dangerous animal.

running—hot and cold together. Up, Mowgli!"

He could not resist the temptation of stealing across the reeds to Mysa and pricking him with the point of his knife. The great dripping bull broke out of his wallow like a shell exploding, while Mowgli laughed till he sat down.

"Say now that the hairless wolf of the Seeonee Pack once herded thee, Mysa," he called.

"Wolf! *Thou?*" the bull snorted, stamping in the mud. "All the Jungle knows thou wast a herder of tame cattle—such a man's brat as shouts in the dust by the crops yonder. *Thou* of the Jungle! What hunter would have crawled like a snake among the leeches, and for a muddy jest—a jackal's jest—have shamed me before my cow? Come to firm ground, and I will—I will . . ." Mysa frothed at the mouth, for Mysa has nearly the worst temper of any one in the Jungle.

Mowgli watched him puff and blow with eyes that never changed. When he could make himself heard through the spattering mud, he said: "What Man-Pack lair here by the marshes, Mysa? This is new jungle to me."

"Go north, then," roared the angry bull, for Mowgli had pricked him rather sharply. "It was a naked cowherd's jest. Go and tell them at the village at the foot of the marsh."

"The Man-Pack do not love jungle-tales, nor do I think, Mysa, that a scratch more or less on thy hide is any matter for a council. But I will go and look at this village. Yes, I will go. Softly now. It is not every night that the Master of the Jungle comes to herd thee."

He stepped out to the shivering ground on the edge of the marsh, well knowing that Mysa would never charge over it, and laughed, as he ran, to think of the bull's anger.

"My strength is not altogether gone," he said. "It may be that the poison is not to the bone. There is a star sitting low yonder." He looked at it between his half-shut hands. "By the Bull that bought me, it is the Red Flower—the Red Flower that I lay beside before—before I came even to the first Seeonee Pack! Now that I have seen, I will finish the running."

The marsh ended in a broad plain where a light twinkled. It was a long time since Mowgli had concerned himself with the doings of men, but this night the glimmer of the Red Flower drew him forward.

"I will look," said he, "as I did in the old days, and I will see how far the Man-Pack has changed."

Forgetting that he was no longer in his own jungle, where he could do what he pleased, he trod carelessly through the dew-loaded grasses till he came to the hut where the light stood. Three or four yelping dogs gave tongue, for he was on

poison not to the bone: Mowgli means something that makes one sick, but isn't really deadly.

the outskirts of a village.

"Ho!" said Mowgli, sitting down noiselessly, after sending back a deep wolf-growl that silenced the curs. "What comes will come. Mowgli, what hast thou to do any more with the lairs of the Man-Pack?" He rubbed his mouth, remembering where a stone had struck it years ago when the other Man-Pack had cast him out.

The door of the hut opened, and a woman stood peering out into the darkness. A child cried, and the woman said over her shoulder, "Sleep. It was but a jackal that waked the dogs. In a little time morning comes."

Mowgli in the grass began to shake as though he had fever. He knew that voice well, but to make sure he cried softly, surprised to find how man's talk came back, "Messua! O Messua!"

"Who calls?" said the woman, a quiver in her voice.

"Hast thou forgotten?" said Mowgli. His throat was dry as he spoke.

"If it be *thou*, what name did I give thee? Say!" She had half shut the door, and her hand was clutching at her breast.

"Nathoo! Ohé Nathoo!" said Mowgli, for, as you remember, that was the name Messua gave him when he first came to the Man-Pack.

"Come, my son," she called, and Mowgli stepped into the light, and looked full at Messua, the woman who had been good to him, and whose life he had saved from the Man-Pack so long before. She was older, and her hair was gray, but her eyes and her voice had not changed. Woman-like, she expected to find Mowgli where she had left him, and her eyes traveled upward in a puzzled way from his chest to his head, that touched the top of the door.

"My son," she stammered; and then, sinking to his feet: "But it is no longer my son. It is a Godling of the Woods! Ahai!"

As he stood in the red light of the oil-lamp, strong, tall, and beautiful, his long black hair sweeping over his shoulders, the knife swinging at his neck, and his head crowned with a wreath of white jasmine, he might easily have been mistaken for some wild god of a jungle legend. The child half asleep on a cot sprang up and shrieked aloud with terror. Messua turned to soothe him, while Mowgli stood still, looking in at the water-jars and the cooking-pots, the grain-bin, and all the other human belongings that he found himself remembering so well.

"What wilt thou eat or drink?" Messua murmured. "This is all thine. We owe our lives to thee. But art thou him I called Nathoo, or a Godling, indeed?"

The
Spring
Running

village: Before the British came (1793), each Indian village was a self-sufficient unit in itself. It only paid tax (usually 1/6 of the crops) and acknowledged the authority of some distant rajah. Cattle were tended by those whose ancestors had been cattle-tenders for unknown generations. The soil was tilled by the tillers, the cloth spun and woven by the hereditary spinners and weavers.

strong, tall, and beautiful: Mowgli was neither the first nor the last boy raised by animals. The founders of Rome were also raised by a wolf. And more recently, Edgar Rice Burroughs created the enormously popular Tarzan, who was raised with, and lived with, the great apes. Did Burroughs model his character on Mowgli? Possibly he was influenced to some degree, for the two are similar in many ways.

147

"I am Nathoo," said Mowgli, "I am very far from my own place. I saw this light, and came hither. I did not know thou wast here."

"After we came to Kanhiwara," Messua said timidly, "the English would have helped us against those villagers that sought to burn us. Rememberest thou?"

"Indeed, I have not forgotten."

"But when the English Law was made ready, we went to the village of those evil people, and it was no more to be found."

"That also I remember," said Mowgli, with a quiver of his nostril.

"My man, therefore, took service in the fields, and at last —for, indeed, he was a strong man—we held a little land here. It is not so rich as the old village, but we do not need much—we two."

"Where is he—the man that dug in the dirt when he was afraid on that night?"

"He is dead—a year."

"And he?" Mowgli pointed to the child.

"My son that was born two Rains ago. If thou art a Godling, give him the Favor of the Jungle, that he may be safe among thy—thy people, as we were safe on that night."

She lifted up the child, who, forgetting his fright, reached out to play with the knife that hung on Mowgli's chest, and Mowgli put the little fingers aside very carefully.

"And if thou art Nathoo whom the tigers carried away," Messua went on, choking, "he is then thy younger brother. Give him an elder brother's blessing."

"*Hai-mai!* What do I know of the thing called a blessing? I am neither a Godling nor his brother, and—O mother, mother, my heart is heavy in me." He shivered as he set down the child.

"Like enough," said Messua, bustling among the cooking-pots. "This comes of running about the marshes by night. Beyond question, the fever has soaked thee to the marrow." Mowgli smiled a little at the idea of anything in the Jungle hurting him. "I will make a fire, and thou shalt drink warm milk. Put away the jasmine wreath: the smell is heavy in so small a place."

Mowgli sat down, muttering, with his face in his hands. All manner of strange feelings that he had never felt before were running over him, exactly as though he had been poisoned, and he felt dizzy and a little sick. He drank the warm milk in long gulps, Messua patting him on the shoulder from time to time, not quite sure whether he were her son Nathoo of the long ago days, or some wonderful jungle being, but

cooking pots: The women of India are wonderful cooks. Each one mixes and grinds her own spices for curry. Try browning lamb or beef in a skillet, then simmering with curry powder in a small amount of water. Add vegetables during the last 20 minutes. Serve over rice, Indian fashion.

glad to feel that he was at least flesh and blood.

"Son," she said at last,—her eyes were full of pride,—"have any told thee that thou art beautiful beyond all men?"

"Hah?" said Mowgli, for naturally he had never heard anything of the kind. Messua laughed softly and happily. The look in his face was enough for her.

"I am the first, then? It is right, though it comes seldom, that a mother should tell her son these good things. Thou art very beautiful. Never have I looked upon such a man."

Mowgli twisted his head and tried to see over his own hard shoulder, and Messua laughed again so long that Mowgli, not knowing why, was forced to laugh with her, and the child ran from one to the other, laughing too.

"Nay, thou must not mock thy brother," said Messua, catching him to her breast. "When thou art one half as fair we will marry thee to the youngest daughter of a king and thou shalt ride great elephants."

Mowgli could not understand one word in three of the talk here; the warm milk was taking effect on him after his long run, so he curled up and in a minute was deep asleep, and Messua put the hair back from his eyes, threw a cloth over him, and was happy. Jungle-fashion, he slept out the rest of that night and all the next day; for his instincts, which never wholly slept, warned him there was nothing to fear. He waked at last with a bound that shook the hut, for the cloth over his face made him dream of traps; and there he stood, his hand on his knife, the sleep all heavy in his rolling eyes, ready for any fight.

Messua laughed, and set the evening meal before him. There were only a few coarse cakes baked over the smoky fire, some rice, and a lump of sour preserved tamarinds—just enough to go on with till he could get to his evening kill. The smell of the dew in the marshes made him hungry and restless. He wanted to finish his spring running, but the child insisted on sitting in his arms, and Messua would have it that his long, blue-black hair must be combed out. So she sang, as she combed, foolish little baby-songs, now calling Mowgli her son, and now begging him to give some of his jungle power to the child. The hut door was closed, but Mowgli heard a sound he knew well, and saw Messua's jaw drop with horror as a great gray paw came under the bottom of the door, and Gray Brother outside whined a muffled and penitent whine of anxiety and fear.

"Out and wait! Ye would not come when I called," said Mowgli in jungle-talk, without turning his head, and the great gray paw disappeared.

"Do not—do not bring thy—thy servants with thee," said

penitent: One who is PENITENT is sorry for something he has done; regretful; in a mood to ask forgiveness.

wood-god: Most Indians are Hindus; the second largest faith in India is Moslem, with about 100 million followers. Hinduism allows broad beliefs; farmers and peasants are inclined to believe in many minor gods, including those of plants, trees, stones and animals. So Messua's belief here would be quite natural.

Messua. "I—we have always lived at peace with the Jungle."

"It is peace," said Mowgli, rising. "Think of that night on the road to Kanhiwara. There were scores of such folk before thee and behind thee. But I see that even in springtime the Jungle People do not always forget. Mother, I go."

Messua drew aside humbly—he was indeed a wood-god, she thought; but as his hand was on the door the mother in her made her throw her arms round Mowgli's neck again and again.

"Come back!" she whispered. "Son or no son, come back, for I love thee—Look, he too grieves."

The child was crying because the man with the shiny knife was going away.

"Come back again," Messua repeated. "By night or by day this door is never shut to thee."

Mowgli's throat worked as though the cords in it were being pulled, and his voice seemed to be dragged from it as he answered, "I will surely come back."

"And now," he said, as he put by the head of the fawning wolf on the threshold, "I have a little cry against thee, Gray Brother. Why came ye not all four when I called so long ago?"

"So long ago? It was but last night. I—we—were singing in the Jungle the new songs, for this is the Time of New Talk. Rememberest thou?"

"Truly, truly."

"And as soon as the songs were sung," Gray Brother went on earnestly, "I followed thy trail. I ran from all the others and followed hot-foot. But, O Little Brother, what hast *thou* done, eating and sleeping with the Man-Pack?"

"If ye had come when I called, this had never been," said Mowgli, running much faster.

"And now what is to be?" said Gray Brother.

Mowgli was just going to answer when a girl in a white cloth came down some path that led from the outskirts of the village. Gray Brother dropped out of sight at once, and Mowgli backed noiselessly into a field of high-springing crops. He could almost have touched her with his hand when the warm, green stalks closed before his face and he disappeared like a ghost. The girl screamed, for she thought she had seen a spirit, and then she gave a deep sigh. Mowgli parted the stalks with his hands and watched her till she was out of sight.

"And now I do not know," he said, sighing in his turn. "*Why* did ye not come when I called?"

"We follow thee—we follow thee," Gray Brother mumbled, licking at Mowgli's heel. "We follow thee always, except in the Time of the New Talk."

"And would ye follow me to the Man-Pack?" Mowgli whispered.

"Did I not follow thee on the night our old Pack cast thee out? Who waked thee lying among the crops?"

"Ay, but again?"

"Have I not followed thee to-night?"

"Ay, but again and again, and it may be again, Gray Brother?"

Gray Brother was silent. When he spoke he growled to himself, "The Black One spoke truth."

"And he said?"

"Man goes to Man at the last. Raksha, our mother, said—"

"So also said Akela on the night of Red Dog," Mowgli muttered.

"So also says Kaa, who is wiser than us all."

"What dost thou say, Gray Brother?"

"They cast thee out once, with bad talk. They cut thy mouth with stones. They sent Buldeo to slay thee. They would have thrown thee into the Red Flower. Thou, and not I, hast said that they are evil and senseless. Thou, and not I— I follow my own people—didst let in the Jungle upon them. Thou, and not I, didst make song against them more bitter even than our song against Red Dog."

"I ask thee what *thou* sayest?"

They were talking as they ran. Gray Brother cantered on a while without replying, and then he said,—between bound and bound as it were,—"Man-cub—Master of the Jungle— Son of Raksha, Lair-brother to me—though I forget for a little while in the spring, thy trail is my trail, thy lair is my lair, thy kill is my kill, and thy death-fight is my death-fight. I speak for the Three. But what wilt thou say to the Jungle?"

"That is well thought. Between the sight and the kill it is not good to wait. Go before and cry them all to the Council Rock, and I will tell them what is in my stomach. But they may not come—in the Time of New Talk they may forget me."

"Hast thou, then, forgotten nothing?" snapped Gray Brother over his shoulder, as he laid himself down to gallop, and Mowgli followed, thinking.

At any other season the news would have called all the Jungle together with bristling necks, but now they were busy hunting and fighting and killing and singing. From one to another Gray Brother ran, crying, "The Master of the Jungle goes back to Man! Come to the Council Rock." And the happy, eager People only answered, "He will return in the summer heats. The Rains will drive him to lair. Run and sing

cold blooded Kaa: Serpents are not the only cold-blooded animals. All reptiles, including lizards, turtles, the horned toad, gila monster, alligator, iguana, chameleon and others, lack a blood-heating system, such as we have. Mammals have a kind of thermostat that regulates internal warmth, regardless of ordinary temperatures outside. The blood of reptiles gets warm or cool, depending on the sun or its absence. When the outside temperature isn't right for them, they burrow, or get into mud or water.

with us, Gray Brother."

"But the Master of the Jungle goes back to Man," Gray Brother would repeat.

"Eee—Yoawa? Is the Time of New Talk any less sweet for that?" they would reply. So when Mowgli, heavy-hearted, came up through the well-remembered rocks to the place where he had been brought into the Council, he found only the Four, Baloo, who was nearly blind with age, and the heavy, cold-blooded Kaa coiled around Akela's empty seat.

"Thy trail ends here, then, Manling?" said Kaa, as Mowgli threw himself down, his face in his hands. "Cry thy cry. We be of one blood, thou and I—man and snake together."

"Why did I not die under Red Dog?" the boy moaned. "My strength is gone from me, and it is not any poison. By night and by day I hear a double step upon my trail. When I turn my head it is as though one had hidden himself from me that instant. I go to look behind the trees, and he is not there. I call and none cry again; but it is as though one listened and kept back the answer. I lie down, but I do not rest. I run the spring running, but I am not made still. I bathe, but I am not made cool. The kill sickens me, but I have no heart to fight except I kill. The Red Flower is in my body, my bones are water—and—I know not what I know."

"What need of talk?" said Baloo slowly, turning his head to where Mowgli lay. "Akela by the river said it, that Mowgli should drive Mowgli back to the Man-Pack. I said it. But who listens now to Baloo? Bagheera—where is Bagheera this night?—he knows also. It is the Law."

"When we met at Cold Lairs, Manling, I knew it," said Kaa, turning a little in his mighty coils. "Man goes to Man at the last, though the Jungle does not cast him out."

The Four looked at one another and at Mowgli, puzzled but obedient.

"The Jungle does not cast me out, then?" Mowgli stammered.

Gray Brother and the Three growled furiously, beginning, "So long as we live none shall dare—" But Baloo checked them.

"I taught thee the Law. It is for me to speak," he said; "and, though I cannot now see the rocks before me, I see far. Little Frog, take thine own trail; make thy lair with thine own blood and pack and people; but when there is need of foot or tooth or eye, or a word carried swiftly by night, remember, Master of the Jungle, the Jungle is thine at call."

"The Middle Jungle is thine also," said Kaa. "I speak for no small people."

"*Hai-mai*, my brothers," cried Mowgli, throwing up his

arms with a sob. "I know not what I know! I would not go; but I am drawn by both feet. How shall I leave these nights?"

"Nay, look up, Little Brother," Baloo repeated. "There is no shame in this hunting. When the honey is eaten we leave the empty hive."

"Having cast the skin," said Kaa, "we may not creep into it afresh. It is the Law."

"Listen, dearest of all to me," said Baloo. "There is neither word nor will here to hold thee back. Look up! Who may question the Master of the Jungle? I saw thee playing among the white pebbles yonder when thou wast a little frog; and Bagheera, that bought thee for the price of a young bull newly killed, saw thee also. Of that Looking Over we two only remain; for Raksha, thy lair-mother, is dead with thy lair-father; the old Wolf Pack is long since dead; thou knowest whither Shere Khan went, and Akela died among the dholes, where, but for thy wisdom and strength, the second Seeonee Pack would also have died. There remains nothing but old bones. It is no longer the Man-cub that asks leave of his Pack, but the Master of the Jungle that changes his trail. Who shall question Man in his ways?"

"But Bagheera and the Bull that bought me," said Mowgli. "I would not—"

His words were cut short by a roar and a crash in the thicket below, and Bagheera, light, strong, and terrible as always, stood before him.

"*Therefore*," he said, stretching out a dripping right paw, "I did not come. It was a long hunt, but he lies dead in the bushes now—a bull in his second year—the Bull that frees thee, Little Brother. All debts are paid now. For the rest, my word is Baloo's word." He licked Mowgli's foot. "Remember, Bagheera loved thee," he cried and bounded away. At the foot of the hill he cried again long and loud, "Good hunting on a new trail, Master of the Jungle! Remember, Bagheera loved thee."

"Thou hast heard," said Baloo. "There is no more. Go now; but first come to me. O wise Little Frog, come to me!"

"It is hard to cast the skin," said Kaa as Mowgli sobbed and sobbed, with his head on the blind bear's side and his arms round his neck, while Baloo tried feebly to lick his feet.

"The stars are thin," said Gray Brother, snuffing at the dawn-wind. "Where shall we lair to-day? for, from now, we follow new trails."

And this is the last of the Mowgli stories.

This is the song that Mowgli heard behind him in the Jungle till he came to Messua's door again:

BALOO—

*F*OR the sake of him who showed
One wise Frog the Jungle-Road,
Keep the Law the Man-Pack make—
For thy blind old Baloo's sake!
Clean or tainted, hot or stale,
Hold it as it were the Trail,
Through the day and through the night,
Questing neither left nor right.
For the sake of him who loves
Thee beyond all else that moves,
When thy Pack would make thee pain,
Say: "Tabaqui sings again."
When thy Pack would work thee ill,
Say: "Shere Khan is yet to kill."
When the knife is drawn to slay,
Keep the Law and go thy way.
(Root and honey, palm and spathe,
Guard a cub from harm and scathe!)
Wood and Water, Wind and Tree,
Jungle-Favor go with thee!

KAA—

Anger is the egg of Fear—
Only lidless eyes are clear.
Cobra-poison none may leech;
Even so with Cobra-speech.
Open talk shall call to thee
Strength, whose mate is Courtesy.
Send no lunge beyond thy length;
Lend no rotten bough thy strength.
Gauge thy gape with buck or goat,
Lest thine eye should choke thy throat.
After gorging, wouldst thou sleep,
Look the den is hid and deep,
Lest a wrong, by thee forgot,
Draw thy killer to the spot.
East and West and North and South,
Wash thy hide and close thy mouth.
(Pit and rift and blue pool-brim,
Middle Jungle follow him!)
Wood and Water, Wind and Tree,
Jungle-Favor go with thee!

BAGHEERA—

In the cage my life began;
Well I know the worth of Man.
By the Broken Lock that freed—
Man-cub, 'ware the Man-cub's breed!
Scenting-dew or starlight pale,
Choose no tangled tree-cat trail.
Pack or council, hunt or den,
Cry no truce with Jackal-Men.
Feed them silence when they say:
"Come with us an easy way."
Feed them silence when they seek
Help of thine to hurt the weak.
Make no bandar's boast of skill;
Hold thy peace above the kill.
Let nor call nor song nor sign
Turn thee from thy hunting-line.
(Morning mist or twilight clear,
Serve him, Wardens of the Deer!)
Wood and Water, Wind and Tree,
Jungle-Favor go with thee!

THE THREE—

On the trail that thou must tread
To the thresholds of our dread,
Where the Flower blossoms red;
Through the nights when thou shalt lie
Prisoned from our Mother-sky,
Hearing us, thy loves, go by;
In the dawns, when thou shalt wake
To the toil thou canst not break,
Heartsick for the Jungle's sake:
Wood and Water, Wind and Tree,
Wisdom, Strength, and Courtesy,
Jungle-Favor go with thee!

Rikki-Tikki-Tavi

9

Rikki—
Tikki—
Tavi

At the hole where he went in
Red-Eye called to Wrinkle-Skin.
Hear what little Red-Eye saith:
"Nag, come up and dance with death!"

Eye to eye and head to head,
    (Keep the measure, Nag,)
This shall end when one is dead;
    (At thy pleasure, Nag.)
Turn for turn and twist for twist—
    (Run and hide thee, Nag.)
Hah! The hooded Death has missed!
    (Woe betide thee, Nag!)

THIS is the story of the great war that Rikki-tikki-tavi fought single-handed, through the bathrooms of the big bungalow in Segowlee cantonment. Darzee, the tailor-bird, helped him, and Chuchundra, the muskrat, who never comes out into the middle of the floor, but always creeps round by the wall, gave him advice; but Rikki-tikki did the real fighting.

He was a mongoose, rather like a little cat in his fur and his tail, but quite like a weasel in his head and his habits. His eyes and the end of his restless nose were pink; he could scratch himself anywhere he pleased, with any leg, front or back, that he chose to use; he could fluff up his tail till it looked like a bottle-brush, and his war-cry as he scuttled through the long grass, was: *"Rikk-tikk-tikki-tikki-tchk!"*

One day, a high summer flood washed him out of the burrow where he lived with his father and mother, and carried him, kicking and clucking, down a roadside ditch. He found a little wisp of grass floating there, and clung to it till he lost his senses. When he revived, he was lying in the hot sun on the middle of a garden path, very draggled indeed, and a small boy was saying: "Here's a dead mongoose. Let's have a funeral."

"No," said his mother; "let's take him in and dry him. Perhaps he isn't really dead."

They took him into the house, and a big man picked him up between his finger and thumb and said he was not dead but half choked; so they wrapped him in cotton-wool, and warmed him, and he opened his eyes and sneezed.

"Now," said the big man (he was an Englishman who had just moved into the bungalow); "don't frighten him, and we'll see what he'll do."

It is the hardest thing in the world to frighten a mongoose, because he is eaten up from nose to tail with curiosity. The motto of all the mongoose family is, "Run and find out"; and Rikki-tikki was a true mongoose. He looked at the cotton-wool, decided that it was not good to eat, ran all round the table, sat up and put his fur in order, scratched himself, and jumped on the small boy's shoulder.

"Don't be frightened, Teddy," said his father. "That's his way of making friends."

"Ouch! He's tickling under my chin," said Teddy.

Rikki-tikki looked down between the boy's collar and neck, snuffed his ear, and climbed down to the floor, where he sat rubbing his nose.

"Good gracious," said Teddy's mother, "and that's a wild creature! I suppose he's so tame because we've been kind to him."

"All mongooses are like that," said her husband. "If Teddy doesn't pick him up by the tail, or try to put him in a cage, he'll run in and out of the house all day long. Let's give him something to eat."

They gave him a little piece of raw meat. Rikki-tikki liked it immensely, and when it was finished he went out into the veranda and sat in the sunshine and fluffed up his fur to make it dry to the roots. Then he felt better.

"There are more things to find out about in this house," he said to himself, "than all my family could find out in all their lives. I shall certainly stay and find out."

He spent all that day roaming over the house. He nearly drowned himself in the bath-tubs, put his nose into the ink on the writing-table, and burned it on the end of the big

revived: When one REVIVES, he becomes conscious; comes back to his senses. Of course one need not be unconscious, but perhaps only very tired and hot. He might then drink some cold lemonade, or eat some ice cream, and say, "Now I feel revived." The word is from the Latin, and means "to live again."

veranda: A roofed porch on one side—or possibly more than one side—of a house. They are popular where, as in India, the weather is very warm. Many of our fine Southern mansions had verandas, where families could sit and enjoy the shade.

man's cigar, for he climbed up in the big man's lap to see how writing was done. At nightfall he ran into Teddy's nursery to watch how kerosene lamps were lighted, and when Teddy went to bed Rikki-tikki climbed up too; but he was a restless companion, because he had to get up and attend to every noise all through the night, and find out what made it. Teddy's mother and father came in, the last thing, to look at their boy, and Rikki-tikki was awake on the pillow. "I don't like that," said Teddy's mother; "he may bite the child." "He'll do no such thing," said the father. "Teddy's safer with that little beast than if he had a bloodhound to watch him. If a snake came into the nursery now—"

But Teddy's mother wouldn't think of anything so awful.

Early in the morning Rikki-tikki came to early breakfast in the veranda riding on Teddy's shoulder, and they gave him banana and some boiled egg; and he sat on all their laps one after the other, because every well-brought-up mongoose always hopes to be a house-mongoose some day and have rooms to run about in, and Rikki-tikki's mother (she used to live in the General's house at Segowlee) had carefully told Rikki what to do if ever he came across white men.

Then Rikki-tikki went out into the garden to see what was to be seen. It was a large garden, only half cultivated, with bushes as big as summer-houses of Marshal Niel roses, lime and orange trees, clumps of bamboos, and thickets of high grass. Rikki-tikki licked his lips. "This is a splendid hunting-ground," he said, and his tail grew bottle-brushy at the thought of it, and he scuttled up and down the garden, snuffing here and there till he heard very sorrowful voices in a thorn-bush.

It was Darzee, the tailor-bird, and his wife. They had made a beautiful nest by pulling two big leaves together and stitching them up the edges with fibers, and had filled the hollow with cotton and downy fluff. The nest swayed to and fro, as they sat on the rim and cried.

"What is the matter?" asked Rikki-tikki.

"We are very miserable," said Darzee. "One of our babies fell out of the nest yesterday and Nag ate him."

"H'm!" said Rikki-tikki, "that is very sad—but I am a stranger here. Who is Nag?"

Darzee and his wife only cowered down in the nest without answering, for from the thick grass at the foot of the bush there came a low hiss—a horrid cold sound that made Rikki-tikki jump back two clear feet. Then inch by inch out of the grass rose up the head and spread hood of Nag, the big black cobra, and he was five feet long from tongue to tail. When he had lifted one-third of himself clear of the ground, he stayed balancing to and fro exactly as a dandelion-tuft balances in the wind, and he looked at Rikki-tikki with the wicked snake's eyes that never change their expression, whatever the snake may be thinking of.

"Who is Nag?" he said. "*I* am Nag. The great god Brahm put his mark upon all our people when the first cobra spread his hood to keep the sun off Brahm as he slept. Look, and be afraid!"

He spread out his hood more than ever, and Rikki-tikki saw the spectacle-mark on the back of it that looks exactly like the eye part of a hook-and-eye fastening. He was afraid for the minute; but it is impossible for a mongoose to stay frightened for any length of time, and though Rikki-tikki had never met a live cobra before, his mother had fed him on dead ones, and he knew that all a grown mongoose's business in life was to fight and eat snakes. Nag knew that too, and at the bottom of his cold heart he was afraid.

"Well," said Rikki-tikki, and his tail began to fluff up again, "marks or no marks, do you think it is right for you to eat fledglings out of a nest?"

Nag was thinking to himself, and watching the least little movement in the grass behind Rikki-tikki. He knew that mongooses in the garden meant death sooner or later for him and his family; but he wanted to get Rikki-tikki off his guard. So he dropped his head a little, and put it on one side.

"Let us talk," he said. "You eat eggs. Why should not I eat birds?"

"Behind you! Look behind you!" sang Darzee.

fledglings: These are young birds, not old enough to leave the nest.

161

Rikki-tikki knew better than to waste time in staring. He jumped up in the air as high as he could go, and just under him whizzed by the head of Nagaina, Nag's wicked wife. She had crept up behind him as he was talking, to make an end of him; and he heard her savage hiss as the stroke missed. He came down almost across her back, and if he had been an old mongoose he would have known that then was the time to break her back with one bite; but he was afraid of the terrible lashing return-stroke of the cobra. He bit, indeed, but did not bite long enough, and he jumped clear of the whisking tail, leaving Nagaina torn and angry.

"Wicked, wicked Darzee!" said Nag, lashing up as high as he could reach toward the nest in the thorn-bush; but Darzee had built it out of reach of snakes, and it only swayed to and fro.

Rikki-tikki felt his eyes growing red and hot (when a mongoose's eyes grow red, he is angry), and he sat back on his tail and hind legs like a little kangaroo, and looked all around him, and chattered with rage. But Nag and Nagaina had disappeared into the grass. When a snake misses its stroke, it never says anything or gives any sign of what it means to do next. Rikki-tikki did not care to follow them, for he did not feel sure that he could manage two snakes at once. So he trotted off to the gravel path near the house, and sat down to think. It was a serious matter for him.

If you read the old books of natural history, you will find they say that when the mongoose fights the snake and happens to get bitten, he runs off and eats some herb that cures him. That is not true. The victory is only a matter of quickness of eye and quickness of foot,—snake's blow against

mongoose's jump,—and as no eye can follow the motion of a snake's head when it strikes, that makes things much more wonderful than any magic herb. Rikki-tikki knew he was a young mongoose, and it made him all the more pleased to think that he had managed to escape a blow from behind. It gave him confidence in himself, and when Teddy came running down the path, Rikki-tikki was ready to be petted.

But just as Teddy was stooping, something flinched a little in the dust, and a tiny voice said: "Be careful. I am death!" It was Karait, the dusty brown snakeling that lies for choice on the dusty earth; and his bite is as dangerous as the cobra's. But he is so small that nobody thinks of him, and so he does the more harm to people.

Rikki-tikki's eyes grew red again, and he danced up to Karait with the peculiar rocking, swaying motion that he had inherited from his family. It looks very funny, but it is so perfectly balanced a gait that you can fly off from it at any angle you please; and in dealing with snakes this is an advantage. If Rikki-tikki had only known, he was doing a much more dangerous thing than fighting Nag, for Karait is so small, and can turn so quickly, that unless Rikki bit him close to the back of the head, he would get the return-stroke in his eye or lip. But Rikki did not know: his eyes were all red, and he rocked back and forth, looking for a good place to hold. Karait struck out. Rikki jumped sideways and tried to run in, but the wicked little dusty gray head lashed within a fraction of his shoulder, and he had to jump over the body, and the head followed his heels close.

inherited: A person may inherit property such as houses or money from someone who has died. But we also speak of inheriting traits. You might inherit your mother's pretty red hair, or your father's square jaw, or even your grandparents' blue eyes. Here Rikki inherited his ancestors' special manner of fighting.

Teddy shouted to the house: "Oh, look here! Our mongoose is killing a snake"; and Rikki-tikki heard a scream from Teddy's mother. His father ran out with a stick, but by the time he came up, Karait had lunged out once too far, and Rikki-tikki had sprung, jumped on the snake's back, dropped his head far between his fore legs, bitten as high up the back as he could get hold, and rolled away. That bite paralyzed Karait, and Rikki-tikki was just going to eat him up from the tail, after the custom of his family at dinner, when he remembered that a full meal makes a slow mongoose, and if he wanted all his strength and quickness ready, he must keep himself thin.

He went away for a dust-bath under the castor-oil bushes, while Teddy's father beat the dead Karait. "What is the use of that?" thought Rikki-tikki. "I have settled it all"; and then Teddy's mother picked him up from the dust and hugged him, crying that he had saved Teddy from death, and Teddy's father said that he was a providence, and Teddy looked on with big scared eyes. Rikki-tikki was rather amused at all

providence: Teddy's father meant that Providence—or Heaven—had sent Rikki.

163

the fuss, which, of course, he did not understand. Teddy's mother might just as well have petted Teddy for playing in the dust. Rikki was thoroughly enjoying himself.

That night, at dinner, walking to and fro among the wine-glasses on the table, he could have stuffed himself three times over with nice things; but he remembered Nag and Nagaina, and though it was very pleasant to be patted and petted by Teddy's mother, and to sit on Teddy's shoulder, his eyes would get red from time to time, and he would go off into his long war-cry of *"Rikk-tikk-tikki-tikki-tchk!"*

Teddy carried him off to bed, and insisted on Rikki-tikki sleeping under his chin. Rikki-tikki was too well bred to bite or scratch, but as soon as Teddy was asleep he went off for his nightly walk round the house, and in the dark he ran up against Chuchundra, the muskrat, creeping round by the wall. Chuchundra is a broken-hearted little beast. He whimpers and cheeps all the night, trying to make up his mind to run into the middle of the room, but he never gets there.

"Don't kill me," said Chuchundra, almost weeping. "Rikki-tikki, don't kill me."

"Do you think a snake-killer kills muskrats?" said Rikki-tikki scornfully.

"Those who kill snakes get killed by snakes," said Chuchundra, more sorrowfully than ever. "And how am I to be sure that Nag won't mistake me for you some dark night?"

"There's not the least danger," said Rikki-tikki; "but Nag is in the garden, and I know you don't go there."

"My cousin Chua, the rat, told me—" said Chuchundra, and then he stopped.

"Told you what?"

"H'sh! Nag is everywhere, Rikki-tikki. You should have talked to Chua in the garden."

"I didn't—so you must tell me. Quick, Chuchundra, or I'll bite you!"

Chuchundra sat down and cried till the tears rolled off his whiskers. "I am a very poor man," he sobbed. "I never had spirit enough to run out into the middle of the room. H'sh! I mustn't tell you anything. Can't you *hear*, Rikki-tikki?"

Rikki-tikki listened. The house was as still as still, but he thought he could just catch the faintest *scratch-scratch* in the world,—a noise as faint as that of a wasp walking on a window-pane,—the dry scratch of a snake's scales on brick-work.

"That's Nag or Nagaina," he said to himself; "and he is crawling into the bath-room sluice. You're right, Chuchundra; I should have talked to Chua."

sluice: A man-made trough for carrying water, used for many purposes. Here the sluice carried off used bath-water. In gold-mining areas, sluices help miners separate gold from the debris and dirt.

He stole off to Teddy's bath-room, but there was nothing there, and then to Teddy's mother's bath-room. At the bottom of the smooth plaster wall there was a brick pulled out to make a sluice for the bath-water, and as Rikki-tikki stole in by the masonry curb where the bath is put, he heard Nag and Nagaina whispering together outside in the moonlight.

"When the house is emptied of people," said Nagaina to her husband, "*he* will have to go away, and then the garden will be our own again. Go in quietly, and remember that the big man who killed Karait is the first one to bite. Then come out and tell me, and we will hunt for Rikki-tikki together."

"But are you sure that there is anything to be gained by killing the people?" said Nag.

"Everything. When there were no people in the bungalow, did we have any mongoose in the garden? So long as the bungalow is empty, we are king and queen of the garden; and remember that as soon as our eggs in the melon-bed hatch (as they may to-morrow), our children will need room and quiet."

"I had not thought of that," said Nag. "I will go, but there is no need that we should hunt for Rikki-tikki afterward. I will kill the big man and his wife, and the child if I can, and come away quietly. Then the bungalow will be empty, and Rikki-tikki will go."

Rikki-tikki tingled all over with rage and hatred at this, and then Nag's head came through the sluice, and his five feet of cold body followed it. Angry as he was, Rikki-tikki was very frightened as he saw the size of the big cobra. Nag coiled himself up, raised his head, and looked into the bath-room in the dark, and Rikki could see his eyes glitter.

"Now, if I kill him here, Nagaina will know; and if I fight him on the open floor, the odds are in his favour. What am I to do?" said Rikki-tikki-tavi.

Nag waved to and fro, and then Rikki-tikki heard him drinking from the biggest water-jar that was used to fill the bath. "That is good," said the snake. "Now, when Karait was killed, the big man had a stick. He may have that stick still, but when he comes in to bathe in the morning he will not have a stick. I shall wait here till he comes. Nagaina—do you hear me?—I shall wait here in the cool till daytime."

There was no answer from outside, so Rikki-tikki knew Nagaina had gone away. Nag coiled himself down, coil by coil, round the bulge at the bottom of the water-jar, and Rikki-tikki stayed still as death. After an hour he began to move, muscle by muscle, toward the jar. Nag was asleep, and Rikki-tikki looked at his big back, wondering which would be the best place for a good hold. "If I don't break his back at the first jump," said Rikki, "he can still fight; and if he fights—O Rikki!" He looked at the thickness of the neck below the hood, but that was too much for him; and a bite near the tail would only make Nag savage.

"It must be the head," he said at last; "the head above the hood; and, when I am once there, I must not let go."

Then he jumped. The head was lying a little clear of the water-jar, under the curve of it; and, as his teeth met, Rikki braced his back against the bulge of the red earthenware to hold down the head. This gave him just one second's purchase, and he made the most of it. Then he was battered to and fro as a rat is shaken by a dog—to and fro on the floor, up and down, and round in great circles; but his eyes were red, and he held on as the body cartwhipped over the floor, upsetting the tin dipper and the soap-dish and the flesh-brush, and banged against the tin side of the bath. As he held he closed his jaws tighter and tighter, for he made sure he would be banged to death, and, for the honour of his family, he preferred to be found with his teeth locked. He was dizzy, aching, and felt shaken to pieces when something went off like a thunderclap just behind him; a hot wind knocked him senseless and red fire singed his fur. The big man had been wakened by the noise, and had fired both barrels of a shot-gun into Nag just behind the hood.

Rikki-tikki held on with his eyes shut, for now he was quite sure he was dead; but the head did not move, and the big man picked him up and said: "It's the mongoose again, Alice; the little chap has saved *our* lives now." Then Teddy's mother came in with a very white face, and saw what was left of Nag, and Rikki-tikki dragged himself to Teddy's bedroom and spent half the rest of the night shaking himself tenderly to find out whether he really was broken into forty pieces, as he fancied.

When morning came he was very stiff, but well pleased with his doings. "Now I have Nagaina to settle with, and she will be worse than five Nags, and there's no knowing when the eggs she spoke of will hatch. Goodness! I must go and see Darzee," he said.

Without waiting for breakfast, Rikki-tikki ran to the thorn-bush where Darzee was singing a song of triumph at the top of his voice. The news of Nag's death was all over the garden, for the sweeper had thrown the body on the rubbish-heap.

"Oh, you stupid tuft of feathers!" said Rikki-tikki, angrily. "Is this the time to sing?"

"Nag is dead—is dead—is dead!" sang Darzee. "The valiant Rikki-tikki caught him by the head and held fast. The big man brought the bang-stick and Nag fell in two pieces! He will never eat my babies again."

"All that's true enough; but where's Nagaina?" said Rikki-tikki, looking carefully round him.

"Nagaina came to the bath-room sluice and called for Nag," Darzee went on; "and Nag came out on the end of a stick—the sweeper picked him up on the end of a stick and threw him upon the rubbish-heap. Let us sing about the great, the red-eyed Rikki-tikki!" and Darzee filled his throat and sang.

"If I could get up to your nest, I'd roll all your babies out!" said Rikki-tikki. "You don't know when to do the right thing at the right time. You're safe enough in your nest there, but it's war for me down here. Stop singing a minute, Darzee."

"For the great, the beautiful Rikki-tikki's sake I will stop," said Darzee. "What is it, O Killer of the terrible Nag?"

"Where is Nagaina, for the third time?"

"On the rubbish-heap by the stables, mourning for Nag. Great is Rikki-tikki with the white teeth."

"Bother my white teeth! Have you ever heard where she keeps her eggs?"

"In the melon-bed, on the end nearest the wall, where the sun strikes nearly all day. She had them there weeks ago."

"And you never thought it worth while to tell me? The end nearest the wall, you said?"

"Rikki-tikki, you are not going to eat her eggs?"

"Not eat exactly; no. Darzee, if you have a grain of sense you will fly off to the stables and pretend that your wing is broken, and let Nagaina chase you away to this bush! I must get to the melon-bed, and if I went there now she'd see me."

Darzee was a feather-brained little fellow who could never hold more than one idea at a time in his head; and just because he knew that Nagaina's children were born in eggs like his own, he didn't think at first that it was fair to kill them. But his wife was a sensible bird, and she knew that cobra's eggs meant young cobras later on; so she flew off from the nest, and left Darzee to keep the babies warm, and continue his song about the death of Nag. Darzee was very like a man in some ways.

She fluttered in front of Nagaina by the rubbish-heap, and cried out, "Oh, my wing is broken! The boy in the house threw a stone at me and broke it." Then she fluttered more desperately than ever.

Nagaina lifted up her head and hissed, "You warned Rikki-tikki when I would have killed him. Indeed and truly, you've chosen a bad place to be lame in." And she moved toward Darzee's wife, slipping along over the dust.

"The boy broke it with a stone!" shrieked Darzee's wife.

"Well! It may be some consolation to you when you're dead to know that I shall settle accounts with the boy. My husband lies on the rubbish-heap this morning, but before night the boy in the house will lie very still. What is the use of running away? I am sure to catch you. Little fool, look at me!"

Darzee's wife knew better than to do *that*, for a bird who looks at a snake's eyes gets so frightened that she cannot move. Darzee's wife fluttered on, piping sorrowfully, and never leaving the ground, and Nagaina quickened her pace.

Rikki-tikki heard them going up the path from the stables, and he raced for the end of the melon-patch near the wall. There, in the warm litter about the melons, very cunningly hidden, he found twenty-five eggs, about the size of a bantam's eggs, but with whitish skin instead of shell.

"I was not a day too soon," he said; for he could see the baby cobras curled up inside the skin, and he knew that the minute they were hatched they could each kill a man or a mongoose. He bit off the tops of the eggs as fast as he could, taking care to crush the young cobras, and turned over the litter from time to time to see whether he had missed any. At last there were only three eggs left, and Rikki-tikki began to chuckle to himself, when he heard Darzee's wife screaming:

"Rikki-tikki, I led Nagaina toward the house, and she has gone into the veranda, and—oh, come quickly—she means killing!"

Rikki-tikki smashed two eggs, and tumbled backward down the melon-bed with the third egg in his mouth, and scuttled to the veranda as hard as he could put foot to the ground. Teddy and his mother and father were there at early breakfast; but Rikki-tikki saw that they were not eating anything. They sat stone-still, and their faces were white. Nagaina was coiled up on the matting by Teddy's chair, within easy striking distance of Teddy's bare leg, and she was swaying to and fro singing a song of triumph.

"Son of the big man that killed Nag," she hissed, "stay still. I am not ready yet. Wait a little. Keep very still, all you three. If you move I strike, and if you do not move I strike. Oh, foolish people, who killed my Nag!"

Teddy's eyes were fixed on his father, and all his father could do was to whisper, "Sit still, Teddy. You mustn't move. Teddy, keep still."

Then Rikki-tikki came up and cried: "Turn round, Nagaina; turn and fight!"

"All in good time," said she, without moving her eyes. "I will settle my account with *you* presently. Look at your friends, Rikki-tikki. They are still and white; they are afraid. They dare not move, and if you come a step nearer I strike."

"Look at your eggs," said Rikki-tikki, "in the melon-bed near the wall. Go and look, Nagaina."

The big snake turned half round, and saw the egg on the veranda. "Ah-h! Give it to me," she said.

Rikki-tikki put his paws one on each side of the egg, and

his eyes were blood-red. "What price for a snake's egg? For a young cobra? For a young king-cobra? For the last—the very last of the brood? The ants are eating all the others down by the melon-bed."

Nagaina spun clear round, forgetting everything for the sake of the one egg; and Rikki-tikki saw Teddy's father shoot out a big hand, catch Teddy by the shoulder and drag him across the little table with the tea-cups, safe and out of reach of Nagaina.

"Tricked! Tricked! Tricked! *Rikk-tck-tck!*" chuckled Rikki-tikki. "The boy is safe, and it was I—I—I that caught Nag by the hood last night in the bath-room." Then he began to jump up and down, all four feet together, his head close to the floor. "He threw me to and fro, but he could not shake me off. He was dead before the big man blew him in two. I did it. *Rikki-tikki-tck-tck!* Come then, Nagaina. Come and fight with me. You shall not be a widow long."

Nagaina saw that she had lost her chance of killing Teddy, and the egg lay between Rikki-tikki's paws. "Give me the egg, Rikki-tikki. Give me the last of my eggs, and I will go away and never come back," she said, lowering her hood.

"Yes, you will go away, and you will never come back; for you will go to the rubbish-heap with Nag. Fight, widow! The big man has gone for his gun! Fight!"

Rikki-tikki was bounding all round Nagaina, keeping just out of the reach of her stroke, his little eyes like hot coals. Nagaina gathered herself together, and flung out at him. Rikki-tikki jumped up and backward. Again and again and again she struck, and each time her head came with a whack on the matting of the veranda and she gathered herself together like a watch-spring. Then Rikki-tikki danced in a circle to get behind her, and Nagaina spun round to keep her head to his head, so that the rustle of her tail on the matting sounded like dry leaves blown along by the wind.

He had forgotten the egg. It still lay on the veranda, and Nagaina came nearer and nearer to it, till at last, while Rikki-tikki was drawing breath, she caught it in her mouth, turned to the veranda steps, and flew like an arrow down the path, with Rikki-tikki behind her. When the cobra runs for her life, she goes like a whiplash flicked across a horse's neck.

Rikki-tikki knew that he must catch her, or all the trouble would begin again. She headed straight for the long grass by the thorn-bush, and as he was running Rikki-tikki heard Darzee still singing his foolish little song of triumph. But Darzee's wife was wiser. She flew off her nest as Nagaina came along, and flapped her wings about Nagaina's head. If Darzee had helped they might have turned her; but Nagaina only lowered her hood and went on. Still, the instant's delay brought Rikki-tikki up to her, and as she plunged into the rat-hole where she and Nag used to live, his little white teeth were clenched on her tail, and he went down with her — and very few mongooses, however wise and old they may be, care to follow a cobra into its hole. It was dark in the hole; and Rikki-tikki never knew when it might open out and give Nagaina room to turn and strike at him. He held on savagely, and struck out his feet to act as brakes on the dark slope of the hot, moist earth.

Then the grass by the mouth of the hole stopped waving, and Darzee said: "It is all over with Rikki-tikki! We must sing his death-song. Valiant Rikki-tikki is dead! For Nagaina will surely kill him underground."

So he sang a very mournful song that he made up all on the spur of the minute, and just as he got to the most touching part the grass quivered again, and Rikki-tikki, covered with dirt, dragged himself out of the hole leg by leg, licking his whiskers. Darzee stopped with a little shout. Rikki-tikki shook some of the dust out of his fur and sneezed. "It is all over," he said. "The widow will never come out again." And the red ants that live between the grass stems heard him, and began to troop down one after another to see if he had spoken the truth.

Rikki-tikki curled himself up in the grass and slept where he was—slept and slept till it was late in the afternoon, for he had done a hard day's work.

"Now," he said, when he awoke, "I will go back to the house. Tell the Coppersmith, Darzee, and he will tell the garden that Nagaina is dead."

The Coppersmith is a bird who makes a noise exactly like the beating of a little hammer on a copper pot; and the reason he is always making it is because he is the town-crier to every Indian garden, and tells all the news to everybody who cares to listen. As Rikki-tikki went up the path, he heard his "attention" notes like a tiny dinner-gong; and then the steady *"Ding-dong-tock!* Nag is dead—*dong!* Nagaina is dead! *Ding-dong-tock!"* That set all the birds in the garden singing, and the frogs croaking; for Nag and Nagaina used to eat frogs as well as little birds.

When Rikki got to the house, Teddy and Teddy's mother (she looked very white still, for she had been fainting) and Teddy's father came out and almost cried over him; and that night he ate all that was given him till he could eat no more, and went to bed on Teddy's shoulder, where Teddy's mother saw him when she came to look late at night.

"He saved our lives and Teddy's life," she said to her

husband. "Just think, he saved all our lives."

Rikki-tikki woke up with a jump, for all the mongooses are light sleepers.

"Oh, it's you," said he. "What are you bothering for? All the cobras are dead; and if they weren't I'm here."

Rikki-tikki had a right to be proud of himself; but he did not grow too proud, and he kept that garden as a mongoose should keep it, with tooth and jump and spring and bite, till never a cobra dared show its head inside the walls.

DARZEE'S CHAUNT

(SUNG IN HONOUR OF RIKKI-TIKKI-TAVI)

Singer and tailor am I—
    Doubled the joys that I know—
Proud of my lilt through the sky,
    Proud of the house that I sew—
Over and under, so weave I my music—so weave I the house that
    I sew.

Sing to your fledglings again,
    Mother, oh lift up your head!
Evil that plagued us is slain,
    Death in the garden lies dead.
Terror that hid in the roses is impotent—flung on the dung-hill and
dead!
    Who hath delivered us, who?
        Tell me his nest and his name.
Rikki, the valiant, the true,
    Tikki, with eyeballs of flame.
Rikki-tikki-tikki, the ivory-fanged, the hunter with eyeballs of flame.

Give him the Thanks of the Birds,
    Bowing with tail-feathers spread!
Praise him with nightingale words—
    Nay, I will praise him instead.
Hear! I will sing you the praise of the bottle-tailed Rikki, with
    eyeballs of red!

(Here Rikki-tikki interrupted, and the rest of the song is lost.)

Toomai of the Elephants

10

Toomai
Of The
Elephants

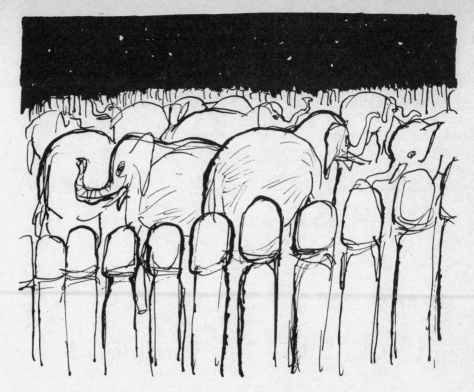

I will remember what I was, I am sick of rope and chain—
    I will remember my old strength and all my forest affairs.
I will not sell my back to man for a bundle of sugar-cane,
    I will go out to my own kind, and the wood-folk in their lairs.

I will go out until the day, until the morning break,
    Out to the winds' untainted kiss, the waters' clean caress:
I will forget my ankle-ring and snap my picket-stake.
    I will revisit my lost loves, and playmates masterless!

ELEPHANTS have lived for 100 years in captivity. Some scientists believe that wild elephants live even longer.

milk tusks: Tusks are specially long teeth, often weighing 150 or 200 pounds each. Elephants lose their baby tusks and grow a second set, just like humans lose their baby teeth.

KALA Nag, which means Black Snake, had served the Indian Government in every way that an elephant could serve it for forty-seven years, and as he was fully twenty years old when he was caught, that makes him nearly seventy—a ripe age for an elephant. He remembered pushing, with a big leather pad on his forehead, at a gun stuck in deep mud, and that was before the Afghan war of 1842, and he had not then come to his full strength. His mother, Radha Pyari,—Radha the darling,—who had been caught in the same drive with Kala Nag, told him before his little milk tusks had dropped out, that elephants who were afraid always got hurt; and Kala Nag knew that that advice was good, for the first time that he saw a shell burst he backed, screaming, into a stand of piled rifles, and the bayonets pricked him in all his softest places. So, before he was twenty-five, he gave up being afraid, and so he was the best-loved and the best-looked-after elephant in the service of the Government of India. He had carried tents, twelve hundred pounds' weight of tents, on the march in Upper India: he had been hoisted into a ship at the end of a steam-crane and taken for days across the water, and made to carry a mortar on his back in a strange and rocky country very far from India, and had seen the Emperor Theodore lying dead in Magdala, and had come back again in the steamer entitled, so the soldiers said, to the Abyssinian war medal. He had seen his fellow-elephants die of cold and epilepsy and starvation and sunstroke up at a place called Ali Musjid, ten years later; and afterward he had been sent down thousands of miles south to haul and pile big balks of teak in the timber-yards at Moulmein. There he had half killed an insubordinate young elephant who was shirking his fair share of the work.

After that he was taken off timber-hauling, and employed, with a few score other elephants who were trained to the business, in helping to catch wild elephants among the Garo hills. Elephants are very strictly preserved by the Indian Government. There is one whole department which does nothing else but hunt them, and catch them, and break them in, and send them up and down the country as they are needed for work.

Kala Nag stood ten fair feet at the shoulders, and his tusks had been cut off short at five feet, and bound round the ends, to prevent them splitting, with bands of copper; but he could do more with those stumps than any untrained elephant could do with the real sharpened ones.

When, after weeks and weeks of cautious driving of scattered elephants across the hills, the forty or fifty wild monsters were driven into the last stockade, and the big drop-gate, made of tree-trunks lashed together, jarred down behind them, Kala Nag, at the word of command, would go into that flaring, trumpeting pandemonium (generally at night, when the flicker of the torches made it difficult to judge distances), and, picking out the biggest and wildest tusker of the mob, would hammer him and hustle him into quiet while the men on the backs of the other elephants roped and tied the smaller ones.

There was nothing in the way of fighting that Kala Nag, the old wise Black Snake, did not know, for he had stood up more than once in his time to the charge of the wounded tiger, and, curling up his soft trunk to be out of harm's way, had knocked the springing brute sideways in mid-air with a quick sickle-cut of his head, that he had invented all by himself; had knocked him over, and kneeled upon him with his huge knees till the life went out with a gasp and a howl,

There are two main types of elephants, the African and the Indian. African elephants are not suited to life in captivity and are never used as beasts of burden. The Indian when tamed, is smart, strong, and friendly. You can tell him from the African elephant by his small ears. The Indian elephant's high point is the middle of its back; the African's is at its shoulders.

Indian Elephant

and there was only a fluffy striped thing on the ground for Kala Nag to pull by the tail.

"Yes," said Big Toomai, his driver, the son of Black Toomai who had taken him to Abyssinia, and grandson of Toomai of the Elephants who had seen him caught, "there is nothing that the Black Snake fears except me. He has seen three generations of us feed him and groom him, and he will live to see four."

"He is afraid of *me* also," said Little Toomai, standing up to his full height of four feet, with only one rag upon him. He was ten years old, the eldest son of Big Toomai, and, according to custom, he would take his father's place on Kala Nag's neck when he grew up, and would handle the heavy iron *ankus*, the elephant-goad that had been worn smooth by his father, and his grandfather, and his great-grandfather. He knew what he was talking of; for he had been born under Kala Nag's shadow, had played with the end of his trunk before he could walk, had taken him down to water as soon as he could walk, and Kala Nag would no more have dreamed of disobeying his shrill little orders than he would have dreamed of killing him on that day when Big Toomai carried the little brown baby under Kala Nag's tusks, and told him to salute his master that was to be.

"Yes," said Little Toomai, "he is afraid of *me*," and he took long strides up to Kala Nag, called him a fat old pig, and made him lift up his feet one after the other.

mahouts: Elephant drivers. They sit on the elephant's neck.

"Wah!" said Little Toomai, "thou art a big elephant," and he wagged his fluffy head, quoting his father. "The Government may pay for elephants, but they belong to us mahouts. When thou art old, Kala Nag, there will come some rich Rajah, and he will buy thee from the Government, on account of thy size and thy manners, and then thou wilt have nothing to do but to carry gold earrings in thy ears, and a gold howdah on thy back and a red cloth covered with gold on thy sides, and walk at the head of the processions of the King. Then I shall sit on thy neck, O Kala Nag, with a silver *ankus*, and men will run before us with golden sticks, crying, 'Room for the King's elephant!' That will be good, Kala Nag, but not so good as this hunting in the jungles."

"Umph!" said Big Toomai. "Thou art a boy and as wild as a buffalo-calf. This running up and down among the hills is not the best Government service. I am getting old, and I do not love wild elephants. Give me brick elephant-lines, one stall to each elephant, and big stumps to tie them to safely, and flat, broad roads to exercise upon instead of this come-and-go camping. Aha, the Cawnpore barracks were good.

There was a bazaar close by and only three hours' work a day."

Little Toomai remembered the Cawnpore elephant-lines and said nothing. He very much preferred the camp life, and hated those broad, flat roads, with the daily grubbing for grass in the forage-reserve, and the long hours when there was nothing to do except to watch Kala Nag fidgeting in his pickets.

What Little Toomai liked was to scramble up bridle-paths that only an elephant could take; the dip into the valley below; the glimpses of the wild elephants browsing miles away; the rush of the frightened pig and peacock under Kala Nag's feet; the blinding warm rains, when all the hills and valleys smoked; the beautiful misty mornings when nobody knew where they could camp that night; the steady, cautious drive of the wild elephants, and the mad rush and blaze and hullaballoo of the last night's drive when the elephants poured into the stockade like boulders in a landslide, found that they could not get out, and flung themselves at the heavy posts only to be driven back by yells and flaring torches and volleys of blank cartridge.

Even a little boy could be of use there, and Toomai was as useful as three boys. He would get his torch and wave it, and yell with the best. But the really good time came when the driving out began, and the Keddah, that is, the stockade, looked like a picture of the end of the world, and men had to make signs to one another, because they could not hear themselves speak. Then Little Toomai would climb up to the top of one of the quivering stockade-posts, his sun-bleached brown hair flying loose all over his shoulders, and he looking like a goblin in the torch-light; and as soon as there was a lull you could hear his high-pitched yells of encouragement to Kala Nag, above the trumpeting and crashing, and snapping of ropes, and groans of the tethered elephants. "*Maîl, maîl, Kala Nag!* (Go on, go on, Black Snake!) *Dant do!* (Give him the tusk!) *Somalo! Somalo!* (Careful, careful!) *Maro! Mar!* (Hit him, hit him!) Mind the post! *Arre! Arre! Hai! Yai! Kya-a-ah!*" he would shout, and the big fight between Kala Nag and the wild elephant would sway to and fro across the Keddah, and the old elephant-catchers would wipe the sweat out of their eyes, and find time to nod to Little Toomai wriggling with joy on the top of the posts.

He did more than wriggle. One night he slid down from the post and slipped in between the elephants, and threw up the loose end of a rope, which had dropped, to a driver who was trying to get a purchase on the leg of a kicking

blank cartridge: A cartridge is made of a charge of powder and a metal bullet held together with a brass casing. When the powder explodes, the bullet is forced out at great speed. BLANK CARTRIDGES don't have this bullet. The powder explodes with a bang, but without a bullet there is nothing to strike a target.

young calf (calves always give more trouble than full-grown animals). Kala Nag saw him, caught him in his trunk, and handed him up to Big Toomai, who slapped him then and there, and put him back on the post.

Next morning he gave him a scolding, and said: "Are not good brick elephant-lines and a little tent-carrying enough, that thou must needs go elephant-catching on thy own account, little worthless? Now those foolish hunters, whose pay is less than my pay, have spoken to Petersen Sahib of the matter." Little Toomai was frightened. He did not know much of white men, but Petersen Sahib was the greatest white man in the world to him. He was the head of all the Keddah operations—the man who caught all the elephants for the Government of India, and who knew more about the ways of elephants than any living man.

"What—what will happen?" said Little Toomai.

"Happen! the worst that can happen. Petersen Sahib is a madman. Else why should he go hunting these wild devils? He may even require thee to be an elephant-catcher, to sleep anywhere in these fever-filled jungles, and at last to be trampled to death in the Keddah. It is well that this nonsense ends safely. Next week the catching is over, and we of the plains are sent back to our stations. Then we will march on smooth roads, and forget all this hunting. But son, I am angry that thou shouldst meddle in the business that belongs to these dirty Assamese jungle-folk. Kala Nag will obey none but me, so I must go with him into the Keddah, but he is only a fighting elephant, and he does not help to rope them. So I sit at my ease, as befits a mahout,—not a mere hunter,—a mahout, I say, and a man who gets a pension at the end of his service. Is the family of Toomai of the Elephants to be trodden underfoot in the dirt of a Keddah? Bad one! Wicked one! Worthless son! Go and wash Kala Nag and attend to his ears, and see that there are no thorns in his feet; or else Petersen Sahib will surely catch thee and make thee a wild hunter—a follower of elephant's foot-tracks, a jungle-bear. Bah! Shame! Go!"

Little Toomai went off without saying a word, but he told Kala Nag all his grievances while he was examining his feet. "No matter," said Little Toomai, turning up the fringe of Kala Nag's huge right ear. "They have said my name to Petersen Sahib, and perhaps—and perhaps—and perhaps—who knows? Hai! That is a big thorn that I have pulled out!"

The next few days were spent in getting the elephants together, in walking the newly caught wild elephants up and down between a couple of tame ones, to prevent them from

Assamese: Assam is the north-easternmost province of India. It's on the Burmese border, near the Himalayas.

giving too much trouble on the downward march to the plains, and in taking stock of the blankets and ropes and things that had been worn out or lost in the forest.

Petersen Sahib came in on his clever she-elephant Pudmini; he had been paying off other camps among the hills, for the season was coming to an end, and there was a native clerk sitting at a table under a tree, to pay the drivers their wages. As each man was paid he went back to his elephant, and joined the line that stood ready to start. The catchers, and hunters, and beaters, the men of the regular Keddah, who stayed in the jungle year in and year out, sat on the backs of the elephants that belonged to Petersen Sahib's permanent force, or leaned against the trees with their guns across their arms, and made fun of the drivers who were going away, and laughed when the newly caught elephants broke the line and ran about.

Big Toomai went up to the clerk with Little Toomai behind him, and Machua Appa, the head-tracker, said in an undertone to a friend of his, "There goes one piece of good elephant-stuff at least. 'Tis a pity to send that young jungle-cock to moult in the plains."

Now Petersen Sahib had ears all over him, as a man must have who listens to the most silent of all living things — the wild elephant. He turned where he was lying all along on Pudmini's back, and said, "What is that? I did not know of a man among the plain-drivers who had wit enough to rope even a dead elephant."

"This is not a man, but a boy. He went into the Keddah at the last drive, and threw Barmao there the rope, when we were trying to get that young calf with the blotch on his shoulder away from his mother."

Machua Appa pointed at Little Toomai, and Petersen Sahib looked, and little Toomai bowed to the earth.

"He throw a rope? He is smaller than a picket-pin. Little one, what is thy name?" said Petersen Sahib.

Little Toomai was too frightened to speak, but Kala Nag was behind him, and Toomai made a sign with his hand, and the elephant caught him up in his trunk and held him level with Pudmini's forehead, in front of the great Petersen Sahib. Then Little Toomai covered his face with his hands, for he was only a child, and except where elephants were concerned, he was just as bashful as a child could be.

"Oho!" said Petersen Sahib, smiling underneath his mustache, "and why didst thou teach thy elephant *that* trick? Was it to help thee steal green corn from the roofs of the houses when the ears are put out to dry?"

181

"Not green corn, Protector of the Poor,—melons," said Little Toomai, and all the men sitting about broke into a roar of laughter. Most of them had taught their elephants that trick when they were boys. Little Toomai was hanging eight feet up in the air, and he wished very much that he were eight feet underground.

"He is Toomai, my son, Sahib," said Big Toomai, scowling. "He is a very bad boy, and he will end in a jail, Sahib."

"Of that I have my doubts," said Petersen Sahib. "A boy who can face a full Keddah at his age does not end in jails. See, little one, here are four annas to spend in sweetmeats because thou hast a little head under that great thatch of hair. In time thou mayest become a hunter too." Big Toomai scowled more than ever. "Remember, though, that Keddahs are not good for children to play in," Petersen Sahib went on.

"Must I never go there, Sahib?" asked Little Toomai, with a big gasp.

"Yes." Petersen Sahib smiled again. "When thou hast seen the elephants dance. That is the proper time. Come to me when thou hast seen the elephants dance, and then I will let thee go into all the Keddahs."

There was another roar of laughter, for that is an old joke among elephant-catchers, and it means just never. There are great cleared flat places hidden away in the forests that are called elephants' ballrooms, but even these are found only by accident, and no man has ever seen the elephants dance. When a driver boasts of his skill and bravery the other drivers say, "And when didst *thou* see the elephants dance?"

Kala Nag put Little Toomai down, and he bowed to the earth again and went away with his father, and gave the silver four-anna piece to his mother, who was nursing his baby-brother, and they all were put up on Kala Nag's back, and the line of grunting, squealing elephants rolled down the hill-path to the plains. It was a very lively march on account of the new elephants, who gave trouble at every ford, and who needed coaxing or beating every other minute.

Big Toomai prodded Kala Nag spitefully, for he was very angry, but Little Toomai was too happy to speak. Petersen Sahib had noticed him, and given him money, so he felt as a private soldier would feel if he had been called out of the ranks and praised by his commander-in-chief.

"What did Petersen Sahib mean by the elephant-dance?" he said, at last, softly to his mother.

Big Toomai heard him and grunted. "That thou shouldst never be one of these hill-buffaloes of trackers. *That* was what he meant. Oh you in front, what is blocking the way?"

An Assamese driver, two or three elephants ahead, turned around angrily, crying: "Bring up Kala Nag, and knock this youngster of mine into good behaviour. Why should Petersen Sahib have chosen *me* to go down with you donkeys of the rice-fields? Lay your beast alongside, Toomai, and let him prod with his tusks. By all the Gods of the Hills, these new elephants are possessed, or else they can smell their companions in the jungle."

Kala Nag hit the new elephant in the ribs and knocked the wind out of him, as Big Toomai said, "We have swept the hills of wild elephants at the last catch. It is only your carelessness in driving. Must I keep order along the whole line?"

"Hear him!" said the other driver. "*We* have swept the hills! Ho! ho! You are very wise, you plains-people. Any one but a mudhead who never saw the jungle would know that *they* know that the drives are ended for the season. Therefore all the wild elephants to-night will—but why should I waste wisdom on a river-turtle?"

"What will they do?" Little Toomai called out.

"*Ohé*, little one. Art thou there? Well, I will tell thee, for thou hast a cool head. They will dance, and it behooves thy father, who has swept *all* the hills of *all* the elephants, to double-chain his pickets to-night."

"What talk is this?" said Big Toomai. "For forty years, father and son, we have tended elephants, and we have never heard such moonshine about dances."

"Yes; but a plains-man who lives in a hut knows only the four walls of his hut. Well, leave thy elephants unshackled to-night and see what comes; as for their dancing, I have seen the place where—*Bapree-Bap!* how many windings has the Dihang River? Here is another ford, and we must swim the calves. Stop still, you behind there."

And in this way, talking and wrangling and splashing through the rivers, they made their first march to a sort of receiving-camp for the new elephants; but they lost their tempers long before they got there.

Then the elephants were chained by their hind legs to their big stumps of pickets, and extra ropes were fitted to the new elephants, and the fodder was piled before them, and the hill-drivers went back to Petersen Sahib through the afternoon light, telling the plains-drivers to be extra careful that night, and laughing when the plains-drivers asked the reason.

Little Toomai attended to Kala Nag's supper, and as evening fell, wandered through the camp, unspeakably happy, in search of a tom-tom. When an Indian child's heart is full, he does not run about and make a noise in an irregular fashion. He sits down to a sort of revel all by himself. And Little Toomai had been spoken to by Petersen Sahib! If he had not found what he wanted I believe he would have burst. But the sweetmeat-seller in the camp lent him a little tom-tom—a drum beaten with the flat of the hand—and he sat down, cross-legged, before Kala Nag as the stars began to come out, the tom-tom in his lap, and he thumped and he thumped and he thumped, and the more he thought of the great honour that had been done to him, the more he thumped, all alone among the elephant-fodder. There was no tune and no words, but the thumping made him happy.

The new elephants strained at their ropes, and squealed and trumpeted from time to time, and he could hear his mother in the camp hut putting his small brother to sleep with an old, old song about the great God Shiv, who once told all the animals what they should eat. It is a very soothing lullaby, and the first verse says:

> *Shiv, who poured the harvest and made the winds to blow,*
> *Sitting at the doorways of a day of long ago,*
> *Gave to each his portion, food and toil and fate,*
> *From the King upon the guddee to the Beggar at the gate.*
> *All things made he—Shiva the Preserver.*
> *Mahadeo! Mahadeo! he made all,—*
> *Thorn for the camel, fodder for the kine,*
> *And mother's heart for sleepy head, O little son of mine!*

kine: A very old-fashioned word for cattle.

Little Toomai came in with a joyous *tunk-a-tunk* at the end of each verse, till he felt sleepy and stretched himself on the fodder at Kala Nag's side.

At last the elephants began to lie down one after another as is their custom, till only Kala Nag at the right of the line was left standing up; and he rocked slowly from side to side, his ears put forward to listen to the night wind as it blew very slowly across the hills. The air was full of all the night noises that, taken together, make one big silence—the click of one bamboo-stem against the other, the rustle of something alive in the undergrowth, the scratch and squawk of a half-waked bird (birds are awake in the night much more often than we imagine), and the fall of water ever so far away. Little Toomai slept for some time, and when he waked it was brilliant moonlight, and Kala Nag was still standing up with his ears cocked. Little Toomai turned, rustling in the fodder, and watched the curve of his big back against half the stars in heaven, and while he watched he heard, so far away that it sounded no more than a pinhole of noise pricked through the stillness, the "hoot-toot" of a wild elephant.

All the elephants in the lines jumped up as if they had been shot, and their grunts at last waked the sleeping mahouts, and they came out and drove in the picket-pegs with big mallets, and tightened this rope and knotted that till all was quiet. One new elephant had nearly grubbed up his picket, and Big Toomai took off Kala Nag's leg-chain and shackled that elephant fore foot to hind foot, but slipped a loop of grass-string around Kala Nag's leg, and told him to remember that he was tied fast. He knew that he and his father and his grandfather had done the very same thing hundreds of times before. Kala Nag did not answer to the order by gurgling, as he usually did. He stood still, looking out across the moonlight, his head a little raised and his ears spread like fans, up to the great folds of the Garo hills.

"Look to him if he grows restless in the night," said Big Toomai to Little Toomai, and he went into the hut and slept. Little Toomai was just going to sleep, too, when he heard the coir string snap with a little "tang" and Kala Nag rolled out of his pickets as slowly and as silently as a cloud rolls out of the mouth of a valley. Little Toomai pattered after him, barefooted, down the road in the moonlight, calling under his breath, "Kala Nag! Kala Nag! Take me with you, O Kala Nag!" The elephant turned without a sound, took three strides back to the boy in the moonlight, put down his trunk, swung him up to his neck, and almost before Little Toomai had settled his knees, slipped into the forest.

fodder: Hay or straw. The word comes from the old English *foda* or food. It means cattle-food.

picket-pegs: Short, pointed pegs were driven into the ground. The elephants were tethered to these pegs.

coir: Cord made from the fiber of the coconut husk.

wild-pepper vines: The pepper
we sprinkle on our food comes
from the dried seeds of the
pepper plant.

pistons: Parts of machines which
move up and down very regularly.
Most American's don't realize it,
but elephants can move very
deftly. There is a saying in
India: "as graceful as an
elephant."

There was one blast of furious trumpeting from the lines, and then the silence shut down on everything, and Kala Nag began to move. Sometimes a tuft of high grass washed along his sides as a wave washes along the sides of a ship, and sometimes a cluster of wild-pepper vines would scrape along his back, or a bamboo would creak where his shoulder touched it; but between those times he moved absolutely without any sound, drifting through the thick Garo forest as though it had been smoke. He was going up-hill, but though Little Toomai watched the stars in the rifts of the trees, he could not tell in what direction.

Then Kala Nag reached the crest of the ascent and stopped for a minute, and Little Toomai could see the tops of the trees lying all speckled and furry under the moonlight for miles and miles, and the blue-white mist over the river in the hollow. Toomai leaned forward and looked, and he felt that the forest was awake below him—awake and alive and crowded. A big brown fruit-eating bat brushed past his ear; a porcupine's quills rattled in the thicket, and in the darkness between the tree-stems he heard a hog-bear digging hard in the moist warm earth, and snuffing as it digged.

Then the branches closed over his head again, and Kala Nag began to go down into the valley—not quietly this time, but as a runaway gun goes down a steep bank—in one rush. The huge limbs moved as steadily as pistons, eight feet to each stride, and the wrinkled skin of the elbow-points rustled. The undergrowth on either side of him ripped with a noise like torn canvas, and the saplings he heaved away right and left with his shoulders sprang back again, and banged him on the flank, and great trails of creepers, all matted together, hung from his tusks as he threw his head from side to side and plowed out his pathway. Then Little Toomai laid himself down close to the great neck, lest a swinging bough should sweep him to the ground, and he wished that he were back in the lines again.

The grass began to get squashy, and Kala Nag's feet sucked and squelched as he put them down, and the night mist at the bottom of the valley chilled Little Toomai. There was a splash and a trample, and the rush of running water, and Kala Nag strode through the bed of a river feeling his way at each step. Above the noise of the water, as it swirled round the elephant's legs, Little Toomai could hear more splashing and some trumpeting both upstream and down—great grunts and angry snortings, and all the mist about him seemed to be full of rolling wavy shadows.

"*Ai!*" he said, half aloud, his teeth chattering. "The elephant-folk are out to-night. It *is* the dance, then."

Kala Nag swashed out of the water, blew his trunk clear, and began another climb; but this time he was not alone, and he had not to make his path. That was made already, six feet wide, in front of him, where the bent jungle-grass was trying to recover itself and stand up. Many elephants must have gone that way only a few minutes before. Little Toomai looked back, and behind him a great wild tusker with his little pig's eyes glowing like hot coals, was just lifting himself out of the misty river. Then the trees closed up again, and they went on and up, with trumpeting and crashings, and the sound of breaking branches on every side of them.

At last Kala Nag stood still between two tree-trunks at the very top of the hill. They were part of a circle of trees that grew round an irregular space of some three or four acres, and in all that space, as Little Toomai could see, the ground had been trampled down as hard as a brick floor. Some trees grew in the center of the clearing, but their bark was rubbed away, and the white wood beneath showed all shiny and polished in the patches of moonlight. There were creepers hanging from the upper branches, and the bells of the flowers of the creepers, great waxy white things like convolvuluses, hung down fast asleep; but within the limits of the clearing there was not a single blade of green—nothing but the trampled earth.

The moonlight showed it all iron-gray, except where some

convolvuluses: Commonly called *bindweed.*

elephants stood upon it, and their shadows were inky black. Little Toomai looked, holding his breath, with his eyes starting out of his head, and as he looked, more and more and more elephants swung out into the open from between the tree-trunks. Little Toomai could count only up to ten, and he counted again and again on his fingers till he lost count of the tens, and his head began to swim. Outside the clearing he could hear them crashing in the undergrowth as they worked their way up the hillside; but as soon as they were within the circle of the tree-trunks they moved like ghosts.

There were white-tusked wild males, with fallen leaves and nuts and twigs lying in the wrinkles of their necks and the folds of their ears; fat slow-footed she-elephants, with restless, little pinky-black calves only three or four feet high running under their stomachs; young elephants with their tusks just beginning to show, and very proud of them; lanky, scraggy old-maid elephants, with their hollow anxious faces, and trunks like rough bark; savage old bull-elephants, scarred from shoulder to flank with great weals and cuts of bygone fights, and the caked dirt of their solitary mudbaths dropping from their shoulders; and there was one with a broken tusk and the marks of the full-stroke, the terrible drawing scrape, of a tiger's claws on his side.

They were standing head to head, or walking to and fro across the ground in couples, or rocking and swaying all by themselves—scores and scores of elephants.

Toomai knew that so long as he lay still on Kala Nag's neck nothing would happen to him; for even in the rush and scramble of a Keddah-drive a wild elephant does not reach up with his trunk and drag a man off the neck of a tame elephant; and these elephants were not thinking of men that night. Once they started and put their ears forward when they heard the chinking of a leg-iron in the forest, but it was Pudmini, Petersen Sahib's pet elephant, her chain snapped short off, grunting, snuffling up the hillside. She must have broken her pickets, and come straight from Petersen Sahib's camp; and Little Toomai saw another elephant, one that he did not know, with deep rope-galls on his back and breast. He, too, must have run away from some camp in the hills about.

At last there was no sound of any more elephants moving in the forest, and Kala Nag rolled out from his station between the trees and went into the middle of the crowd, clucking and gurgling, and all the elephants began to talk in their own tongue, and to move about.

Still lying down, Little Toomai looked down upon scores

rope-galls: Scores, made by the rubbing of ropes.

188

and scores of broad backs, and wagging ears, and tossing
trunks, and little rolling eyes. He heard the click of tusks as
they crossed other tusks by accident, and the dry rustle of
trunks twined together, and the chafing of enormous sides
and shoulders in the crowd, and the incessant flick and *hissh*
of the great tails. Then a cloud came over the moon, and he
sat in black darkness; but the quiet, steady hustling and
pushing and gurgling went on just the same. He knew that
there were elephants all round Kala Nag, and that there was
no chance of backing him out of the assembly; so he set his
teeth and shivered. In a Keddah at least there was torch-
light and shouting, but here he was all alone in the dark, and
once a trunk came up and touched him on the knee.

Then an elephant trumpeted, and they all took it up for
five or ten terrible seconds. The dew from the trees above
spattered down like rain on the unseen backs, and a dull
booming noise began, not very loud at first, and Little Toomai could not tell what it was; but it grew and grew, and Kala
Nag lifted up one fore foot and then the other, and brought
them down on the ground—one-two, one-two, as steadily as
trip-hammers. The elephants were stamping altogether now,
and it sounded like a war-drum beaten at the mouth of a
cave. The dew fell from the trees till there was no more left
to fall, and the booming went on, and the ground rocked and
shivered, and Little Toomai put his hands up to his ears to
shut out the sound. But it was all one gigantic jar that ran

through him—this stamp of hundreds of heavy feet on the raw earth. Once or twice he could feel Kala Nag and all the others surge forward a few strides, and the thumping would change to the crushing sound of juicy green things being bruised, but in a minute or two the boom of feet on hard earth began again. A tree was creaking and groaning somewhere near him. He put out his arm and felt the bark, but Kala Nag moved forward, still tramping, and he could not tell where he was in the clearing. There was no sound from the elephants, except once, when two or three little calves squeaked together. Then he heard a thump and a shuffle, and the booming went on. It must have lasted fully two hours, and Little Toomai ached in every nerve; but he knew by the smell of the night air that the dawn was coming.

The morning broke in one sheet of pale yellow behind the green hills, and the booming stopped with the first ray, as though the light had been an order. Before Little Toomai had got the ringing out of his head, before even he had shifted his position, there was not an elephant in sight except Kala Nag, Pudmini, and the elephant with the rope-galls, and there was neither sign nor rustle nor whisper down the hillsides to show where the others had gone.

Little Toomai stared again and again. The clearing, as he remembered it, had grown in the night. More trees stood in the middle of it, but the undergrowth and the jungle-grass at the sides had been rolled back. Little Toomai stared once more. Now he understood the trampling. The elephants had stamped out more room—had stamped the thick grass and juicy cane to trash, the trash into slivers, the slivers into tiny fibers, and the fibers into hard earth.

"Wah!" said Little Toomai, and his eyes were very heavy. "Kala Nag, my lord, let us keep by Pudmini and go to Petersen Sahib's camp, or I shall drop from thy neck."

The third elephant watched the two go away, snorted, wheeled round, and took his own path. He may have belonged to some little native king's establishment, fifty or sixty or a hundred miles away.

Two hours later, as Petersen Sahib was eating early breakfast, his elephants, who had been double-chained that night, began to trumpet, and Pudmini, mired to the shoulders, with Kala Nag, very foot-sore, shambled into the camp.

Little Toomai's face was gray and pinched, and his hair was full of leaves and drenched with dew; but he tried to salute Petersen Sahib, and cried faintly: "The dance—the elephant-dance! I have seen it, and—I die!" As Kala Nag sat down, he slid off his neck in a dead faint.

But, since native children have no nerves worth speaking of, in two hours he was lying very contentedly in Petersen Sahib's hammock with Petersen Sahib's shooting-coat under his head, and a glass of warm milk, a little brandy, with a dash of quinine inside of him, and while the old hairy, scarred hunters of the jungles sat three deep before him, looking at him as though he were a spirit, he told his tale in short words, as a child will, and wound up with:

"Now, if I lie in one word, send men to see, and they will find that the elephant-folk have trampled down more room in their dance-room, and they will find ten and ten, and many times ten, tracks leading to that dance-room. They made more room with their feet. I have seen it. Kala Nag took me, and I saw. Also Kala Nag is very leg-weary!"

Little Toomai lay back and slept all through the long afternoon and into the twilight, and while he slept Petersen Sahib and Machua Appa followed the track of the two elephants for fifteen miles across the hills. Petersen Sahib had spent eighteen years in catching elephants, and he had only once before found such a dance-place. Machua Appa had no need to look twice at the clearing to see what had been done there, or to scratch with his toe in the packed, rammed earth.

"The child speaks truth," said he. "All this was done last night, and I have counted seventy tracks crossing the river. See, Sahib, where Pudmini's leg-iron cut the bark of that tree! Yes; she was there too."

They looked at each other, and up and down, and they wondered; for the ways of elephants are beyond the wit of

quinine: A bitter-tasting medicine that is used to treat malaria.

191

any man, black or white, to fathom.

"Forty years and five," said Machua Appa, "have I followed my lord, the elephant, but never have I heard that any child of man had seen what this child has seen. By all the Gods of the Hills, it is—what can we say?" and he shook his head.

When they got back to camp it was time for the evening meal. Petersen Sahib ate alone in his tent, but he gave orders that the camp should have two sheep and some fowls, as well as a double-ration of flour and rice and salt, for he knew that there would be a feast.

Big Toomai had come up hot-foot from the camp in the plains to search for his son and his elephant, and now that he had found them he looked at them as though he were afraid of them both. And there was a feast by the blazing camp-fires in front of the lines of picketed elephants, and Little Toomai was the hero of it all; and the big brown elephant-catchers, the trackers and drivers and ropers, and the men who know all the secrets of breaking the wildest elephants, passed him from one to the other, and they marked his forehead with blood from the breast of a newly killed jungle-cock, to show that he was a forester, initiated and free of all the jungles.

And at last, when the flames died down, and the red light of the logs made the elephants look as though they had been dipped in blood too, Machua Appa, the head of all the drivers of all the Keddahs—Machua Appa, Petersen Sahib's other self, who had never seen a made road in forty years: Machua Appa, who was so great that he had no other name than Machua Appa—leaped to his feet, with Little Toomai held high in the air above his head, and shouted: "Listen, my brothers. Listen, too, you my lords in the lines there, for I, Machua Appa, am speaking! This little one shall no more be called Little Toomai, but Toomai of the Elephants, as his great-grandfather was called before him. What never man has seen he has seen through the long night, and the favour of the elephant-folk and of the Gods of the Jungles is with him. He shall become a great tracker; he shall become greater than I, even I, Machua Appa! He shall follow the new trail, and the stale trail, and the mixed trail, with a clear eye! He shall take no harm in the Keddah when he runs under their bellies to rope the wild tuskers; and if he slips before the feet of the charging bull-elephant that bull-elephant shall know who he is and shall not crush him. *Aihai!* my lords in the chains,"—he whirled up the line of pickets,—"here is the little one that has seen your dances in your hidden places—the sight that never man saw! Give him honour, my lords! *Salaam karo*, my children. Make your salute to Toomai of the Elephants! Gunga Perhad, ahaa! Hira Guj, Birchi Guj, Kuttar Guj, ahaa! Pudmini,—thou hast seen him at the dance, and thou too, Kala Nag, my pearl among elephants!—ahaa! Together! To Toomai of the Elephants. *Barrao!*"

And at that last wild yell the whole line flung up their trunks till the tips touched their foreheads, and broke out into the full salute—the crashing trumpet-peal that only the Viceroy of India hears, the Salaamut of the Keddah.

But it was all for the sake of Little Toomai, who had seen what never man had seen before—the dance of the elephants at night and alone in the heart of the Garo hills!

SHIV AND THE GRASSHOPPER
(THE SONG THAT TOOMAI'S MOTHER SANG TO THE BABY)

Shiv, who poured the harvest and made the winds to blow,
Sitting at the doorways of a day of long ago,
Gave to each his portion, food and toil and fate,
From the King upon the guddee to the Beggar at the gate.
    All things made he—Shiva the Preserver.
    Mahadeo! Mahadeo! he made all,—
    Thorn for the camel, fodder for the kine,
    And mother's heart for sleepy head, O little son of mine!

Wheat he gave to rich folk, millet to the poor,
Broken scraps for holy men that beg from door to door;
Cattle to the tiger, carrion to the kite,
And rags and bones to wicked wolves without the wall at night.
Naught he found too lofty, none he saw too low—
Parbati beside him watched them come and go;
Thought to cheat her husband, turning Shiv to jest—
Stole the little grasshopper and hid it in her breast.

    So she tricked him, Shiva the Preserver.
    Mahadeo! Mahadeo! turn and see.
    Tall are the camels, heavy are the kine,
    But this was least of little things, O little son of mine!

When the dole was ended, laughingly she said,
"Master, of a million mouths is not one unfed?"
Laughing, Shiv made answer, "All have had their part,
Even he, the little one, hidden 'neath thy heart."
From her breast she plucked it, Parbati the thief,
Saw the Least of Little Things gnawed a new-grown leaf!
Saw and feared and wondered, making prayer to Shiv,
Who hath surely given meat to all that live.
    All things made he—Shiva the Preserver
    Mahadeo! Mahadeo! he made all,—
    Thorn for the camel, fodder for the kine,
    And mother's heart for sleepy head, O little son of mine!

The Miracle of Purun Bhagat

11

The Miracle Of Purun Bhagat

The night we felt the earth would move
　　We stole and plucked him by the hand
Because we loved him with the love
　　That knows but cannot understand.

And when the roaring hillside broke,
　　And all our world fell down in rain,
We saved him, we the Little Folk,
　　But lo! he does not come again!

Mourn now, we saved him for the sake
　　Of such poor love as wild ones may,
Mourn ye! Our brother will not wake,
　　And his own kind drive us away!

Dirge of the Langurs

Prime Minister: In many countries, the highest official next to the actual king or president. Sometimes he has more power than the nominal head of State himself.

Brahmin: This is the highest caste in India; from the BRAHMINS come the priests and holy men, as well as the scholars and government officials.

THERE was once a man in India who was Prime Minister of one of the semi-independent native States in the northwestern part of the country. He was a Brahmin, so high-caste that caste ceased to have any particular meaning for him; and his father had been an important official in the gay-colored tag-rag and bobtail of an old-fashioned Hindu Court. But as Purun Dass grew up he felt that the old order of things was changing, and that if any one wished to get on in the world he must stand well with the English, and imitate all that the English believed to be good. At the same time a native official must keep his own master's favor. This was a difficult game, but the quiet, close-mouthed young Brahmin, helped by a good English education at a Bombay University, played it coolly, and rose, step by step, to be Prime Minister of the kingdom. That is to say, he held more real power than his master, the Maharajah.

When the old king—who was suspicious of the English, their railways and telegraphs—died, Purun Dass stood high with his young successor, who had been tutored by an Englishman; and between them, though he always took care that his master should have the credit, they established schools for little girls, made roads, and started State dispensaries and shows of agricultural implements, and published a yearly blue-book on the "Moral and Material Progress of the State," and the Foreign Office and the Government of India were delighted. Very few native States take up English progress altogether, for they will not believe, as Purun Dass showed he did, that what was good for the Englishman must be twice as good for the Asiatic. The Prime Minister became the honored friend of Viceroys and Governors, and Lieutenant-Governors, and medical missionaries, and common missionaries, and hard-riding English officers who came to shoot in the State preserves, as well as of whole hosts of tourists who traveled up and down India in the cold weather, showing how things ought to be managed. In his spare time he would endow scholarships for the study of medicine and manufactures on strictly English lines, and write letters to the "Pioneer," the greatest Indian daily paper, explaining his master's aims and objects.

At last he went to England on a visit, and had to pay enormous sums to the priests when he came back; for even so high-caste a Brahmin as Purun Dass lost caste by crossing the black sea. In London he met and talked with every one worth knowing—men whose names go all over the world—and saw a great deal more than he said. He was given honorary degrees by learned universities, and he made speeches and talked of Hindu social reform to English ladies in evening dress, till all London cried, "This is the most fascinating man we have ever met at dinner since cloths were first laid."

When he returned to India there was a blaze of glory, for the Viceroy himself made a special visit to confer upon the Maharajah the Grand Cross of the Star of India—all diamonds and ribbons and enamel; and at the same ceremony, while the cannon boomed, Purun Dass was made a Knight Commander of the Order of the Indian Empire; so that his name stood Sir Purun Dass, K. C. I. E.

The
Miracle
Of Purun
Bhagat

dispensaries: These are stations or small offices where medicine and medical supplies are given out.

medical missionaries: Health workers, such as physicians, nurses and technicians, sometimes go to foreign lands on behalf of various churches. They make little or no charge for their services. This is one way churches help the poor. These health workers are usually called MEDICAL MISSIONARIES.

That evening, at dinner in the big Viceregal tent, he stood up with the badge and the collar of the Order on his breast, and replying to the toast of his master's health, made a speech few Englishmen could have bettered.

Next month, when the city had returned to its sunbaked quiet, he did a thing no Englishman would have dreamed of doing; for, so far as the world's affairs went, he died. The jeweled order of his knighthood went back to the Indian Government, and a new Prime Minister was appointed to the charge of affairs, and a great game of General Post began in all the subordinate appointments. The priests knew what had happened and the people guessed; but India is the one place in the world where a man can do as he pleases and nobody asks why; and the fact that Dewan Sir Purun Dass, K. C. I. E., had resigned position, palace, and power, and taken up the begging-bowl and ocher-colored dress of a Sunnyasi or holy man, was considered nothing extra-ordinary. He had been, as the Old Law recommends, twenty years a youth, twenty years a fighter, — though he had never carried a weapon in his life, — and twenty years head of a household. He had used his wealth and his power for what he knew both to be worth; he had taken honor when it came his way; he had seen men and cities far and near, and men and cities had stood up and honored him. Now he would let these things go, as a man drops the cloak he no longer needs.

Behind him, as he walked through the city gates, an antelope skin and brass-handled crutch under his arm, and a begging-bowl of polished brown *coco-de-mer* in his hand, barefoot, alone, with eyes cast on the ground—behind him they were firing salutes from the bastions in honor of his happy successor. Purun Dass nodded. All that life was ended; and he bore it no more ill-will or good-will than a man bears to a colorless dream of the night. He was a Sunnyasi—a houseless wandering mendicant, depending on his neighbors for his daily bread; and so long as there is a morsel to divide in India neither priest nor beggar starves. He had never in his life tasted meat, and very seldom eaten even fish. A five-pound note would have covered his personal expenses for food through any one of the many years in which he had been absolute master of millions of money. Even when he was being lionized in London he had held before him his dream of peace and quiet—the long, white, dusty Indian road, printed all over with bare feet, the incessant, slow-moving traffic, and the sharp-smelling wood smoke curling up under the fig-trees in the twilight, where the wayfarers sit at their evening meal.

coco-de-mer: French for "coconut."

incessant: Continuous, not ever stopping.

When the time came to make that dream true the Prime Minister took the proper steps, and in three days you might more easily have found a bubble in the trough of the long Atlantic seas than Purun Dass among the roving, gathering, separating millions of India.

At night his antelope skin was spread where the darkness overtook him—sometimes in a Sunnyasi monastery by the roadside; sometimes by a mud pillar shrine of Kala Pir, where the Jogis, who are another misty division of holy men, would receive him as they do those who know what castes and divisions are worth; sometimes on the outskirts of a little Hindu village, where the children would steal up with the food their parents had prepared; and sometimes on the pitch of the bare grazing-grounds, where the flame of his stick fire waked the drowsy camels. It was all one to Purun Dass—or Purun Bhagat, as he called himself now. Earth, people, and food were all one. But unconsciously his feet drew him away northward and eastward; from the south to Rohtak; from Rohtak to Kurnool; from Kurnool to ruined Samanah, and then up-stream along the dried bed of the Gugger river that fills only when the rain falls in the hills, till one day he saw the far line of the great Himalayas.

Bactrian Camel

Then Purun Bhagat smiled, for he remembered that his mother was of Rajput Brahmin birth, from Kulu way—a Hill-woman, always homesick for the snows—and that the least touch of Hill blood draws a man at the end back to where he belongs.

"Yonder," said Purun Bhagat, breasting the lower slopes of the Sewaliks, where the cacti stand up like seven-branched candlesticks—"yonder I shall sit down and get knowledge"; and the cool wind of the Himalayas whistled about his ears as he trod the road that led to Simla.

The last time he had come that way it had been in state, with a clattering cavalry escort, to visit the gentlest and most affable of Viceroys; and the two had talked for an hour together about mutual friends in London, and what the Indian common folk really thought of things. This time Purun Bhagat paid no calls, but leaned on the rail of the Mall, watching that glorious view of the Plains spread out forty miles below, till a native Mohammedan policeman told him he was obstructing traffic; and Purun Bhagat salaamed reverently to the Law, because he knew the value of it, and was seeking for a Law of his own. Then he moved on, and slept that night in an empty hut at Chota Simla, which looks like the very last end of the earth, but it was only the beginning of his journey.

He followed the Himalaya-Thibet road, the little ten-foot track that is blasted out of solid rock, or strutted out on timbers over gulfs a thousand feet deep; that dips into warm, wet, shut-in valleys, and climbs out across bare, grassy hill-shoulders where the sun strikes like a burning-glass; or turns through dripping, dark forests where the tree-ferns dress the trunks from head to heel, and the pheasant calls to his mate. And he met Thibetan herdsmen with their dogs and flocks of sheep, each sheep with a little bag of borax on his back, and wandering wood-cutters, and cloaked and blanketed Lamas from Thibet, coming into India on pilgrimage, and envoys of little solitary Hill-states, posting furiously on ring-streaked and piebald ponies, or the cavalcade of a Rajah paying a visit; or else for a long, clear day he would see nothing more than a black bear grunting and rooting below in the valley. When he first started, the roar of the world he had left still rang in his ears, as the roar of a tunnel rings long after the train has passed through; but when he had put the Mutte-eanee Pass behind him that was all done, and Purun Bhagat was alone with himself, walking, wondering, and thinking, his eyes on the ground, and his thoughts with the clouds.

One evening he crossed the highest pass he had met till then—it had been a two days' climb—and came out on a line of snow-peaks that banded all the horizon—mountains from fifteen to twenty thousand feet high, looking almost near

affable : Good-humored, pleasant and friendly.

borax: This mineral has many uses. It is used in glass making, enamel, printing inks, dyes, rust inhibitors and dental powders. One half the entire world's supply comes from the Mojave Desert in California.

lamas: The small mountain country of Tibet has many monks—possibly a third of the population. Only a very few monks—who excel in higher studies—become lamas.

enough to hit with a stone, though they were fifty or sixty miles away. The pass was crowned with dense, dark forest—deodar, walnut, wild cherry, wild olive, and wild pear, but mostly deodar, which is the Himalayan cedar; and under the shadow of the deodars stood a deserted shrine to Kali—who is Durga, who is Sitala, who is sometimes worshiped against the smallpox.

Purun Dass swept the stone floor clean, smiled at the grinning statue, made himself a little mud fireplace at the back of the shrine, spread his antelope skin on a bed of fresh pine-needles, tucked his *bairagi*—his brass-handled crutch—under his armpit, and sat down to rest.

Immediately below him the hillside fell away, clean and cleared for fifteen hundred feet, where a little village of stone-walled houses, with roofs of beaten earth, clung to the steep tilt. All round it the tiny terraced fields lay out like aprons of patchwork on the knees of the mountain, and cows no bigger than beetles grazed between the smooth stone circles of the threshing-floors. Looking across the valley, the eye was deceived by the size of things, and could not at first realize that what seemed to be low scrub, on the opposite mountain-flank, was in truth a forest of hundred-foot pines. Purun Bhagat saw an eagle swoop across the gigantic hollow, but the great bird dwindled to a dot ere it was half-way over. A few bands of scattered clouds strung up and down the valley, catching on a shoulder of the hills, or rising up and dying out when they were level with the head of the pass. And "Here shall I find peace," said Purun Bhagat.

Now, a Hill-man makes nothing of a few hundred feet up or down, and as soon as the villagers saw the smoke in the deserted shrine, the village priest climbed up the terraced hillside to welcome the stranger.

When he met Purun Bhagat's eyes—the eyes of a man used to control thousands—he bowed to the earth, took the begging-bowl without a word, and returned to the village, saying, "We have at last a holy man. Never have I seen such a man. He is of the Plains—but pale-colored—a Brahmin of the Brahmins." Then all the housewives of the village said, "Think you he will stay with us?" and each did her best to cook the most savory meal for the Bhagat. Hill-food is very simple, but with buckwheat and Indian corn, and rice and red pepper, and little fish out of the stream in the valley, and honey from the flue-like hives built in the stone walls, and dried apricots, and turmeric, and wild ginger, and bannocks of flour, a devout woman can make good things, and it was a full bowl that the priest carried to the Bhagat. Was he going to stay? asked the priest. Would he need a *chela*—a disciple —to beg for him? Had he a blanket against the cold weather? Was the food good?

Purun Bhagat ate, and thanked the giver. It was in his mind to stay. That was sufficient, said the priest. Let the begging-bowl be placed outside the shrine, in the hollow made by those two twisted roots, and daily should the Bhagat be fed; for the village felt honored that such a man— he looked timidly into the Bhagat's face—should tarry among them.

That day saw the end of Purun Bhagat's wanderings. He had come to the place appointed for him—the silence and the space. After this, time stopped, and he, sitting at the mouth of the shrine, could not tell whether he were alive or dead; a man with control of his limbs, or a part of the hills, and the clouds, and the shifting rain and sunlight. He would repeat a Name softly to himself a hundred hundred times, till, at each repetition, he seemed to move more and more out of his body, sweeping up to the doors of some tremendous discovery; but, just as the door was opening, his body would drag him back, and, with grief, he felt he was locked up again in the flesh and bones of Purun Bhagat.

Every morning the filled begging-bowl was laid silently in the crutch of the roots outside the shrine. Sometimes the priest brought it; sometimes a Ladakhi trader, lodging in the village, and anxious to get merit, trudged up the path; but, more often, it was the woman who had cooked the meal overnight; and she would murmur, hardly above her breath: "Speak for me before the gods, Bhagat. Speak for such a one, the wife of so-and-so!" Now and then some bold child would be allowed the honor, and Purun Bhagat would hear him drop the bowl and run as fast as his little legs could carry him, but the Bhagat never came down to the village. It was laid out like a map at his feet. He could see the evening gatherings, held on the circle of the threshing-floors because that was the only level ground; could see the wonderful unnamed green of the young rice, the indigo blues of the Indian corn, the dock-like patches of buckwheat, and, in its season, the red bloom of the amaranth, whose tiny seeds, being neither grain nor pulse, make a food that can be lawfully eaten by Hindus in time of fasts.

When the year turned, the roofs of the huts were all little squares of purest gold, for it was on the roofs that they laid out their cobs of corn to dry. Hiving and harvest, rice-sowing and husking, passed before his eyes, all embroidered down there on the many-sided plots of fields, and he thought of

appointed: Someone or something set apart or "spoken for." A person may be APPOINTED to a particular office—as where the Mayor appoints a Vice-Mayor, or a Governor appoints someone a Judge. So too, a place may be set apart and reserved, as here, for Purun Bhagat.

husking: Stripping the leaves that tightly enfold cobs of corn is called HUSKING or "shucking." In early American times, farm people had husking bees, where everyone gathered at one place to husk mountains of corn.

them all, and wondered what they all led to at the long last.

Even in populated India a man cannot a day sit still before the wild things run over him as though he were a rock; and in that wilderness very soon the wild things, who knew Kali's Shrine well, came back to look at the intruder. The *langurs*, the big gray-whiskered monkeys of the Himalayas, were, naturally, the first, for they are alive with curiosity; and when they had upset the begging-bowl, and rolled it round the floor, and tried their teeth on the brass-handled crutch, and made faces at the antelope skin, they decided that the human being who sat so still was harmless. At evening, they would leap down from the pines, and beg with their hands for things to eat, and then swing off in graceful curves. They liked the warmth of the fire, too, and huddled round it till Purun Bhagat had to push them aside to throw on more fuel; and in the morning, as often as not, he would find a furry ape sharing his blanket. All day long, one or other of the tribe would sit by his side, staring out at the snows, crooning and looking unspeakably wise and sorrowful.

After the monkeys came the *barasingh*, that big deer which is like our red deer, but stronger. He wished to rub off the velvet of his horns against the cold stones of Kali's statue, and stamped his feet when he saw the man at the shrine. But Purun Bhagat never moved, and, little by little, the royal stag edged up and nuzzled his shoulder. Purun Bhagat slid one cool hand along the hot antlers, and the touch soothed the fretted beast, who bowed his head, and Purun Bhagat very softly rubbed and raveled off the velvet. Afterward, the *barasingh* brought his doe and fawn—gentle things that mumbled on the holy man's blanket—or would come alone at night, his eyes green in the fire-flicker, to take his share of fresh walnuts. At last, the muskdeer, the shyest and almost the smallest of the deerlets, came, too, her big rabbity ears erect; even brindled, silent *mushick-nabha* must needs find out what the light in the shrine meant, and drop her moose-like nose into Purun Bhagat's lap, coming and going with the shadows of the fire. Purun Bhagat called them all "my brothers," and his low call of *"Bhai! Bhai!"* would draw them from the forest at noon if they were within earshot. The Himalayan black bear, moody and suspicious—Sona, who has the V-shaped white mark under his chin—passed that way more than once; and since the Bhagat showed no fear, Sona showed no anger, but watched him, and came closer, and begged a share of the caresses, and a dole of bread or wild berries. Often, in the still dawns, when the Bhagat would climb to the very crest of the pass to watch the red day

the Himalayan black bear has a light-colored crescent shaped mark on his chest. He lives in the forest, mainly on fruits and nuts.

dole: Something—money or food —given in charity. Usually this is a small gift to a very poor person. During the great depression of 1931 in the United States, money paid out by the government to the unemployed was called a DOLE.

walking along the peaks of the snows, he would find Sona shuffling and grunting at his heels, thrusting a curious fore-paw under fallen trunks, and bringing it away with a *whoof* of impatience; or his early steps would wake Sona where he lay curled up, and the great brute, rising erect, would think to fight, till he heard the Bhagat's voice and knew his best friend.

Nearly all hermits and holy men who live apart from the big cities have the reputation of being able to work miracles with the wild things, but all the miracle lies in keeping still, in never making a hasty movement, and, for a long time, at least, in never looking directly at a visitor. The villagers saw the outline of the *barasingh* stalking like a shadow through the dark forest behind the shrine; saw the *minaul*, the Hima-layan pheasant, blazing in her best colors before Kali's sta-tue; and the *langurs* on their haunches, inside, playing with the walnut shells. Some of the children, too, had heard Sona singing to himself, bear-fashion, behind the fallen rocks, and the Bhagat's reputation as miracle-worker stood firm.

Yet nothing was further from his mind than miracles. He believed that all things were one big Miracle, and when a man knows that much he knows something to go upon. He knew for a certainty that there was nothing great and nothing little in this world; and day and night he strove to think out his way into the heart of things, back to the place whence his soul had come.

So thinking, his untrimmed hair fell down about his shoul-ders, the stone slab at the side of the antelope skin was dented into a little hole by the foot of his brass-handled crutch, and the place between the tree-trunks, where the begging-bowl rested day after day, sunk and wore into a hollow almost as smooth as the brown shell itself; and each beast knew his exact place at the fire. The fields changed their colors with the seasons; the threshing-floors filled and emptied, and filled again and again; and again and again, when winter came, the *langurs* frisked among the branches feathered with light snow, till the mother-monkeys brought their sad-eyed little babies up from the warmer valleys with the spring. There were few changes in the village. The priest was older, and many of the little children who used to come with the begging-dish sent their own children now; and when you asked of the villagers how long their holy man had lived in Kali's Shrine at the head of the pass, they answered, "Always."

Then came such summer rains as had not been known in the Hills for many seasons. Through three good months the

miracles: Something that is done beyond the normal power of man may be a MIRACLE. Unlike magic, miracles usually are for good or holy purposes. Christ raising Lazarus from the dead is considered a miracle.

threshing floor: To get wheat or other grain kernels free of stems and leaves, it must be THRESHED. The common method was to throw the cuttings on a smooth hard floor, and hit at it with flails—handles with free-swinging rods on the ends. This broke up the stems and the edible grains could be easily separated for later use.

valley was wrapped in cloud and soaking mist—steady, unrelenting downfall, breaking off into thunder-shower after thunder-shower. Kali's Shrine stood above the clouds, for the most part, and there was a whole month in which the Bhagat never saw his village. It was packed away under a white floor of cloud that swayed and shifted and rolled on itself and bulged upward, but never broke from its piers— the streaming flanks of the valley.

All that time he heard nothing but the sound of a million little waters, overhead from the trees, and underfoot along the ground, soaking through the pine-needles, dripping from the tongues of draggled fern, and spouting in newly torn muddy channels down the slopes. Then the sun came out, and drew forth the good incense of the deodars and the rho-dodendrons, and that far-off, clean smell which the Hill people call "the smell of the snows." The hot sunshine lasted for a week, and then the rains gathered together for their last downpour, and the water fell in sheets that flayed off the skin of the ground and leaped back in mud. Purun Bhagat heaped his fire high that night, for he was sure his brothers would need warmth; but never a beast came to the shrine, though he called and called till he dropped asleep, wondering what had happened in the woods.

It was in the black heart of the night, the rain drumming like a thousand drums, that he was roused by a plucking at his blanket, and, stretching out, felt the little hand of a *langur*. "It is better here than in the trees," he said sleepily, loosening a fold of blanket; "take it and be warm." The monkey caught his hand and pulled hard. "Is it food, then?" said Purun Bhagat. "Wait awhile, and I will prepare some." As he kneeled to throw fuel on the fire the *langur* ran to the door of the shrine, crooned, and ran back again, plucking at the man's knee.

"What is it? What is thy trouble, Brother?" said Purun Bhagat, for the *langur's* eyes were full of things that he could not tell. "Unless one of thy caste be in a trap—and none set traps here—I will not go into that weather. Look, Brother, even the *barasingh* comes for shelter!"

The deer's antlers clashed as he strode into the shrine, clashed against the grinning statue of Kali. He lowered them in Purun Bhagat's direction and stamped uneasily, hissing through his half-shut nostrils.

"Hai! Hai! Hai!" said the Bhagat, snapping his fingers. "Is *this* payment for a night's lodging?" But the deer pushed him toward the door, and as he did so Purun Bhagat heard the sound of something opening with a sigh, and saw two slabs of the floor draw away from each other, while the sticky earth below smacked its lips.

"Now I see," said Purun Bhagat. "No blame to my brothers that they did not sit by the fire to-night. The mountain is falling. And yet—why should I go?" His eye fell on the empty begging-bowl, and his face changed. "They have given me good food daily since—since I came, and, if I am not swift, to-morrow there will not be one mouth in the valley. Indeed, I must go and warn them below. Back there, Brother! Let me get to the fire."

The *barasingh* backed unwillingly as Purun Bhagat drove a pine torch deep into the flame, twirling it till it was well lit. "Ah! ye came to warn me," he said, rising. "Better than that we shall do; better than that. Out, now, and lend me thy neck, Brother, for I have but two feet."

He clutched the bristling withers of the *barasingh* with his right hand, held the torch away with his left, and stepped out of the shrine into the desperate night. There was no breath of wind, but the rain nearly drowned the flare as the great deer hurried down the slope, sliding on his haunches. As soon as they were clear of the forest more of the Bhagat's brothers joined them. He heard, though he could not see, the *langurs* pressing about him, and behind them the *uhh! uhh!*

of Sona. The rain matted his long white hair into ropes; the water splashed beneath his bare feet, and his yellow robe clung to his frail old body, but he stepped down steadily, leaning against the *barasingh*. He was no longer a holy man, but Sir Purun Dass, K. C. I. E., Prime Minister of no small State, a man accustomed to command, going out to save life. Down the steep, plashy path they poured all together, the Bhagat and his brothers, down and down till the deer's feet clicked and stumbled on the wall of a threshing-floor, and he snorted because he smelt Man. Now they were at the head of the one crooked village street, and the Bhagat beat with his crutch on the barred windows of the blacksmith's house as his torch blazed up in the shelter of the eaves. "Up and out!" cried Purun Bhagat; and he did not know his own voice, for it was years since he had spoken aloud to a man. "The hill falls! The hill is falling! Up and out, oh, you within!"

"It is our Bhagat," said the blacksmith's wife. "He stands among his beasts. Gather the little ones and give the call."

It ran from house to house, while the beasts, cramped in the narrow way, surged and huddled round the Bhagat, and Sona puffed impatiently.

The people hurried into the street—they were no more than seventy souls all told—and in the glare of the torches they saw their Bhagat holding back the terrified *barasingh*, while the monkeys plucked piteously at his skirts, and Sona sat on his haunches and roared.

"Across the valley and up the next hill!" shouted Purun Bhagat. "Leave none behind! We follow!"

Then the people ran as only Hill folk can run, for they knew that in a landslip you must climb for the highest ground across the valley. They fled, splashing through the little river at the bottom, and panted up the terraced fields on the far side, while the Bhagat and his brethren followed. Up and up the opposite mountain they climbed, calling to each other by name—the roll-call of the village—and at their heels toiled the big *barasingh*, weighted by the failing strength of Purun Bhagat. At last the deer stopped in the shadow of a deep pine-wood, five hundred feet up the hill-side. His instinct, that had warned him of the coming slide, told him he would be safe here.

Purun Bhagat dropped fainting by his side, for the chill of the rain and that fierce climb were killing him; but first he called to the scattered torches ahead, "Stay and count your numbers"; then, whispering to the deer as he saw the lights gather in a cluster: "Stay with me, Brother. Stay—till—I —go!"

There was a sigh in the air that grew to a mutter, and a mutter that grew to a roar, and a roar that passed all sense of hearing, and the hillside on which the villagers stood was hit in the darkness, and rocked to the blow. Then a note as steady, deep, and true as the deep C of the organ drowned everything for perhaps five minutes, while the very roots of the pines quivered to it. It died away, and the sound of the rain falling on miles of hard ground and grass changed to the muffled drum of water on soft earth. That told its own tale.

Never a villager—not even the priest—was bold enough to speak to the Bhagat who had saved their lives. They crouched under the pines and waited till the day. When it came they looked across the valley and saw that what had been forest, and terraced field, and track-threaded grazing-ground was one raw, red, fan-shaped smear, with a few trees flung head-down on the scarp. That red ran high up the hill of their refuge, damming back the little river, which had begun to spread into a brick-colored lake. Of the village, of the road to the shrine, of the shrine itself, and the forest behind, there was no trace. For one mile in width and two thousand feet in sheer depth the mountain-side had come away bodily, planed clean from head to heel.

And the villagers, one by one, crept through the wood to pray before their Bhagat. They saw the *barasingh* standing over him, who fled when they came near, and they heard the *langurs* wailing in the branches, and Sona moaning up the hill; but their Bhagat was dead, sitting cross-legged, his back against a tree, his crutch under his armpit, and his face turned to the northeast.

The priest said: "Behold a miracle after a miracle, for in this very attitude must all Sunnyasis be buried! Therefore where he now is we will build the temple to our holy man."

They built the temple before a year was ended—a little stone-and-earth shrine—and they called the hill the Bhagat's Hill, and they worship there with lights and flowers and offerings to this day. But they do not know that the saint of their worship is the late Sir Purun Dass, K. C. I. E., D. C. L., Ph. D., etc., once Prime Minister of the progressive and enlightened State of Mohiniwala, and honorary or corresponding member of more learned and scientific societies than will ever do any good in this world or the next.

A SONG OF KABIR

Oh, light was the world that he weighed in his hands!
Oh, heavy the tale of his fiefs and his lands!
He has gone from the guddee and put on the shroud,
And departed in guise of bairagi avowed!

Now the white road to Delhi is mat for his feet,
The sal and the kikar must guard him from heat;
His home is the camp, and the waste, and the crowd—
He is seeking the Way as bairagi avowed!

He has looked upon Man, and his eyeballs are clear
(There was One; there is One, and but One, saith Kabir);
The Red Mist of Doing has thinned to a cloud—
He has taken the path for bairagi avowed!

To learn and discern of his brother the clod,
Of his brother the brute, and his brother the God.
He has gone from the council and put on the shroud
("Can ye hear?" saith Kabir), a bairagi avowed!

BACKWORD

Rudyard Kipling:
the Indian Story Teller

India is big country.

It has steaming rice fields and hard-baked deserts. It has pine forests and mountains capped with snow. Men wear brightly colored turbans, and women wear delicately pleated saris. In the bazaars there are piles of tropical fruits: mangos, papayas, yellow bananas as big as a finger and red ones as big as half an arm.

Rudyard Kipling was born in Bombay, a great city on India's western coast. His father was principal of the Bombay School of Art. At that time India was part of the British Empire. Englishmen came out to India to work for the Empress, Queen Victoria. They built railroads, they dammed rivers, they started schools. The native Indians called them *sahibs*.

Young Rudyard was a sahib, and he knew it. He ruled his small, safe, nursery world. It was a world of light and color, full of interesting things to do. Early in the morning he walked with his ayah, or nurse, to the market, and they chose the fruit for the day. When there was a wedding procession, they stopped to watch it: the bride in a covered litter carried by six men, and the groom riding behind on a white horse.

Sometimes Rudyard visited his father's art school. He played with bits of clay, and watched the students painting.

One of Rudyard's friends was Meeta, the bearer, He was a big boy, a Hindu. Often he took Rudyard with him when he went to pray at the little Hindu temple. Meeta told wonderful stories; stories about the Ranee that was turned into a tiger, or about Rama and his long search for Sita. He told stories about the jungle-people, too; about the monkeys and the elephants and how the leopard got his spots.

Living in England

The Indian climate was not safe for children. Most Englishmen who lived in India sent their children to live in England while they were growing up. When Rudyard was six his parents took him across the ocean. They left him with a Mrs. Holloway who lived in a dark, ugly house in Southsea.

His parents meant well. They tried to find a good home for him. But Mrs. Holloway was a terrible, narrow minded woman. When Rudyard told the stories he had learned from Meeta and the ayah, she said he was a little heathen. She beat him. She told him God would send him to Hell. When Rudyard asked questions, she scolded him for showing off. Everything he did was wrong.

Rudyard's mother and father didn't know what was happening to him. They were far away in India. Finally, his mother came to England for a visit. She was horrified.

Years later, Rudyard wrote a story about that dreadful time. It's called "Baa Baa, Black Sheep." You can probably find it in any collection of his stories, because it's one of the best he ever wrote. The story ends, the way it ended in real life, with Rudyard happily living in the country with his mother.

Return to India

When he was nearly seventeen, Rudyard returned to India. He had a job on an Indian newspaper. He lived with his father and mother in the ancient city of Lahore, in the northwest part of India. At last the family was together again!

Now he was a man, with a man's work. As a newspaper reporter, he really got to know India. At night he wandered through the city, talking with all sorts of people: Hindus and Moslems and Sikhs and Afghans. He talked with Englishmen about their work. On one railroad trip he stopped at the deserted city of Amber, which later became the Cold Lair of "Kaa's Hunting."

The Jungle Book

After seven years in India, Kipling travelled to London. His short stories and poems about Indian life were already creating a sensation. In London he met an American girl, Carrie Balestier, and married her. They went to live in New England. While they were there, waiting for their first child to be born, Kipling started to write his first book of children's stories.

He asked his father to send him exact information about Indian animals. Kipling wrote to friends for pictures of the Seeonee district, which he had never visited. He reached back into memories of his own childhood, when he was part of India—and he wrote the Jungle Book.

The Lure of Kipling's Lore

A person who reads Kipling's "Jungle Book" enters a different world. He is never the same again. When he daydreams, he pictures himself as Mowgli, running through the forest. When he looks at his mother, he wonders how she compares with a wolf. When he sees a cobra in a zoo's reptile house, he mentally snarls—like plucky Rikki-tikki-tavi. And if a wrinkled elephant steps out of line in a circus performance, he secretly knows that tiny Toomai could make the oversize beast behave.

More Real Than Our Friends

Kipling's animal characters seem as real as our actual friends and acquaintances. Shere Khan, the treacherous tiger, is a playground bully magnified a thousand times. Bagheera, the faithful black panther, is an older brother who gives us advice, and sees that no one pushes us around. Baloo, Akela, Kaa—they're all three-dimensional. We feel as though we've known them always.

Since the vision is so entrancing, we ask ourselves: Are animals truly as fascinating as Kipling portrayed them? Have there honestly ever *been* any striplings like Mowgli, the Man-cub? We'll answer the question about animals in a moment. First, let's look at some interesting legends about "wolf children."

Children Who Growled

More than a hundred years ago, a British Army colonel reported five separate cases of children supposedly reared by wolves in India. All of the youngsters were said to have walked on all fours, growled like dogs, and been unable to speak. One, captured with two furry companions when drinking at a riverbank, later wasted away in an insane asylum.

In 1920, an Anglican minister in India claimed he had rescued two small girls who had been surviving somehow in a den with three wolves. His "proof" was a diary, plus several blurry photographs. The girls, placed in an orphanage, soon died—as did the minister, before all details of his story could be checked.

A Phony Gazelle Boy

Since then, there have been unconfirmed reports of children living with baboons. After World War Two, a "gazelle boy" was featured in LIFE Magazine. However, a sharp-eyed reader noted that the supposedly wild youth had been wearing a T-shirt for some time before being "captured" and photographed, as evidenced by a distinct sunburn pattern on his neck and arms.

Discounting the gazelle boy, who was obviously a fake, what are we to *think* of wolf children and baboon children? Is it possible for a child to be reared by wild animals? Believers say yes. Skeptics say no. The evidence is conflicting.

For example, small children *are* carried off by wolves each year in India . . . just as an occasional child is carried off by a bear in Wisconsin. The odds are against its survival. Many babies found alive in the vicinity of wolves undoubtedly toddled or crawled there by accident.

Mowgli Did Not Live in a Jungle

There are several types of forest in India. Mowgli and his four-legged companions did *not* live in a rain forest, or dense monsoon jungle, as is commonly thought. Though the vast sub-continent has rain forests, they're not present in the central portion of the country, where the stories take place. Father Wolf, Mother Wolf, and the others lived in what's known as a "dry tropical" forest.

Trees in a dry tropical forest resemble oaks and maples rather than lush jungle vegetation. They even shed their leaves, as do oaks and maples in America, but they do so one leaf at a time, not all at once. A hike through the forest in which the Man-cub dwelled would not be too different from a hike through trees in upper Michigan, though the temperature would be considerably warmer.

Let's return to the question, are India's wild animals really as fascinating as they seem in the Jungle Book. The answer is yes. In fact, they're even *more* intriguing now, because we know more about them than did the imaginative young author with the bristling moustache. Let's begin with Shere Khan, the "Big One" . . . the limping tiger who prowled near the Waingunga River.

Cats Cannot Chew

Being a cat, slinky Shere Khan was absolutely unable to chew anything. He had to forcibly tear off jagged chunks of flesh and swallow them in great gulps. No cat—whether it's a purring tabby or a coughing leopard—can chew. Grinding molars are needed for this process, and cats have only a trace of molar teeth. A cat's scissors-like dental structure is perfect for piercing, slicing, and cracking hard bone, but is as ineffective as a powder puff when it comes to chewing.

What kind of animal *is* a tiger, anyway? Here are some odd facts, sprinkled with a few vital statistics: The tiger is the big cat of India, as the lion is the big cat of Africa. A lion may survive thirty years; a tiger seldom passes its nineteenth birthday. Though they don't live as long as their African cousins, tigers are larger and tougher. If a lion and tiger are pitted against each other, the tiger balances on its hind legs and viciously swings both of its front paws. The lion also balances on its hind legs, but swings only one paw, and usually loses the fight.

Tigers Suffer From The Heat

It's hard to accept the fact that tigers originated in eastern Siberia, where the temperature sometimes dips to seventy below zero, but it's true. Some of these striped animals still live there. Indian tigers are unhappy descendants of ancestors who moved south many years ago. They suffer intensely from the heat. They cool off by swimming whenever possible.

So much for the muscular Shere Khan, who was flattened into a tattered rug by stampeding cattle. What about sinewy Bagheera, the jet black leopard? Why did his eyes glow in the dark? For the same reason that the tiger's eyes glinted balefully. The inner wall of any cat's eye is coated with tiny silver or gold particles called guanin, which catch, intensify, and reflect back any light that strikes their surface. The tinsel-like particles make it easier for a cat to see in the dark. Though fiction writers would have us believe otherwise, the glow vanishes shortly after the outside source of light is cut off. Big cats don't stalk around with eyes flashing like automobile headlights.

Bagheera was black, but probably had spotted parents, for the ebony color is a mutation. Black leopards — sometimes called black panthers — are fairly common in India, but extremely rare in Africa. Spotted or black, leopards are solitary hunters. Strangely enough, vultures, who normally gorge on any dead creatures, shun the remains of any "kills" these shadowy carnivores store in tree branches.

Baloo Really a Sloth Bear

One of the most likeable of Mowgli's friends was Baloo, the sleepy brown bear. Kipling meant well, but his facts were hazy, and he was mistaken about Baloo in at least one respect. The Indian word "bhalu" means sloth bear, and refers to a shaggy creature that's glistening black, not teddy bear brown. What's more, a sloth bear has a rather unbelievable naked gray face, plus a startling white chevron on its broad chest.

The bhalu is well on its way to developing into an overgrown anteater. Although it will placidly chew on leaves and flowers, it prefers to swallow enormous quantities of squirming termites, or the larvae of bees. Since this is a soft diet, akin to jello or tapioca in texture, teeth are not needed. Therefore, the sloth bear's have become small and virtually useless. In fact, there are only two of them left in the front of its upper jaw.

In the Mowgli tales, Kipling favored elephants with no more than a passing mention. Yet he was fascinated by them, and gave them feature billing in his heart-warming story about Toomai. If some of the facts about the sloth bear seem weird, so do some of the facts about the Asiatic pachyderm — a bulky gray giant that's radically different from its African relative.

Elephants Wear False Tusks

In the first place, the Indian elephant frequently wears false tusks when carrying dignitaries in gaudy processions. Why? Because genuine ivory tusks are not as commonplace as they are with African elephants. Females seldom grow them, and many males are oddly toothless in this respect. Since an elephant without tusks is like a car without wheels, wooden shafts are substituted, usually painted a convincing dirty white.

In both species, there are more than 40,000 muscles in the trunk. In both species, the growth rate and life-span are identical to those of man. Neither species sucks water up through the trunk and into the mouth, as though the wrinkled tube were a gigantic soda straw. Instead, an elephant draws water into its trunk, then forcefully squirts the liquid into its mouth, garden hose fashion.

If the habits of an elephant are interesting, the habits of a mongoose—as depicted by Kipling—are downright dramatic. What could be more thrilling than the concept of a nondescript little animal, no larger than a loaf of rye bread, courageously attacking a cobra, and winning? It's as unbelievable as a grade school gym class challenging Big Ten champions to a football scrimmage in the Rose Bowl, and thrashing them. Yet, it's true . . . at least occasionally.

Cobras Strike Slowly

Why can Rikki-tikki-tavi nimbly dance around Nag, the cold-eyed cobra, and artfully dodge the forward thrust of that venomous mouth?

Because cobras strike slowly. Rikki wouldn't have a ghost of a chance against a rattlesnake—or any other pit viper, for that matter. This was proven when someone attempted to make a motion picture of a mongoose shadowboxing with a deadly South American bushmaster. Eight outclassed mongooses were promptly killed in the process.

Naturalists doubt if mongooses ever *deliberately* pick fights with poisonous snakes. They'd much rather eat insects, chickens, or rats. Because of their formidable reputation as rodentkillers, they were gratefully introduced into Hawaii and the West Indies. The rats promptly scurried up the trunks of palm trees and stayed there, and the mongooses promptly raided every available chicken coop. To this day, they're absolutely forbidden to enter the United States.

The devoted reader of the Jungle Book is unaffected by the fact that mongooses are unwelcome here. His loyalty to Rikki-tikki-tavi remains unshaken. It doesn't matter a snap that Kipling made wolves wiser than they really are, and gave a normally untrustworthy panther the kindliness of a scoutmaster. In his mind, Akela will always be infinitely wise, and Bagheera will forever be Big Brother to a little brown boy who was nicknamed "The Frog" by his animal brethern. We all desperately need an Akela, a Bagheera, and a shuffling Baloo in our lives. Kipling has delightfully supplied them for us, and we will brook no petty arguments about this magical truth!